REVERSION

ALSO BY AMY ROGERS

Petroplague

REVERSION

AMY ROGERS

ScienceThrillers Media

SCIENCETHRILLERS MEDIA

REVERSION. Copyright ©2014 by Amy Rogers. All rights reserved. For information, contact ScienceThrillers Media, P.O. Box 601392, Sacramento, CA 95860-1392.

www.ScienceThrillersMedia.com
Publisher@ScienceThrillersMedia.com

First edition, 2014

Library of Congress Control Number 2014916243

FIC028110 FICTION/Science Fiction/Genetic Engineering
FIC031040 FICTION/Thrillers/Medical

ISBN 978-1-940419-01-5 (trade paperback)
ISBN 978-1-940419-02-2 (ebook)

Cover design by Ian Koviak, TheBookDesigners.com

To Jason

CHAPTER 1

Fifty thousand US dollars, sealed in watertight stacks of $100 bills, was peculiar baggage for a hike in the foothills of the Sierra Madre del Sur.

Cristo Castillo slowed his pace to a walk on the rain-slickened dirt footpath and shifted the weight of the backpack on his shoulders. The battered pack smelled of wet leather and the sweat of previous bearers. Birds sang high in the sparse, waxy trees, and rustled in the thin, semi-arid underbrush. A brief, late-summer thunderstorm had resurrected the fragrance of soil and blue gum trees and sun-baked rocks.

He paused to breathe and to savor the wildness of this place, far from fluorescent-lit laboratories and Rolex-wearing clients. He'd played hide-and-seek in these mountains as a child. Thirty years ago he didn't know that the full name of his favorite tree was *Eucalyptus globulus,* or that its leaves synthesized glucose from air and sunlight. A college education had deepened his appreciation for this ecosystem. Coming to this place restored him.

Which is why he regularly offered to do this errand for his boss, even though it was a far cry from his real job at the Palacio Centro Medico.

The first few times Cristo made the exchange of backpacks, the couriers from the Zeta cartel counted every single bill. Now that the Zetas trusted him and Vargas, they randomly opened and counted only a couple of stacks of hundreds. It was faster to do it that way, and if they later discovered anything was wrong with the cash, they knew where to find Dr. Vargas. Manuel

Vargas's elite medical center was no secret. The private hospital was famous not only in the Acapulco area of Mexico, but around the world.

Sun broke through the clouds and Cristo felt steam rise from his quick-drying shirt. The meeting place was a few hundred meters ahead. He couldn't see it; tall trees blocked his view. But he knew every step of the winding path that led uphill and then down into one of the many valleys along this trail.

Being outdoors put him at ease. Perhaps too much at ease for this kind of business. He reminded himself to stay alert.

He smelled their cigarette smoke before he saw them. Two men sat on boulders in the narrow, concealed valley below. A third meandered along the trail, carrying a rifle. He recognized them as Zetas, the same ones who'd made the delivery last time. His shadow, lengthened by the early morning sun, caught the seated men's attention as he crested the hill. They stood up. One plucked a handgun from his belt and held it loosely against his belly. The other lifted a tattered pack identical to the one Cristo carried.

"*Buenos días.*" Cristo unzipped his pack and showed them the money. In turn, they let him check the packets of white powder in their bag. He felt a pang of yearning when he touched the cool, pliable pouches.

He knew this powder. How it tasted. How it puffed dust into the air, the way flour does. He knew the best way to package it inside a capsule or dissolve it in solution. He knew how a little bit could smooth the rough edges of life. It was the Palacio's special house narcotic. Everyone called it *plack*.

Plack was Vargas's painkiller of choice for patients after surgery. He claimed it wasn't as addictive as morphine. He said eventually the drug would be legal in both Mexico and the United States, once the ponderous regulatory agencies finally got around to approving it. In the meantime, the Palacio Centro Medico had clients who needed plack, and Dr. Vargas wasn't the type to wait around for permission from some bureaucrat.

"*Bueno?*" said the Zeta.

"*Sí,*" Cristo replied. He reached forward to trade packs with the courier.

A sharp *crack* and its echoes shattered the morning calm. Startled, Cristo jerked back. Two meters away, the rifle-toting Zeta guard toppled to the ground. Wet drops sprayed Cristo's bare arm. Blood.

Rapid repeated rounds followed. Chips of stone splintered from a nearby boulder. The courier dove for cover behind a rock. He nudged his weapon over the top and returned fire. The third Zeta sprinted into the scrub. Cristo glanced up the hill he'd just descended and saw movement. Three men. Not Zetas.

Adrenaline kicked in. Blood surged through his arteries.

Move!

He swung the moneybag over his shoulder and ran.

Voices shouted behind him. Who called? What did they say? It didn't matter.

Get to the next valley. Get out of sight. Out of the line of fire.

Something snagged his backpack, yanking him to the left. He stumbled and his palm struck the dirt. He wriggled out of the shoulder strap and saw a hole in the pack. The tug he'd felt was the impact of a bullet. It had struck just off-center enough to miss his body.

He cast the bag aside. Maybe the attackers would pick up the money and let him flee into the wilderness alone. A kilo or two lighter, he covered ground faster.

He reached the rim of the valley and glanced back. The Zeta who'd sheltered behind the rock was down on one knee on the trail. Three men surrounded him. One of them lashed out with a kick. The Zeta's head hit the ground. An attacker pressed a foot into the drug dealer's back and aimed a pistol at his head. With a loud report, he scattered the man's brains across the dirt.

Cristo choked and ran like an Olympian, holding nothing back. Terror masked any physical discomfort from the exertion. After seeing the gunmen, he knew the abandoned cash wouldn't save him. The killer was bald and bore a scalp tattoo so large Cristo had read it clearly. Two huge, Gothic capital letters: MS.

The Mara Salvatrucha.

The most ruthless, most violent gang in the western hemisphere. They would hunt him down and kill him. They didn't need a reason.

Running downhill into the next valley, he allowed his stride to lengthen dangerously. He prayed he wouldn't slip. For the moment, the MS boys couldn't see him. Could he outrun them, staying one slope ahead so they couldn't shoot him in the back?

But already his thighs were burning. He was a scientist, not an athlete or a thug. His pursuers looked like they were practically kids, ten years younger than he was. If his life depended on a flat-out chase, he was finished.

He ran by an unnatural tower of small stones next to the trail. A cairn. Decades ago, he and his friends explored up here, making piles like that one to mark their discoveries. Then he remembered. It had been a long time but he knew it was nearby. Could he find it?

He attained the lip of the next ridge just as the Mara Salvatruchas entered the valley behind. *Where? Where?*

There, at the low point of the canyon: an overgrowth of ferns.

The feathery fronds marked a stream that trickled out of the mountain. He sped to the ferns and plunged up hill, off the trail, following the water. Sucking air into his lungs to feed his overwrought muscles, he noticed a cool draft that stank like chicken coop mixed with moldy root cellar.

The stench of salvation.

He ducked deeper into the trees and didn't look back. The ferns thrived on the humidity near the stream. Their broad, green fronds concealed an old rockfall underneath. He scrambled over the uneven ground and twisted an ankle on a hidden rock. The entrance was near.

Another cairn peeked through the leaves. That had to be the place. Someone had marked the cave entrance. He knocked down the rock tower and spotted a fissure in the base of the mountain. The opening was two meters wide but less than half a meter high at its tallest point. If the MS weren't local—and he doubted they were, this was Zeta territory—they wouldn't know about the cave, and they probably wouldn't see it in the shadow of all those ferns. Gulping one last breath of outside air, he extended his arms and forced his head and shoulders into the crevice.

It was a tight squeeze. If they found him now, they could fill him with bullets and leave him like a cork in a bottle. He crawled into the earth, hands grasping soft, wet mud. The crevice funneled into a tunnel and the sunlight dimmed. Odors he had whiffed outside now overwhelmed, a foul, dense, ripe miasma mixed with only a trace of fresh air.

Ever narrower and darker, the tunnel forced him to wriggle like a worm. His shoulders scraped an unyielding stone roof. Too wedged to look back at his feet, he guessed he was inside, his whole body swallowed by the mountain. So far, he hadn't been shot.

The earth muffled sounds from outside. No way to tell if the Mara Salvatruchas had seen him, if they were closing on the entrance to the cave. He pressed forward into diminishing light. If he reached the chamber, his chance of survival would increase exponentially.

"Ooof." Groping through total blackness, he struck his forehead on a low-hanging rock. Warm blood trickled down the side of his nose. To avoid more obstacles, he probed the invisible path ahead with one arm. Jagged rock above, wet clay below. He traveled a few more meters. The tunnel widened. He reached out, literally not seeing his hand in front of his face, and felt the floor slope sharply down.

The cave.

One more push and he slid down the slippery slope like a penguin on ice. On his belly, blind and accelerating head first, he lost control. Had he misremembered the height—

His face plowed into raw muck with a horrible stench. Bat guano. Piles and piles of it.

He lurched to his knees and dry heaved. The inside of his shirt was all he had to wipe the filth from his face. Stale air and total darkness made him dizzy. He listened. The uselessness of his eyes made his hearing more sensitive, but the only sounds were his breathing and a distant drip-drip of water. In the silence, his brain manufactured a ringing in his ears.

No sound of pursuit.

He relaxed a little. If the MS entered the tunnel, he would hear them. Unless they had flashlights, they'd be as blind as he was. And if they were waiting for him to come out, he could make them wait a very long time.

A faint whisper of sound and breeze attracted his attention. He spun his head around but saw nothing. The profound blackness affected more than his vision. He could feel it, like a woolliness inside his skull. Disoriented, he tried to recall the chamber's shape.

Something brushed his cheek and chittered softly.

He pulled back in revulsion, but the touch came again from another direction. Flinging his hands up to protect his face, he bumped something in the air. Something small and soft.

Bats.

At this time of year? The cave was always empty in the summertime. In warm weather, the bat colony migrated north.

Already hunted and half-sick, he felt a new distress. His father always said a summer bat was a bad omen. Cristo was now a grown man, an educated man, and he didn't believe in omens. It wasn't his father's fortune-telling that filled him with dread when he pondered why the bats were here out of season.

What worried him was rabies.

Rabies affected animal behavior. A colony of bats infected with rabies might migrate at the wrong time or place. It could explain why the bats were here now.

He huddled in the sludge and covered his head with his arms. Because of the unique nature of his work at the Palacio, he had a fighting chance against the rabies virus. Against the Mara Salvatrucha, he had nothing.

Bats or no bats, I'm staying put.

Time passed. He started to shiver. Anxiety blossomed in his chest with every flap and squeak. His phone was lost with the backpack so it was impossible to tell how long he'd been in the cave. Minutes? Hours?

Be patient.

The year-round chill of the cave gradually vanquished his sweaty exertion. He shivered and his teeth chattered. Gingerly he stood up. If memory served, the chamber was big enough to move about, to get his blood moving. He stretched his arms and hopped in place.

He must have struck one of the bats. Or maybe the group was startled by the movement which they could "see" even without light. He didn't know. The only certainty was he'd made a mistake.

What had been an occasional whisper of a wing exploded into a hurricane of flying mammals. Bat wings, fur, claws touched him everywhere at once. He recoiled but no direction was safe. The entire invisible space around him became thick with bats. He swatted at them, trying to keep his head in the clear. Bats scratched the skin on his arms and face. He whirled in place, losing all sense of direction. He was on his knees. His elbow struck a rock. He flailed in a black void, drowning in a sea of bats.

By chance he found the waist-high opening in the wall. He scrambled up and plunged into it on his belly. The swarm went with him. Pinned in the tunnel, he couldn't keep them off. As he squirmed ahead, bats nipped his arms and bit his ankles. He kicked and crushed a bat against the roof of the tunnel. Then another. Warm wetness from the animals' bodies seeped into his sock. He gasped. Was the air getting fresher?

Bats swept past him. Yes—the tunnel was lightening. He could *see* the bats fly ahead. Towards the outside.

Recklessly he pushed forward, and burst into blinding daylight.

On his hands and knees, Cristo dragged himself into the ferns at the mouth of the cave. Water trickled peacefully in the adjacent stream. The bats dispersed like smoke. He wavered in the hot air and bright sun, trying to open eyes adapted to total darkness. His stomach heaved with disgust as he scraped the mashed carcass of a bat off the front of his shirt.

"This one is a very big *murciélago*, eh? But he has no wings," said a voice with the timbre of sandpaper.

Cristo's heart skipped a beat. He was not alone.

He lifted his head and blinked furiously, struggling to bring his vision into focus.

The unknown man chuckled savagely. "Maybe he's a rat, not a bat. Good thing I brought a trap." More voices laughed in agreement.

The cold steel of a gun barrel pressed against the back of Cristo's head, forcing his gaze groundward. He thought about the rats he'd sacrificed at the lab and doubted his own death would be as humane.

"Rats can crawl. Crawl. This way."

A kick landed on his backside, encouraging him to move. Keeping his head down, he crawled painfully over the rockfall to the path.

He deeply regretted leaving the cave. The bat storm was horrifying but he would've survived. Now the Mara Salvatrucha had him. Men grabbed his arms and yanked them behind his back. He sank back to sit on his heels, and his chest dropped to his knees.

They handcuffed his wrists. The gun barrel stayed glued to his skull.

A pair of snakeskin boots entered his limited field of view. A worn leather backpack plopped into the dust between him and the boots, stirring a small cloud.

"Zetas are rats," the voice said.

Cristo glimpsed the shadow of the speaker's arm in motion. The gun was pulled away from his head. The man reached forward, grabbed Cristo's chin, and lifted to face him.

Cristo glanced left and right. Not far off, he spied a helicopter. He was surrounded by at least seven or eight men. Gangsters. Several sported the elaborate three-color tattoos of the MS on their faces and bald heads. All the men were armed.

He thought of his elderly mother, and how she would mourn for him.

The leader, in those snakeskin boots and a pair of jeans, let go of his chin. He was a hard, slender man, shorter than average, clean-shaven, with close-cropped black hair. He had no facial ink, only a modest mark on his left forearm. His age was indeterminate, fifties maybe, unless the gray hairs and furrowed skin were premature. Cristo guessed that the Mara Salvatrucha worked for his group, whatever that was, probably as hired thugs.

"You're no Zeta," the leader said. "Who are you?"

He saw no use in lying. In fact, his association with a powerful friend might be the key to getting out of this alive.

"My name is Cristo Castillo. I work for Dr. Manuel Vargas. Of the Palacio Centro Medico. He's a good customer." Hastily he added, "For anyone. We buy plack. For cash. No risk."

His interrogator studied him and did not respond. Cristo swallowed hard.

The man took a step and turned his attention to something behind Cristo, to his left. Cristo heard a whimper, and looked.

The one surviving Zeta courier kneeled in the dirt. The center of his face was painted with blood, apparently streaming from a broken nose. Like Cristo's, his hands were bound behind his back. Two men pointed rifles at him. His whole body trembled as the rival gang leader approached.

"Is this true?" the leader asked.

The Zeta wagged his head up and down and blubbered 'yes.'

"A new client for Sinaloa?"

More blubbering. Despite fear for his own safety, Cristo pitied the courier. He sensed the tide was turning against this fellow.

The scratchy voice of the kingpin continued. "Because this is Sinaloa territory now. Zeta rats are...not welcome. Right boys?"

The gangsters shouted their assent, raised their arms, and fired bullets into the air. For a moment, Cristo shut his eyes.

When he opened them, a pistol had appeared in the leader's hand. The man brandished it as he addressed his troops.

"Maybe he's not a rat. Let's find out."

He gestured to one of his men. Cristo held his breath in terror as the man came toward him. But he did not lay a hand on him. Instead, he put on a work glove and picked up a half-dead bat that twitched, flightless, on the ground nearby.

The leader said, "I don't think a bat will bite a rat. Do you?"

The men laughed. The one holding the bat brought it close to the Zeta's face. The bat screeched a soft, high-pitched wail. The Zeta arched his back to pull his head away.

"Or, does a rat bite a bat?" the leader asked. He looked at his prisoner. "Which should we try? Who bites?"

The Zeta sobbed and pleaded. A Mara Salvatrucha thug moved behind him and held his shoulders.

"Let him bite the head off the bat," the leader said. "I've always wanted to see that."

Horrified, Cristo saw the amusement in the leader's expression as his lackey pressed the bat, head first, toward the Zeta's face. The Zeta sealed his mouth closed, and twisted and moaned.

In a flash, the injured bat lashed out and bit the prisoner's lip. Startled, the gangster lost his grip on the animal. It hung there like a ghastly beard, squealing and mixing with the blood that dripped from the courier's chin.

The Zeta screamed. His captor let go of his shoulders and stepped aside, laughing.

Please don't let them torture me before I die.

When the Sinaloa boss fired his weapon point-blank at the Zeta's head, Cristo felt a small measure of relief that his own death might be swift.

The gruesome pair of man and bat collapsed to the ground. The drug lord turned to Cristo. Cristo's back stiffened.

"Sinaloa knows of Vargas," the leader said. He tapped the courier's backpack with his toe. "Sinaloa has something Vargas needs."

Desperate to justify his own existence, Cristo spoke up. "Vargas has much to offer. The Palacio is the finest hospital in Mexico. I can—"

"You can't. So shut up."

He shut up. The man stowed his weapon into a shoulder holster and stroked his chin. "The Palacio…"

Was he pondering a deal? Cristo wondered, but he dared not open his mouth again.

The drug lord ambled toward the corpse. The bullet had missed the bat, which flopped where it had fallen to earth. He lifted his boot and stomped his heel on the creature, smashing what life remained. He crossed his arms and looked at the sky. Then he gestured to his men and strode swiftly toward the helicopter. Hope flickered in Cristo's mind.

The leader's back was turned to him as he walked away. He called out, "Tell your boss he will hear from Luis Angel de la Rosa."

Several gangsters trailed after de la Rosa and boarded the helicopter with him. The three Mara Salvatruchas who had originally arrived on foot and ambushed the plack deal, lingered. One approached Cristo with a sneer on his face. He raised his fist and Cristo braced for a blow. Instead, the man laughed scornfully, stepped behind Cristo and unlocked one of his hands. Cristo fought back tears of relief as the trio picked up the pack of money and walked away.

He put some distance between himself and the dead Zeta, and sat against a rock, nervously fiddling with the handcuffs still locked to his right wrist. He lingered until the bat bites on his body had crusted over and the sun was low in the sky. Then hoping his tormentors were gone, he followed in their footsteps down the trail.

CHAPTER 2

Noise-canceling headphones muted the high-decibel din inside the helicopter, but Dr. Tessa Price didn't make small talk with the pilot. She took her eyes off the screen of her laptop only once, to glance out the window. Infinite hues of blue colored the placid waters below. A strip of intense green decorated the shore where the Pacific Ocean met Mexico. In the distance, green transitioned to brown as scrub-covered mountains rose from the coastal lowlands. A lovely sight. She wished she were here on vacation, to relax and enjoy it.

The unfinished text on her computer beckoned. She thought for a moment, then typed. *Sample size not adequate for stated confidence interval. Additional studies needed to support authors' conclusions.*

Tessa felt a twinge of guilt, just like every other time she'd advised a peer-reviewed journal to decline publication of a research paper. She knew first-hand how much time, money, sweat, and passion went into preparing a scientific manuscript. But wanting a submission to be brilliant didn't make it so.

Reviewer recommendation: REJECT.

Too harsh? she wondered. No. Publishing experimental data in her field wasn't an academic game. The research had real-world consequences. Handing out smiley face stickers for mediocre work did nothing to save the lives of sick kids.

The helicopter pilot pointed over the water. "The Palacio."

"Already?" she said. They'd taken off from Acapulco only twenty minutes ago.

It seemed a waste to fly such a short distance, but Dr. Manuel Vargas, founder and director of the Palacio Centro Medico, didn't allow guests to arrive by land. At first she thought this policy was pretentious, designed to create a sense of exclusivity. Then she'd heard about the drug-related violence on the road.

Vargas knows his business. Kidnapped clients don't pay their bills.

Ahead she saw the peninsula owned and occupied by the medical center. Rocky cliffs ringed the finger of land formed long ago by some now-extinct volcano. Thick forest covered the table-like top of the peninsula. The tree cover was broken by a few holes of golf, two glittering swimming pools, and the main hospital tower. The helicopter aimed for a landing pad on the tower's roof, marked with a huge red "H" inside a white cross.

Though her mission was deadly serious, she felt a thrill to be admitted into this private club, one that catered to rich globetrotters with health problems.

Before she decided to work with Vargas, she had done her homework. The Palacio was one of many medical tourism centers around the world that combined resort amenities with elective health care. Patients trying to escape the high prices, long queues, and abysmal customer service at hospitals in Canada, the US, and Great Britain, could buy quality care at a fraction of the cost in Costa Rica, Thailand, and India. Medical tourism was a growth industry. Cash customers could get a root canal done in Monterrey, angioplasty of the coronary arteries in Kuala Lumpur, or a hip replacement in Bangkok. She'd even stumbled on a South African company that offered patients "surgery and safari."

The Palacio matched or exceeded them all in luxury. More importantly for her, this gorgeous Mexican facility offered something the others didn't.

The helicopter touched down with a gentle bump. She felt the vibration and noise decrease as the rotor blades slowed. Out on the roof, a man stood in a doorway that led into the building. He unrolled a crimson mat across the pavement.

Red carpet service. She glanced at her black travel skort and running shoes, and visualized her rumpled, chestnut-colored crop cut. *What, do patients show up in Oscar de la Renta?*

The man wasn't wearing a tux but he was dressed in the most stylish clothes she'd ever seen at a hospital: a double-breasted seersucker suit with pale blue stripes, and a natty pair of boat shoes. She felt a glow of appreciation. Vargas himself had turned up to meet her. She climbed out of the aircraft and filled her lungs with sultry tropical air.

"Welcome, Dr. Price." Vargas grasped her hand with both of his. His brown skin was soft and smooth; his two-handed grip was gentle and reassuring. "*Bienvenido a México.*"

"*Gracias*, Dr. Vargas," she said. "It's great to finally see this place."

His English word choices were perfect but his pronunciation was accented Spanish. "I am sorry it took a crisis to convince you to come."

She'd met Vargas in person once before, back in the United States, when they negotiated their agreement to run her clinical research trial at the Palacio. He was decent-looking for a man his age, but his charisma went way beyond his looks. A real charmer, even more so in this exotic setting. She caught herself calculating the age gap from her thirty-six to his fifty-something.

Knock it off. The last thing you need is to get involved with a surgeon again.

He touched her shoulder and steered her along the red carpet toward the entrance.

"Wait. I don't want to miss this view." She walked to the edge of the roof to survey the campus from on high.

The Palacio had all the appearance of a five-star resort, with gardens, walking paths, and outdoor dining shaded by colorful umbrellas. A wall surrounded the hospital, separating mundane service functions like trash pickup from the luxurious areas where Palacio guests played. A road ran along the wall. One branch of the road descended a steep slope and connected the peninsula to the Mexican mainland. This lifeline passed an airstrip before crossing the outermost security fence and disappearing into the coastal forest.

As attractive as it all was, her focus was on business. "Is that your research facility?" She pointed at the only other multi-story structure on the peninsula, a smaller, lower building a few hundred yards to the north.

"Yes. The Palacio's crown jewel," he said. "My competitors can fix knees and enlarge breasts as well as we do. But only the Palacio can give hope."

Hope. The most valuable health care product of all. Thank God Vargas had allowed her to be part of this vision. The Palacio Centro Medico was unique in the industry because Vargas sponsored medical research. He reached out to people who'd been failed by conventional medicine, but rather than exploit these sometimes desperate, vulnerable patients with irrational, New Age alternatives, he offered experimental therapies with a basis in real science. Most of the Palacio's cutting-edge treatments were not approved in the United States, and some, such as her gene therapy, were available nowhere else in the world. Doubtless many of them did not work. But all offered a fighting chance.

A boy like Gunnar deserved a fighting chance.

A breeze dissipated the helicopter's engine fumes and Tessa smelled the fragrance of flowers and wet earth. The treetops rustled and birds squawked. *So peaceful.* Unlike home, no highway noise, leaf blowers, or distant sirens. The ambient sounds here were like spa music.

She turned away from the edge. "Manuel, I don't think I can trust your outcomes data." He gave her a quizzical look. "The placebo effect is too strong. All your patients are bound to feel better."

Vargas smiled. "When you see Gunnar, you will not think the weather caused the change."

Her heart skipped a beat. "How is he? Before Cristo got sick, he told me Gunnar was looking a lot better."

"That was two weeks ago." They strolled back to the red carpet. Vargas opened the door for her. "When Cristo returns, he will not recognize the boy."

Her excitement faded. "So Gunnar's worse again."

"*Ay Dios mío*, Doctor, do you always have such black thoughts? No. Cristo witnessed only the first signs of progress. Now your experiment is looking more like miracle than science."

Was it possible? Might her gene therapy actually be reversing the boy's terrible disease? Six months ago she sent Gunnar and his mother Sigrun to the Palacio. For six months, the colleagues she'd trained had been treating the boy with the therapeutic virus she designed. For six months they scrutinized him for any sign of improvement. Until a few weeks ago, all they could say was Gunnar hadn't gotten any worse, which was a victory of sorts for a child with Batten disease. The relentless genetic killer tore the patient ever downward. Stability was a blessing.

Any recovery, no matter how small, would be unprecedented. But not un-hoped for. Besides his mother, no one was more emotionally committed to saving Gunnar than Tessa Price.

Tessa entered a short hallway with plush chocolate-colored carpet that led to an elevator with elegant wooden doors. In the center of each door was the Palacio's logo, a clever fusion of an Aztec serpent image and a caduceus, the classical snakes-and-wings symbol for the medical profession.

I wonder how much that design cost him. The Palacio's director clearly had refined taste. She suddenly felt under-dressed and out of place in this haven for the rich.

Instead of pressing a button, Vargas summoned the elevator by placing his palm on a molded hand-shaped panel. "I will have my people check you in. You brought your vaccination record?"

Her stomach flipped at the memory of getting her shots. The Palacio required all visitors to be up-to-date with their immunizations. She'd been more than a little behind with hers. If the need to travel to the Palacio had been any less compelling, she would never have consented to the jabs.

Vargas didn't need to know she had to be sedated before she got them. She simply replied, "Yes."

The elevator stopped on the ground floor. They exited into what looked like the lobby of a fine hotel with Meso-American decor. She vaguely recognized Mayan and Aztec glyphs carved onto the walls and pillars of the expansive space. The glyphs portrayed simple animal and human figures as well as abstract maze-like shapes. Flowering vines, some real, some fake, climbed the pillars. Arches built of tan-colored bricks connected the lobby to hallways paved with natural-looking stone tiles. The faux-archeologic effect was stylish and evoked a sense of adventure.

Too bad Gunnar can't see it, she thought. A kid would love this stuff.

"Dr. Price!" someone called from across the room.

Vargas smiled and kissed her cheek. "I will leave you in good hands."

She turned toward the voice. A slight, black-haired man wearing khaki shorts and of all things, a bowtie, skipped in her direction.

Dr. Sameer Desai.

The last time she saw this baby-faced young physician from India was during the coldest days of winter in her American lab. A native of the tropics, Sameer was always cold during that time, even while working indoors. She smiled and remembered the down-filled vest he never took off. It puffed him to twice his normal size.

"Hey, Sameer. You've shrunk." She made a gesture to suggest the barrel shape of the vest.

Sameer Desai beamed. He reached to shake her hand, then changed his mind and wrapped a skinny arm around her in a half-hug.

"You made it! How was your trip?" The British intonation of his words lilted in the musical fashion of English speakers from the subcontinent.

"Uneventful," she said. "It's good to see you."

"I, too, am glad you're here," he said.

Oh Lord, he's blushing. Six months later and he's still carrying a torch for me?

"I hoped you would come sooner," he said.

She heard the suppressed yearning in his voice. When Sameer was working with her in the US, she was emotionally drained by divorce proceedings. Maybe she would see him with fresh eyes now.

"I knew you and Cristo had things under control," she said.

"We did. You trained us. But—" He searched for a compelling excuse. "We had histopathology slides for you to see."

That's romantic, she thought sarcastically. "I would've come but Vargas has that stupid vaccination policy."

"What is wrong with his policy?"

"Well, he won't let anybody visit the Palacio unless they've had shots for everything, whether they need it or not."

Sameer looked aghast. "You don't believe in vaccines?"

"Of course I do. They're one of the most important medical achievements of all time. It's just that…"

What? What's the big deal with a little stick?

She had no rational answer to this question. But the facts were, merely thinking about a hypo pricking her skin set her stomach churning, and made her feel faint. She pictured her baby Benjamin, pierced and probed in every part of his tiny body.

For me, needles puncture more than flesh. They stab my soul.

But she wasn't ready to share this. She said, "I didn't come until I had to."

She had stayed in the US until Cristo was too sick to do his job. Only for Gunnar's sake had she taken the shots—while drugged.

She and Sameer ambled to a quiet corner and sat on a rattan settee under a softly turning palm leaf ceiling fan. Sameer said brightly, "We might not need you after all. I talked to Cristo this morning and he's feeling much better. He may be back soon." He leaned closer and lowered his voice. "Which is quite fortunate if you ask me. He told me a secret."

"A secret? About what?"

"His illness. Three weeks ago he was bitten by a bat. I think possibly several bats."

Eew! Not only gross, very dangerous. Was there a connection to his illness? "How did that happen?"

"He was chased into a cave by drug runners. The bats were there out of season. Naturally his first thought was rabies."

Tessa's first thought was, *I'm glad I came by helicopter.* "Cristo's been vaccinated against rabies. It's part of our research protocol."

"I know. He followed the guidelines and gave himself two booster shots. But even that is no guarantee. When the headaches started, he was very worried."

"He didn't ask you for help? Or did he see a different doctor?"

"What would be the point? If prevention fails, there is no cure for rabies. Cristo knows this." Sameer smiled. "No need to worry. Whatever made him sick, it is leaving him. So maybe this will be a vacation for you, yes?"

I'm not here to have fun. "Rumor has it he's not the only one on the mend," she said. "Gunnar."

"Yes. The miracle patient."

That word again—miracle. Dr. Sameer Desai was directly responsible for clinical care of patients in research studies at the Palacio. She valued his opinion more than Vargas's. "Is he really getting better?"

"Better is a relative term. Patients with Batten disease are the sickest of the sick. But I am on my way to remove his G button," he said triumphantly. "The child can swallow again."

"No way. He hasn't been able to eat for eight months."

"Wrong. Gunnar has been taking all his food by mouth for the last week."

Her mouth dropped open. *And no one told me?* "Why didn't you tell me?"

He shrank a little and folded his hands in his lap. "If it is not too presumptuous to say, I know how you feel about this case. The changes in the boy's condition have been sudden. They might reverse just as quickly. Your trip here was already planned. I thought if the patient stayed on this path, you would see for yourself. If not—I did not want to disappoint you."

"You should have told me."

She thought she spoke gently, but he wilted like a pansy in the summer sun. She'd learned during the month Sameer and Cristo spent working in her lab that Sameer was sensitive to criticism, especially from her. That made it hard to rigorously teach him the techniques. She'd persevered because these two men were going to run her gene therapy trial at the Palacio. Gunnar's life depended on their being the best.

She patted his shoulder. "Don't worry about it. Can you take me to see him?"

"Of course, Doctor."

"You know you can still call me Tessa."

There was nothing subtle about the redness that flushed his cheeks. "Yes, Tessa. When I show you, you will understand why you must see to believe."

CHAPTER 3

Acid rain dripped off the yellow plastic tarp that covered the street vendor's stall, filling nearby potholes with muddy water. The open-air marketplace was crowded with sellers, but too few buyers. A wrinkled Latina wearing stretchy black pants and a faded pink tee shirt rearranged a display of counterfeit handbags and dolls dressed in frilly princess dresses, pulling her wares into a narrow zone of dryness.

A young man, nineteen years old, watched her from across the street. He lifted a cigarette to his mouth with an arm entirely covered in three-color tattoos. He took a drag from the cigarette and reflected that he didn't like what he saw. He didn't like that woman working out here, every day from dawn to dusk in the dirty air.

The woman caught him staring at her.

"*Mijo!*" she shouted. "Go find your sister!"

Mama. Always telling me what to do.

He tossed the smoking butt into the gutter and went to find the girl. When he returned, he would explain to his mother that he was going away for a while.

She thinks I'm good for nothing. That my friends will get me in trouble. When I show her the money, she'll have to admit she was wrong.

How much would he give her? Not all of it. He deserved to keep some for himself. After all, he was the one who was going to suffer. But he'd give her enough to keep her out of that godawful stall for at least a year.

He found his little sister flirting with a much-too-old stranger who had cozied up with her under his nice, oversized umbrella. He grabbed her arm and dragged her away.

"Hey!" She slapped him and tried to keep up in her high heels.

With the money, he'd buy her a nice *quinceañera* party. She'd be turning fifteen soon. He would decide which boys to invite.

"Mama is looking for you."

"So what? I can do what I want. Just like you."

"Stay away from that man. He's not Sinaloa."

"Are you saying I can only date your friends?" She spat at the ground. "Your friends don't have any money."

They arrived back at their mother's stall and found the merchandise unattended. His mother was nowhere to be seen.

"Mama!" he called. *Stupid woman. Someone will steal everything.*

At that very moment a van pulled up. One tire dropped into a deep rut and splashed him and his sister with filthy runoff. He wondered if the driver had seen the empty stall and was coming to take what he could.

The rear doors opened and four men jumped out. One went straight up to his sister and seized her. It was the older man again, the one with the umbrella.

"Get away from her," he said, reaching for his gun.

Too late. The other three men surrounded him, pinned his arms, and shoved him toward the van. As he wrestled with them, he saw their gang-identifying tattoos.

Zetas. What the hell are they doing on this street? This is Sinaloa territory.

He shouted for help from his homies, but the operation was swift. In seconds, both he and his sister were bundled into the van. The doors closed and the vehicle lurched away at high speed. Duct tape was slapped over his mouth and around his wrists. Just before they covered his eyes, he saw the Zetas shove his sister to the floor next to a woman similarly bound, her eyes wide with fear.

His mother.

Umbrella Man whispered into his ear. "We want you to deliver a gift."

CHAPTER 4

Tessa and Sameer crossed the lobby of the Palacio, passing pots of flowering hibiscus plants and spherical topiary shrubs that looked like green lollipops on giant sticks. Sameer paused to pour her a glass of lemon-infused water from a crystal beverage dispenser.

She was thirsty from the trip but hesitated. "Is it safe?"

"As safe as from your tap at home. Vargas would not settle for anything less."

A porter scurried by, pushing a cart loaded with matching pieces of Louis Vuitton luggage of every shape and size. Other Palacio employees, wearing tropical floral shorts or skirts, hustled about, pushing wheelchairs, carrying drinks. Tessa saw Vargas visiting with an elderly couple seated at a table. The woman's right hand was inside a shiny black dome about the size of half a basketball.

"What's that thing on the table?" she asked Sameer.

"Hand scanner. Part of the arrival protocol. We use a combination of fingerprints and hand vascular patterns to identify guests. People like it much better than wearing a hospital ID bracelet. It also means no one has to carry a key. All the doors are locked and unlocked by handprint."

"Convenient."

"At the time of admission we also draw blood and do low-resolution genome sequencing. That gives us a genetic profile of each patient's blood type and alerts us to certain disease risks. We can also use the DNA sequence to predict the right dose of medicine for each person based on whether they have fast or slow metabolism. So we see fewer side effects from the drugs we prescribe here."

"Personalized medicine. Nice. I bet the patients love it."

"The technology is mainstream but other hospitals can't afford to use it on everyone," he said. "Look, they're done. I can process you now before we see Gunnar."

"But I'm not a patient. You don't need to admit me."

"It doesn't matter. Vargas screens everyone in the building, including employees, to monitor for infections and immune responses. You'll need a hand scan to get into your room and to eat in the restaurants. The menus are personalized to each client's dietary requirements."

She felt goosebumps rising on her arms. "You can scan my hand. But you're not doing a blood draw. Not even a teeny, tiny one."

"A personal genome analysis is worth at least a thousand dollars. Vargas gives it to you free. It's one of the benefits of working here."

"Forget it, Sameer. Not gonna happen."

"But—"

A booming male voice speaking English with a Texas twang reverberated through the lobby.

"Then I said, 'Jack, that's not my ex-wife, it's yours!'" The speaker belly-laughed at his own punchline. A woman at his side giggled.

Tessa stared at an odd parade. A big white man, tall and wide and with an exuberant stride, marched in with a beautiful Latina twenty, maybe thirty, years younger. The word "statuesque" came to mind. The woman was tall and chiseled, with perfectly symmetric facial features and golden skin as smooth as polished marble stretched over well-developed muscles. Lustrous auburn hair cascaded over her shoulders and swayed as she moved like a cat next to her grizzly bear escort.

"Excuse me," she heard Vargas say to the elderly couple. "It appears Mr. Simmons's plane landed early." He didn't wait for their response and headed toward the new arrivals.

"Dixie. *Ablegen!*" the big man said.

Then Tessa noticed a dog marching calmly at the man's left side. It was a German shepherd as graceful as the man's human companion. The animal responded instantly to the German command and sank to the floor, head up, ears erect, utterly focused on its master. The dog wore a black leather collar adorned with red gemstones. No leash was in sight.

Vargas pumped hands with, and practically bowed to, the newcomers. They exchanged pleasantries, and Vargas led them to Sameer. "Dr. Desai, I'd like you to meet Mr. Lyle Simmons."

The big man thrust his hand forward. "Pleasure to meet you, Doc. Vargas here tells me y'all are in charge of the experimental stuff. Which makes you my fairy godmother." Lyle Simmons laughed at his own joke, a deep, hearty laugh. Tessa got the impression this was the only kind of laugh he had. "Y'know, making wishes come true and all that. My girl's wishes, too. By the way, let me introduce you to my lovely companion."

Tessa and Sameer turned toward the beautiful woman, but Lyle knelt and stroked the dog's head.

"This is Dixie," Lyle said. "She's been with me a long time."

The human female made a tsk-tsk sound and brushed the hair from her face. "Like most of his jokes, this one is old. My name is Isabella Branco and I wonder if I made a mistake letting him come here."

Her voice was creamy and low. She spoke with a Portuguese accent. Tessa guessed she was probably from Brazil.

"You don't mean that, honey. You need this procedure as much as I do." Lyle slipped an arm around her waist and yanked her body close to his. "You *want* it."

Isabella gave him a stern look for several seconds, just long enough for the confident smile on his face to start to wither. Then she wrapped her hands around his neck and mashed her mouth against his.

Sameer, who had yet to say a word, shifted nervously from one foot to the other as the kiss went on and on. Tessa was amused by Sameer's discomfort. Only Dixie appeared unmoved by the public display of affection.

"Of course I want it," Isabella said, disengaging at last. "Can this doctor give it to us?"

Sameer snapped to attention. "Yes. Well. You are here for one of our exclusive Pioneering Procedures?"

"That's what your brochures call 'em," Lyle said. "Pudendal artery stent for me and cataract surgery for my dog." He laughed and elbowed the Indian. "I'm calling this our ball trip."

"Why is that, Mr. Simmons?" Sameer said. Tessa could practically see him sweat.

"'Cause the dog's getting new eyeballs and I'm getting my balls fixed!"

Sameer's face turned its reddest yet. Lyle, Isabella, and Dr. Vargas all cracked up. Tessa had to laugh, too. She didn't know what medical procedure this guy was getting but she had a pretty good idea what part of his anatomy was being tended to.

Sameer cleared his throat. "Sir, I supervise all the Pioneering Procedures. Our success rates for your treatment are excellent. I sincerely hope you're pleased with the outcome."

Isabella peeled one arm off Lyle, reached out and brushed Sameer's cheek with her fingers. "I'm sure we will be."

Heat radiated from Sameer. "My colleague and I must check on a patient," he said. "Your surgeon will come to your room to answer any questions you may have."

Sameer grabbed Tessa's wrist. She nearly tripped as he pulled her away.

"No blood sample from me, then?" she teased.

"I can draw it later." He released her and hurried toward an exit.

She flipped a thumb in Lyle's direction. "What's his story?"

Sameer sighed. "He's here for an experimental therapy. Like yours, it is not approved in the US."

"I gathered that. What is it?"

"I cannot tell you—patient privacy. But I can say he is a VIP even for the Palacio. Vargas told me about him. That woman has several hundred million reasons to tolerate his behavior."

They made their way toward a pair of sliding screen doors framed with sandalwood. The doors automatically parted at their approach, releasing them into a lush, jasmine-scented garden. Tessa marveled at colorful butterflies attracted by platters of freshly-cut oranges and bananas. She turned toward a buzzing sound and saw a hanging hummingbird feeder. The red bulb was surrounded by brilliant green little hummers, each sporting a ruby throat. They darted and squabbled for access to the nectar.

"This is lovely, but where are we going?" From what she could see, the garden was completely enclosed by a stucco wall.

"To the Research Annex, where Gunnar is. Most people use the tunnel. I prefer to walk outside."

He explained that the Serenity Garden served as main entrance for the few clients who arrived by airplane instead of helicopter. As they got closer to the eight-foot-high wall, she saw a door. A metal plate was mounted next to it.

"After we scan your hand it will give you access to this door." He put his palm against the plate and an LED switched from red to green. With a click and a mechanical whir, the door opened.

On the other side of the wall, it was no serenity garden.

A motion-detecting camera mounted above the door they'd just exited locked on to them and followed their movements. A cracking hum drew Tessa's gaze upward, where she saw five rows of wire strung on posts leaning out from the top of the wall. At intervals along the wall were yellow signs in English and Spanish warning of an electric fence. She thought the universal graphic was more effective than any words: a picture of a hand contacting a lightning bolt.

Note to self: no climbing.

A two-lane road hugged the wall as it arced around the main hospital. Two soldiers dressed in green camouflage and black boots patrolled the road, armed with what Tessa could only describe as big guns. The weapons rested on their shoulders while they marched.

"Rough neighborhood," she said.

"Why do you think Vargas brings his clients in by air?" Sameer said. "I think he has special arrangements with the drug gangs. They leave us alone on the peninsula. But security is important. On any day, we have scores of rich foreigners here."

Not only rich, but also old and disabled, she thought, picturing the elderly couple that had just checked in. All of the guests were preoccupied by their own pains or pleasures. Talk about a soft target.

"Vargas keeps the security hidden from our clients as much as possible. You have to remember the people who come here are tourists. They also have medical problems. If there is the smallest hint of danger, who would come?"

She had an answer for that. Sigrun Baldursdottir and her son Gunnar would come. Because death stalked them wherever they went.

Sameer raised a hand in greeting to the soldiers. One acknowledged with a curt nod.

They walked down the road to the only intersection, which was protected by a guard house. Several more armed soldiers loitered around it. Tessa recognized this as the branch of the road that went to the mainland—the only road in or out. Uninvited vehicles trying to get into the Palacio would have to get past the guards and the tire shredders she saw beneath a black-and-yellow-striped gate arm.

The phone in Sameer's pocket jangled. The guards looked up.

"You can get that. I don't mind." She suspected that unlike most people he was too polite to text or talk in her presence.

"Thank you, I will just…" He lifted out the phone and read a message. His face clouded as his finger swept over the screen.

"Something wrong?"

Hastily he tapped a reply. "I'm sorry, but we must delay our visit to the patient. I may need your help with an urgent matter in the animal facility."

Vargas keeps research animals? That seemed weird but maybe one of his experimental treatments used antibodies from mice or something. "Problem with your rodents?"

He quickened his pace. "No. One of the chimps."

Tessa froze. "Chimpanzees? You're kidding, right?"

Sameer didn't slow as he headed down the road toward the Research Annex building.

He never makes jokes. She hurried to catch up.

"The chimps arrived a month ago, before Cristo went out sick," he said, avoiding eye contact. "Five females and one male. All elderly. Vargas has a patron who wants to use them in a research trial. They're testing a new treatment for dementia."

"There's no way keeping chimps here is legal." *Not to mention ethical.* Vargas couldn't just wake up one day and decide to house a chimpanzee troop unless he planned to lock them in cages unsuitable for apes. "I can count on one hand the number of facilities authorized to do chimp research in the States."

"Which is precisely why the donor came to Vargas," he said. "If I may say, it is the same reason you came. You know the American regulatory agencies don't always consider the greater good when they make decisions."

"We're talking about primates, Sameer, not microbes or fruit flies. Chimpanzees are more like humans than some teenagers. Keeping chimps is a big deal. A huge deal. You need experts. Money. Space."

"Vargas has money. And there is more space than you think. The animal facility in the Annex has rodent rooms, but we also have kennels for dogs and pigs. Vargas terminated the swine research to make room for the chimpanzees."

That was just plain wrong. "You're keeping chimps in a pigsty?"

They'd reached the Research Annex. Sameer paused to face her, his expression a mix of anger and embarrassment.

"It was not my decision."

"But you're involved."

"As Director of the Palacio's research programs, yes, I'm involved. But Cristo is responsible for day-to-day management of the animal facility."

"This must be a violation of some international treaty. How do you think that's going to affect your chances of getting an American medical license? Is it worth compromising your dream?"

Sameer's facial muscles tightened. "As much as it was when I carried your gene therapy vector with me into Mexico."

She flinched. "That was different."

"How, Doctor? The paperwork I gave to Customs told a half-truth about your virus. We knew they would never detect it; the molecular biology is too complex. You lied in the documents. And I broke the law."

"To save a child's life."

"You think the chimpanzee work is for fun? The goal is also to save lives." He gestured with his hand and his phone passed into her field of view. She glimpsed the text. "The research is important and Vargas is doing it according to reasonable ethical standards. The animals won't be subjected to invasive procedures. They're well-cared for."

"Then why is one of them dead?"

Too late he covered the screen of his phone. His shoulders slumped. "I don't know."

As she stepped up to the entrance, Tessa noted that architecturally the Research Annex was a smaller version of the Palacio's main hospital. It had the same Mayan design elements, with arches and carvings, though the decoration wasn't as elaborate. Sameer placed his hand in the scanner at the door. After a flash of white light, the door unlocked and they entered.

"Our research labs are in this building," he said. "The animal facility is in the basement. Most patients come over just for their medical procedures. We have a few rooms for long-term residents. At the moment, your experimental subject is the only one."

"He has a name," Tessa said. "It's Gunnar." It drove her crazy when medical people objectified sick children. Gunnar was a real, live person. With a name. Not "the patient" or the "experimental subject." It had been that way with Benjamin, too. Some of the hospital staff never used her son's name. She knew why. It protected them from the pain. But that didn't make it okay.

Sameer was too distracted to react to her scolding. "I must go to the animal lab. The techs are panicking without Cristo. Will you…"

He didn't flat-out ask for her help. No surprise considering the way she'd lit into him about the chimps. Sameer carried himself with humility, but he had a proud heart.

Tessa was a PhD scientist but she'd spent some time in medical school before dropping out. She also had years of experience working with laboratory animals. If there was a medical problem in the animal facility, she was a good person to have around.

"Of course," she said. Gunnar wasn't going anywhere.

They passed empty sofas and chairs in the small reception area and boarded the elevator. Sameer used his handprint again to gain access to the basement.

The doors opened. She recognized the drab features of a typical changing room: fluorescent lighting, brown vinyl flooring, cream-colored walls, and a constant seventy-two degrees. Several backless metal benches were mounted to the floor, and a central drain lay ready to accept waste water when the place got hosed down. Two pairs of reinforced doors led out of the room. One had a window. The other had a keypad lock built into the handle.

She heard the rumble of the ventilation system on overdrive. Fresh air was cycling into the facility but it failed to overcome a persistent sewer smell.

"You can use the dressing area." Sameer pointed at a curtain that hung from a track on the ceiling. It enclosed one corner of the room for privacy.

She'd been in enough animal facilities to know the drill. Change out of your street clothes into scrubs. Put on a disposable paper gown, shoe and hair covers, gloves, and a face mask. In the American labs where she'd worked, the animals came from certified disease-free breeders or they spent time in quarantine. This guaranteed that the animals didn't carry any germs. These clothing precautions were designed to protect the animals from germs on the humans, not the other way around.

But illegal chimpanzees were another story, especially if they were sick. She grabbed extra gloves, gown, and mask from a stainless steel cart.

Sameer reached into a large plastic bag marked with autoclave tape that meant the contents had been sterilized. He pulled out a set of green hospital scrubs and handed them to her. As she expected, both top and pants were one-size-fits-none. She ducked behind the curtain and undressed.

As she cinched up the oversized waist of the scrub pants, she heard something crash on the other side of the locked, windowless door. The crash was followed by a bizarre, muffled shriek.

She folded her clothes and slid the curtain aside. "What was that?"

Sameer snugged a surgical mask against his nose. "Nothing good."

She stuck close behind him as he entered a six-digit code in the keypad lock. The door opened with a *whoosh*.

The sounds that had been muffled by the door grew loud and monstrous—deranged, howling, freakish cries unlike anything she'd heard before. A horrible smell nearly overcame her.

"Dr. Desai!" A short, round Mexican woman rushed toward them, pulling a clean paper gown over her soiled scrubs as she ran. "We call you. Big problems with the chimps!"

Tessa tracked the odor of human excrement to the smears on the woman's garments.

"You put this on," the woman said as she forced an extra gown into Sameer's hands. "They go crazy in there!"

What am I getting into?

Tessa quickly oriented herself. The space was an oversized hallway, a staging area that led to the chambers where the animals lived. She counted three doors. Metal shelves stacked with supplies were the only things in the room.

Sameer stiffened as the woman grabbed his arm and dragged him toward the door at the end of the hall. The howls were coming from that direction. Tessa braced herself as the woman opened the door. Animal noises filled her ears, along with the clang of metal striking metal. A man shouted in Spanish.

They entered the primate room.

She'd thought the stench was bad in the outer rooms but in here it was truly awful. She couldn't breathe through her nose. Sameer cursed in Hindi.

In a flash she took in the layout of this room. On either side were individual "cages"—clearly pig stalls retrofitted to house chimpanzees. Floor-to-ceiling steel mesh separated one stall from another. Only one of the stalls had a chimpanzee inside. The rest of the apes were straight ahead, at the end of the room, in a single large enclosure. Four howling chimps jumped and tussled in a frenzy inside the communal cage.

This is totally messed up. Unhealthy for the chimps, dangerous for the caregivers.

Another tech in filthy scrubs—a man—came wild-eyed to Sameer. "They kill her," he said, pointing.

Killed?

With morbid curiosity she approached the cage and looked inside.

A furry, bloody mess lay on the floor: the mangled body of a chimpanzee. The rest of the cage was in riot as chimps wailed and leaped about. One banged a metal food dish against the steel mesh. Another stood erect on a wooden plank, baring its teeth. It was a large male, presumably the troop leader. Tessa couldn't help staring at its outlandish genitals. The chimp stared back, its eyes smoldering with intelligent fury.

Sameer finished tying his extra gown. "What happ—*ugh*." He stepped back from the cage.

Tessa looked away from the chimp. Something brownish-red, slick, and amorphous was plastered to Sameer's gown. It matched the color of the fleshy pile around the dead chimp.

"I've got it." One of the technicians plunged a needle into a pharmacy bottle and drew a clear liquid into the syringe.

Tessa saw the needle and instantly felt ill.

The male chimpanzee exploded with screams. It sprang from the plank and slammed into one of the females who was hanging from a steel bar near the front fence, tossing her aside. The other chimps responded with more cries and unrest.

She backed away. The tumult and stink were making her dizzy. She wasn't familiar with chimpanzee behavior, but these animals didn't seem merely angry. They seemed more like inmates in an asylum, driven by madness, acting out with violence. Had they murdered one of their own?

"Coming through," the tech said.

Her attention locked on to the needle in his hand. It seemed cartoonishly long. She closed her eyes for a moment and tried to banish the image of the needle from her thoughts. *Pull it together, Tessa. Sameer could use some help here.*

Then something warm and wet smacked her shoulder. Automatically her head turned in that direction. She saw what it was and gagged.

Oh God. They were throwing feces. She had chimpanzee shit on her.

The horror of it scattered what was left of her wits. *Get it off! Get it off!*

She spun around and bolted from the room.

CHAPTER 5

Tessa waited by the elevator in the changing room. The chaotic sounds from the primate lab had subsided some time ago. Once or twice she heard a dog bark. Vargas must house dogs behind another door in the interior hallway. She guessed he probably kept rats in the animal facility as well.

Why couldn't Sameer have had a problem with the rats? She could deal with rats. Not apes.

Her soiled garments were now sealed inside a plastic bag that failed to block the septic stench. Or maybe the smell was permanently imprinted on her senses. She couldn't tell.

I need a shower. Now.

Ashamed of her weakness and just plain grossed out, she desperately wanted to get out of the animal facility. She was kind of grateful that a hand scan was needed to operate the elevator. Given the choice she would've ditched, but she didn't want to do that to Sameer. At least, not any more than she already had.

I'm amazed he stayed, and the techs, too. Maybe they were used to offal and dung. Sameer would've worked with dead bodies in gross anatomy class as a med student. And the animal care techs had been cleaning up after those chimps for a month already.

Then again, maybe they were just tougher than she was.

I don't even own a pet to clean up after, she thought. And the only diapers I've changed…well, Benjamin's sickly little output during his weeks in the perinatal intensive care unit hardly qualified as poop.

She lay back on one of the hard benches to settle her queasy stomach. Her reward was a headache.

At last the door opened and Sameer returned. The stink accompanied him. Without speaking he went to the corner of the room and drew the curtain to undress.

"I'm sorry," she said. "I could *not* handle that."

The usual lilt in his voice had gone flat. "It's okay. Nothing you could do. My problem."

"So what happened?"

He reached around the curtain for a clean set of scrubs, which told her he was in no condition to put his regular clothes on.

"Maria and Juan—the techs—say the chimps were agitated yesterday. At the time they thought nothing of it. Today the troop was aggressive, fighting each other. They tried to separate them into individual pens but the animals wouldn't leave the community cage, not even for treats."

"What about the dead one?"

He sighed. "They don't really know what happened. At some point, one of the females ended up on the floor. They think she was injured. Then—"

"What?"

"They say the male attacked her. And the rest of the females followed his lead." Pause. "They ripped her to pieces."

She remembered the glob stuck to Sameer's gown in the chimp room. "Is that what they threw at you?"

He pulled the curtain aside, dressed in hospital green. "A bit of liver, I think."

"That's horrible."

"And bad news for Vargas. This behavior may be a reaction to the Alzheimer's drug we're testing. I don't know. A veterinarian will have to figure it out."

Sameer escorted her to a locker room and shower on the second floor of the Research Annex building. As cheap, heavily-scented shampoo trickled into the drain, the chimp smell finally faded from Tessa's nostrils. She pondered what she'd seen and blamed Vargas for it.

I can't believe he brought in chimpanzees. Way out of his league. Now some vet who probably makes a living delivering piglets is supposed to do a necropsy on what's left of the dead female? No primatologist would touch this mess with a ten-foot pole. The poor things. Whatever sent them off the deep end—moving into that abysmal facility, or exposure to the experimental drug—I don't see any easy fix. Vargas will probably have to euthanize the whole troop.

Infuriating. It wasn't the apes' fault. They never should've been brought to the Palacio. She hated it when people mistreated helpless creatures.

Which reminded her that Gunnar's room was somewhere on this floor.

She pictured the invalid child chewing and swallowing real food, and it gave her comfort. Such a simple action, fundamental to life, taken for granted by mothers and sons everywhere. Batten disease had robbed Gunnar of this and much more. Would her work—her imagination, her dedication, her risks—give it back to him?

God, she hoped so. She wanted so badly to save this boy.

She knew this dream was irrational. It didn't take a psychiatrist to see her obsession was rooted in the loss of her own child to a genetic disease. Her gene therapy research was some kind of psychic compensation, a transfer of her maternal instincts from the son who died to another woman's son who was fated to die. She was aware of this subconscious motivation. Her husband had been, too, and he didn't accept it. He questioned why she allowed this obsession to drive her professional life. Why invest yourself in an impossible task? he'd asked. Batten disease kids are going to die. Period. Why not have another baby of your own and move on?

She was never able to answer him. After a miscarriage and then a pregnancy that resulted in the short, tragic life of Benjamin, she'd been diagnosed with a rare genetic disorder. Two of her forty-six chromosomes had swapped genes, a so-called balanced translocation. This molecular oddity had no effect on her own health, but any child she conceived had a one-in-four or higher chance of inheriting a lethal assortment of the wrong DNA.

Her luck was no good. Two pregnancies, two dead babies. She would not risk those odds again.

Technically, she didn't have to. Let's do *in vitro*, her husband had said. We can afford it. They'll test the embryos and only implant healthy ones.

In vitro fertilization involves needles. A lot of needles.

I want to be a father, he said. Don't you want to be a mother?

Of course I want to be a mother.

Don't I?

She turned off the water and exited the shower. The air was so humid that the clean towel she plucked from a shelf felt damp.

I guess I didn't want it badly enough.

She'd rejected the reproductive technology that might have given them a healthy child. Her work in the laboratory became her child, the object of her nurturing and devotion. But guilt dogged her: guilt for causing Benjamin's death; guilt for failing her husband; guilt for not being willing to make the sacrifices necessary to give him a healthy son or daughter.

Choosing the most hopeless cause for her research, and giving herself fully to it, was expiation for her sins. The fight to save Gunnar was personal.

––––––––––

Tessa felt her heart beating as she followed Sameer to Gunnar's room. Two years had passed since she'd tested her experimental gene therapy in animals. She'd used a laboratory strain of mice with a genetic mutation similar to the one in Gunnar's DNA. In mice, her treatment slowed the progress of the disease but did not cure it. Slowing the relentless advance of Batten disease from disability to death would be a welcome first step if the therapy also worked in humans. But her mice never *improved*. What was she to make of the news that her first human patient was getting better?

"He has a corner room," Sameer said. "Very nice."

The door to Gunnar's room was open and fresh air spilled from it into the hallway. Before entering she glimpsed a piece of artwork on the wall, a colorful carving of a toucan in a palm tree.

Wound tight with expectation and uncertain hope, she went in.

A blond-haired boy, small and underweight for his seven years, sat in a lounge chair wearing Spider Man shorty pajamas. His eyes were glued to a cartoon on a large-screen TV. In his hands he held maracas painted with the red, white, and green of the Mexican flag.

For an instant it seemed her heart stopped. She gaped while cataloguing a list of all the things "wrong" with this picture. This was a changeling child. Surely not the boy she met in the United States ten months ago.

"Dr. Price, you came!" Sigrun Baldursdottir, Gunnar's mother, hurried forward and wrapped her arms around Tessa. "Look at him. Can you believe it?" Though she'd lived in the US for a decade, she retained a Scandinavian accent from her native Iceland.

Tessa reciprocated the hug. Then she did look at Gunnar, intensely, critically.

Like his mother, Gunnar had a pale complexion, slender nose, and delicate cheekbones. Something on the TV tickled him. He squealed and shook the maracas.

It cannot be.

"But…but…he's *blind*," Tessa stammered. "When we tested him, he could make out light and dark. That was all."

"Not any more." Sigrun kissed the top of his head. "He can see the shapes of things. He can tell the difference between these," she said, holding up a plush lion and a panda bear.

Sameer touched Tessa's wrist. In her distraction, she'd clutched his arm. Embarrassed, she let go and sat down on the sofa next to Gunnar's chair.

"It's a miracle," Sigrun said. "You made it happen. You and Dr. Desai and Cristo. You gave my son a chance."

She struggled to take it all in. Others had hinted at signs of improvement in the boy, but no one had prepared her for changes as dramatic as this. Blindness was one of the first symptoms of Batten disease. Partial recovery of vision was unheard of. Like everything else about this degenerative disease of the brain, the vision loss was irreversible. But there was more. Sameer said the boy had regained the ability to swallow. Also "impossible." The way he was sitting up in the chair, without support—definitely an improvement in his core muscle strength. His hands—Gunnar was grasping the handles of the maracas. Ten months ago, he couldn't do anything purposeful with his hands.

Sigrun sat down beside her and squeezed her fingers. "After his first seizure, he was scared. I told him I would take care of him. I told him not to be afraid. But *I* was afraid. The doctors told me I was going to lose my son. Slowly. The seizures were only the beginning. They said his personality would change, that he would lose control of his body and mind—"

Sigrun flung her arms around Tessa again.

Tessa knew those doctors weren't exaggerating. The Batten disease mutation in Gunnar's DNA, a rare defect slightly more common in Scandinavians, made it impossible for his nervous system to dispose of waste. His brain was like New York City during a sanitation strike. Every day, garbage piled up a little deeper inside his cells. Over time, the effect was toxic. Neurons malfunctioned or died, disrupting vision, muscle control, sleep, speech, and ultimately all the higher cognitive functions. His future: total mental and physical incapacity. For lack of a better term, he would become a vegetable. Then, most likely, he would die before his fifteenth birthday.

The image was too painful to contemplate. Her own anguished death watch over Benjamin lasted only thirty-two days. How could a mother endure for a decade or longer? Fervently she hoped Sigrun wouldn't have to find out.

"When did you first notice any improvement?" she asked.

"A few days after Cristo went home sick," Sigrun said. "By the way, how's he doing?"

"Much better, I hear. I expect we'll see him soon."

"Good, good. I remember because Gunnar came down with a little fever about the same time. I figured he had whatever Cristo had."

"And then?"

"Gunnar got over it right away. But he didn't just go back to normal. He had more energy. He wanted me to put him up in the chair all the time. Then he started asking for food. Dr. Desai—" she nodded at Sameer, who was kneeling next to the boy, "was worried he would choke but we tried some soft foods and he was able to get them down."

She marveled at the news. "All this in the last two or three weeks?"

"Yes. Before, you know I was happy just because he wasn't getting any worse. Now I think maybe, maybe this will work. I started taking him out for walks in the wheelchair, to see the ocean. Once he even got to see the monkeys."

"There are monkeys in the forest around here?"

"No, the monkeys in the basement. That nice lady who takes care of them heard that Gunnar loves animals. She gave us a tour. We saw the dogs and the monkeys."

Sweet little monkeys, eh? Not the demon-possessed, shit-flinging murderers I had the pleasure of meeting today? "They're chimpanzees, actually."

"Yes," Sigrun said, "Gunnar visited the chimpanzees. He loved it. I hope when Cristo gets back he'll let us visit them again."

That's not gonna happen. She turned to the child. "Gunnar?"

Sigrun rose and turned off the TV. Gunnar made a sound not unlike a chimp howl, though nowhere near as loud. "Gunnar, Dr. Desai and Dr. Price are here. They want to talk to you."

Gunnar dropped the maracas with a rattle and a crash, then impishly curled up and covered his head.

"What did he say?" Tessa asked. The boy's garbled speech was unintelligible.

Sigrun placed a hand on her son and whispered in his ear. He nodded. She whispered some more. Gunnar sat up and looked Tessa in the eye.

"Hello, Gunnar. Do you remember me?"

"Hi." That word came out clearly.

"I hear you're eating things. What's your favorite food here?"

The boy covered his head again and said something only his mother could understand.

"That's okay," she said to Sigrun. "I'm a stranger. I'll get out of the way and let Dr. Desai do his thing."

She stepped aside and observed while Sameer coaxed Gunnar to sit up. He played a game that got the boy to lift his shirt and even to laugh a little. She saw the gastrostomy button in Gunnar's belly through which they'd been feeding him. Sameer traced his fingers around the button and pressed gently on the boy's abdomen. Gunnar giggled.

"With your permission, Ms. Baldursdottir, I'm going to remove the feeding tube," he said. "I can do it here on the bed. It will only take a minute."

Sigrun had tears in her eyes when she nodded.

"I'll wait outside," Tessa said. She didn't know if Sameer would use a needle in this procedure, but she wasn't going to stick around and find out.

———

The Palacio's lobby was quiet when Tessa and Sameer returned to finish checking her in. She sat down at the table with the biometric scanner and discovered the tabletop was inlaid with a beautiful mosaic of a Mayan calendar. She traced her fingers over the colored tiles which formed a kind of sundial. In the center was a distorted representation of a face sticking out its tongue.

"Does this table tell me when the world's going to end?" she said.

"I believe the 2012 predictions were based on a particular tablet found at Tortuguero—"

"I'm kidding, Sameer."

He didn't laugh. "Put your right hand inside the dome. Make sure your fingertips are in the notches. Just relax, don't press down unless I tell you."

An intense band of light started at her wrist and migrated into the dome. Sameer operated a computer as the device recorded her hand's vascular pattern. She had to admit the technology was pretty cool. She'd left hotel keys inside rooms before but she'd never forgotten to take her hand with her.

"You will have access to all the Palacio's facilities," Sameer said. "The restaurant will give you a personalized menu. Our weight loss surgery clients are not always happy about that. Do you have any dietary restrictions?"

"Make a note that I only eat chocolate."

"I cannot write that."

"Fine. No restrictions."

He typed. "Your hand will open all exits, all doors in the Research Annex including laboratories and the animal facility, the tunnel, the pool showers. And of course your room."

"Right."

The scanner went dark. She removed her hand and stood up. "Which way to my room?"

"First I need to take a small blood sample," he said.

She pushed the chair under the table. "Not on your life."

"We do this for everyone. A personal profile of your genome and your immune system is quite valuable."

"What about my right to privacy?"

"The data are for internal use at the Palacio. Vargas does not share with anyone unless you ask him to."

"Doesn't matter. No needles." She crossed her arms.

"You're serious," he said, perplexed. He punched a few keys and furrowed his brow. "I cannot activate your account without blood test results." Pause. "I can use a fingerstick instead of venipuncture. We will not be able to assess your immunity but the test should generate enough information to satisfy the computer."

"No, Sameer. No blood. No sticks. Period. If that's a problem, I'll stay at a motel."

"A motel? That is not possible."

"I know. So figure something out. Or I'm on the next helicopter back to Acapulco."

She could tell from the expression on his face he wanted to argue, but he didn't.

"Maybe I can generate a metabolic profile," he said.

"Fine. Just make up some numbers in the normal range."

"For some values there is more than one kind of normal. These data will be false."

"I'm not a patient. Nobody's going to look at my file."

He looked like he'd just swallowed cod liver oil. "Very well. I'll show you to your room and then I will see Gunnar again. Do you agree that pathology specimens from him would be useful at this time?"

"Absolutely." A look through the microscope at some of Gunnar's nerve tissue could prove this wasn't a dream. They ought to see changes in the cells reflecting the changes in the boy's symptoms. If she was ever going to publish the results of this research, some pathology slides would be objective evidence of his improvement. "If you get them, I'll process them."

———

After a one hour nap in her luxurious room, Tessa was ready to head over to the lab and do what she came for.

The experimental gene therapy treatment she'd designed for Gunnar wasn't a drug. It was a living thing, a virus that she'd genetically modified to carry a bit of human DNA. Every day Gunnar got a dose of this virus. Because the virus was alive, it had to be made fresh on a regular basis. She'd personally trained the only person at the Palacio who had the specialized skills needed to make it. That person was Cristo. When he fell ill and stopped coming to work, the clock started ticking for Gunnar.

This was the crisis that brought her to Mexico. She couldn't let the boy's medicine run out.

Her rumbling stomach reminded her she ought to eat a quick meal before shutting herself up in the lab. As the afternoon sun streamed hot and bright, she put on sunglasses and headed for the poolside restaurant.

She exited from the lobby to the pool area. Suddenly sick children and psychotic chimps seemed a million miles away. *Wow.* Vargas had really put hospitality into a hospital. The Palacio was paradise. Two perfect swimming pools, one shallow and decorated with sea turtle mosaics, one deep with whales tiled on the bottom. Wheelchair lifts and shallow, sloping shores in the pools made them accessible for elderly or infirm visitors. Soft reggae music played from speakers hidden inside artificial rocks. Meticulously groomed palm trees shaded the paths. Birds of paradise, orchids, and many plants she couldn't identify filled the gardens. There was even a bar complete with tiki torches she was sure would be lit at dusk.

"*Setzen!* Hello, Doc. Y'all care to join us?"

The man from the lobby—the one who irritated Sameer—had his legs stretched out next to a table a few steps away. He wore long swim trunks and a massive gold watch. His German shepherd reclined on a cushioned lounge chair at his left, jeweled collar sparkling in the sun. His girlfriend sat on the opposite side of the table. She was dazzling in a broad white straw hat, white sunglasses with dark lenses, and a strappy white swimsuit that contrasted nicely with her brown skin. On the table stood two colorful drinks with tiny paper parasols.

Tessa became acutely aware of her practical but boring attire. "Mr. Simmons, is it?"

"You got a better memory than me. Call me Lyle. This is my girl—" The woman glared at him, daring him to introduce the dog again. "My girlfriend Isabella."

"A pleasure, Doctor..."

"Tessa Price." She shook Isabella's hand. The woman even had beautiful fingers.

"Have a seat," Lyle said, "unless you don't like dogs. Dixie can smell dog-haters."

"Thank you, I like dogs." *They don't judge you by your looks.* "But I don't have much time, I'm on my way to work."

"Doc, doc, it's happy hour." Lyle rose and pulled a chair out for her. She sat.

"Do you work with Dr. Vargas?" Isabella asked.

"Not directly. My partner is Dr. Desai."

"Dezzy!" Lyle said. "The doc with a rod up—"

"He's a good friend," Tessa said. She wished she'd taken a seat by herself.

Lyle slapped her shoulder. "Of course he is. I'm just kidding. By tomorrow afternoon he'll be one of my favorite people." He winked at Isabella.

"What do you do at the Palacio, Doctor?" Isabella asked.

A waiter delivered a bowl of shrimp ceviche garnished with fresh cilantro leaves. Tessa was impressed. *Vargas promises the best. As long as I'm here, I might as well enjoy it.*

"I'm a visiting scientist, not one of the Palacio's physicians," she said as she ladled the cold seafood mix onto a small plate. "My specialty is genetics. I'm working on a new treatment for diseases people inherit from their parents."

"Diseases like small bank accounts?" Lyle said.

Isabella laughed, but Tessa noticed an unexpected intensity in the way she was listening. Like she actually cared about Tessa's answer.

"There's a little boy here who has a mutation in his DNA. The mutation is making him sick. I'm testing a treatment that fixes it."

"Gene therapy," Isabella said.

Tessa was taken aback. "Yes."

"Very interesting," Isabella said. "Does it hurt?"

"What do you mean?"

"Is the boy in pain? Do you have to give him medicine for the pain?"

What a strange question. "No, he inhales the treatment through his nose."

"Lovely," Isabella said and sipped her cocktail.

"Does the boy like dogs?" Lyle said. "Maybe I'll bring Dixie by for a visit. She's a certified *Schutzhund*, level three. Born and trained in Germany. Tracking, obedience, protection: the whole package. She's smarter than most people and more disciplined than most soldiers. She can rip off a man's arm but if I tell her to, she'll cradle a kitten in her jaws." He switched to baby talk and nuzzled the dog. "Not that I'd do that to you, would I, girl? Really, she's great with kids."

"I'm sure he'd love to meet Dixie."

"She's no spring chicken any more. Old girl is getting cataracts removed tomorrow morning. Human-level care for a human-level animal, I say. That's what I told Vargas. That's why I brought her down here. She'll have both a vet and an MD working on her. Bella, darling, is your drink as watered-down as mine?"

"It's personalized, my love. The computer tells them how much you can have."

"Bull. Vargas is cheaping out to save a few pesos. I'll have to talk to him."

"Excuse me," Tessa said, rising from her chair. "I have work to do."

———

Rules are for little people. Which makes things complicated when two big people make a deal.

Dr. Manuel Vargas didn't build Mexico's finest—and most profitable—medical tourism center by following the rules. When the Palacio's research program made its first major discovery—something he considered inevitable—patients clamoring for help wouldn't ask if he'd adhered to a thousand pages of regulations. Results were what mattered, to Vargas, to his investors, and to his patient-clients.

Likewise, Luis Angel de la Rosa didn't become head of the most powerful—and most feared—organized crime syndicate in the Americas playing by the book, not even by a drug dealers' book.

Vargas reflected, both of us have a vision for the future, and goals for our organizations. Both of us judge results, not intentions.

Which made the stakes of their new relationship very high.

Beyond his office windows on the sixth floor of the Palacio main hospital, blue ocean waves rolled and rolled, sending energy across vast stretches of the Pacific, leaving no imprint on the water a few feet below the surface. The Palacio is like that, Vargas thought. Turmoil could roll over Guerrero state, but he would use his smarts, his money, and his influence to keep his work here below the surface. If he managed the transition properly, he saw no reason why he couldn't work under the Sinaloa cartel as well as he'd worked under the Zetas, who controlled this part of Mexico until a few weeks ago. These drug bosses were all the same: street smart but uneducated, insecure, greedy. And violent too, of course, but only as a consequence of the rest. Give them what they want, show submission, and they'll leave you alone.

His position was precarious, though. He was blindsided by Sinaloa's move to take over the region. Worse, Sinaloa had sent in the Mara Salvatrucha, or MS, a loathsome band of hired guns, as the first boots on the ground. This intelligence failure nearly cost him the life of Cristo Castillo, his multitalented employee. Miraculously, Cristo had survived the MS raid on their weekly plack deal. From now on the Palacio would buy plack from Sinaloa. Prices were going up with the regime change, but he could afford to pass on the cost to his clients. Plack would remain the pain-control drug of choice at his hospital because it was a wonderful narcotic. Being a high-volume, regular customer also helped the Palacio to build a relationship with the cartel—and buy some protection.

Vargas turned on his computer and scanned the register of clients currently on the peninsula. Unfortunately the census was high. Getting everybody out was going to take time and cost a lot of money, not to mention the loss of goodwill among those who weren't ready to go. At the very least, he'd have to reimburse every patient for airline ticket change fees and other expenses for early departure. Would a discount on a future visit to the Palacio be a good marketing move? Maybe if he made the discount transferable to a friend…

His cell phone rang. Luis Angel de la Rosa had a businessman's punctuality.

"We have a donor," de la Rosa said in a gravelly voice. "The day after tomorrow."

"Luis, I have to move two hundred people for you," Vargas said. "If you arrive in the morning, I can't guarantee the Palacio will be empty of nonessential personnel. Give me forty-eight hours—"

"Manuel. I'm a busy man. I don't have time for dialysis, and I don't have time to wait for you to clean house. You agreed that if Sinaloa supports you, you would give me what I want. At your hospital. Anytime."

"Absolutely. We'll give you the best."

"You will give it to me the day after tomorrow. If I don't like the people still there when I arrive, I will kill them."

"Understood. Hospital staff only. Medical, kitchen, and housekeeping. Full service."

"No guards. My MS will handle security."

Vargas swallowed hard on that morsel but had to accept. A stiff reed breaks in the wind, he reminded himself. Go with the flow. Luis Angel de la Rosa was bringing the Mara Salvatrucha to his hospital.

He'd better start the evacuation now.

CHAPTER 6

Tessa felt comfortable in the cell culture room, a small, windowless space off the main laboratory in the Research Annex. The ventilation system cocooned her in white noise. Solitude, clarity, no distractions—her preferred work environment.

She placed a three-inch plastic dish under a microscope, taking care not to splash the liquid in the dish. The microscope's two eyepiece lenses nestled against her face. With her right hand she twirled a knob to raise the dish toward the magnifying lens. A flash of light in the lenses told her the focus point was close. Switching to the fine focus knob she adjusted the height of the stage more precisely. A layer of cells coalesced into view.

Beautiful. The cultures she'd set up last night were growing well. The cells were uniform and plump. Things were on track to synthesize Gunnar's next treatment.

"Find everything?"

Her hand jerked. A bit of the cell culture liquid spilled warm and sticky on her latex glove. She'd thought she was alone in the lab. Who had—

"Cristo! You're back!" She covered the cells with a plastic lid and returned them to the incubator, disinfected the spill, took off her gloves, and finally was able to give her colleague a hug. "How do you feel?"

"Like I'm back from the dead," Cristo said.

"Sameer told me you were getting better but I didn't expect to see you so soon."

She looked him over. He'd definitely lost weight, and he didn't have a lot to lose to begin with. Good color in his cheeks, though. But what was with his eyes? The pupils were tiny pinpoints, much too small for this dim room.

"Are you sure you're okay? Maybe you could use a few more days on the couch."

He shrugged as they strolled into the main laboratory. "Vargas called. He needs me to take care of something."

Gee, I can't imagine what that might be. "The chimpanzees."

"*Sí.* You know about that?"

She wanted to lecture him about how bringing chimps to the Palacio was all wrong, that it was bound to lead to trouble. But there was no point; Vargas was the one who needed talking to. "I was in the facility yesterday. I saw it."

Taciturn as ever, Cristo opened a freezer and dug in the inch-deep frost, searching for something.

"I started the next batch of gene therapy for Gunnar," she said. "If you want to take over, I won't be offended."

He closed the freezer door. "I'll stay away from rabies for a while. You do it."

The bat attack, she thought. It had him spooked.

"Cristo, the virus we're using is rabies in name only. You know we knocked out the genes that make it dangerous. The thing can't even reproduce on its own."

Disabling the virus was standard procedure when using a virus as a tool in gene therapy. Yes, her clinical trial used a rabies virus, but the virus was designed to be nothing more than a courier that delivered a package of DNA to a specific cellular address. It didn't behave like natural rabies, and it definitely did not make the patient sick. She'd taken great pains to guarantee the safety of her genetically-engineered virus. She had deleted the genes that allowed it to cause disease, and she had crippled the virus's reproduction. Outside the laboratory, it could not copy itself. Which was the reason Gunnar needed to be treated on a regular basis. The gene therapy virus died off, was cleared from his body, and had to be replaced over and over.

"I know," was Cristo's only reply.

If she could use a different virus, she would, but rabies had a uniquely strong attraction to the brain, making it the ideal delivery system for Gunnar's condition. It homed in on neurons, the cells that Gunnar most needed fixed.

"Were you able to test the bat that bit you?" she asked, knowing he had the skill to do it.

He grimaced slightly. "One of them. The first test was positive."

"You've been vaccinated."

"And I gave myself booster and gamma globulin shots," he said.

"So you're immune to rabies now."

"But not immune to fear." He dragged a wheeled stool to the lab counter-top. The stool's casters squeaked in protest.

Not much she could say to that. *He better get over it. I need him to take responsibility for the project again. I can't be away from my own lab forever.*

They each turned to their labors in silence until the roar of a jet engine rattled the room's racks of glass test tubes. Taking off from the Palacio's airstrip, she figured. Minutes later, a clicking sound at the lab's main door rippled through the quiet. After a second or two, it repeated. The noise was coming from the electronic lock. She looked up, curious about the function of the fancy security system. Finally someone rapped an old-fashioned knock.

"I'll get it." She crossed the lab and opened the door.

A woman wearing scrubs stood with arm raised, palm hovering over the scanner. Her hand was shaking. It took Tessa a moment to connect the woman's full, round face with the eyes and mask she'd seen in the animal facility. She was one of the technicians.

"Sorry. The door not open for me." The tech looked past her and spoke rapidly to Cristo in Spanish.

He rose from his stool. "I'm going to check on the animals. You want to come?"

"No thanks." She'd smelled enough chimp dung. "I guess I'll head back to the hospital."

The tang of disinfectant clung to the technician's clothes. Not a pleasant odor but better than the alternative.

Tessa offered her hand. "I'm sorry, yesterday was pretty crazy. I didn't get to meet you. I'm Tessa Price."

The woman extended her hand. Tessa noticed the hand quivered at rest. When the woman lifted her arm, the twitching grew worse. By the time their hands clasped, the motion was so bad she had no need to "shake."

"I'm Maria." The tech broke contact and hid her hands behind her back.

Poor thing, Tessa thought. I wonder if she's got Parkinson's disease.

They exited the lab and walked down the hall together. Cristo and Maria were deep in conversation. They turned a corner and Tessa jumped backward in surprise, bumping into her companions as they were ambushed by a fierce snarl and ferocious bark.

"*Platz!* Ah Doctor, so sorry." Lyle Simmons stroked his German shepherd Dixie, who was on a leash this time. Dixie showed her teeth. "She's not herself. But y'all don't have to worry. I've got her."

The dog was wearing a giant protective cone collar. Tessa had seen such collars many times, but she'd never seen a dog blindfolded. Dixie's eyes were covered by dressings held in place by black eye patches. Her appearance was both comical and spooky.

A low growl rumbled in the *Schutzhund's* throat. She pointed her nose at Maria, the animal technician, and tensed her muscles as if to spring.

Lyle shortened the leash. "She just had cataract surgery. Still coming off the anesthetic. Kind of loopy, you know?"

Tessa took one more step back. A highly-trained attack dog, cranky and hallucinating, was not something she wanted to be close to. "I bet she smells the animals."

"What animals?" Lyle said.

"I take care of the chimps." Maria cowered behind Cristo. "Maybe she no like that."

I guess if I were a dog, and woke up blind, strapped in a goofy collar, high on drugs, and smelling apes, I'd be freaked out, too.

"Chimps?" Isabella glided forward. Tessa noticed she'd had her teeth whitened this morning. "Vargas keeps chimpanzees here? Where?"

Cristo gave Isabella a hard look. "Our research facility is not open to the public."

The tech fidgeted. Tessa wondered what Cristo would say if he knew Maria had let Gunnar take a tour.

Isabella drifted closer, her gaze fixed on Cristo. She was as tall as he and looked directly into his eyes. She glanced at Tessa's eyes once, then seemed to focus her full attention on Cristo. She slinked deep into his personal space. Cristo's expression softened.

"I don't really care about monkeys." She draped her fingers on the back of his neck and pulled his ear close to her lips.

Whatever she whispered was drowned out by the noise of another jet landing at or taking off from the Palacio's airstrip. Color rose in Cristo's face and he blinked several times. Once, he turned to look at her in disbelief. She smiled and whispered some more.

Dixie whined, then made a high-pitched, pathetic yelp.

"We've gotta go, darlin'," Lyle said.

Isabella released Cristo and floated back to Lyle. "What's your name?"

"Cristo Castillo."

"See you later, Cristo." The couple and their dog continued on their way.

"What was that all about?" Tessa said. *I can't believe she'd flirt like that right in front of her man. And he didn't seem to care.*

Cristo said nothing.

Tessa left Cristo and Maria to deal with the chimpanzee debacle and exited the Research Annex, a nice, fresh lunch in an outdoor restaurant on her mind. Tropical sunlight filtered through the canopy of palm trees, dappling the road that led back to the main hospital. The low thrum of the electric fence and ocean breezes rustling through the trees made a gentle soundtrack for the short walk.

"Pare! Quien eres? Adónde vas?"

One of the guards on patrol had spotted her and shouted in Spanish. He jogged forward, unshouldering a rifle as he moved.

Dang. Touchy. She stopped and put her hands out at her sides. "I'm sorry, I don't speak Spanish. *No comprendo.* Is there a problem?"

Carelessly, the guard rested the long weapon in the crook of one arm and pointed it vaguely in her direction. That was not cool. She was at a high-end resort hospital, not a crime-ridden 'hood. Had she broken some major rule that Sameer forgot to tell her about?

Then she realized the guard wasn't like the ones she'd seen yesterday. Instead of a green camouflage uniform, this man wore jeans and a white tank top. His exposed shoulders and arms were covered in tattoos, all the way to his hands. Instead of a beret, he had a baseball cap on his head. She looked past him toward the guard station at the gate and saw the other security men looked just as thuggish.

Now she was getting worried. Where'd the soldiers go?

Again he spoke harshly to her in Spanish. She glanced around for another Palacio staff member or guest, but except for the guards, she was alone on the road.

"Okay, I'm sorry, am I not supposed to be out here?" She pantomimed that she was headed for the Palacio entrance, that she would key herself in with her hand. "Please? *Por favor?*"

He pointed to the entrance and fired more questions. She could only smile and shrug and try not to pee her pants. *What the hell is this, Vargas?*

Apparently her display of deference worked. The tattooed guard stepped back and waved his rifle in the direction she wanted to go. Permission granted?

"*Gracias.*" Frightened and angry, she walked briskly toward the entrance to the hospital. Her back prickled as she felt the man's stare until she was through the gate and on the other side of the wall. Standing in the Serenity Garden, she felt distinctly *not* serene.

Vargas better reconsider hiring goons like that. Bad for business.

The garden was empty. She followed the path toward the Palacio's reception area. Yet another airplane, a small propeller-driven one, swooped right overhead. She glanced up. That made at least three or four flights so far today. Seemed like a lot.

The airplane passed but tranquility did not follow. Noisy commotion leaked through the sliding screen doors ahead. An electric eye saw her coming and the doors opened.

I made a wrong turn to Grand Central Station.

The lobby, so elegant and orderly the day before, was overflowing with a tumultuous crowd. Scores of people milled about, crowding the few sofas and lounge chairs. Some of the people were in wheelchairs. Others had surgical dressings taped to faces or necks. For a moment she wondered if she'd walked in on a fire drill. Then she saw the suitcases lined up against one wall of the room.

"What the heck?" she muttered.

The air was thick with discontent. Feet tapped impatiently. Voices rose in irritation. She saw one of the uniformed Palacio staff arguing with a patient.

Vargas was there. He caught sight of her and weaved toward her through the throng. "Dr. Price. We need to talk."

He waved off a question from one of his overwhelmed workers and led Tessa through a stone archway to a cool, flagstone-lined patio. "Wrap things up in the lab. You're going to have to leave for a few days. Maybe a week."

"What? Why?"

He glanced back at the chaotic scene in the lobby. His lips were drawn tight. "I'm evacuating the campus. Everyone, except a few key personnel, must go."

"But—"

"This is an emergency. We detected bacteria in our water early this morning. Something happened to my well. Or pipes. Or purification systems. I can't explain it. Until we make repairs, the water is not safe to drink or use. I'm transporting all patients and nonessential staff to Acapulco hospitals or hotels at my own expense."

"But what about Gunnar?"

"Everyone goes."

"Not Gunnar. This is the only place on earth where he can get his treatment."

"He will have to go without for a short time."

This startling news infuriated her. "A short time? You can't promise that. For all you know you might have to dig up half the campus to fix this. It could take weeks. Or longer."

He glanced at his jeweled watch. "You must go. I don't have time to discuss it."

She blocked him as he moved to leave. "Manuel, the kid is turning around. You said yourself it's like a miracle. We're using an experimental protocol. Nobody knows what'll happen if he misses even one dose of his medicine. I came down here to make sure we wouldn't find out." She gestured at the clients gathered in the lobby. "We're not talking about a nose job. A boy's life is at stake."

Vargas leaned forward and got in her face. "What would you have me do, Doctor? This peninsula is isolated. We do not have an alternate water supply."

"If it's bacterial contamination, we can boil enough water to get by just fine. Cripes, you've got autoclaves over in the Research Annex. Use those."

"For over two hundred people, many of them needing medical care?"

"Not for two hundred. For one. Gunnar. Plus me, or Sameer, and maybe his mother."

"I can't start making exceptions."

Her muscles tensed. "Why not?"

"I don't expect you to understand business decisions."

"This isn't a business question. It's medical ethics."

The smooth-talking, ingratiating Dr. Jekyll who had met her on the roof yesterday transformed into *Señor* Hyde.

"Don't lecture me about ethics. You're a med school dropout who ran to Mexico to hide her illegal experiments on humans."

He might as well have slapped her. She felt her mouth hang open. No words came out.

Pointing a finger at her he walked away. "You have until tomorrow afternoon to do what you want with the boy. After that, you'll be with him on the last flight out."

CHAPTER 7

Vargas hurried to the helicopter pad on the roof of the Palacio feeling fatigued and stressed. He knew Luis Angel de la Rosa was ruthless and a killer. De la Rosa's Sinaloa cartel littered its territory with corpses—often with the heads, hands, and feet hacked off. Anyone who stood up to them, whether gang rivals, federal police, or civilians, was a target. Sinaloa-sponsored violence in Mexico, the United States, and other countries of Central America was legendary for its amoral brutality. If de la Rosa wanted all the patients out of the hospital today, Vargas would get them out.

He fumed about the raw deal he was getting. When Sinaloa recently took control of this region, he made an amiable agreement to buy plack from them and to give the gang's leaders access to medical care. He hadn't anticipated a total evacuation on short notice, or the tremendous cost involved. The list of his expenses was long and growing. Cost of the flights, which had continued into the night because he couldn't get enough planes and helicopters. Cost to reimburse evicted guests. Cost of lost business during de la Rosa's stay. Particularly galling was the cost to his reputation, falsely besmirched by the cover story about contaminated water. He took pride in the Palacio's high-quality services, including the water. And he'd likely incur more costs while the Mara Salvatrucha enforcers patrolled his campus.

Bunch of yahoos. They'll probably trash the place. He made a mental note to "evacuate" as much of the bar's liquor as possible on the next flight.

Engine noise and a rush of wind heralded the arrival of a chopper. He looked on with contempt as it dropped into view. Clearly the helicopter was not one of his. It was beat-up, dented and dirty, and had what looked like bullet holes on one panel. He'd never transport his clients in a craft like that.

It settled on the landing pad and three young men got out. All were tattooed and looked prematurely old. He guessed their chronological age was early twenties. They walked with a jaded, confrontational swagger. He knew the type. They were worthless kids filled with testosterone and rage against their own worthlessness. Quick to take offense. Prone to violence. Extremely dangerous.

The trio differentiated into individuals as they approached. One walked slightly ahead of the others. He had a hunted look and swiveled his head from side to side, like a gazelle crossing lion territory. A bruise, about three days old judging by the color, stained his left chin and nose. The other two toughs paid no attention to the surroundings and kept their eyes on their companion.

Vargas was pleased to see the donor wasn't handcuffed or otherwise restrained. Means of persuasion may have been employed to get the youth here, but at least he didn't have to see them. Hopefully de la Rosa was going to pay the kid well. Actually, the kid might be getting some good out of this. Gangbanger with no job, no education, no social skills, no future except a bullet or a prison cell. What assets did he have?

Two young, healthy kidneys, Vargas thought. He only needs one. Why not sell the other?

No doubt the kid was terrified, though. The prospect of major surgery does that to people. Vargas vowed to give him the best medical care possible. The transplant surgeon he hired had flown in this morning. The surgeon wasn't the best in the world—a truly famous surgeon would ask awkward questions about donor consent—but he was damn good. He'd do right for both donor and recipient.

Maybe I'll kick in a little extra cash. Help the kid pay for school or something when he goes back to whatever squalor he came from.

This thought gave him a warm, affectionate feeling.

Good idea. A little largesse could change a life.

"Vargas?" asked one of the escorts.

"*Aquí.*"

"*El donante.*" He gave the donor a little push.

Vargas put on his most comforting, most compassionate expression. "*Bienvenido, mijo.*" He laid his arm around the youth's shoulders and gently guided him down the red carpet to the waiting elevator.

———

Tessa willed Vargas to answer her call.

Talk to me, dammit! Or have the guts to tell Gunnar's mother to her face that you're banishing her son.

No good. Over the last fourteen hours she'd tried phone, text, voicemail, and real-life visits to Vargas's office without making contact. He did not respond and she didn't run into him anywhere in the hospital or Research Annex. Whether she liked it or not, he was carrying out his plan. Late into the previous night the Palacio campus swirled with the controlled chaos of people and planes in motion. After a lull in the wee hours, the evacuation began again early this morning.

She finished a cup of coffee made with boiled water and went back to the laboratory. If she was forced to leave after noon today, she had to work quickly without compromising quality. For Gunnar's gene therapy, "good enough" wasn't good enough. The next batch of virus she prepared for his treatment might be the last one he got for a long time.

Or maybe not, God willing. Sameer had told her Vargas was keeping a few "essential staff" on campus, including him. With a fresh batch of her virus, Sameer could care for Gunnar for up to a week, whether she was around or not.

That is, if she could convince Vargas to let the boy stay. She tried to come up with an irrefutable argument. But the way he'd treated her yesterday made her doubt he'd listen to anything she said.

I can't believe he treated me like that. Rather than discuss or even argue about Gunnar's status, he'd pretty much accused her of doing something wrong, something immoral, by trying to save the child's life. Even if he was under a lot of pressure, his comments were inexcusable. Heck, on paper, he was as complicit in the gene therapy project as she was.

I guess I'm too trusting. Especially of charismatic men. Just look at my ex-husband.

By noon the virus was ready. She measured out Gunnar's daily dose, loaded it in a nasal spray, and set it on ice. Then she surveyed the equipment in the lab to make sure everything could be left untended for a week—carbon dioxide tanks full, water baths turned off, hazardous waste bagged for disposal. Cristo didn't know whether Vargas had him staying or going. Somebody had to stick around to care for the animals, but Vargas hadn't told them who it would be. If he sent both Cristo and Tessa packing, the research laboratory would be empty.

She heard planes and helicopters take off or land every half hour or so. The airplanes she glimpsed were small, carrying at most a dozen passengers. No wonder it was taking so long for Vargas to evacuate all the patients.

When she had secured the lab, it was time to visit Gunnar.

She texted Cristo to meet her at the boy's room. They administered the gene therapy as a nasal spray. The best part of that? No needles. She could treat Gunnar herself. But the boy was used to Cristo and Sameer. No sense disturbing the routine. Batten patients were emotionally unstable, prone to outbursts, and she didn't know whether that aspect of his condition had gotten any better.

Ice bucket in hand, she waited for the elevator. It opened, revealing Lyle Simmons with his two- and four-legged female companions. She was relieved to see Dixie was back to her usual disciplined self. Today her eyes were uncovered and the large cone collar had been replaced with a much smaller one.

"Howdy, Doc. Going up?"

"Yes, Mr. Simmons." She forced herself to make small talk. "How are you doing today?"

"I'm feelin' hurry-scurry, if you know what I mean. With this water thing and all. Me and my girls got evicted from our suite. That rascal Vargas tried to put us on a plane last night."

"But you're still here." Had Lyle convinced Vargas to let him stay? Could he get Gunnar permission to stay, too?

"Damn right. The eye surgeon and vet fixed up Dixie just yesterday and I hadn't had my work done yet."

"So you're staying."

"Only 'til the last flight out today. Vargas gave a cold shoulder to a hot pile of my cash. Said we had to git."

She deflated. If Vargas couldn't even be bribed into letting one of his VIP clients stay, what chance did Gunnar have?

"My sawbones did me at oh-dark-hundred this mornin'. Just got the O-K to head out and kill some time in a regular room," Lyle continued. "We were hoping to enjoy this place for a while, but at least we got done what we came for."

No visible cuts, bandages, or bruises. She was curious to know more about his experimental treatment. "Was your procedure a success?"

Isabella answered. "The doctor told him he should wait a few days before we find out."

"To hell with that," Lyle said. "I think we'll have a go tonight in Acapulco." He squeezed Isabella's shapely butt and pecked her cheek.

"It's too soon, you must let it rest," Isabella said.

A lascivious smile spread on Lyle's face. "*I* decide when to test drive my equipment."

It dawned on Tessa that she might not want to know any more about his "medical" problem.

Lyle pointed at the ice bucket she was holding. "By any chance you fixin' to see that boy you told us about?"

"I'm on my way to his room now."

"Well shucks, we've got nothin' to do. How about we take Dixie to meet the little fella?"

Gunnar's blue eyes opened wide when the parade of people and a dog waltzed into his room.

"Hi!" he said. An energetic string of not-quite-decipherable words followed.

Tessa stared. Gunnar was standing. Granted, he slouched against the side of the bed and his mother Sigrun was supporting him. But he was on his feet.

The timing of this evacuation couldn't be any worse, she thought. He really is getting better. What'll happen to his progress if he misses treatments?

"Gunnar, I brought some friends for you to meet," she said.

The boy's eyes locked on to the German shepherd. Lyle patted Dixie's shoulder.

"Like dogs, do you, son? This dog's mighty special. North of fifty thousand dollars special, to be exact. Wanna see some of her tricks?"

Gunnar squealed and squirmed, causing his legs to buckle. Sigrun caught him and carried him into a chair. He tugged at his shirt, smiling.

"I'll take that as a yes. Dixie. *Fuss!*"

Tessa watched in admiration as the dog positioned herself precisely at Lyle's right side.

"*Gib laut!*"

Dixie barked, a full-bellied, alarm-raising dog noise with a threat of violence. A sound sure to scare the pants off any intruder. Gunnar stuffed his face into a pillow.

"A little too much, maybe. How 'bout this: *kriech!*"

Lyle pointed at Gunnar. Dixie crouched her lean body against the floor as low as the cone around her neck allowed. Ears flat, she crawled to the boy and halted motionless, plastered to the ground. Gunnar laughed.

"*Legen.*"

Dixie rose to a normal lying position, more relaxed but still poised for action, like a soldier going from attention to parade rest.

Impressive, Tessa thought. Kind of scary, too. I'm sure some of her trained behaviors aren't as cute.

"*So ist brav,*" Lyle said in a soothing tone. He gave Dixie a rub on the head. She gave him a long-tongued kiss. "Would you like to pet her?"

While Gunnar and Dixie got to know each other, Cristo entered the room.

"Ready for—" He stopped, startled to see the visitors. "I can come back later."

"No, no," Isabella said, smiling. "Do your job. We are just saying hello. Darling, should we go?"

Gunnar's face was lit with delight. Tessa knew the dog was the reason and she hated to break the spell. "Please, stay. The treatment only takes a second."

They lifted Gunnar onto his bed. He struggled and shouted "aaah aaah" until Lyle guided Dixie to within reach of his hand. Then he quietly settled his head against the pillow. Everyone except Cristo stepped aside.

"How's the boy doing?" Lyle asked.

"Pretty amazing, actually," Tessa said.

"So you'll be in the news one of these days? Become a celebrity?"

She almost laughed. In contemporary culture, the words *celebrity* and *scientist* went together about as well as oil and water. "I suppose anything is possible."

Wearing gloves, Cristo took one of the two small syringes from the ice bucket she'd brought from the lab.

"What's in the secret sauce?" Lyle said.

She got a kick out of the shock value of saying, "Rabies."

Both Lyle and Isabella looked at her in wide-eyed horror. Cristo smirked a little.

She explained. "A harmless form of it, that carries a gene our young friend needs. We have to get it inside his brain. Fortunately for him, part of the brain sticks out and is easy to reach."

Cristo spoke softly to Gunnar and brought the syringe toward the boy's face.

"Which part is that?" Isabella said.

"The first cranial nerves. Otherwise known as the olfactory bulbs." She touched a finger to her nose. "Right inside here."

In the blink of an eye, Cristo placed the nozzle of the syringe into Gunnar's left nostril, pressed the plunger, and expelled a droplet of liquid deep into the boy's sinuses. The kid didn't even flinch. Then he repeated the motion with the second syringe into the right side.

"That's it," he said.

Sigrun smothered her son in kisses, even though Gunnar's attention was entirely on the dog.

Tessa remembered the gentle kisses she'd given Benjamin during his short time in this world. *Love him for as long as you can.*

Cristo disposed of the syringes and gloves in the room's biohazard bin. To Tessa's surprise, he sidled over to Isabella. They exchanged a few words too quietly for her to hear. He reached into a pocket and pulled out a tiny plastic pouch of white powder. He slipped it into Isabella's hand.

What the heck, she wondered. Some random synapse in her brain remembered Cristo's pinpoint pupils yesterday. Wasn't that a sign of—

Cristo's phone rang. She heard a frantic voice yelling in Spanish, and pandemonium in the background. He headed for the door with the phone to his ear.

"Excuse us," Tessa said, following him out of the room.

In the hall he stashed his phone and broke into a run.

"What's wrong?"

"Maria's gone crazy," he said tersely. "She let the animals out."

CHAPTER 8

Maria? The tech from the animal facility? Tessa couldn't believe it. *Why?* Not willing to wait for the elevator, she followed Cristo as he leaped down the stairs toward the animal facility in the basement of the Research Annex. The reverberation of an alarm reached her ears, louder with each flight she descended.

Maria wouldn't have freed the chimps, would she?

They landed at the bottom of the stairwell. Cristo slapped his hand on a scanner and burst through the fire door. The klaxon hit her with full volume. A red light flashed.

The stairwell dumped them into a cavernous concrete bunker or garage, not inside the animal lab itself. She took it in and drew a mental map. This was an underground receiving area for deliveries. The floor sloped upward to the left, a wide driveway leading to a warehouse door at ground level. To her right was a loading dock that she calculated must connect to the animal lab changing room.

Jarring warning beacons tinted the space red. Brighter light streamed down from ground level. Sunlight. The warehouse door to the outside stood open. Movement caught her eye. She gasped.

A pair of chimpanzees crouched in the opening, dark silhouettes against the dazzling sun. For an instant, the chimps froze.

The humans froze, too. *They see us.*

One ape broke for freedom and disappeared. The larger lingered. *The male.*

Her toes curled when it looked her squarely in the face. Cage-free for the first time in who knew how long, it rose on its hind legs and bellowed a challenge. Then it followed the female chimp into the forest.

Cristo shouted curses.

Tessa turned toward the loading dock. A pair of reinforced steel doors separated the animal facility from the loading bay. These doors were open, too. She saw straight through to the changing room.

Her eyes snapped back to the loading dock. More movement. Only a few feet away. Near to the ground. Something scuttling for cover.

Rats.

Cristo swore some more and bounded up to the loading dock. He tried to swing the heavy doors shut, pulling one with all his might. It separated from its hinges and crashed against the concrete, crushing a rat.

"Shit. Maria must've loosened the hinges to keep them open." He glanced back at the open maw of the exit to the outdoors. "Then she raised the warehouse door. That's what triggered the alarm. You're never supposed to have both doors open at the same time."

He entered a code in a panel on the wall. The garage door started to descend.

As the sunlight was steadily pinched out it occurred to her that whatever was left inside the facility was now trapped—whether it was inside a cage or not.

"Let's go." Cristo sprinted into the changing room.

That smell. She'd learned the hard way what it was—and who made it. Rats on the run weren't a problem. They'd flee from people and hide in darkness. But the day before yesterday, the chimpanzees had murdered one of their own. What would they do to a human?

She trailed behind Cristo. "Do you have a tranquilizer gun or something?"

"This isn't a movie. Be careful."

The last time she was here, with Sameer, a locked door separated the changing room from the "clean" area that led directly to the animals. Today that door was propped open. So were the other doors, to rooms where the dogs and rodents were kept. She peeked around the corner into the rodent room. Clear shoebox-shaped rat cages had been taken from the shelves and laid on the floor. Their wire covers were off, allowing the rats to escape if they wished. Shredded bedding and food pellets were scattered about. She saw dozens of rats still in the room, some hiding in their open cages, others on the floor.

A bloodcurdling scream emanated from the final chamber at the far end. The chimpanzee room.

An animal sound? No, human. Possibly female.

Cristo didn't waste time gowning up to protect the animals. Isolation had been broken. He raced into the primate zone.

She put on a paper gown. It was an excuse to hesitate while she screwed up her courage.

Come on, Tessa, they need your help in there.

But she couldn't erase the image of the mutilated chimp and the strewn offal on Sameer's gown.

Then a distraction. A low-pitched rumble behind her. A familiar sound— she'd heard something similar recently—

The growl progressed into a snarl. Heart pounding, she turned toward the sound. A dog. Bared teeth, fur on back erect. Medium-sized. Some kind of beagle mix.

At least it wasn't a German shepherd—or a chimpanzee. But it barked viciously, and charged at her.

She raced after Cristo into the primate room and slammed the door behind her.

The stench of ape feces, so similar to human, hung thick in the air. Nothing moved in the cages. Either they were empty, or the occupants were dead.

Maria, the chimp caretaker-turned-liberator, screamed again.

She was crouched on the floor in a corner, arms wrapped around her knees, rocking back and forth like an autistic kid. Her head was down, her hair a matted mess. The elastic band of a paper hair cover dangled from one ear. Juan, the other animal tech stood nearby, wary. Both of them were grubby with animal filth.

"*No me toque,*" she shrieked.

Tessa saw why Juan was keeping his distance. Maria brandished a screwdriver. At random moments her agitation peaked and she stabbed the air with it while mumbling like a schizophrenic.

Juan and Cristo talked to the poor woman in soft, comforting tones. They inched toward her from opposite sides.

She wriggled backward, tightening herself into the corner, crying out and swinging the screwdriver. Her arm shook uncontrollably—the Parkinson's symptom Tessa remembered from the other day. The tool dropped, clattered and rolled toward the floor drain. Maria folded up again and moaned.

This isn't some animal rights activist stunt. Something is terribly wrong—medically—with that woman.

Her conclusion was reinforced when she saw blood smeared on the walls of the corner and realized Maria's paper gown wasn't merely soiled. It was soaked with blood in several places.

Cristo spoke to Juan in Spanish.

Tessa couldn't follow. "What happened?"

Cristo translated. "She was late for work. Juan fed and watered the rats alone and went for an early lunch break. When he was in the elevator on his way back, the alarm went off. He thinks she propped open the doors and opened the cages. Then she raised the garage door. By the time he got here, the chimps and dogs were loose."

Gagging, Maria flopped onto her hands and knees. Her belly contracted and she vomited, adding another layer of odious stench to the air.

Tessa slapped on a pair of gloves and a face mask, some small protection for her next move. "We have to get her to the hospital."

She spoke gently to the suffering woman and stepped toward her with her palms out. Maria saw her coming. She shouted and fumbled for the dropped screwdriver.

"I want to help," Tessa cooed. Another step. Maria shrunk back. One more step.

Maria lashed out with a feeble, unsteady arm.

"Let me hold your hand," Tessa said. "It's okay."

In a last, wild effort the stricken tech flopped and reached for the screwdriver. Before she could wrap her fingers around it, Cristo and Juan swooped forward. They dragged her upright. Juan got behind and wrapped her in a giant bear hug. She exploded in fury, shaking her head, legs thrashing, screaming. Cristo kicked the screwdriver away and grappled her from the front.

"Open the door," Cristo yelled as the two men dragged the technician toward the exit.

Tessa put a hand on the knob. "There's a dog loose out there."

"The dogs are fine. Open the door!"

She took a quick peek through the window. The dog wasn't in view. She took an extra second to pick up the screwdriver, and then opened the door.

Maria's frenzy gave her surprising strength. The two men struggled to control her. Tessa saw her head twist to an unnatural angle. Juan cried out and loosed his grip around her chest. Somehow she'd managed to bite his arm. Cristo lost his grip on her as well. Maria stumbled the rest of the way into the changing room by herself.

Into the waiting jaws of the beagle.

Woman and dog shouted and snarled. They wrestled and flailed in a crazed, maddened jumble. Cristo managed to land a ferocious kick into the beagle's side. It tumbled, rolled, got to its feet again, a furry ball of fury.

That kick had to break some ribs. Yet it keeps coming.

Like Maria, the dog had gone mad.

The beagle snapped at Juan's legs. Its teeth connected and Juan cried out. Frantic, Tessa looked for something to use as a shield—

Palacio employees, some wearing scrubs, poured into the room from the loading dock. One was armed with a gun.

A single gunshot drowned out the chaos. Eerie silence followed. Blood was splattered on a wall beside the body of the beagle. The dog twitched a few times and then moved no more. Even Maria was momentarily stunned. Cristo spoke quickly in an authoritative voice. Some of the newcomers surrounded Maria. Tessa couldn't see whether one of them gave Maria a sedative, but the poor woman was subdued without further incident. They carried her out.

"They'll use the tunnel to get her to the hospital," Cristo explained, breathing hard, as the group disappeared into the stairwell.

Juan pressed a clean paper gown against the bite wound on his calf. He sat heavily on a bench and gave instructions to the assembled group.

Tessa surveyed the mess. In addition to the dead dog, there was animal waste, bedding, kibble, broken glass and water. An overturned cart spilled boxes of supplies and spray bottles of disinfectant. Rats scampered in the shadows. She pictured the dead chimpanzee from the other day, and imagined the confusion of the ones who were on the loose. What a terrible waste of resources, of animals' lives. Data gone. Experiments ruined. The escaped dogs and chimps were dangerous. Vargas would likely have them hunted down and killed.

Dangerous—but in how many ways?

"Cristo, tell me you weren't doing any infectious disease research down here."

"No," he said indignantly. "Does this look like a containment facility?"

"No, but it doesn't look like a primate house either."

He righted the supply cart. "I told Vargas we weren't equipped to handle chimps. He didn't care. Said we could learn. But I swear, he would never allow germs."

"Because he's so rule-abiding?"

"Because he wouldn't put his hospital clients at risk."

That made sense. Vargas probably never considered the chimps a hazard to anyone outside the animal facility. "Were all the escaped animals specific pathogen-free?"

"The rats were. Totally clean. The dogs and pigs didn't come from laboratory breeders so they didn't have the SPF label. But they were healthy. Our vet screened them for common parasites and viruses. They were cleaner than most farm animals."

"Whoa. Did you say pigs? You didn't still have pigs in there, did you?"

"Two. We had one week left of their experiment."

"So they were in the same room with the chimpanzees?"

He nodded and picked up a broom.

"Oh for God's sake." She hadn't even noticed the pigs, which was understandable given the chimpanzee situation during her first visit. "What about the chimps? Did they come from a reputable source? Did you test them for infections?"

"You know how it is with primates. You can't test for everything. As far as we know, they were healthy."

"Obviously you're not counting psychiatric issues. Even in animals, murder isn't a sign of mental health."

He slammed a chunk of broken bottle into a trash bin. "You asked about infectious diseases. I tell you the escaped animals are not infected with anything." He turned his back to her. "Unless you're going to pick up a mop, you should get on the next plane. I have work to do."

Belatedly she realized her questions sounded more like accusations.

It's not his fault. Vargas brought those chimps here. Poor Cristo is just out of a sick bed and now he has to deal with this.

They were both upset and frustrated. She needed to find another way to channel her feelings. Better leave Cristo to his job and figure out her next move with Gunnar.

"Take care of yourself, *amigo*." She patted him on the shoulders. He grunted.

She exited through the loading dock. That fecal smell—almost but not quite human—was really getting to her. But it wasn't only the physical stench.

Sure, the chimps might've gone crazy because of the woefully inadequate housing. They were caged, bored, and improperly fed.

But that couldn't explain what happened to Maria. Or the dog.

This whole situation stinks.

There were lots of reasons why primate research was heavily regulated in the US. Most of the regulations were intended to protect the animals. But some were for their keepers' benefit. Chimpanzees were similar enough to humans that some of their germs could infect people. Case in point: HIV, the virus that causes AIDS.

Perhaps leaving the Palacio for the next week wasn't such a bad thing, even for Gunnar.

CHAPTER 9

Vargas swept past the swimming pool bar and into the Palacio's main lobby. He saw no patients, and one approved staff member. *Good.* Then he spotted two brutish thugs carelessly handling automatic weapons. *Not good. But expected.*

For the past two hours, he'd been personally supervising last-minute preparation for Luis Angel de la Rosa's arrival. Through heroic effort he'd cleared the main hospital of patients in time. As the deadline approached he had overloaded the outgoing flights. Not all his clients departed with their luggage, and few departed happy. Some were in no condition to travel but he shipped them to a hospital in Acapulco anyway. Those folks were going to cause him trouble later despite the money he spread around to assure they were well cared for until they went home.

He'd cross-checked the list of staff approved to be on campus during Luis Angel de la Rosa's stay and talked to each employee in person. Of course he explained to them the Palacio's water was as safe as always. Then he emphasized the importance of discretion and doing exactly as they were told for the next several days. The word Sinaloa was never spoken, but the workers were smart enough to recognize that drug money—big drug money—was involved in this upheaval at the hospital. They'd toe the line. He saw it in their faces. Most of them were terrified.

As if he didn't have enough problems, now he had to worry about renegade chimpanzees, dogs, and even a couple of damn pigs. Sometimes he wondered what the hell he was paying people for. The woman responsible—Maria?—he'd serve her head on a platter. If she survived, that is. Sameer Desai examined her and said she probably had advanced encephalitis, an infection in her brain. Medically, nothing could be done for her. Fine. He sent her back to the Research Annex. She'd get strapped in the next (and last) flight out with the rest of the clean up crew from the animal lab. Along with Tessa Price, the kid, and the kid's mother. Tessa had been bugging him all day. He ignored her. She needed to chill out. One week wasn't going to make any difference for the kid. Batten disease played out over decades, not days. If her gene therapy was the miracle drug she hoped, that miracle could come a week later. If not, well, what mattered was the data—and the survival of the Palacio.

He felt sticky with sweat. *Wish there was time for a shower. You only get one chance to make a first impression*. His goal when he met de la Rosa was to convey a fine balance between power and submission. Competence with service.

For the second time today Vargas stood on the roof of the Palacio waiting for a helicopter's blades to stop spinning. The blades kicked up a hot wind in the late afternoon air. He ran his fingers through his hair. Unlike the aircraft that delivered the donor, this was a first-class 'copter. A military model, it bristled with weapons and was probably armored.

His knees wobbled. For one of the few times in his life, he felt vulnerable. If it suited them, Sinaloa would crush him and his entire life's work. Not merely crush. Torture, disfigure, and dismember. This organization's violent acts were so obscene the press hardly reported a simple mass execution. Killing wasn't newsworthy unless decapitation and identity obliteration were involved, preferably with a victim count in the high double digits.

What's a genius like me doing associating with a bunch of brainless killers?

There was no turning back now. He told himself that a physician does not judge the moral shortcomings of his patients. De la Rosa was coming to him for needed medical attention. He had a responsibility to provide it.

He took a deep breath and closed his eyes to resurrect his trademark self-confidence. His hospital was ready. The donor had arrived safely and was being prepped. The surgeon and necessary support staff were trained and capable. With a new kidney, they would give Luis Angel de la Rosa his life back. The drug lord would be grateful. Maybe he'd reward them generously. At the very least, Vargas expected de la Rosa would leave the Palacio alone and keep the hospital supplied with plack. That was enough.

The helicopter door slid open. Vargas smoothed his shirt. *Just another high-maintenance client.*

Tessa stared at the text message on her screen, willing the letters to rearrange themselves into words she wanted to read.

"8:05 PM departure for Acapulco. Take the boy and his mother with you. Not negotiable. If all 3 not on plane I terminate the project. Vargas"

The bastard didn't even have the guts to talk to me.

She stomped each step as she climbed to Gunnar's floor. They had to go. One hour to pack and wheel Gunnar out to the airstrip down the hill at the base of the peninsula.

How am I going to explain this to Sigrun?

To her surprise, Lyle, Isabella, and Dixie were still in Gunnar's room. Apparently the dog had won over the family, as she was now snuggled up in Gunnar's bed. Sigrun was nowhere to be seen.

Lyle and Isabella were in a most awkward and unexpected posture. For a moment she thought she'd walked in on a very private activity, but both of them were fully clothed.

Isabella's long, lean body was draped over the windowsill, hanging literally halfway out the window. Lyle was gripping one of her wrists with both hands, his feet braced, to keep her from falling.

"Is it him?" he said.

"Yes," Isabella replied. She shifted her weight and Lyle hauled her back into the room. In her free hand she held a pair of binoculars. "Oh," she said, surprised to see they were not alone.

Lyle helped her to her feet and turned to Tessa. "You're back, Doc. About time for all of us to get out of Dodge."

"The plane leaves in an hour. The last flight, I hear."

"We got the same news." Lyle slid an arm around Isabella's waist. The binoculars had disappeared. "We're traveling together, then."

"Traveling?" Sigrun entered the room. "Vargas wouldn't change his mind?"

"I'm sorry," Tessa said. "I tried. He isn't making any exceptions. The Palacio is closing for a week. Maybe less. We're going to Acapulco."

"They don't have his medicine there," Sigrun said.

"He'll get great care. You and I will both make sure of that. But he will miss a couple of doses."

"I thought he needed it every day. It doesn't stay in his body."

"It doesn't."

Sigrun's eyes pleaded. A look of resignation came over her face. Silently she turned to a dresser and started selecting garments to pack.

To her surprise, Tessa felt Lyle's hand on her shoulder.

"It's for the best," he said. "You don't want to be around the Palacio right now." He gestured to the German shepherd. "Dixie. *Hier!*"

Isabella and the dog took their places at either side of Lyle and they walked out.

Lyle's comment baffled Tessa. *What does he know about it?*

Vargas felt pounding in his arteries as he speed-walked to the clinical lab. The tech who ran the blood tests had paged him. Urgent news about the kidney donor. The news wasn't good.

This was an unwelcome development. When the donor arrived, they drew blood for the Palacio's usual panel of tests, plus a few extras specific for transplantation. Luis Angel de la Rosa had found and delivered the donor, but Vargas wasn't going to take it on the drug lord's word that the donor was suitable. It was possible to transplant a kidney that wasn't a close immunologic match for the recipient. But to prevent rejection of an unmatched organ, the recipient would need to take immunosuppressive drugs. De la Rosa was a poor candidate for that. The whole point of this transplant was to break the old man's dependence on doctors. Being hooked up to a machine three times a week for several hours of dialysis was not compatible with his lifestyle. Neither was constant monitoring for rejection.

If Vargas transplanted a poorly-matched kidney, it'd be his fault when the organ crashed. De la Rosa would undoubtedly fail to take the immunosuppressant drugs. His body would reject the kidney. It would look like *Vargas* had failed.

He didn't want to think about the consequences of failing Sinaloa's boss.

The clinical lab was on the second floor of the main hospital. He hand-scanned himself into the room. It was a typical analytical lab: fluorescent lights, refrigerators, glass beakers, floor centrifuges that looked like washing machines, and an array of automated equipment with complex control panels.

A rotund woman wearing a lab coat peeled off her latex gloves with a snap. "Look at this."

She handed him a stack of printouts. He hyperventilated as he flipped through.

"This is impossible. Repeat everything. And this time, do proper controls."

She snorted. "I already did. These results are reproducible. What you're reading is the truth."

He looked more closely. The young man chosen to give a kidney to the drug lord was a good immunologic match—same blood type including major and several minor antigens, enough matching tissue markers to make the risk of rejection low.

But based on the other blood tests, they wouldn't be able to use him.

"Hepatitis B, hepatitis C, *and* HIV?" Vargas said. Three different viruses. All slow-acting. All transmitted in blood. All lethal.

"He must be an IV drug user."

"Maybe."

It didn't make sense. Surely when de la Rosa's people typed and cross-matched the donor, they screened for blood-borne diseases. He studied the profile of antibody subclasses.

"These numbers say he's having acute antibody responses. That means he was exposed to all three viruses within the last two weeks. Possibly even the last few days." He tapped a finger on the pages. "What are the odds of that?"

The tech pressed a button on her mouse and printed out another document. She frowned and handed it to Vargas.

"Jesus, he's got malaria too?" he said.

A parasite that infects red blood cells *and* three blood-borne viruses? And all contracted very recently, because the kid didn't have symptoms yet.

The donor's blood was poison.

The situation was improbable to the point of impossibility

Vargas crumpled the paper in frustration. "Somebody did this."

The Tenochtitlan Suite occupied twelve hundred square feet of the top floor of the Palacio main hospital. Like the lost Aztec capital city it was named after, Tenochtitlan was fit for royalty with designer fabrics, hardwood floor, granite countertops, an enormous flat screen TV, floor-to-ceiling windows with expansive views of the ocean, gardens, and pool area.

None of which was going to placate Vargas's most important client ever.

I need a drink, Vargas thought. Or better yet, a hit of plack.

Normally the area outside the suite was manned by Palacio staff in friendly floral uniforms—nurses, aides, a personal concierge. He missed them. His staff didn't leave oily, disassembled gun parts on the counters, nor did they spill chips and beer and leave grimy fingerprints on the white leather couch. With Mara Salvatrucha enforcers all over the place, instead of freshly-cut jasmine, the antechamber smelled like a locker room.

Two of the MS guards threw down their poker cards and got up to intercept him.

"I need to talk to de la Rosa," Vargas said.

"What makes you think *El Jefe* wants to talk to you?"

"I'm his doctor." Mentally he added, *you moron.* He brandished a sheaf of papers. "Don't give me crap. I've got urgent medical matters to discuss."

Their little exercise of power satisfied, the MS let him pass. Part of him wished they'd stopped him, driven him back into the elevator. Anything to avoid the conversation he was about to have with the patient.

Get a grip, man. You can salvage this thing. Sinaloa must have a backup plan, a second-choice donor.

The hand scanner at the side of the door beckoned, but out of courtesy he knocked instead. The door to the suite was a large framed window with a privacy blind. His knock triggered the whir of an automatic motor and the blind lifted, revealing a pair of dark, tailored pants. Rising further, it exposed a pair of large hands hanging beside hip holsters filled with two handguns and a smart phone, followed by a white shirt clinging to a flat, muscled belly, and broad shoulders. Last came a face. Icy. Professional. Nothing like the buffoons watching *fútbol* in the foyer.

De la Rosa's bodyguard opened the door. "Come in, Doctor."

Vargas strode into the suite. Two more bodyguards closed in on him.

"Arms up."

He did as he was told, holding the laboratory printouts over his head while the guards frisked him.

"This way."

They passed an abstract painting by a contemporary Mexican artist. Vargas had paid ten thousand US dollars for it.

How much would it cost to convince *El Jefe* not to shoot the messenger?

A sectional sofa, modified to incorporate a hospital bed at one end, arced around the magnificent windows that met at the corner of the building. They were one story higher than the tree canopy, six stories above the ground. As Vargas and the guards approached the sofa from behind, someone triggered the sheer curtains to descend. The top of a head, black buzz-cut hair richly mixed with gray, barely stuck up over the back of the furniture. A bodyguard went around and respectfully whispered to the head.

"Vargas." Luis Angel de la Rosa's voice was raspy. "You have something to say?"

He was nervous earlier in the day when the Sinaloa boss arrived. By now, with de la Rosa admitted to his hospital and depending on him for survival, he had expected to be more in control. Instead, he felt like he was falling from a high wire without a safety net. His job was to give the drug lord an organ transplant. Without a donor, he had nothing to offer. Luis Angel de la Rosa held all the cards.

After a nod of approval from the guard, he shuffled over to face his patient. "Sir."

Tongue-tied? Me?

Mexico's most-wanted man sat propped up by cushions, his short wiry frame dwarfed by the oversized sofa. Vargas knew the man's bones were weakened from chronic kidney disease and he could see swelling in the man's ankles. Despite these signs of physical debility, de la Rosa was a predator. He radiated power the way an alpha wolf sprays pheromones over his pack. Vargas could practically smell his own vulnerability. He wondered if de la Rosa smelled blood.

"Sir, we—I—have examined your donor."

"Your surgeon is ready?"

"Yes—well—the surgeon is here. He's at your service. But—"

Luis Angel de la Rosa didn't smile, or ask him to have a seat, or make any unnecessary gestures. His narrow, unforgiving eyes drilled into Vargas. He did not speak.

Vargas fingered his goatee. "There's a problem." *Make it clear that it's not your fault!* "The donor you delivered is unfit. He's a great match, your people did well to find him. But he's infected with several diseases. Diseases of the blood. There's no way to clean them out of the kidney. If we transplant his organ into you, you will die."

No reaction.

He felt compelled to show the data. He laid a couple of pages on the ottoman. "We're very thorough here at the Palacio. I'm sure your people did many of these tests already but we repeated them. Our methods are highly advanced. Capable of detecting the lowest concentrations of a virus in the blood. Very sensitive. Though the young man has developed a slight fever now. Anybody could see that."

God, shut up, man! You're blathering like an idiot.

He waited for a reply.

"Phone." De la Rosa raised a hand and a guard instantly placed a cell phone in his palm.

Awkwardly standing there, ignored, Vargas felt like a schoolchild in the principal's office. Or maybe an innocent man facing a hanging judge.

De la Rosa muttered an occasional word to someone on the phone. Vargas gleaned the one-sided conversation was about the donor. The drug lord grunted and rid himself of the phone.

"What happened?" de la Rosa asked as Vargas apparently became visible again.

"I can assure you he did not acquire any infections here at the Palacio. And our diagnostic tests are extremely reliable. We repeated—"

"What happened before he came here?" de la Rosa said. "My doctor in Mexico City claims he tested everything."

"I don't know."

"Guess."

He'd been asking himself this question for an hour. How did the donor simultaneously get cancer, AIDS, malaria, and more?

"I'd say, sir, the only explanation is someone injected him on purpose."

"I think you're right. Someone is trying to kill me." De la Rosa laughed, a brief, menacing laugh. "What a surprise."

"Do you have a backup donor?"

"I do. We will bring him in. But first, I want to know who has gone to such trouble to put germs in my blood." He snapped his fingers. "Bring me the donor."

Vargas wagged his head from side to side. *Is he talking to me? He wants the donor up here?* His mind finally caught up to the brutal logic of what might be coming.

"Sir, be careful. The man's blood is infectious."

"They say you cannot get AIDS by shaking hands, Doctor." He addressed two of his men. "Go with him."

Vargas led the two bodyguards to a less ostentatious room on a lower floor. The scared, skinny youth was lying in bed, watching TV. Though the room was warmer than the rest of the hospital, he'd wrapped himself in two layers of fleece blankets. Fever's getting worse, Vargas thought. Whoever plotted this miscalculated how long it would take for the kid to show symptoms. No doctor would transplant from a febrile donor.

The donor put on a show of bravado. "You're early. *El Jefe* and I go under the knife tomorrow."

"How do you feel?" Vargas asked.

The kid puffed himself up and put on a show of vigor. "I'm ready whenever you are, *Señor*."

He's lying, Vargas thought. I can see he feels like shit. Why lie about it? Then he realized. *The kid knows.*

"There's been a change in plans," he said. "We think you're coming down with something. It's best for you and *El Jefe* if we delay the operation."

"No!" The young man lurched up in his bed. "Do it today if you think I'll be sick tomorrow."

"That's not the way it works. If there's an infection in your body, it'll travel with the kidney. We don't want *El Jefe* to catch something."

"Take it! Take it out now!" He got to his feet and wobbled. "Give him my kidney!"

De la Rosa's bodyguards grabbed him by the arms. They gave the kid no explanation and guided him out of the room in his robe, allowing him to put on a pair of slippers first. The youth walked with them, dragging his feet a little. Whether this was intentional resistance or merely weakness, Vargas couldn't tell.

The MS goons in the foyer barely looked up when Vargas and the others came back with the donor. They entered the Tenochtitlan Suite.

De la Rosa had moved to the kitchen area. He sat upright in a high-backed dining chair upholstered in crimson fabric. The bodyguards brought the donor before him. Three took positions behind the youth and at his sides. They did not touch him. The donor stood, trembling.

"*Mijo*," de la Rosa said in a kindly, paternal voice. "I had hoped to invite you here to say *gracias*. But sadly the deal is off."

"*Mi padre*, I'm ready. Tell this doctor to do the operation."

"Your mind is ready but your body is not. They tell me you're very sick."

"I'm not sick!" De la Rosa fixed his gaze on him and said nothing. "A little sick maybe. That's okay. This is a hospital."

"You don't feel it yet. But you are dying," de la Rosa said.

What was left of the color in the donor's cheeks faded away. His teeth chattered. "*Padre*, I need the money very badly."

"Is that all?"

The youth's hunted look returned. He touched the bruise on the side of his face and stared at the floor.

"What did they do to you?" de la Rosa said.

No response.

With unexpected vitality, de la Rosa leaped from his chair. He grabbed the youth's chin and pulled until they were looking each other in the eye, even though the drug lord was several inches shorter.

"They are trying to kill me by killing you. I know. The doctors here tested your blood. No matter what you do, I will not use your kidney."

The donor choked back sobs. "They took my mother and my sister."

De la Rosa released his chin. "Was it the Zetas?"

The donor nodded. Now Vargas understood. The Zeta cartel was Sinaloa's main rival. Until Sinaloa took over a few weeks ago, the Palacio was in Zeta territory. The Zetas must have learned about the kidney donor. They shot him up with all kinds of nasty things. The biological contamination was an elaborate assassination plot.

"What happened?" de la Rosa asked.

Again, no response. Vargas willed the youth to answer the questions. He did not want the situation to get out of hand.

De la Rosa sat down. "I can send our brothers to save your mother. If you tell me everything."

The youth wiped his tears. "They took us off the street, in a van. They put me to sleep." He choked again. "When I woke up, they told me if I didn't give you a kidney, they would kill my *madre*. They told me not to tell anyone I'd been with them."

"Where did this happen?"

"Barrio Tepito."

"*Gracias, mijo.* We will find your women. And this doctor will help you." He gestured and the bodyguards escorted the donor out of the suite.

De la Rosa turned to Vargas. "My expert in Mexico City recommends a—what do you call it—MRI scan of the boy. He thinks the information will be useful."

"A magnetic resonance image? Of the donor?" Vargas was perplexed. "That won't tell us anything about the infections. We might pick up some kind of tumor, but—"

De la Rosa raised a finger to silence him. "I want an MRI scan of the donor. You will do it for me. You have one of these machines, yes?"

"Of course."

"Do it now."

"What about your transplant? When will the new donor arrive?"

"Soon. Take me to the scan. I want to watch."

CHAPTER 10

Tessa towed two small rolling suitcases out of the Annex into the long shadows of evening. Gunnar carried a duffle bag and a package of snacks on his lap. Sigrun pushed his wheelchair.

He'll be fine, Tessa told herself. Any setbacks will be temporary.

She watched Gunnar lift a corn chip to his mouth. Her experimental treatment had restored his ability to feed himself. Once they returned to the Palacio and resumed his inoculations, more miracles would follow.

They had to.

Sigrun looked warily at the shady-looking mercenaries who now patrolled the road in great numbers. "Who are these people?" she whispered.

"I don't know." Why would Vargas bring in special guards for plumbing repair?

"I hope they're gone when we get back."

"Me too."

Four of the gun-toting men approached and loosely grouped themselves around the women and child.

If this is supposed to be protection, it doesn't feel like it.

The guards accompanied them toward the airstrip. They followed a paved footpath through the forest that clung to the sides of the peninsula. It was a steep descent for a wheelchair, from the plateau down to the airstrip at sea level. Earlier Tessa had seen golf carts going this way, shuttling guests to their flights, but no one was left to assist them.

"It's creepy," Sigrun said. "This place used to feel like a resort. Now it feels more like a terrorist camp."

I hope Sameer and Cristo stay out of trouble. "Let's get to the plane."

Thick tropical vegetation crowded in on both sides, blocking much of the waning light. The air was uncomfortably still. Buzzing insects swirled around her head. She swatted a mosquito on her bare forearm. Too late. Blood streaked the spot.

The forward guard paused. Sigrun brushed bugs away from her son. The guard snapped a few words to his comrades. They lifted their weapons and pointed them into the forest.

"Do you hear that?" Sigrun said.

Sounds of birds and distant humans were muffled by the foliage. No wind stirred the treetops, which arched silently over their heads. She heard a mild scuffle in the forest. Crackle, like the snapping of a twig. Grunts.

She remembered the dead chimpanzee and suddenly was glad for the company of armed thugs.

A wide smile slithered across the face of the leader. He raised his weapon and took aim into the trees.

Crack!

The single shot transformed the scuffle into a brawl. Something—something large—moved in the underbrush, shaking the broad leaves of tall ferns. It was coming their way.

The man fired again, this time in repeating mode. She covered her ears against the deafening reports and crouched low in fear.

A creature stumbled out of the forest on to the path just ahead. Blood poured from holes all over its body. It was a pig, large, brownish-pink. Not a native wild peccary. Livestock grade.

An escapee from the lab.

The other three men took the opportunity to dump rounds of ammunition into the dying animal. Gunnar cried out a guttural protest against the noise.

Their fun over, the men stopped firing and leaned over the pig to admire their work. The pig had inconveniently collapsed in the middle of the path, and now the heavy carcass blocked their way. The guards made a half-hearted attempt to shove it aside. It didn't budge. The leader stepped over the dead swine and kept walking.

Sigrun looked helplessly at Tessa.

"Excuse me." Tessa pointed at the wheelchair. "We need help."

"*Ayuda,*" Sigrun said.

Two men gracelessly hefted Gunnar's chair over the pig while Sigrun frantically reached to keep the boy from falling out. Tessa dragged the suitcases, trying to avoid the pig's spilled blood. She failed and for the next couple of yards, one of the wheels traced a thin red line on the path.

Just before the path started to slope downward, they reached the Palacio's outer wall. She pushed to the front of the group and laid her hand on the scanner to open the gate.

"I'll help you brake," she said to Sigrun.

Cautiously, they guided Gunnar's chair down the hill. Minutes later, the ground flattened out and they emerged from the leafy tunnel at the sea-level airstrip. A nondescript white jet in desperate need of a good washing waited on the short runway. She counted eight passenger windows on the near side.

Lyle, Isabella, and Dixie were already there, waiting to board. They had only two small bags—considerably less luggage than when they arrived. Lyle saw them and hurried over.

"Are y'all okay?" he said, his brow tight with concern. "We heard gunshots."

They nodded. Sigrun said, "They killed a wild pig."

"Not wild," Tessa corrected. She told them about the incident in the animal facility. Isabella joined them and listened carefully.

"Another good reason to get out of here," Lyle said. "Killer chimps."

A handful of other stragglers, all Palacio staff, turned up for the flight. Last to arrive was a patient on a wheeled stretcher, the collapsible kind used in ambulances. Juan, the animal technician, pushed it with the help of another man.

"Sorry we're late," he said. "Had some trouble getting around a dead pig."

The men rolled the stretcher forward to load it first on to the plane. Tessa got a look at the patient.

It was Maria, her face like death.

Sameer Desai slumped into one of the comfy chairs in the Palacio's main lobby. The room looked like a ballroom after a wedding reception: abandoned cups and glasses, chairs out of place, miscellaneous trash about, floor rugs askew. But it was also quiet, at last. The past day and a half of his life was a blur of triage, writing prescriptions, transferring medical records, organizing flights. He felt like the lower-caste servants in his parents' home: underpaid, overworked, and disrespected. To make it worse, amid the chaos of clearing the hospital Vargas had issued orders but told half-truths. It took Vargas a full day to get around to telling him there was nothing wrong with the Palacio's water supply, that it was an excuse to get everybody out. For the privacy of a VIP, Vargas said. And that was all the explanation he gave.

A VIP, huh? As if being very rich also made one very important. Sameer had been forced to send patients out against his medical judgment. For the convenience of some rich guy? It ran counter to everything he believed. Every time he arranged for a patient to transfer to a hospital in Acapulco, he had to lie to the admitting physicians about why he was dumping these people on them. He hated that.

Then the mysterious soldiers replaced the Palacio's usual police force. He started to suspect that something was amiss. That Vargas had left out some important information about this mystery guest.

Now the job was done, the hospital empty of patients. To his regret he'd been too busy to spend any time with Tessa since that first horrible day with the chimps. Now it was too late. She was on the last flight, scheduled to depart in a few minutes. He was already thinking about her return. For what it was worth, Vargas said this foolishness wouldn't drag out any longer than a week. He knew how worried Tessa was about the impact this separation would have on Gunnar. For her and her patient, he hoped Vargas was telling the truth this time.

His phone rang. *Speak of the devil. It's Vargas.* Maybe the boss would finally explain to him what was really going on.

"Sameer, I need your help to do an MRI. Meet me at radiology in five minutes."

That's it? Scut work? No summary of the patient's medical history or the purpose of the imaging scan? Just 'do this,' like I'm a janitor or something?

He swallowed his pride. "I can be there. The evacuation logistics are nearly complete. One of the—"

"*Bueno.* Five minutes." *Click.*

What, no thank you?

Peeved, he marched to the MRI suite with half a mind to tell Vargas he could do his own darn procedures. He was the first to arrive.

They'd shut down the MRI scanner during the evacuation. The suite was dark and over-chilled from lack of activity in the constant air conditioning.

Muttering with irritation, he turned on the lights and computers. Sound and energy flowed through the room again.

He sat at the MRI control console, which was behind a viewing window triple-layered with safety glass and shielding. Power hummed through the hidden metal coils that generated the machine's magnetic field as the system came online.

The door opened. Vargas pushed in a wheelchair bearing a stringy young Mexican man wearing a Palacio patient robe. These two were accompanied by four dark-suited heavyweights and a short, leathery, old man. The old one was in a wheelchair too but got to his feet as soon as they entered.

Sameer jumped up. Introductions would have to wait until safety protocols were followed.

"Stop, please, stay where you are. This facility uses an extremely powerful magnet to take pictures. The magnet will grab anything with even a trace of magnetic metal in it. I've seen a watch leave a man's wrist and fly across the room with the speed of a bullet. The effect is stronger the closer you get." He gestured. "This is our safe zone. The wheelchairs will stay outside and you must remove anything that has metal. Rings, jewelry, watches, belts, boots." He looked at the four tough guys and added, "Weapons of any kind."

He guessed that the younger man in Vargas's care was the one to be scanned. He extended a hand in greeting and was about to ask the patient if he had any medical implants, like a pacemaker or artificial joint.

Vargas stepped between him and the young man. "I've screened them. The patient's ready. I'll get him in the machine. You operate the controls."

So I don't even get to introduce myself. He vowed to have a fierce conversation with Vargas later. But not now in front of the patient—that would be unprofessional.

"What are we doing?" he asked.

"Chest and abdominal scan," Vargas replied.

He could see the patient shivering and wondered why Vargas wasn't paying more attention to the client's comfort. *Is this how you treat a VIP?* The patient also looked scared. Fortunately the Palacio used an open MRI scanner. No narrow, tight tube of the kind that gave many people intense claustrophobia. With this scanner, patients lay on an open table. The table slid between a pair of huge, round magnets suspended horizontally, like a hamburger patty between two halves of a giant bun. No part of the patient's body was ever fully enclosed during the scan.

Vargas helped the patient onto the table. Because movement ruined magnetic resonance images, the table was equipped with padded restraints for the ankles, wrists, and head. Normally they only used one of these, whichever was nearest the body part being scanned. Sameer was surprised to see Vargas engage all the restraints. When Vargas tightened the straps, the patient whimpered.

Sameer held his tongue again. Yet another issue to raise later with his boss. If Vargas was going to do advanced procedures himself, he ought to know the proper methods. The restraints were intended to be more psychological than physical. Patients were instructed to lie as still as possible. You didn't literally tie them down; that only made them more fidgety.

The strange guests did not speak this entire time. They clustered around him in the control room, making him uncomfortable. The older man seemed to be in charge. Were the others bodyguards? Maybe the patient was this man's son?

Vargas gave the patient a few words and a pat on the arm, then left the vicinity of the scanner. He joined Sameer behind the viewing window. "Begin."

The motors that drove the table whirred. The old man leaned forward and rested a hand on the console. Sameer didn't like it but chose not to react. This was Vargas's show. He turned his attention to the patient, who squirmed on the table. His teeth were chattering.

Good thing we're not trying to get head images, he thought. They'd be too blurry.

The scanner emitted a rapid series of loud, low-frequency noises—*brrrt brrrt brrrt*—as the magnets inside the machine moved. The table on which the patient lay slid closer to the magnets. In a few seconds, his torso would be between the scanner halves. That was the point of maximum magnetic field strength, where they got the best images.

The youth grunted. His fingers lifted as he pulled against the wrist restraints. The old man at Sameer's side pressed closer to the viewing window.

A rumble, then a hum and a series of *buh-buh-buh* sounds came from the machine as Sameer fired up the electromagnets.

The patient screamed.

A paint ball exploded in the scanner. Except it wasn't paint. Blood spattered on the magnets, the walls, the ceiling. A few drops reached all the way to the viewing window, perfect red circles that dripped into lines.

"No! No!" Sameer cut the power to the electromagnets. It would take minutes for the field to drop. The patient wailed and flailed but couldn't break free of the restraints. The fabric of his robe had been torn away from his belly. A red stain was growing.

No one else said anything. Vargas took a step backward, his face aghast. Sameer saw him stare at the old man. The old man lifted his hand from the console and stood upright. His face was bizarrely unexpressive.

Sameer didn't have time to interpret the strange reactions of the others. He was working on reflex.

"Vargas! Get the cart!" He reversed the movement of the table to slide the patient away from the scanner.

I heard something. Simultaneous with seeing the blood. A metallic strike. Something solid had flown at the magnet.

He ran out of the control room to the scanner. The patient continued to scream vigorously, which was a good sign. A fresh wound had opened in the right lower quadrant of his belly. The skin was torn, jagged, irregular. It held a pool of blood that dribbled over and puddled on the table. Sameer had seen wounds like this before. Exit wounds, where bullets had passed through a person's body. The magnets had ripped something out of the youth.

"He had an implant!" Why the hell didn't Vargas know that? Vargas said he'd screened the patient. He should've looked for scars. Asked about previous surgery. He should have known.

Did he know?

Sameer looked up. Vargas hadn't moved from his position behind the control console. No cart. No help.

"Damn it, Manuel, I need gauze!"

An unfamiliar voice came over the microphone from the control room. Sameer peered through the window. The old man was talking.

"Thank you, Doctor. Your work here is done."

"Who the hell are you? Vargas, bring me the cart!" He moved to examine the wound.

"Don't!" This time Vargas spoke. "The patient's HIV-positive. Get out of there until we've got proper blood-borne pathogen control."

He hesitated. He wasn't wearing the standard protective gear against infection. Didn't even have gloves on. He was dressed to run the computers, not to deal with trauma.

The old man and his bodyguards came out from behind the shielded wall. "I said you're done." The old man's tone was threatening.

That was too much. *Threaten me, will you? I'm a doctor. This patient has a serious medical problem.* He'd had enough being pushed around lately. No matter who this man was, he had no right to interfere with patient care.

"Get out of here," Sameer said. "This man needs a doctor."

One flick of the old man's wrist, and a burly guard clamped his hands on Sameer. Sameer's arms were pulled behind his body and lifted slightly, putting pressure on his shoulders. He could tell that if the guard tugged even a little harder he'd be in a lot of pain. Another guard exited the suite. Vargas continued to cower in the control room.

De la Rosa stepped to the MRI scanner and examined the surface of its overhead arm. Sameer followed his gaze and saw a small bloody object, about the size of a pack of gum, plastered against the magnet. At that moment, the field strength decreased enough to drop the object. De la Rosa glanced at it and walked away.

"A live GPS tracking device," the drug lord said. "Found and removed in one step. But destroyed too late, I'm sure. *Amigos*, the Zetas know where we are."

The Zetas. Finally Sameer put the pieces together and realized who he was dealing with. The reason for the evacuation. Why Vargas had been behaving strangely. The Palacio had been taken over by organized crime.

The Sinaloa boss spoke again. "The gods of my ancestors demanded blood sacrifice. We have kept this tradition."

Heads around him nodded. Sameer listened in disbelief.

De la Rosa continued. "The Aztecs slew their enemies and burned their hearts. The bodies of their victims, they ate."

The fourth guard returned. He held a handgun.

The injured youth, still strapped to the table, struggled furiously at his bonds. De la Rosa walked wide to avoid the blood splashing from the donor's belly wound. He stopped at the youth's head and leaned over, eye to eye with the terrified victim.

"Don't worry. Your body is contaminated. We will burn it."

Another swift, silent gesture from de la Rosa to his men. Then he walked to the door and took a seat in his wheelchair. The guard with the gun moved.

"The magnet," Sameer warned, but both he and the guard knew the magnet was now weak. Too weak to support the weight of the tracking device the Zeta cartel had implanted in the donor's abdomen.

Definitely too weak to wrench a gun from a man's hand.

No invisible magnetic force acted on the bullet as it blasted from the barrel. It traveled true to aim, penetrating the donor's forehead and exiting in a straight line into the table.

Out on the tarmac, Tessa looked at Maria unconscious on a stretcher and cursed silently.

Vargas! Couldn't you even take care of your own people?

She swatted another mosquito—too late again—while the stretcher bearing Maria rode up the belt of a baggage lift to the rear door of the airplane. Juan stood at the bottom, guarding against mishap.

Lyle picked up the duffle bag from Gunnar's lap. "Can I give you a hand, ladies?"

"Thanks," Tessa said. She cocked an ear toward an odd noise, a kind of screech in the distance. The screech grew a bit louder and ended with a pop. Isabella stiffened.

Another screech. Much louder, moving fast. The pitch rose as it got closer.

"Get down!" Isabella screamed. She dropped to the pavement. Lyle threw himself over Gunnar.

Hell broke loose on the airstrip.

The first explosion was far down the runway. A flash of light like day, then the clatter of broken pavement falling from the sky.

Tessa shook her head. Whatever was happening was happening faster than she could process it.

The rolling *pa-wah-ow-ow* of the blast echoed. No, not an echo. Another gigantic hole appeared in the pavement. Closer than the last. Belatedly she dropped to her knees. *Get down. Hands on head.*

From that moment, the blasts fell in rapid succession, overlapping, indistinguishable. The shock waves created their own wind. Gravel stung her exposed skin.

The armed guards fled up the hill into the forest.

What about the plane? She glanced. The baggage lift had tipped over, throwing Maria's stretcher upside down, under the fuselage. Juan crawled on his hands and knees. Another flash and the wing was severed from the plane. It crashed *crack-rattle* on the tarmac. Liquid sprayed from the tail of the jet.

"Doc!" Lyle yanked her arm and dragged her to her feet. "Get out of here!"

Confused. Shocked.

He shook her. "Run for it! Back to the Annex!"

A switch flipped in her head. Clarity. "I can't leave Gunnar."

"I'll carry the boy. Go!"

Questions. *Who? What? Why?*

More Doppler-warped screeches. A concussion knocked her to the ground. Pain in her left elbow and hip and head. Blood.

"Sigrun!" she shouted.

Gunnar's chair overturned. *He's crying.* Sigrun on top of him. Isabella pulling her off.

Dixie standing still. Nose quivering.

A new sound. *Puh-whoof*, deep, loud. A wave of heat. Constant roar. The jet engulfed in flames. Juan running away, barely ahead of the fire.

She stumbled to Sigrun and added her pull to Isabella's. They got Sigrun on her feet. Lyle lifted Gunnar.

Brick-sized pieces of tarmac landed a few feet away. A bigger one. Closer.

"Dixie! *Voraus!*"

The German shepherd led the way. Back into the sheltering darkness of the forest. Screeches and explosions here, too. Shredded leaves floating in mid-air. A slender tree trunk across the path. Isabella followed the dog, holding Sigrun's hand. They let Lyle shuffle-run past with Gunnar in his arms. Tessa brought up the rear. Stunned. Scared. Wanting to sprint past the others, to get away. The grade of the slope felt unbearably steep. She breathed hard, sucking in black smoke that followed them uphill.

The top of the hill. Everyone stopped at the gate to the main campus. Locked. She came forward, hand extended.

Only red light.

Oh God, is the system down?

Green light. Click.

"Inside! Everybody!" She held the gate. Last to enter.

Scrambling over the dead pig, not caring about congealed blood. To the road. Armed guards swarming, not seeing them. No screeches right here, right now. Commotion rising from the airstrip.

The Palacio main hospital was big and sturdy. She turned that way.

"No!" Isabella pushed her in a different direction. "Back to the Annex!"

The tone was commanding. She obeyed.

They entered the Research Annex. She closed the door and the pandemonium outside was muffled. Palm fans rotated gently on the ceiling. She counted the company: all present. Lyle set Gunnar on a couch. The child croaked as he inhaled long and deep. Then he released all his breath at once—in a scream. Sigrun enveloped him, trying to console. Dixie took a position in front of Gunnar. He touched the dog. The screams diminished to whimpers.

"Damn it," Lyle said. He pressed a hand against his groin and lay on the floor.

Isabella was instantly at his side. She unbuttoned his shorts and unzipped his fly. Plaid boxers exposed.

For a surreal, disoriented second Tessa didn't understand. *Really, people?* Then she noticed the red stain against the navy and green stripes.

Lyle caught her staring. He winked through a grimace. "Ladies, I think we just extended our stay."

CHAPTER 11

Slack-kneed, Sameer supported himself against the wall of the MRI suite. The bodyguards wheeled de la Rosa out of the room. Vargas materialized from the control center. Sameer tried to catch his eye, to silently share the horror of what they'd just seen. But Vargas kept his head down. No eye contact.

Guilty, Sameer thought. Damn him. His lies made me complicit in the injury and death—no, *murder*—of a patient.

He felt an utterly unfamiliar urge to hit the man.

Vargas slinked away without a word, leaving Sameer alone with the body. An HIV-positive body, no less. Who was going to clean this up? Even fully staffed, the Palacio wasn't equipped to handle a bloody corpse. They didn't have a morgue. Palacio patients didn't *die*.

The deafening blast of the handgun that ended the patient's life echoed in his ears.

He listened. No, not an echo. A real sound. The MRI suite was heavily shielded. One rarely heard anything through the shielding. Yet he heard something. Bangs, cracks?

Chilly air wafted through the suite. He considered the dead body. It could lie there for a little while. He scooted out of the room.

In the hall, the noises intensified. Coming from outside—somewhere on the campus. Fireworks? Then the sounds reminded him of—of—*BBC radio.* Journalists broadcasting from a war zone. *Gunfire? At the Palacio?*

His throat tightened. The drug lord had said, the Zetas know where we are. Was a rival gang attacking the hospital?

A drug war? Here? Unthinkable. He tried to steady himself, to assess the situation. *I'm a man of medicine. So is Vargas.*

Correction: Vargas used to be part of my profession. I don't know what he is now.

Then he realized that based on what he'd just witnessed, a drug war at the Palacio wasn't unthinkable. It was likely.

Not knowing where to go or what to do, he ran toward the voices in the lobby. A small army of thugs had gathered, each man laden with firearms. The drug lord was there, shouting orders from his wheelchair.

A heavy hand clasped his shoulder. Vargas.

"They're bombing my airstrip," Vargas said.

Not, *they murdered that man*, or, *I'm sorry about what happened.* "My" airstrip.

Vargas went on. "De la Rosa's men say the Zeta cartel targeted the plane. They're at the bottom of the hill, with rocket-propelled grenade launchers. They'll try to keep Sinaloa pinned down. I don't think they've got the range to reach my hospital—"

"The last flight." Sameer swatted Vargas's hand away. "What happened to the plane?"

"Destroyed."

The lights in the lobby flickered. He smelled burned powder.

"Shot down?"

"Not sure if it took off. The wreckage is on the tarmac."

Tessa!

He grabbed and shook Vargas. "Is anybody out there to help the injured?"

Vargas snorted. "The Zetas are at the wall with RPGs. Mara Salvatrucha isn't the fucking Red Cross."

Sameer didn't wait for another word. He sprinted for the exit to the Serenity Garden and beyond.

———

The modest sitting area inside the entrance to the Research Annex reverberated with the sound of explosions beyond the walls. As Tessa's heartbeat slowed, the pace of her thoughts accelerated. So many unanswered questions.

Isabella straddled Lyle, her knees on the floor. There was an intensity in her eyes. No panic. Determination. Not the reaction Tessa would've predicted from a sugar baby.

"Are you hit?" Isabella said.

"I don't think so," Lyle replied. "Just a bleeder."

Isabella put her hands in Lyle's boxers. She grasped the opposite sides of his fly, gave him a quick smile, and ripped the fabric apart. "Good thing you're not shy."

"Whaddya mean? I'm a regular shrinking violet."

Lyle's exposed privates didn't grab Tessa's attention. The jet of blood did. It spurted from his groin in rhythm with the contractions of his heart. An arterial bleed.

"Dr. Price."

She no longer heard the violence outside. Her vision darkened. She smelled the phenolic disinfectant of a surgical suite.

She was back in medical school. A barrage of F-words—noun, verb, adjective—spewed from the general surgeon in charge of the case. They were doing a gut resection. Her arm was numb from holding the retractor for an hour, afraid to move. Deep folds of the patient's abdominal fat weighed against her wrist. The patient's flesh felt warm against the cold air of the sterile room.

Then the blood. Spurting like a fountain. A hot, red, water show. It sprayed across the front of her surgical gown. It strafed her face mask. It pulsed in time with the patient's heartbeat. An arterial bleed. All of a sudden, breathing felt like sucking molasses into her lungs. The surgeon's language reached new lows of vulgarity. Hands holding suture needles—sharp, smooth, curled points like fish hooks without the barb—moved quickly.

Too quickly.

The goal of the first-year medical student was to be invisible. She had succeeded. The surgeon didn't notice his needle stab her glove. He didn't see her hands shake, nor could anyone in the room see the color drain from her face behind the mask. The surgeon did notice when the patient's fat drooped into his field of view, freed from the retractor that clanged on the steel table as she fainted.

"Tessa!"

It was a woman's voice. Not the surgeon's. Isabella.

"Yes?"

"Give me some paper towels!"

Coming to her senses, she dashed to a dispenser behind the nurse's station counter. She handed a stack to Isabella, who pressed the paper against the wound in Lyle's groin.

"Is he okay?" Sigrun said. She sat wide-eyed and trembling next to Gunnar.

Yeah, he's hunky-dory, Tessa thought. Bleeding like a stuck pig.

"I don't think it's shrapnel," Isabella said. "It's from his operation." She stacked her hands on the towels and leaned down with her full weight.

"My secret's out," Lyle said. His voice was nothing like the bellow she'd first heard in the lobby two days ago.

"What did they do to you?" she asked.

An awkward smile and chuckle. "I'm man enough to tell the truth," he said. "I've got a bad case of whiskey dick. Vargas's guy said he could fix it. No more blue pills. No implants. No shots. Doc did a Roto Rooter on the arteries to my penis this morning."

She couldn't help but smile. Lyle had a gift for getting straight to the point.

Isabella scowled and when she spoke, her Portuguese accent was stronger than ever. "They did the procedure through an artery in his groin. He had to lie down for hours until the hole closed. I think running and carrying the boy broke the clot."

"We have to get him over to the main hospital," Tessa said. "Dr. Desai—Sameer—is still here. He'll take care of him."

"No. We stay in this building."

"Why? There's nobody over here, except maybe Cristo, and he's not a medical doctor, either."

"The hospital is too dangerous." There was an uncompromising certainty in the way Isabella spoke that left Tessa silent.

"I'm fine," Lyle said. "Just need to lie still for a while."

Tessa took a long, hard look at Lyle's face. She wasn't a physician but she had picked up a few things during that year of medical school. If Lyle lost too much blood, he'd go into shock.

Look for signs. Cold skin. Weak pulse.

She put two fingers on his wrist and two on his neck, feeling his heartbeat. His heart wasn't ticking any faster than hers. *Probably he's all right. Just make sure he drinks a lot. Not the contaminated water. Look for juices or something?*

"Are you two okay?" she asked Sigrun and Gunnar. Sigrun nodded.

She took a deep breath to center herself. The shelling had stopped but the sudden silence felt anything but peaceful. What next?

The paper towels were turning red. "I'll go find some proper dressings for that," she said to Isabella. "We should move away from the entrance."

Isabella nodded. If she had any additional information about what was happening, she wasn't sharing. Tessa left to rummage through a cabinet for supplies. As her fight-or-flight response subsided, her mind went into analytical mode.

Fact: Vargas emptied the hospital of all patients—including Lyle Simmons, who offered to pay a lot of money to stick around—even though they could have scraped by with sterilized water. Fact: While all the paying clients were being shipped out, strange and unpleasant new guards—lots of them—were coming in. They needed clean water to drink, didn't they? Fact: The Palacio was under attack.

She found sterile gauze, bandages, and a gurney, but no answers. Her intuition leaped to bridge the gap between what she knew and what she suspected.

Opinion: *There's more to this contaminated water story than I've been told.* Opinion: *Drug money is involved.*

Conclusion: *We need to stay out of sight and pray we don't end up as collateral damage in somebody else's war.*

"Let's get him up here," she said as she rolled the stretcher into the sitting area. The room smelled of spent explosives, like a parking lot after a Fourth of July show. Sigrun nervously stroked her hair. Gunnar seemed content with Dixie nearby.

Thank God for that dog.

Isabella wrapped her arms under Lyle's shoulders and Tessa grabbed his feet to lift him on to the gurney. She felt like she was performing slapstick as they floundered with the tall man's bulk.

"You're gonna bust my head," Lyle complained. He brushed them aside and climbed up himself. Red oozed down his leg. "There. Y'all can take it from here."

Tessa mentally prepared herself for the sight of blood. Isabella removed Lyle's shorts, and Tessa covered the torn incision with a sterile dressing.

Isabella kept pressure on it with an open palm. "Where do we go?"

Tessa considered their options. Gunnar's room was familiar, large, and comfortable, but it was too exposed. Big windows. Wide view. Great for seeing what was happening outside but lousy if a shell landed close by. And they could be seen from other parts of the campus. Anywhere on the first floor seemed poorly defensible. Better choices were an interior room on the second floor, or the basement.

She couldn't stomach the idea of hiding in the basement animal facility. The stink, the claustrophobia—no way.

Unlike the patient rooms, the laboratory upstairs had no windows. Safe from shrapnel and prying eyes.

"To the elevator. This way."

Paradise had become a battlefield. Sameer sprinted down the road, ignoring the Mara Salvatruchas clustered in sloppy formation around the guard house. He plunged into the forest, following the footpath toward the airstrip. The tree canopy gave the illusion of shelter. Oily black smoke in the fading light obscured his way. He squinted, scanning up and ahead, until his eyes burned and he was forced to close them.

"Oof." His shin collided with something massive and mushy, pitching him to the ground. The palms of his hands abraded on pavement. Lucky—no broken wrist. But he was tangled in a big, sticky carcass. Wiry hair. A dead pig.

High-pitched shrieking sound. Incoming. He crouched behind the gruesome swine shield. The bomb blast squeezed his heart. He felt clods strike the pig's bulk. He took a moment to assemble his courage. He scrambled to his feet and kept going.

The gate at the crest of the hill had been knocked out of joint. No more electronic security. He passed through without a hand scan. The downhill slope gave him unnatural speed. Shredded palm leaves and sheared branches covered the path. The smoke swirled and writhed. He glimpsed the pitted airstrip ahead. Explosions agitated his gut and threatened to burst his eardrums. He plugged his ears while he ran. If a bomb flew his way, would he hear it? Could he dodge it?

Not likely.

Puh-wump. Another hit. A rain-like tinkle of shattered concrete sprinkled the ground.

Don't think. Just run.

"Tessa!" he shouted as he broke into the open of the airstrip.

Hot. Burning jet fuel. The fluctuating light of the fire lit the area. He coughed and lifted his shirt to cover his face. He had to get closer to the devastated airplane.

He saw a smoldering stretcher with a blackened human figure still strapped to it. The plane was enveloped in flames. Both wings broken. Frantic, he searched for a way up or in. None. He backed away from the heat.

Another smoking body, under the plane's nose, below the cockpit door. A pilot's hat inexplicably unscathed on the pavement nearby.

A horrible certainty struck him. If Tessa was on that plane, she was dead.

He looked beyond the wreck and saw a pile of debris. After wiping his eyes he realized it was more than torn tarmac. Some of the shapes were abandoned luggage. Carry-on size. And an overturned wheelchair. Hunching low, he scampered to check the tags.

The sun had set but there was enough light to read by.

S. Baldursdottir. Gunnar's mother. Tessa would've been with her.

He skipped the Louis Vuitton cases and read another tag. *Dr. Tessa Price.*

Maybe they hadn't boarded the plane. If the attack came while they were waiting, still outside—maybe they fled to the Research Annex. He took one more look around the area for injured survivors and saw no one. The shrieking whistle of a fast-approaching projectile—

Time to go.

He sprinted up the hill. Too much smoke burned his lungs. *Breathe less. Control panic. Move slower.*

A shadowy shape in the sooty darkness ahead, slouching, scurrying. Gunnar's height but bulkier. It stopped in the middle of the path.

He blinked the stinging from his eyes and slowed to a walk. The shape took on a defined form. Arms scraped the ground. Long fingers scratched its head.

One of the chimpanzees blocked his way. Judging from the size, a female.

With death behind and danger ahead, he stood still. *How close do I dare to get?* The forest wasn't thick. If he had to, he could go around, bushwhack off the path. But certainly the chimp would be aware of him. And what if there were more apes with her?

He took a step closer. The chimp fidgeted. A flash of white in its face: bared teeth. He remembered the disemboweled primate on the floor of the cage. Sweat dripped from his chin.

The whistle of another missile. Getting louder. Getting closer.

His courage failed him. He cried out and sank to the ground, uselessly covering his head with thin arms.

The shell struck. Flaming plant debris fell around him. A branch hit his head. His body quivered like gelatin and any thought he'd had of Tessa evaporated in the furnace of his fear.

Seconds later he looked up. The chimp was gone. He clambered to his feet. Clutching his bleeding scalp, he dashed toward safety.

———————

Tessa led the group to the laboratory on the second floor of the Research Annex. The windowless interior room, with familiar smells of yeast and rubbing alcohol, made her feel safe. There was plenty of space for everyone, and they could use the lights without fear of detection. Yes, this was the right choice for now. Until they had more information about what was going on, her group needed to be unknown and invisible.

Which meant the mess in the entryway was a problem. Lyle's blood on the floor was a dead giveaway that someone was in the building. While Sigrun crept around gathering blankets and other comfort items for the lab, Tessa found a flashlight and went downstairs to clean up the mess.

She found a bucket and mop in a janitor's closet. Keeping the flashlight beam low and away from windows, she filled the bucket and wheeled it to the entryway. The still-wet blood wiped easily off the bamboo floor, turning the water in her bucket crimson. A few red spatters stained the upholstery in the sitting area. She flipped the cushions over. Good enough. Her goal was to eliminate obvious clues. If soldiers entered the Annex with the intention of searching the building, she and her companions would be found no matter what she did.

Something scratched at the door. Her heart stopped. She flicked off the flashlight. *Hide? Flee?* The bucket of hot water would give her away. How much time until they broke down the door?

The electronic deadbolt clicked. It was an authorized entry. The door opened, a hand slapped the room lighting controls. She blinked against the sudden brightness.

"Tessa!"

Sameer staggered into the room and threw his arms around her. The intensity of his embrace shocked her. He smelled of oil, smoke, and sweat.

Warm wetness dripped from his chin to her cheek. After a second or two she realized it wasn't perspiration.

"Let me see." She broke from his arms and parted his hair to get a look at the head wound. It wasn't deep but it sure did bleed. "Wait here. I'll get some gauze."

He leaned over her bucket to catch the falling drops of blood. "I went to the airstrip to find you."

"I was there. With Gunnar and Sigrun, Lyle and Isabella. And the dog."

"You weren't on the plane." His voice was thick with feeling.

She pressed an absorbent pad against his scalp and gave him a towel to wipe his hands. "Another ten minutes and we would've been. And we'd all be dead. As it is, when the bombing started we ran back here." The panic faded from his eyes. "You're lucky this is all you got," she said of his wound. "What were you thinking, going out there?"

He looked at the floor. "I'm glad you're safe."

Warmth blossomed in her cheeks. The prim and reserved Indian had rushed headlong into danger to save her.

She turned off the lights. "I'm glad you're okay too. Do you know what this is all about?"

While she put away the mop and bucket, he told her about the Sinaloa drug cartel and its boss Luis Angel de la Rosa. He related the story of the MRI magnet ripping a tracking device out of a patient. In the darkness she couldn't see his expression but his voice filled with anguish when he described the subsequent murder.

"Who was the kid?" she asked.

"Vargas hasn't told me anything but I examined the old man with my eyes. He has an arteriovenous graft in his arm."

"Which means what?"

"He's on dialysis. Chronic renal failure. I think he is here for a kidney transplant, and the man he murdered was supposed to be his donor."

That is messed up. Thank God Isabella told us to come here, not the main hospital.

"Sameer, they can't know we're here."

He nodded. "I must go back. Vargas will be looking for me. I will tell them I saw the plane and that all of you were killed."

"Do you think the Zeta cartel is attacking us?"

"De la Rosa thinks so."

"What do they want?"

"They want *him*." He headed for the stairs. "I'll take the tunnel. I met one of the chimps on my way here. She was not friendly. You and the others must stay indoors."

No worries there. She wouldn't set foot outside unless the building was on fire. Not with a gang of armed murderers running the Palacio, another gang in control of the low country on their border, and a troop of liver-ripping chimpanzees on the loose in between.

She suddenly felt a desperate need for a hug.

"Be careful." This time, she put her arms around him.

———————

Sameer fretted about Tessa's safety as he descended to the Annex's lower level. White lab rats scrambled under the stairs as he passed. The stairwell smelled of rat, and their droppings littered the concrete floor.

He'd been around wild rats growing up in India. Later, he worked professionally with inbred strains of laboratory rats. In his experience, rats were smart, tenacious, and surprisingly compressible. They could chew a tiny hole in anything and then squeeze through it. Despite the fire doors, he was pretty sure some of them would find their way into the tunnel to the main hospital.

He reached the bottom of the stairwell and paused when he heard voices in the animal facility. He recognized Cristo's voice. Agitated. Raised. The scientist was arguing with another man. Sameer crossed the loading dock and entered the animal facility.

He opened the door to a bizarre scene.

Cristo was in the changing room with Juan, the lab tech. Juan had his back in a corner. He faced Cristo and in his right hand he brandished a broken water bottle from a rat cage. His whole arm trembled.

Both men started when Sameer entered. Cristo gave a slight nod of surprised acknowledgement but kept his focus on the technician.

"Hey man, it's okay. We're safe here," Cristo said.

Juan whimpered and slurred a few words. The jagged glass lowered as his hand drooped.

Sameer didn't move. He knew psychosis when he saw it.

Cristo explained in a low voice. "I came down here when the bombing started. He was supposed to be on the flight to Acapulco with Maria but he showed up a few minutes ago, all freaked out."

Sameer pictured the burned corpse on the tarmac. "He saw her die. This may be acute hysteria triggered by traumatic stress."

"Maybe. Except Maria didn't get shot at before she snapped."

The broken bottle fell from Juan's fingers and shattered into fragments. His hand shook uncontrollably.

Why is he comparing Juan to Maria? Sameer wondered. "Maria was like this?"

"Just like. When she let the animals go."

"I didn't know she was delusional."

"Totally off her rocker. They took her over to the hospital. Didn't you see her?"

"Someone else did. Vargas had me evacuating patients."

Juan put his hands on his head and sobbed. Gingerly Sameer inched to the man's side. The tech allowed him to put an arm around his shoulders.

"He needs medical help. I'll take him to the hospital," Sameer said. Briefly he told Cristo his own story. "Tessa and the others are in the lab upstairs. Perhaps you should join them."

A pair of rats chased each other across the room.

"Yeah," Cristo said. "I sure as hell don't want to stay down here."

CHAPTER 12

Vargas kept as far back as possible from the expansive windows of the Tenochtitlan Suite. He didn't share Luis Angel de la Rosa's confident estimate of the range of the Zetas' attack. And he had no need to indulge in the *machismo* of parading in front of the vulnerable glass.

De la Rosa wasn't parading, either. He sat in a wheelchair wearing long warmup pants that hid his swollen ankles. Vargas watched him scratch his legs, and noted the fishy odor of the drug lord's breath. All symptoms of chronic renal failure. Observing this made Vargas itchy, too. De la Rosa was going downhill. Something had to be done—soon.

One of the bodyguards stopped talking into his mobile phone headset and turned to his boss. "We've got MS in positions along the hill. Patrols are on the cliffs. If the Zetas come by sea, we'll pick them off before they reach the top."

Vargas wanted to keep himself useful. "My security cameras cover all access points to the peninsula. You can—"

"We're using the cameras," de la Rosa said. "Several were lost during the assault on the airstrip but I've got men in the area. Congratulations on your design, Manuel. The Palacio is a strong position to defend. My people on the outside tell me the Zetas control the road but we can hold them off here for some time. Until I can muster a force."

"You're not going to try to leave, then?" Vargas hoped his voice didn't convey his desire that Sinaloa get the hell out of his hospital.

De la Rosa leaned over and spent several seconds rubbing his legs. "We don't know what air coverage the Zetas have. They have not hit your helicopter pad. It may be safe for us to use it. I came here for a kidney. You have not yet given me one."

"How can I do that without a donor?" Vargas sputtered.

"Let's try again, shall we?" De la Rosa snapped his fingers and whispered to a bodyguard, who nodded and stepped aside, headset activated. "The backup donor is on his way."

"How?"

"By helicopter."

"What if—"

"It seems an ideal way to find out what the Zetas are capable of. The pilot has been waiting for my signal. Chopper should be here in twenty minutes."

Vargas nodded. He didn't like it, not one bit, but he had no say in the matter. The transplant surgeon was somewhere in the building, probably hiding in the basement with the few remaining staff. He'd find him and tell him to get the surgical suite ready. If the donor made it to the Palacio alive, Vargas wasn't going to waste time on screening tests. De la Rosa would get whatever kidney walked through the door.

———

Sameer rubbed his eyes as if he could wipe away the weariness of a sleepless night. It wasn't the first time he'd dedicated an entire sleep cycle to the care of a patient, but he'd never had a patient like this one. And he'd never been forced to work in secret before.

Juan thrashed in the hospital bed. Last evening, Sameer had managed to coax him out of the animal facility and down the tunnel into the main hospital. Then with the help of a swiftly-placed sedative injection, he got the patient into a bed in one of the Palacio's many empty rooms. Because of the violent dementia Juan exhibited over in the Annex, he tied him to the bed with loose straps. He didn't like using restraints, but it was to protect both of them. If Juan escaped all crazy and had an encounter with the Mara Salvatrucha, they'd kill him in a heartbeat.

He splashed some cold water on his face. Good thing he'd followed his instincts and used restraints. The last ten hours, Juan lived a semi-waking nightmare. The patient cried of stabbing pain in his head, screamed at unseen terrors, and struggled against demons conspiring to carry off his soul. Sameer gave him pain medicine and more sedative, hoping the psychiatric crisis would pass. But then Juan's temperature began to rise, and Sameer knew the delusions weren't all "in his head." He probably had an infection in his brain. Sameer placed an IV and started infusing the drugs he had at hand. Even if the Palacio's full pharmacy had been open, a tourist hospital like this didn't carry the kinds of heavy-duty antibiotics Juan needed.

If, indeed, any kind of drug could save him. This looked more and more like a case of acute encephalitis, which could be caused by a long list of different viruses. None of those viruses could be cured with antibiotics.

Sameer pointed a thermometer in Juan's ear. The fever was holding high and steady at 102.4 degrees.

Trying to give some comfort, he held a cup of water to Juan's dry lips and poured. The water touched the patient's tongue. He recoiled as if the liquid scalded him. Bubbles foamed at the corners of his mouth. The water dribbled down, unswallowed.

"Sorry, my friend." He stroked the technician's head. Based on what Cristo had told him, both Juan and Maria were stricken with the same malady. The probable diagnosis: viral encephalitis.

Two workers in the same animal facility, home of six recently imported chimpanzees of poorly documented origin. Chimps that themselves had shown abnormal, aggressive behavior just before Maria released them.

Chimps that had slopped excrement and body parts on the two victims. An excellent method for spreading disease.

Of course Juan and Maria weren't the only people exposed to the mad apes.

He told himself it's normal to have a headache after staying up all night.

His pager went off. No time to dwell on this worry. Vargas was calling for him.

———

According to the clock, dawn was breaking. Not that Tessa could tell, inside the windowless lab on the second floor of the Palacio's Research Annex. She couldn't stand the stuffy darkness another minute, and turned on a few downward-pointing countertop lights over her research bench. The light disturbed the fragile slumber of her companions, or maybe they'd been lying awake, too. Bodies that had shifted restlessly during the night rose wearily: Sigrun, Lyle, Isabella, and Cristo, who had showed up some hours ago. Gunnar stirred but stayed on the cushions his mother had arranged for him on the linoleum floor.

There'd been no explosions since about eleven o'clock. Tessa wondered if that meant a victory, a stalemate, or a pause before a larger assault.

Lyle got to his feet.

"Shouldn't you stay down?" she said, thinking of his groin bleed.

"My back hurts so bad if I don't get up now, I'll never walk again," he said. "I'll take it easy."

"Mama. I'm hungry."

She froze in mid-stretch. That was the first decipherable sentence she'd ever heard Gunnar speak. Clear words. A clear thought.

My God, he's still getting better. An elated thrill passed through her. They were trapped, with danger all around, but at least in this place she could continue to give the boy his treatments. His life was changing before her eyes.

Cristo noticed the extraordinary words, too, and made wide-eye contact with her as he folded a bedsheet.

Sigrun leaned over and hugged her son. "It's too early for breakfast." She took the laboratory beaker they were using as a cup and gave him a drink. "I'll get you something soon."

Then she looked imploringly at Tessa. All of them were hungry. They'd missed dinner last night. Problem was, all the Palacio's kitchens and restaurants were in the main hospital. Normally they delivered meals to patients in the Annex by way of the tunnel. That wasn't going to happen today.

"I need to get out of here." Isabella ran her fingers through her long auburn hair, which was gorgeous even when mussed. "And Dixie needs a walk."

"You can't go outside," Tessa said. "I think it's all right for us to move around this floor during daylight, as long as we stay away from windows. But no one should leave the building."

Lyle grumbled. "If I have to do the time, I'd at least like the pleasure of doing the crime."

"Can we boil water in here?" Sigrun asked.

"That's one thing we don't have to worry about," Tessa said. "Sameer told me there's nothing wrong with the Palacio's water. The contamination story was a cover for the evacuation. Vargas emptied the place for a drug kingpin. A really big boss named Luis Angel de la Rosa. Head of the Sinaloa cartel. Those are his thugs patrolling the grounds."

"Vargas kicked us out for a drug dealer?" Sigrun said indignantly.

"Bastard," Cristo said. "He almost got us all killed."

"Sameer says it was de la Rosa's enemies who attacked the Palacio last night." She paused. "He also told me these people are dangerous. They don't want any outsiders here. And they think we're dead. If they find us, we're in deep trouble."

"Does Sameer know why de la Rosa is at the Palacio?" Isabella asked.

Once again she'd miscalculated the Brazilian beauty. Isabella didn't seem surprised, or shocked, or even scared by the news. "He needs a kidney transplant."

"Hmm." Isabella scratched Dixie. Dixie said thanks by licking her arm.

Tessa puzzled for a moment and made a guess about Isabella's prescience. "You already knew about de la Rosa. How?"

"Wasn't that hard," Lyle said. "We saw him arrive on the roof when everybody else was leaving."

"But—"

"Hey, the whole contaminated water story smelled like two-day-old catfish. When Bella and I saw that fancy helicopter and all the bodyguards, we guessed what Vargas's game was. Decided it was definitely time to git." He rubbed Dixie's neck, ruffling the fur still pressed down where the cone had been. "Where you gonna do your business, girl? No nice grass indoors."

"Do you think we'll be safe if we stay here?" Sigrun asked.

"I hope so." Tessa's stomach rumbled. Water was no longer an issue but if they were stuck inside the Annex for very long, they'd have to get mighty creative about meals. But it wouldn't be long, would it? There was a war going on here. Surely the Mexican authorities would intervene.

"There's a toilet down the hall and a patient room with a full bathroom just past that. Help yourself. I'll go scavenge something for us to eat. Lyle, be sure to drink lots of water."

The big man touched his forehead in salute.

"I'll go with you," Cristo said. Isabella, too, followed Tessa out of the lab.

Because the Annex building was limited to research and experimental medical procedures, it didn't have many patient beds. Still, she remembered from her med school days that any place you had patients and nurses, you'd find stashes of nonperishable snacks.

"There's a supply closet near reception on the first floor," Cristo said.

"Let's try it."

They took the stairs down and emerged into the sunlit lobby where they'd found refuge last night. Isabella searched behind the main desk. Tessa noticed Cristo wince and cover his eyes in the brightness.

"Stay away from the windows," she reminded them.

There were no signs of life in the lobby or outside. They dashed into the cover of the hall.

In the shadows, the floor wriggled. White rats were fleeing the humans, leaving a trail of rat droppings and cake crumbs.

"I think we found it." Of course the rats, with their exquisite senses, had found the food storage first and somehow worked their way into the closet.

A *locked* closet, she discovered. No fancy palm scanner to let her in. If you couldn't use the secret rat entrance, an old-fashioned key was needed. "Maybe the key's in a drawer at the front desk."

Isabella examined the lock mechanism. "Step aside," she said.

Tessa glanced at Cristo and they both stepped back. Isabella poised herself in front of the door, one foot forward, one back. She took four short breaths and hopped in place. Then with a grunt, her rear foot flew up and kicked with the heel. The door slammed inward, its feeble lock ripped from the frame.

Isabella brushed herself off and looked into their stunned faces. "Tae-kwondo," she said. "Since I was a child."

Tessa swallowed. "Thanks."

Basic supplies—sheets, towels, small plastic basins, toilet paper, packs of sterile scissors, gloves, and other medical miscellany took up most of the shelf space. But there was also a woven basket of packaged cookies, crackers, and salty treats. One last rat scurried away. Tessa snatched the goody basket.

"There's probably more somewhere," she said. "We should search the building and collect any food before the rats get it."

"Wait. What is this?" Isabella asked.

Just down the hall a door marked Security piqued Tessa's interest, too. Weapons?

Hiding is our best defense, she thought. I've never used a gun. But if somebody comes after Gunnar...

Yesterday morning the thought would've seemed ludicrous. Now she was mentally preparing for it.

She put her hand on the doorknob. "Let's check it out."

Ironically, this room wasn't locked. Apparently management was more worried about the staff pilfering potato chips than whatever was in here. Which didn't bode well for finding anything to defend themselves with.

The door swung into a dark room. They entered and she groped for a light switch.

"Ach," Cristo complained, shielding his eyes. "Turn that damn thing off."

The room wasn't much bigger than a closet. It was a station for watching security camera feeds. Two rolling office chairs pressed against a narrow shelf-like table facing a wall of six monitors. She needed barely half a minute to be disappointed in her search.

Mall cops, she thought. No weapons.

"Well." Isabella took a seat. "Let's see what's happening outside." She pushed some buttons and the screens flickered to life.

If we can see the campus, maybe we can find a way to get to the mainland.

She sat down in the other chair. Cristo leaned over between them.

The control menus were straightforward. Soon they were looking at live images of the Annex's rear loading dock, the road in front of the Annex, and a series of views from cameras mounted on the walls that protected the high ground of the Palacio's peninsula.

"Can you get a view of the airstrip?" Tessa said.

Isabella rolled the mouse. A blackened wreck appeared on all six screens. Something was moving in the shadow of the plane. Image resolution was poor. She peered closer.

A flock of crows. The birds were picking at the bodies on the tarmac.

Her stomach flipped and she looked away. *Damn you, Vargas. You made a deal with the devil and others are paying the price.*

"There, beyond the plane," Isabella said. "The perimeter security fence. The Zetas were shooting from the other side."

"It's quiet now. Maybe we could make a run for it?"

"No. Quiet, yes, but they have not gone away. Look at this." Isabella's hand moved. A few screens went black, then new images appeared. "They took out the cameras on the perimeter fence but they missed some on the wall at the top of the hill. This one looks inside, toward the Palacio."

Tessa saw Mara Salvatruchas, heavily armed, gathered around the entrance gate. Another camera captured guards distributed in pairs along the inner wall.

Isabella pointed at a screen. "The MS position at the top of the hill, where they control the wall, is very good. They can defend against a stronger force." She moved her finger. "This area between the two sides—the forest, hill, and airstrip—is no man's land. If you try to go that way, either Sinaloa or Zeta will shoot you."

And that would not improve my situation. "Cristo, do you think—" She turned to make eye contact with him and was startled to see his face wet with sweat. It was a little close in the room with all three of them, but it certainly wasn't hot. "Hey, are you okay?"

"Why? What's your problem?" Cristo said.

"Me? Nothing. I just—"

"Then shut up and mind your own business."

What the heck? She looked at him more closely. Something was strange about his eyes. The pupils. Instead of being small like the other day, they were abnormally large, even for a dimly-lit room. She made a quick comparison to Isabella's eyes. Definitely Cristo's pupils were dilated. And he seemed to be trembling, too.

"We should go back to the lab," she said, adding as an excuse, "the others are waiting for breakfast."

"Action at our back door," Isabella interrupted. She pointed to a view of the Annex's rear loading dock.

Tessa watched. For some reason, two Mara Salvatruchas patrolling the service road behind the Annex had stopped and aimed their rifles into the forest.

They must have heard something. Too bad there's no audio.

After a moment they put their weapons away. Then an odd thing happened. One MS turned away from the forest. Without any reason that Tessa could see, he shoved his buddy. The buddy stumbled a couple of steps backward and responded in kind, rushing forward with his hands out. He plowed into the first guy and knocked him to the ground. As the fight grew chaotic, details blurred in the image. She saw the butt of a weapon strike an ankle. Both men tumbled to earth. They wrestled and flailed with fists flying. The long rifles strapped to their bodies flopped. She expected one to accidentally go off at any second. *Damn fools.*

One man smashed his feet into the other's chest. The combatants rolled apart. One shakily got up on a knee. He reached for his gun.

Tessa tensed. Was she about to witness a murder?

The business end of the rifle was halfway around the man's body before the other MS, still on his back, fortuitously got his rifle in his hands first. He fired, hitting his partner in the shoulder. The attacker got to his feet. Three strides later he was standing over his former ally. For a long moment that froze in Tessa's memory, he held his weapon with quivering arms—and then dispatched his "buddy" to the afterlife.

She gasped, imagining the sound of the gunshot. The killer stood over his victim, rifle wobbling in his hands. His arms were shaking.

Like Maria.

Nothing on the silent screen could tell her what had prompted the Mara Salvatruchas to turn on each other. But if this kind of senseless violence was typical for the MS, she and her friends better damn well stay out of sight.

Something moved in the forest on screen. "What is that?" Isabella said.

Squat objects approached fast from several directions, dark blurs that converged on the survivor. Tessa identified the shapes. Four chimpanzees.

She recognized the male chimp by its size. Cristo lobbed obscenities at the screen.

The "victorious" MS had no time to raise his rifle. His kicks and punches into their dense bodies had no effect. The chimps swarmed and tore him to the ground, easily overwhelming him with their muscular bulk. A part of Tessa's brain told her to close her eyes but she couldn't help watching.

They worked as a team. The three females pinned the man. The male climbed atop his chest. Like a miniature King Kong on the screen, it opened its mouth and exposed sharp teeth. Tessa remembered the chimp's ferocious howl and her brain filled in the sound in this silent movie. The beast looked into the man's face. She imagined the terror written there.

As if to give a deadly kiss, the chimp leaned forward. Then the taunting ended. It lurched down and tore the man's lips from his mouth. She covered her open mouth in horror as blood sprayed, and human flesh hung from the ape's maw.

The Mara Salvatrucha's nose was next. With one powerful rip after another in rapid succession, the chimp systematically chewed off the man's face.

The lack of audio feed from the camera was now a relief. At some indecipherable signal, the females joined in the carnage, mauling the man's hands and feet. Someone in the security room cried out.

She realized *she* had screamed.

The screen went dark as Isabella turned off the monitors. "We've seen enough."

Tessa, Cristo, and Isabella left the security room. Tessa tried to stop thinking about who the man was. Whether he had any family. Even though he'd just committed murder and his death by chimp could be viewed as swift, primal justice, she didn't think anyone deserved to die like that.

They scoured the building for anything edible, adding a few items to what they'd found in the closet. The collection was a pitiful amount considering the number of people in their group. They returned to their hideout in the laboratory, disappointed by their haul.

"Cristo!" Gunnar said when they entered. The boy was sitting in a pile of pillows and sheets arranged like a nest on the floor. Sigrun wandered the room nearby. Lyle was missing.

"Got something for you, buddy," Cristo said. Sweat plastered his wavy bangs against his forehead. He handed Gunnar a package of cookies.

Tessa watched closely to see what Gunnar would do with the package. A month ago, he could barely use his fingers. Automatically, Sigrun reached to open it for him.

With a petulant look, Gunnar twisted away from her. "I can."

And he could. Sigrun refrained from jumping in as her son struggled with the plastic. A minute passed. His fingers slipped. He tried again, grasping as much of the wrapper as he could.

The bag split open. Chocolate chip cookies and crumbs tumbled around his nest. Tessa clapped her hands.

Gunnar grinned. "Want one?" he said, offering a cookie to Cristo.

"No thanks. Not hungry. You eat it."

Tessa distributed small servings to Sigrun and Isabella. Cristo declined any food and lay down with his eyes closed. Just when she started to worry that Lyle had wandered off or done something foolish, the big man and his dog came back.

"This dog's so well trained, she would not do her business on the floor," he said.

"You didn't go outside, did you?" Tessa asked in alarm.

"Nah, I finally took her down to the basement. There's enough dog smell there to convince her it was okay. But next time we might try going out the back door—"

"No you won't." She told him about the chimp attack.

"I'm a glass half full kind of guy," Lyle said. "Killer chimps ought to keep those Sinaloa boys away from us. Our own monkey bodyguards."

"As long as they're out there and we're in here. With heavy doors and good locks keeping it that way," Tessa agreed.

"Until the police come," Sigrun said. "Someone will rescue us, yes?"

"I expect so," Tessa said.

"Don't count on it," Isabella said. "This is between the drug gangs. The local police will stay out of it until they know which side is stronger."

Tessa didn't like the sound of that. "What makes you think so?"

"The Zeta cartel controlled this region for two years," Isabella said. "They are, as you say, in bed with the police. Now Sinaloa has moved in. The police don't dare to get involved. They must work with whoever is the most powerful."

"So we're stuck in the middle until one side wins."

"Or until de la Rosa leaves. He's a major player. If the Mexican Federal Police find out he's here, they might come."

"And as long as the Zetas are out there, the only way de la Rosa can leave the Palacio is—"

As if on cue, she heard the *thump-thump* of a helicopter approaching.

CHAPTER 13

For the first time ever, Vargas forgot to unroll the red carpet.

The normal protocol for welcoming guests at the Palacio's rooftop helipad was far from his mind as Sinaloa's chopper approached. Most of his brain was preoccupied with telling his body not to run and hide. The rest of his mental power was spinning possible scenarios, trying to anticipate events. He figured staying one step ahead increased his chances of coming out alive.

He hung back in the covered hallway that led to the rooftop elevator. Sinaloa men patrolled the roof. So far, he'd seen no obvious response to the helicopter from the Zetas. But the rival gang was out there, just beyond the security walls. He wasn't taking chances unless he had to. He wouldn't be up here on the roof, exposing himself to danger, except de la Rosa had ordered him to meet the new kidney donor. The drug lord had temporarily vacated the Tenochtitlan Suite, one floor below the landing pad, in case the helicopter was fired upon or crashed.

Vargas tried to calculate what would happen if the Zetas did have the ability to take down an aircraft with a surface-to-air missile. If the 'copter smashed into the roof of the Palacio, how many floors would be damaged? Which hospital systems would be affected? Would there be fire? How much would it cost to repair?

Losing the backup donor on board would also mean he was stuck with de la Rosa and his cronies. Bad situation. The old man was in end-stage kidney failure. If they couldn't transport a donor in, and they couldn't get de la Rosa out, what then?

He rubbed his temples with both hands. *It'll be fine. We'll get the donor. My transplant surgeon will do the operation. Sameer Desai will assist. Sinaloa will beat off the Zetas, and de la Rosa will fly away in two days. I can get the*

airstrip re-paved—tell people we had to dig up some pipes—and declare the
water problem cured. Back in business.

Probably have to get the MRI machine serviced...

The Sinaloa men, along with a few of their hired Mara Salvatruchas, took up defined positions around the roof, pointing their weapons at unseen enemies in all directions. Vargas's eyes picked up a speck in the distance before he heard the noise of the rotor. First he could make out the shape of the helicopter. As it got closer he saw its olive green sides and blue underbelly. When the craft was nearly over the Palacio, he could see the pilot. The helicopter was less than fifty meters above the roof and descending. He started to exhale.

Ka-blam!

The noise of the helicopter had drowned out the missile's approach, but the impact on the tail was loudest of all. The helicopter spun out of control. The pilot struggled with the controls and the 'copter lurched away from the hospital's roof, still maintaining its altitude. Vargas strained for the best view possible without leaving cover. The pilot still had some influence over his craft. Maybe he could bring it down on the service road?

A second hit, on the cockpit, eliminated that chance. Smoke, then fire obscured his view of the pilot.

The helicopter went into a death spiral, veering away from the rooftop landing pad. It was headed for the cliffs and the ocean beyond.

At least it's not crashing into my hospital. He ran out and peered over the edge of the roof.

The aircraft was falling fast. It wasn't going to reach the ocean before it hit.

In the windowless laboratory of the Annex, Tessa heard a helicopter fly by the building. Could this be what they were hoping for—a ride for Luis Angel de la Rosa to get him away from the siege? Or a raid by the Mexican Federal Police?

Or had the Zetas found a way to finish their assault on the Palacio?

Violence was possible. Better take precautions.

"Everybody get under cover," she ordered.

The lab provided a surprising number of sheltered spots. It was equipped with long stretches of heavy, solid countertops. Drawers and cabinets filled much of the space under these workbenches, but there were also gaps with plenty of room for a crouching adult. Quickly she shoved some of Gunnar's pillows into one of these cubbies and set him inside. Dust bunnies and hairballs, stains from spilled laboratory reagents, and the cobweb she found were less hazardous to the boy than shrapnel would be. Sigrun looked askance at the space but squeezed in with her son.

The rotor noise passed in the direction of the main hospital. Isabella and Dixie were stashed in a hideout. Lyle moved a rusty old beaker stand to make room for himself in another space. Tessa squatted and waddled into the last available spot. *Ah, what about Cristo? He's asleep--*

Too late to wake him. The violence began with an explosion. Was the aircraft hit, or was it firing at the Palacio? She covered her head with her hands.

The rhythm of the rotor noise broke. A second explosion. *Thump-thump* became an irregular metallic screech. Her heart beat faster. A hit *on* the helicopter.

Engine noise louder. It was coming. She cowered back as far as she could.

Something hit the Annex. Not one noise, a series. Crunches, bangs, and cracks in rapid succession. The building convulsed. A thick manual of laboratory protocols slid off a shelf and landed in front of her. Glass shattered, one-two-three-more, like hits in a video game, as unsecured bottles and glassware tumbled to the floor around the room. Dust shuddered from ceiling panels and clouded the air. She smelled alcohol and the fruitiness of spilled cell culture medium. *God, I hope Cristo has the toxic chemicals in a secure cabinet.*

The crash-sounds ended and the fire alarm began. She lifted her head and blinked.

Now what? Did they dare to leave the building? If there was a fire, did they dare to stay?

Lyle's legs strode past her hiding place.

"Wait!" she said.

The Texan put his palm on the closed door that led to the hallway, feeling for heat. "Jet fuel burns hot and fast. There's only one way out of this room. If that route's compromised, we're screwed."

He cracked the door. The fire alarm screamed.

"Dixie, *komm!* The rest of you stay here."

Tessa ignored Lyle's command and followed him into the hallway. She plugged her ears and wondered how the German shepherd could stand the clamor of the alarm and look so calm. Supposedly dogs had super-sensitive hearing.

Sensitive smell, too, but she didn't need a dog's nose to tell her there was smoke in the building.

Lyle didn't waste time arguing about her presence. "We need to know where the chopper hit. Fire's more dangerous to us below than above."

"I'll go upstairs."

"Dixie and I will scope out this floor and down. Let's hustle."

She sprinted for the stairs. Fire doors sealed off the stairwell. In here she could barely smell the smoke as she skipped steps up to the third floor.

A draft carried black smoke from the southwest corner of the building into the common area. She covered her nose with her shirt and followed the smoke trail, her shoes crunching broken glass on the floor. An excess of natural light. A smoke-filled breeze. No fire.

She found the source of the smoke. The helicopter had slashed this corner of the building. Chunks of drywall lay below a gash in the wall. Smoke was being drawn in from outside. The gash dove below her feet, down to the second floor.

The hole left her exposed to view from the outside. She pressed against the intact wall and inched toward the opening until she could get a glimpse of the crash.

The aircraft was directly below. Part of it had penetrated the first floor of the Annex building. The blades were crumpled. Flames rose from the misshapen wreck. She didn't see any survivors, but down the road people were coming.

Mara Salvatrucha.

Minutes had passed since she left Lyle. She ran back to the lab.

Sigrun, pale and trembling, crowded her when she burst in. "What should we do?"

Before Tessa answered, Dixie and Lyle rushed in and closed the door behind them.

"We stay put," Lyle shouted over the alarm.

"But I smell smoke."

"The helicopter crashed into the first floor. It's burning but most of the wreck is outside the building. The automatic sprinklers are on. I think it's enough to contain the fire."

"You think? I'm not gambling my son's life on your guess." Sigrun went to pick up Gunnar.

Isabella put a hand on her shoulder. "Sigrun, there are other dangers to consider."

Lyle nodded. "The MS are on their way. If we leave the building—or even go down to the lower floors—they'll find us."

"Better that than burning up."

"We're not going to burn up," Isabella said gently. "We stay here and wait. Until it's truly safe to leave."

"Mama, can we see the fire?" Gunnar crawled out of his hiding place. Despite her fear, Tessa thought, we crawl before we walk. Will Gunnar walk again?

The group nervously settled in. Sigrun curled up with her arms around Gunnar. Lyle and Isabella huddled in conversation. Tessa prayed the alarm would stop, and that the fire was out, and that they wouldn't be found. As a distraction she picked up a broom and dustpan and started sweeping up debris. Moving about the laboratory, checking for damage or leaks, she came upon Cristo.

He was lying on the floor in a fetal position, his blanket tossed aside. Sweat soaked the back of his shirt and his limbs twitched. With each spasm, he moaned.

She leaned her broom against the wall and knelt beside him. The poor guy picked a lousy time to get sick. She wondered if the stress of the past days had brought on a relapse of the illness that had kept him home for weeks. "Can I do anything for you? Bring you some water?"

He shook his head without looking up.

They'd chosen this room because it was windowless and enclosed. It occurred to her those virtues were vices if whatever Cristo had was catchy.

I shouldn't have him in the same space with Gunnar.

Maybe they could move Cristo to another room on this floor. As long as he stayed in bed, he wouldn't be seen from outside.

The fire alarm went silent. She felt the absence of sound physically, as if the air pressure had decreased. It let her relax a little.

No, Cristo had to stay put. Until the drug gangsters cleaned up the helicopter mess, nobody—including Cristo—should leave this room.

Pretend you're in grad school. Living in the lab, pulling all-nighters.

But she had a hard time overlooking one rather terrifying difference between this camp-out and those in her past. Her PhD thesis adviser didn't carry an AK-47.

———

Vargas chased the Mara Salvatruchas to the crash site. Now they had proof that the Zetas controlled the skies. De la Rosa wouldn't be departing by air. But dead or alive, Sinaloa had delivered the backup donor to the Palacio. In the next few minutes Vargas would know whether he'd be doing an organ transplant today—or not.

The helicopter had gone down near the Research Annex. As he ran along the service road, he saw smoke billowing up from the front of the building. Rounding the bend, the Annex came fully into view.

His monument to cutting-edge medical research was wounded, and bleeding money. A massive gouge ran from the ground all the way to the third floor. At the lowest level the hole was big enough to drive a car through, though the space currently was occupied by the downed aircraft. He momentarily wondered if the damage to the building was more cosmetic or structural. Structural damage would mean the end of most of his research programs. He didn't have the cash to rebuild the whole Annex.

Debris was piled atop the helicopter and flames licked out of the heap. He quickened his pace. They were going to need speed and luck to salvage a kidney from this.

The wreck crackled and a small explosion shifted the pile. The Mara Salvatruchas hesitated.

Vargas swore at them. "Get in there! Dig out the side door!"

It was entirely possible that the donor had survived the impact and was now trapped or unconscious inside the chopper. As long as his heart was still beating and he hadn't taken a hit to the side of his body, they could harvest a kidney. A decisive injury to the man's head would be ideal. Brain-death was the ordinary trigger for organ donation. In this case it would be convenient. He didn't want to deal with a patient recovering from both trauma and surgery. Yes, it would be best all around if the donor had had a nice skull-breaker at the moment of impact.

But the fire was getting hotter. Baked kidney would be useless.

"Hurry!" he screamed. He even bent over and tugged at a piece of rebar himself.

Which revealed to him the futility of the effort. This motley group of thugs lacked the equipment and resourcefulness to handle an emergency like this. The fallen pieces of the building were too heavy to lift by hand, so the MS did nothing.

Frustrated with failure and disgusted by the fools around him, he let fly every verbal insult he knew in three languages. If you needed something shot at, these were your guys. Meaningful, complex tasks were beyond them.

Another blast popped under the chunks of concrete. His skin burned and he couldn't keep his eyes open. First one, then the rest of the MS fell back from the intense heat. Vargas had no choice but to follow.

It was over, then. The kidneys were lost.

———————

Dixie deserves a medal, Tessa thought.

Not for anything the expensive German shepherd had been *trained* to do. There were shelter rescue pets who could've accomplished the same feat. It was a simple formula: dog + boy = peace. Dixie kept Gunnar amused—and quiet—while the group holed up in the lab.

Two hours after the helicopter crash, claustrophobia was setting in. Tessa knew she had advantages over the others. The laboratory environment was familiar to her, and while here she could immerse herself in useful tasks. She prepared Gunnar's next dose of gene therapy. Sameer had taken some tissue samples from the boy earlier in the week and they needed to be processed. Lab work was a distraction that only she could enjoy.

The others suffered the passive torture of boredom and isolation. At first, fear of fire had them all on edge. When that threat receded, they tiptoed around the room in fear of discovery by the Mara Salvatrucha. They could neither hear nor see anything happening outside, and every unexplained sound made them freeze in anticipation of a raid on their refuge.

Sigrun grew fatigued from whispering stories to Gunnar. Gunnar, with his newly-recovered strength, was restless. Dixie's company was the only thing that prevented him from having a meltdown and a noisy fit. Such a fit could betray them if the MS were still in the building. Lyle tried to rest. Isabella paced like a caged tiger. Cristo tossed and turned amid his blankets on the floor. His muted groans stoked everyone's anxiety.

And everyone was hungry.

Tessa readied the syringes for Gunnar's nasal spray and tidied up the workbench. *How long can we keep the peace in here? We may be stuck for days.*

Her thoughts drifted to the story of Anne Frank and her family, who hid from the Nazis in a Dutch attic for *years*. The thought gave her courage. If people could endure that in a civilized way, certainly this crew could keep it together for one lousy week.

"Time for your medicine," she said to Gunnar. He lay his head on his mother's lap. Tessa squirted the solution into his nostrils.

A knock on the door. *Da-d-d-da-da, da-da.* Just loud enough to hear, a voice on the other side said, "It's Sameer."

Tessa's heart leaped. She disposed of her latex gloves and let him in.

The Indian looked haggard. Probably a mirror of herself, she thought. Whatever Sameer's condition, his concern was entirely for the others.

"Praise God," he said. "You're all right?"

He set a bag of single-serving nut packages on a desk. He put his hands on her shoulders and looked her over from head to toe.

"You're my hero," Tessa said, giving him a hug. "We're okay. What about you? Is it safe for you to be here?"

"For a few minutes. I came through the tunnel. No one saw me leave. I had to come, I was so worried. I knew they didn't find you. But I had to make sure you were not injured by the crash."

"Scared by it, that's all. We're fine except poor Cristo. He's gotten sick again. Could you take a look at him while you're here?"

He raised his eyebrows. "Sick?"

"Yeah. He was real cranky earlier. No appetite. Then he got aches and started sweating a lot. Muscle pain, too, with some spasms."

The good doctor's face clouded and he seemed oddly reluctant to examine Cristo. Tessa took his hand and led him to Cristo's corner. Sameer observed, but didn't bend over, touch, or speak to the sick man. Then he pulled Tessa aside.

"This is bad," he said.

"Do you think it might be a relapse of the infection he got from the bats?"

Again he hesitated. "No. Cristo isn't the only person sick. Over at the hospital Juan lies near death. Before him, it was Maria."

She drew a sharp breath. "All the animal lab staff."

"It cannot be a coincidence. I think they were exposed to something the animals carried."

"The only new animals in the facility were the chimps."

He nodded. "Science knows of many viruses that jump from apes to humans. I fear we may have met another."

She remembered the horrid smell of chimpanzee dung. The body parts flung from the cage. Sameer smeared with chimp offal.

Then she realized why his face was tightly drawn. "The day I arrived, when the chimp died. You may have been exposed."

"And to some extent, you as well."

Her mind raced. What did she know about zoonoses, diseases that afflict animals and humans with equal ease? A lot, actually, since rabies was one example. Unfortunately, there were no universal rules governing the behavior of germs like these. If a new disease had come from the chimps, anything was possible. It might spread only upon contact with body fluids, or bites. Or it might be in the air. It might travel from chimp to human and go no further, or it might spread from person-to-person as well. And what about other animals?

The dog.

She wasn't thinking of Dixie, but the research dog, the beagle shot dead in the animal facility on that fateful day when Maria opened the doors. The dog had been extremely aggressive. At the time, she attributed it to the chaos, and being out of its cage. Maybe there was more to the behavior than that.

Sameer leaned in close to her ear. "The sickness affected Juan's brain. He got paranoid and violent. I had to restrain him. If the same thing happens to Cristo..."

My God. And I was worried about Gunnar going stir-crazy in here.

"What should we do?" she asked.

"I wish I knew." He took her hands in his. "So many if's. I would stay and help you but Vargas would send the drug men to look for me. My only advice is take care of *yourself.*"

"And Gunnar," she added.

"If you can." They walked toward the door. "If Cristo has encephalitis, there's nothing you can do to help him. Your responsibility is to make sure he cannot do harm to *you*."

"Okay." She choked a little as she spoke.

He grasped both her hands and fixed his eyes on hers. "The most important thing is to stay out of sight. The cruelty of these people—I cannot describe it."

Sameer squeezed her once and left, gently closing the door behind him. His warnings about both the drug cartel and the possible zoonosis left her reeling. If there was a new infection, and Cristo had it, the drug men might be the lesser of the threats to Gunnar.

She rubbed her eyes and sighed. *Note to self: next time you see apes and you're not at a zoo, get the hell out of there.*

It was too late stay away from the chimps now. If Cristo caught a virus from the primates, her priority had to be containment. This was no head cold that they were dealing with. Difficult choices had to be made.

They had to get Cristo out of here. Now.

Quickly she gathered the other adults and conferred quietly on the far side of the room from Cristo. They agreed on a plan that she hoped would not become one of the great regrets of her life. Too much tenderness for her friend could get them all killed.

Isabella slipped out to collect surgical masks from elsewhere on the floor. Sigrun moved Gunnar as far away from Cristo as possible.

There is one thing I can do, Tessa thought. It probably wouldn't help Cristo but it might help others. She searched the lab and found what she needed.

Isabella returned and everyone put on a mask and gloves, some small protection against a possible infection.

Tessa knelt beside Cristo. In her imagination, the seemingly empty air between them teemed with deadly virus particles. But she had to act.

He tossed and turned with his eyes closed, somewhere between sleep and waking.

"Cristo, I'm going to swab your nose. Try not to move."

He didn't acknowledge. She opened a sealed sterile package with a long cotton swab inside. Timing her movement to catch him immobile and facing her direction, she touched the cotton tip to the inside of his nose. He allowed her only a second to swirl for a specimen before his eyes flew open.

He seized her arm. His hand was slick with sweat. "What the hell are you doing?" he demanded

"I'm—"

"Don't touch me!"

His grip tightened as he leveraged himself to a sitting position. The whites of his eyes were streaked with red and the pupils were grossly enlarged.

"Let go. You're hurting me," she pleaded, unconcerned about his strength but terrified of contact. The cotton swab in her hand, wet with mucus and possibly virus, was trapped in the air between them.

"Who do you think you are? You think you're better than me?" He grabbed a fistful of her hair with his other hand. "This is all your FAULT!"

"Please, Cristo, calm down—"

A growl over her right shoulder shifted Cristo's attention. Tessa smelled Dixie's dog breath and felt its warmth at her cheek.

Lyle towered over them all. "Sir, let go of the lady."

The German shepherd growled with greater ferocity. From the corner of her eye—she dared not move—Tessa saw sharp white teeth.

Lyle kept his voice even. "I said let her go, or my partner will make you."

Cristo was in the grip of some madness, but his primal fear of predators remained intact. He released Tessa. She backed away and packed the swab in sterile saline.

"Now we're gonna take a little walk," Lyle said. "Get up."

Her heart was in her throat. She hated doing this. Cristo was a friend. How could she?

No choice. She had to protect Gunnar. And herself.

Vargas! Her anger blazed at him, the architect of this whole situation.

Lyle was calm but firm. "I said get up."

"No," Cristo replied.

Please, just do it, Tessa thought. Before Cristo grabbed her, she was worried he'd be too weak to walk. Now she just wanted him to comply.

"Dixie. *Nimm.*"

The *Schutzhund* sprang forward and latched her jaws on Cristo's forearm. He cried out.

"Don't hurt him!" Tessa said.

Through his surgical mask, Lyle's Southern drawl was soothing and threatening at the same time. "She won't hurt him unless I say. Now, mister, I suggest you get up."

Cristo staggered to his feet with the dog clinging to him. He looked terrible. His nose was running and his skin prickled with goosebumps. "Where we going?"

"Someplace safe."

Isabella led the way. Dixie walked backward, maintaining her lock on her prisoner's arm, tugging him in the direction her master wanted him to go. Tessa put on some gloves and shoved Cristo's bedding into a trash bag. She followed Lyle into the hallway, carrying the contaminated linens. Cristo winced and covered his eyes with his free hand.

They managed to get him into the stairwell. Somehow Dixie navigated down the steps without letting go. Past floor one, all the way to the basement. At the loading dock behind the animal facility, Cristo dropped to his knees.

"*Lass,*" Lyle said. Dixie released Cristo and stood stock-still.

Cristo moaned and heaved. Crouched on all fours, he vomited. Isabella, Lyle, and Tessa all reflexively took a step away and waited.

"You okay, son?" Lyle said. "We're almost there."

Cristo cursed in Spanish. Lyle allowed him another minute to recover. "Let's go."

It took Dixie's persuasion again to get Cristo moving. They passed from the loading dock into the abandoned animal facility. It stank. Tessa told herself that Cristo had spent many hours working down here. He was used to the smell. It wouldn't bother him as much as it bothered her.

Sure.

They entered the room that used to house the dogs. Some of the enclosures were mere cages. Others had long concrete runs for the dogs to exercise a bit. Isabella chose the cleanest one of these and opened the door. Tessa tossed in the pillows and blankets she carried.

"In you go," Lyle said.

"Are you crazy?" Cristo said. "You're gonna lock me in there like a dog?"

"I treat dogs well," Lyle said. "This is for your protection and ours."

It was horrible, horrible what they were doing. But she didn't have a better idea. The Annex building didn't have a proper infection control facility, much less a psychiatric ward to put him in case he became violent. If they tied him to a bed, how would he use the toilet? If he went mad and started screaming, he might be heard outside. And he would breathe or spit or poop contagion all around him.

No, the only option was to secure him down here, away from the rest of them. On his own.

Sameer said medically there's nothing we can do. She fetched some buckets. Some she filled with fresh water for drinking. Others she left for collecting waste, if he retained control of his bodily functions. She arranged the buckets in the cage.

Cristo swore a blue streak. On Lyle's command, Dixie snapped at him, making light contact on his buttocks until he retreated into the cage. Isabella locked the door.

Tessa's heart ached. "I'll be back to check on you. I'll bring food, if I can."

Cristo's rage and his strength were spent. Her last image of her friend was Cristo huddled on the concrete floor, trembling.

Vargas finished the physical exam and draped his stethoscope around his neck.

His conclusion: Luis Angel de la Rosa was dying.

The drug lord and his entourage had permanently moved out of the luxurious Tenochtitlan Suite. Its location on the top floor of the hospital was too exposed in light of the Zetas' surface-to-air missile capability. The gang took up residence in the modest accommodations of a Palacio standard suite on a lower floor on the other side of the building. Same comfortable bed, fine linens, and marble bathroom, but smaller and with no kitchen. In this room, the bodyguards allowed Vargas to examine his patient.

He found no surprises in the examination. Patients who lacked functioning kidneys needed dialysis three times a week. Without dialysis, toxic wastes—products of metabolism normally filtered out by the kidneys—built up in their blood. Without dialysis, they died. It was as simple as that.

Today was the third day since de la Rosa had been dialyzed. Vargas didn't want to do it, didn't want the responsibility, but it was either dialyze de la Rosa or take the blame for the Sinaloa boss's death.

"I know it's getting late, but we shouldn't wait until tomorrow," he said to de la Rosa. The treatment would take at least three hours, into the evening. Not that any of them had plans to go anywhere tonight.

"What are you afraid of?" de la Rosa said.

"Afraid?"

"I can smell a man's fear." De la Rosa's voice was croaky and he now scratched himself constantly. "You are afraid of me. That is wisdom. Or are you afraid of yourself? Afraid that you will fail in a task that should be easy for you?"

Vargas felt heat in his cheeks. The old man was good.

"I am afraid of nothing," de la Rosa said. "Not even your incompetence." He lifted his skinny arm, showing the place where weeks before a surgeon had implanted an artificial blood vessel—an arteriovenous graft—to make dialysis easier. "You stick the needles in here. If you can't do it, give me the needles and I will."

"My team and I will take excellent care of you," Vargas said, faking his usual suave manner as best he could while reminding himself to have Sameer and the transplant surgeon in the room in case anything went wrong. "I'll see you downstairs in fifteen minutes."

He tramped through the vacant halls of his hospital, mentally reviewing the dialysis procedure. They didn't do dialysis very often at the Palacio. Occasionally they'd get a patient who was on regular dialysis and came to Mexico for some other medical procedure. Or when they did a kidney transplant, they normally dialyzed the recipients when they arrived, before the surgery. But they only did a handful of these living donor transplants in a year. De la Rosa talked big but he was ignorant. Dialysis was a common medical procedure. That didn't make it simple or trivial. Or risk-free.

Over the course of several hours, a dialysis machine pumps all the blood out of a patient's body and then puts it back in. While the blood is outside the body and inside the machine, toxins diffuse out of the blood and into a solution called dialysate. When the procedure is over, the patient's blood is clean. The dialysate becomes like urine and is thrown away.

De la Rosa didn't understand any of this. Vargas wondered if he even knew that each kidney patient needed his own special formula of dialysate, prescribed by a kidney doctor.

De la Rosa's handlers had brought his prescription. The Palacio had enough of the life-saving liquid for two rounds of dialysis.

Today. And one more.

Which meant that in the next seven days, de la Rosa would either leave the Palacio, or get a new kidney, or he'd die.

Vargas arrived at the dialysis suite. Sameer helped him prep the machine. Rogelio, the transplant surgeon, was there too.

"This isn't what I do," Rogelio said. "Dialysis will cost you. On top of my hourly fee for being stuck in this shit-storm."

Vargas bristled. Rogelio was good with his hands, but his mouth was another story. He lacked the most basic social graces. All he talked about was himself, and money. From the moment the Zetas attacked the hospital, his primary concern was how much Vargas owed him for the change in plans. The original deal was for Rogelio to come to the Palacio, do the transplant—no questions asked—and get whisked out again within twenty-four hours.

He did not understand the delicacy, and danger, of the situation. De la Rosa required careful handling. Vargas had been keeping Rogelio away from him.

"It's not what I do either," Vargas said. "Is it too hard for you? Maybe I can get one of my janitors in here to do your part."

"Fuck you."

"Yes, I think I will. Why don't you go back to your room and watch TV?"

Rogelio ripped off his paper gown, threw it on the floor, and spit on it. "Your janitor can clean up, too." He stormed out of the room.

Vargas picked up the gown. Sameer stared at him.

"He's a problem when the patient is awake," Vargas said. "I didn't want him in the room. We don't need him."

"If you say so," Sameer said.

Vargas ignored him. *Why am I the only person around here who can handle a little stress?*

He had finished arranging the equipment when de la Rosa's bodyguards wheeled their boss into the room. They made him comfortable in the chair next to the dialysis machine. Vargas handed de la Rosa a remote control for the television mounted on the wall. He didn't take it. He just fixed Vargas with a piercing gaze, challenging him with his eyes.

Vargas refused to be swayed. He set the remote on the table at the side of the chair and got down to the business of hooking the patient up.

Think you're tough, don't you? Well, I'm in control here. Your life is in my hands.

He considered intentionally missing the vein on the first couple of needle sticks just to torture de la Rosa. But his pride was bigger than his desire for petty vengeance. Smoothly he placed the needles with complete accuracy the first time.

Pasting on a fake smile, Vargas said, "Is there anything else we can do for you?"

De la Rosa glared at him, then shook his head. Vargas watched the tube in the drug lord's arm turn red as blood drained from his body. The sight made Vargas feel powerful. For the next thirty minutes he hovered over the patient, monitoring his vital signs and appearance. Then as boredom and sleepiness grew, he put Sameer in charge of this routine drudge work.

"I'll be in there," he said, gesturing to an adjacent lounge area. He went into the room and lay down on a sofa to rest his eyes for a few minutes.

The next thing he knew, Sameer was shaking him awake. He looked at the clock. He'd been asleep almost an hour.

"Dr. Vargas. The patient says he feels cold."

"Get him a blanket," Vargas said. Sameer frowned. Apparently it wasn't that kind of cold. Feeling a chill in his own gut, Vargas went to examine the patient.

De la Rosa's steely expression was as cold as ice.

Businesslike, Sameer checked the monitoring devices. "His heart rate has increased."

Vargas put his fingers on de la Rosa's wrist and felt the pulse for himself. It was fast. And the drug lord didn't look good. "How are you feeling, *señor*?"

"I feel that you screwed up. You didn't make the machine warm enough. Now my blood runs cold."

I wish. It's not the temperature of the dialysis machine that's causing your problem.

He pulled Sameer aside and conferred with him quietly. "What's his blood pressure doing?"

"Decreasing."

He was pretty sure of the answer to his next question. "Temperature?"

"Rising."

"Damn. He's having a pyrogenic reaction."

Sameer nodded.

"If it gets any worse, we'll have to stop the procedure."

"Yes, Dr. Vargas."

It was rotten, rotten luck. He'd never had a Palacio patient get a pyrogenic reaction before. Such reactions were generally preventable. But somehow a tiny quantity of bacterial body parts had gotten into his dialysis machine, tubing, or solution. From there the microscopic debris had passed into de la Rosa's blood. While it couldn't cause an infection, it provoked an immune response that looked like one, which explained de la Rosa's sudden fever and chills.

He curled his fists. He wanted so badly to chastise Sameer for failing to disinfect the machine properly, but they'd performed the task together. The cause was probably the Palacio's water. With a hefty sense of irony, he realized his lie about a contaminated water supply was a little bit true. For some reason, today the water contained more of the trace pyrogenic chemical. Or else de la Rosa was unusually sensitive to it.

The sound of chattering teeth made him look up. De la Rosa had started to get shaking chills.

"We're done. Stop the draw and get his blood back in," Vargas said.

Sameer obeyed.

Luis Angel de la Rosa said nothing while Sameer disconnected him from the machine. Within minutes, he stopped shivering. He looked daggers at Vargas.

Vargas pretended not to notice. He focused on the problem. Today's dialysis session had been too short. It had partially cleaned de la Rosa's blood but the effect wouldn't last the usual two or three days until another treatment was needed. With only one dose of dialysate solution left, that put them under some time pressure. He figured they could avoid the pyrogenic reaction next time by doing an additional ultrafiltration of the sterilized water. But it wouldn't give them back the time they'd lost.

Vargas was pretty sure the Sinaloa boss didn't know about the limited supply of dialysate. He was not about to tell him. If de la Rosa was so powerful, his people on the outside ought to be able to break the siege in time. As long as in the next four days they got Sinaloa's leader out of the Palacio, or resumed deliveries into the facility, he'd be fine.

But in case the stalemate lasted longer, Vargas needed a plan B.

CHAPTER 14

Fear of contagion broke the fellowship in the Annex.

With the possibility that the virus might spread through the air and no way to tell who might be infected, Tessa had recommended to Lyle, Isabella, and Sigrun that they not all sleep in the same room. Lyle and Isabella had moved out of the lab and found a dark corner in the hall away from any windows. As an act of kindness, they left Dixie with Gunnar. The boy was unhappy and too young to understand why everyone had to stay silent and hidden. Like all of them, he was hungry. The dog gave him some comfort.

Tessa rose from her makeshift bed and tried to clear the lingering traces of disturbing dreams from her mind. She stretched her stiff body and her joints cracked. Her mouth felt pasty and her stomach was as empty as the night before.

God, she wanted some breakfast.

What else did she miss this morning? Toothpaste, a shower, and coffee, and a mattress, and—well, the list of inconveniences went on. A distraction from her bigger problems.

The surgical mask and N95 respirator had slipped away from her mouth sometime during the night. The elastic bands irritated the skin behind her ears. She tore off the mask and threw it away. Was there any point in donning a fresh one? A mask couldn't filter out a virus from the room's air.

More as a talisman than protection, she strapped on a new mask.

Gunnar, Sigrun, and Dixie were still asleep. She turned on a desk lamp and aimed the light at her workspace on the lab countertop. Her stomach growled, loud in the silent room. They'd searched the Annex as thoroughly as possible and collected a few more packages of snacks. Little was left. By unanimous agreement, what food they had belonged to Gunnar. Even Dixie was about to go on a diet. Lyle had given her a bit of dry dog food he found in one of the cages last night. None remained.

Look on the bright side. Fasting can be a purifying experience.

What bothered her more than the feeling of hunger was that she had no food to take to Cristo. Bringing him something to eat would show that she cared. She wanted him to know that she was worried about him, even though she dreaded going down to the basement to check on him. Part of that dread was fear of catching the disease. More of it was fear of what she might see. Would he be sicker? Out of his mind? Dead, even? She had nothing to offer except fresh water and a reminder that he had not been abandoned. Hopefully that would be enough.

I'll visit him as soon as Sigrun wakes, she decided. In the meantime she could do some science. She had the swab from Cristo's nose, which might carry DNA or RNA from the germ that was making him sick. With luck she could analyze it and find out what microbial family it belonged to.

While the first steps in the nucleic acid extraction were incubating, she had time to work on Gunnar's condition. Given his tremendous clinical improvement, she expected to see microscopic evidence that the gene therapy was working. Over the last several weeks, Sameer had taken tiny tissue specimens from Gunnar. Ultra-thin slices of the tissue on glass microscope slides hadn't been studied yet because that was Cristo's job, and he'd been out sick.

Sameer's precise handwriting marked a slide box with the dates of the most recent samples, exactly the way she'd taught him to do it. She stained the slides to give the cells color and definition. She worked quietly, opening the sink faucet to a gentle trickle, taking care not to clink glassware or to slam cabinet doors so as not to wake Gunnar and Sigrun. At the microscope she decided to look at older slides first, ones Cristo had stained in previous months, to get a sense of what Gunnar's nerve cells looked like *before* his amazing improvement.

She slipped a slide onto the microscope stage, adjusted the distance to the lens, and brought the cells into focus. A perfect circle of bright light hit her eyes. She blinked and searched the strange micro-landscape for familiar patterns. There they were—cells. She rotated the precision focus knob to get a clear view of the cells' internal structure.

Gunnar's cells showed typical signs of Batten disease. The Batten mutation affected his cells' waste disposal systems. Lacking the ability to take out the trash, his cells were piled high with molecular garbage. She could see the waste as inclusions--blobs of material stored where it didn't belong. Batten disease inclusions were fluorescent. When she switched from the microscope's regular light bulb to a fluorescent one, the blobs glowed like white T-shirts under black light.

No news here. Gunnar has Batten disease.

But what would the recent slides reveal?

She removed the old slide and filed it in a narrow vertical slit of a slide box. Her mind tingled with anticipation. It was foolish, perhaps, to put such emphasis on the scientific data when the boy himself was a living miracle. But she wanted so badly for Gunnar to get better, she didn't trust her clinical judgment.

Memories can lie. Maybe he hasn't changed that much. Maybe I'm seeing only what I want to see, not how he really is.

She knew about this kind of blindness. Impossibly, irrationally, her baby Benjamin's death had come as a shock to her, even though she "knew" he was dying.

She could not allow herself to believe Gunnar's progress was real or permanent until she saw proof under the microscope. With trembling fingers, she laid the newest specimen on the microscope stage. As she clicked the fluorescent bulb into place she forced herself to take a deep breath. Then she put her eyes on the lenses.

The field of view was dark.

She inhaled and didn't breathe out while she systematically made adjustments to the focus, the position, the illumination of the slide. Still nothing.

The glowing trash heaps were gone. No sign of Batten disease.

Warmth washed over her from head to toe and her eyes filled with tears. She muted the sounds of her sobs but didn't resist the tears. This was something worth crying over.

Gunnar's improvement wasn't the mad hallucination of a desperate mother and an idealistic scientist. It was real.

Eagerly she swept through more slides. Discovering a few glowing Batten inclusions was actually a relief because it confirmed that the microscopy was working. Without question, the number and size of the inclusions had decreased dramatically in the past few weeks.

She lifted her head and stared into the unlit lab. Amid this darkness, a light of hope. Torn between terror in the present and rejoicing for the future, she felt her heart might burst.

The gene therapy worked. She'd found a cure.

The scientist in her fired a dozen questions in quick succession. *Is the effect permanent? How much of his vision will he regain? Will he need to be on the therapy his whole life?*

She ignored the questions to savor the moment. Then she slowed her racing thoughts and started a thorough examination of each slide. Observe. Record. Miss nothing.

Slide after slide showed fewer Batten inclusions. She fiddled with the microscope's lighting to get the best views.

What's this? Her heart skipped a beat. There was some kind of anomaly in the image.

Eye strain. I'm seeing things.

She rubbed her eyes, stretched her arms over her head, flexed her neck. Looked in the 'scope again.

Her pulse quickened. *That doesn't make sense.*

Regular incandescent light bulb: on. Slide specimen: recent. Observation: cellular inclusions. Trash heaps.

But...

She flipped to fluorescent light. The trash heaps disappeared. The opposite of what she should see with Batten disease.

She leaned back in her chair. *Think.*

The fluorescent marker of Batten disease had vanished from Gunnar's nerve cells. Yet under regular light, she could see the outlines of *other* abnormal accumulations. Trash heaps that did *not* glow. What could they be?

An idea crawled into her brain. Her dewy eyes dried and she felt ice in her belly.

Pictures. I need to look up some pictures.

The chair squeaked as she scrambled away from the benchtop. Sigrun stirred. *Books. Where does Cristo keep his books?*

A desk. Above it, shelves. Laboratory notes, three-ring binders, medical journals. Textbooks.

She scanned the titles. Cristo owned several excellent atlases of histopathology. Books with color pictures of microscopic structures, images of every kind of normal and abnormal cell imaginable. She snatched a volume that specialized in nerve tissue.

Index. Her finger slid down the alphabet to "N." Negri bodies. Page forty-two. Heart pounding, she tugged the arm of a desk lamp to bring the light closer to the page.

Printed on the page were pictures taken through a microscope, pictures of neurons with oval-shaped blobs of stuff that didn't belong inside a cell.

The trash heaps looked like the ones she had just discovered in Gunnar's most recent tissue samples.

She scooted back to the lab bench with the book. Sigrun stood up, stretched, and wandered toward her.

The pounding of her heart in her ears deafened her to other sounds. *Not now, Sigrun.*

She had to be sure. Microscope power: on. Neurons scrolled through the microscope field as she moved the stage. Once every few seconds she paused and squinted, trying to glean every scrap of visual information from the magnification. One slide. Two slides. More. Sigrun hovered but did not speak.

A last glance at the textbook to confirm that what she saw on the slide matched what she saw in the book. The images were identical. If she had a camera hooked up to the microscope, she could get a textbook photo of her own.

There were Negri bodies in Gunnar's cells. A classic diagnostic sign of—

She slammed the textbook shut.

Sigrun jumped. "What's wrong?"

She wanted to be gentle but frustration and anger bled into her voice. "Your son has rabies."

Vargas didn't waste his breath asking the man for his real name.

"What do they call you?" he said.

He didn't care if the gangbanger said Adolf Hitler. Truth was irrelevant. What mattered was consistency. The name should match what the previous

Mara Salvatrucha guy said was this one's call sign. A biometric hand scan would confirm identity in the end. He just needed a name, any name, to type in the computer and let him quickly find the donor later.

God, why do they all stink? The Palacio has showers. Do these people know what soap is?

The man squirmed in the plush chair, rubbing his greasy palms over the padded armrests. Vargas mentally added another expense to this ill-fated venture: new chairs for the client reception area.

The MS flashed an excessively jovial grin at his peers milling about in an unstructured queue in the Palacio's elegant main lobby. Vargas recognized nervousness in the gesture. Despite their forced bravado and experience with real-life violence, most of these boys were naïve and uneducated. Never went to a doctor. Terrified of needles.

The tough guy mumbled his nickname. With academic curiosity, Vargas confirmed the pattern. The name was another variant on what appeared to be Mara Salvatrucha standard form: an adjective describing either a physical trait or the kid's hometown followed by a slangy noun of violence, like "killer" or "slasher." As if they were American boxers or professional wrestlers.

"Put your hand in the dome," he said.

The MS had watched a dozen others do this already. He didn't jump at the flash of light as the scanner recorded his hand's vascular pattern.

When the hand came out of the scanner Vargas noticed it was trembling. How ironic, he thought, that this young man may have committed murder but he's afraid of a needle prick.

"Left hand."

The small square of alcohol-soaked cotton turned grimy as Vargas wiped off the finger. To his surprise, the finger bore a simple wedding band. Vargas's cultivated glibness kicked in.

"You and your wife have any kids?"

The MS looked at him. "Two."

The quaking of the finger faltered fractionally. *Perfect.* Vargas clicked the trigger on the disposable pen-like device in his hand. The man's whole body jerked, but the deed was done. Vargas had his blood sample. He stretched a little bandage over the tiny wound. The MS grinned when he realized it was over, that he'd survived the procedure.

He dismissed the man with a wave. "Next."

His foot tapped the floor under the broad desk. How many did he need? To find a tissue match for an organ donation, how many unrelated people did you have to screen? He didn't know the exact statistics but he was sure the number of MS flunkies wandering the Palacio didn't come close to being enough. The odds were against them. He—and de la Rosa—would need luck to pull this off. Luck, or some armed support to break the siege and get the drug lord out of here before the unfiltered poisons in his blood killed him.

Another swaggering Mara Salvatrucha slouched into the chair. Vargas wanted to slap him. Then out of the corner of his eye he noticed Sameer scurrying across the lobby from one wing of the hospital to another.

He'd had enough of this job. It was time to check on de la Rosa anyway. Sameer could do the screening.

He called out, "Dr. Desai! Come here."

Sameer froze and looked around as if there were another Dr. Desai nearby. Vargas knew the Indian physician well, knew his habits and gestures. There was something furtive about his movements. Suspicious. Without a word to his "patient," Vargas got up and cornered Sameer, who shifted a small object from one hand to the other.

"I need you to take over," he said. "We have to screen everyone Sinaloa brought in. One of them might have to give up a kidney."

Sameer's forehead wrinkled. "I can help you later."

This hardworking underling never shirked the tasks Vargas gave him. What was going on?

"You're busy with something?" Vargas asked.

The hand holding the object slipped behind Sameer's back. "Yes."

That's it? No explanation?

Vargas crossed his arms. "Something more important than finding an organ for our patient?"

A flash of anger. Sameer squared his shoulders. "I'm taking care of a patient."

"De la Rosa is our only patient."

Sameer didn't reply.

"Give it to me," Vargas said, holding out his hand. Like a teenager busted by his parents, Sameer reluctantly placed a small glass vial in Vargas's waiting palm. It was from the Palacio pharmacy. Vargas recognized it immediately. The vial contained plack, his favorite illegal narcotic.

Vargas's face tightened. "What the hell are you doing?" He leaned toward his associate.

Sameer didn't flinch. "Until a few hours ago I was trying to save a man's life. Now I'm trying to ease his passing."

"What—"

"Not here," Sameer said. "Come."

Nobody told Vargas what to do—except de la Rosa, of course—but he bowed to the certainty in Sameer's voice and followed him out of the grand lobby. A scraping sound drew his gaze to the carpet. A white rat sprinted along the wall and squeezed through an impossibly small crack. Sameer saw the rat too and cringed.

"From the lab," Vargas said. *There's one major screw up I can't blame on Sinaloa.* Rodent extermination was going to be yet another expense. "I should start trapping the damn things."

"Stay away from them." Sameer hastened on. "They might be carriers."

Carriers?

Before he could ask, he heard a choked cry from a patient room off the hall just ahead. A barely-human gurgling and a groan of inexpressible agony. The sound was chilling. When Sameer opened the door, the heightened clarity and volume of the sound injected ice into his core.

"Quickly," Sameer said. "Sinaloa mustn't know." He closed the door behind them.

Vargas saw the source of the noise.

In a bed lay a Mexican man with all four limbs tied to the rails. He thrashed about, rattling the joints and springs. Foamy liquid leaked from between his gritted teeth. A long strip of tape spiraled around one arm, securing an IV.

Vargas stepped back in shock. "*Dios mío.*"

"Give me the drug," Sameer said. "He's in pain."

Vargas treated the ailments of the rich, not cases of demonic possession. He handed the vial back to Sameer.

"Who is this?" he said.

"Juan Aguilar. A tech from your animal facility." Sameer opened a drawer in a cart near the bed. Plastic crinkled as he tore the seal off a sterile syringe. He jabbed the needle into the vial.

One of the techs…

Vargas remembered the sick woman he'd offloaded during the evacuation. She died when the Zetas attacked the airstrip. He hadn't tended to her himself but from the way his staff had described her condition, if she hadn't been killed, she might have ended up looking like this.

Sameer said carriers…

"Viral encephalitis," he concluded.

Sameer nodded as he injected plack into Juan's vein. "I think it came from the chimpanzees. The apes were the first to show symptoms. Agitation, aggression. Death."

"You think it jumped species?"

"This is enough evidence for me," Sameer said, pointing at Juan. "It infects humans. The rats and dogs? I don't know."

Juan's grim cries died and the limb restraints went slack as the narcotic circulated through his body. Fury flared in Vargas. Everything in his carefully tended private universe was spinning out of control.

"Who gave you permission to bring this man here?" he demanded. "This is *my* hospital and I do *not* treat infectious diseases."

"If he lives, I'll gladly put him on the next plane out," Sameer said. "In the meantime—"

Vargas backed toward the door. "In the meantime, you've been exposing yourself to an unknown pathogen. I want no part of this. And I don't want to be anywhere near you."

"That is acceptable to me as well," Sameer said.

The tone was insolent. Vargas wagged a finger at his subordinate but didn't move any closer. "Nobody keeps secrets from me—"

Commotion approached in the hall outside. Men shouting for a doctor. Thumping feet, bodies banging against the walls. Vargas stared at the door, wondering what could possibly happen next. The tumult passed. He cast a dirty look at Sameer but spoke no more as he left the room.

A fresh trail of smeared blood slicked the elegant tile floor. Vargas slipped and blundered into the wall, catching himself before he fell. His hand touched blood on the wall.

Voices rose in the lobby ahead.

"Damn it." He wiped his hand with a tissue and drenched his skin in alcohol gel. Then he trotted down the hall as briskly as he could while maintaining a dignified manner.

Guns and dirty gang members overran the Palacio's grand lobby. The blood trail led to a group of men clustered around something on the rug in front of the check-in desk. One of the men saw Vargas and called his name.

"What's going on?" Vargas snapped. A dozen men spoke at once. He didn't bother to decipher the babble while he stepped forward. The cluster parted before him.

He would've preferred ten Juan Aguilars to what he saw on the rug.

CHAPTER 15

*G*unnar *has rabies.*

The proof was on the microscope slide.

Bitterness rose in Tessa's throat. This emotional roller coaster was too much. Her thoughts flitted like mosquitoes.

When will he show symptoms? Is there any treatment we can provide? How much time does he have left?

One thing she did *not* wonder was how he got infected. She knew where the rabies virus came from. And she knew it was her fault.

Her imagination fast-forwarded to the future. Like Batten disease, rabies was uniformly lethal. The boy would die. His mother would grieve. Tessa would be consumed by guilt. Another child dead because of his association with her.

She put her hands on the side of her head to stifle the memory of Benjamin's cries. Benjamin, her poor, beautiful, damaged child. She'd defiled his innocence with her flawed DNA, and he died. Now in her attempt to save another boy and spare another mother that cruel loss, she'd hastened the outcome she most wanted to avoid.

She'd given Gunnar the virus. Rabies virus was the cornerstone of her experimental gene therapy. In the laboratory, she had modified rabies to carry the healthy gene Gunnar needed to survive. She'd used every molecular safeguard in the book to disable the virus. As a backup, she'd also vaccinated Gunnar against rabies. Everyone working with the modified virus had taken the rabies vaccine too, in case through some one in a billion chance, the virus overcame its genetic handicaps and found a way to breed. In case the virus reverted to wild type.

All these precautions were in vain. Right in front of her eyes, on the microscope slide, was proof that rabies virus was growing inside Gunnar's brain.

She bowed her head.

Sigrun spoke. "If this is what rabies looks like, I wish he'd gotten it a long time ago."

Wallowing in despair, she'd nearly forgotten the boy's mother was standing right there. "Sigrun, you don't understand. This tissue section—"

"I don't care about that. Look at my son. Not at some little piece of him. At *him*." She pointed across the room. "He's getting better."

Sigrun's eyes were bloodshot and her hair was disheveled, but there was triumph in her voice. "I'm not a scientist. I can't explain why that thing you're looking at is a lie. All I can say is I'm his mother and I know your treatment is working."

"But—"

"But nothing. You believe what you want. Maybe that microscope knows my son better than I do. But my proof isn't in there. It's out here." Her voice quavered. "I never thought he'd speak again. Last night he said, 'I love you.'" She sniffled and rubbed her nose through the surgical mask. "Cristo might have some terrible germ. But not my son. He's getting better."

"Mama?" Gunnar's voice across the room. He was awake. "I'm hungry."

Tessa looked toward the small figure as he sat up in his rumpled pile of bedding. He held his head high. The boy who a month ago could barely keep himself up while leaning against a bedstead now sat bolt upright. Nothing supported his torso—no chair back, no caregiver's arms. His tender soprano voice was strong and his words were clear.

All her life she'd put her faith in science, clinging to data that could be quantified, represented in a graph, analyzed with statistics. When did she begin to doubt her senses? To ignore the real world in favor of the constructed world of a laboratory experiment?

She turned off the microscope. Sigrun was right.

———

The trail of blood merged with a growing stain on the vintage Mexican rug in Vargas's lobby. A fragment of his attention fixated on the damage to the rug. The majority was seized by the source of the damage.

A mangled human body.

Gradually Vargas absorbed the sight. Two legs in a pair of camo fatigue pants, blood-spattered but oddly intact. One boot was missing. He saw one and a half arms attached to the torso and half an arm detached, lying on a flat belly. The number of fingers on the associated hand was unclear amid shredded fabric and gore. He counted six puncture wounds in the neck. Possibly more but the ragged edges of the wounds were torn and were consolidating into larger lacerations. The face—

He shut his eyes and turned away. Took four conscious breaths to steady himself. Looked again.

Neither whole numbers nor fractions could describe what remained of the face. Chunks of flesh and bone were missing. The mouth was barely identifiable thanks to a dangling portion of lip in the general vicinity. Skin had been peeled back from the orbital area around the one remaining eye, exposing nerve and bleeding muscle. Hair from the scalp had somehow been inverted to the jaw. A piece of bone was embedded in bloody soft tissue. From the skull?

"*Jesucristo*," he muttered. Gang members tugged at him, dragging him to the body. They expected him to do something with this, this ruin of a man. As if that man would even *want* to live after being pieced back together like Frankenstein's monster. "What the hell happened?"

"Monkeys," several said. "Two of them. One big, one smaller."

"We came but they work fast," said another.

"I think maybe I shot one."

"They ran away."

Vargas shook free of the men's pawing grasp. He put his hands on his hips and shook his head. Blood no longer spurted from any of the man's wounds. It oozed, moving in response to gravity, not the push of a beating heart. "There's nothing I can do."

Then the blood drained from his own face as shock wore off and rational thought resumed. *Sameer said there was a virus.* That it came from the chimpanzees and drove them mad. He said the lab techs were infected. Down the hall at this very moment, the virus was killing one of them.

The sodden corpse on the carpet was more than a mess. It was a grubby, seeping biohazard.

"Was anyone else hurt?" He looked around the assembly. Bloody clothing was the uniform of the day. He couldn't tell what was splatter from the victim and what was actual injury.

Two men gestured. Ah, yes. Now he discerned the ripped shirt and the bleeding scalp.

"Come with me." As he led these two toward a treatment room, he said to the disquieted group, "Use the rug to roll up the body. Take it outside and bury it. While you're out there, find those apes and kill them."

No one moved. Vargas and his two new patients left the lobby.

He followed the blood trail back to the room where he'd left Sameer with the sick tech. If Sameer was so eager to practice a little infectious disease medicine, here were two more customers for him. Vargas sure as hell wasn't going to touch them. Without knocking, he put his palm on the entrance scanner.

Red light. The door was privacy-locked from the inside.

"Sameer! It's Vargas! Open up."

There was no reply. He pressed his ear against the door and heard nothing. The bastard had to be in there. No way that half-dead, strapped-down patient had activated the lock.

He pounded his fist on the door. "Sameer!"

The door clicked open. "Keep it quiet," Sameer said. His eyes widened when he saw the two injured Mara Salvatruchas. "Why are they here?"

"They need a doctor and you're the one playing Father Damien," Vargas said. "Not my problem."

The animal tech in the bed was quiet. Maybe he was dead. Vargas spun on his heel and left the lepers in there together. He squirted a triple shot of sanitizer gel into his hands and scrubbed. Whatever this infection was, he wanted nothing to do with it.

The ersatz daylight of the fluorescent lights in the windowless laboratory made Tessa hunger for sunshine. But that hunger was as dangerous to fill as the hunger for food that gnawed at her. At this time of day, her body expected breakfast. After a thirty-six hour fast she deserved a box of doughnuts. She'd even settle for a single doughnut hole.

Sigrun gave Gunnar the last of the packaged crackers. Seeing him eat like a normal kid—chewing, swallowing—was food for the soul, at least.

It was so unfair that right after the artificial feeding button was removed from his stomach, Gunnar was cut off from the pleasure of food. When they got out of here, when the drug gang relinquished the Palacio, she wondered what he would want to eat first.

"Dixie needs a walk," Sigrun said.

The German shepherd's ears pricked up and her pink tongue hung from her mouth. Gunnar stroked her head. "I walk too," he said.

Was Gunnar able to walk? Tessa was willing to believe it possible.

Sigrun apparently didn't think he could. "We better let the doggie's master and mistress do it," she said. "Mama's too tired."

Tessa took the obedient dog out of the lab to find Lyle and Isabella. The air in the hall smelled of yesterday's fire.

They found Lyle stretched out on his back on the floor, his head propped by a crumpled white sheet. Isabella sat cross-legged in a meditative pose. When Dixie saw them she made a joyful skip. Lyle sat up at the sound of her claws scratching the floor. True to her discipline, the dog stayed at Tessa's side until Lyle called her forward. Wagging her tail, she smeared Lyle's face with affectionate licks.

To avoid contact, Tessa kept back. She noticed the couple had ditched their surgical masks. "Get any sleep?"

Lyle got to his feet. "I wanted to sleep but the lady here insisted we test the new equipment. Being a gentleman I couldn't let her down. Not the second or third time, either."

Isabella rolled her eyes. "I'd say *in your dreams* but I don't think you slept enough to have any." She looked at Tessa. "We both had a restless night."

"How's his groin wound?" Tessa asked.

"As flattering as it is to have two beautiful women discussing my privates, this is a little awkward," Lyle said.

"It looks okay," Isabella said, ignoring him. "As long as he behaves himself I don't think it'll bleed again."

"Fine, fine," Lyle said. "And how's yours? Maybe I oughtta examine you."

"How is the boy and his mother?" Isabella said.

"They're okay," Tessa replied. She saw no reason to raise the issue of what she saw under the microscope. She couldn't explain it to herself, much less somebody else. "They're hungry."

"Last night I did some—how do you say—*reconnaissance*?" Isabella said.

"You didn't leave the building!"

"No, no. No one could see me. I looked for food. I'm sorry, I didn't find any."

"We don't need it. As long as the gangs don't know we're here, we'll survive."

Isabella nodded. "I have another idea. For a long time I watched video from the security cameras."

"Did you find a way off the peninsula?"

"No. The only way is a long ocean swim, or to go through the battle lines. Sinaloa men patrol the plateau on this side. I think Zetas control the mainland," Isabella said. "But I see maybe a way to get something to eat."

"We can't use the tunnel to the Palacio."

"Not the tunnel," Isabella said. "Outside."

"That's suicide. Between the cameras and the patrols, they'll see us," Tessa said.

"Not this spot," Lyle said, joining in. "We think there's a food depot behind the Annex. It's not in view of any of the security cameras."

"We'll be invisible," Isabella said.

"If you can't see this thing, what makes you think there's food out there?"

"I watched a chimpanzee on the cameras. She came from one side and disappeared. When she came back on a screen on the other side, she was dragging a box of snacks."

"It happened twice," Lyle said. "Must be a storage shed back there. Or maybe a truck they didn't unload. Something."

"Even if you're right, it sounds dangerous." *To say the least. The chimp attack we saw—well, that guy even had a gun, and look what happened to him.*

"The chimps don't come often. I speeded through eight hours of video. They came only two times. Alone."

"We'd have to exit the building through the crash site," Lyle said. "The Annex's main and rear entrances are on camera. We estimate the food depot's maybe thirty yards away. Ten seconds. That's nothing."

"Safe after dark," Isabella said.

"I'll talk to Sigrun about it," Tessa said, "but for now it's not worth the risk. We're all hungry, but we're a long way from starving to death. Take care of your dog. I'm going to check on Cristo."

Lyle's face clouded. "Y'all can't do anything for him. Might be best if you didn't breathe the same air."

"He's my friend," Tessa said. "I promised I'd check on him. He might need water." *And I need to know if he's still alive.*

Lyle nodded. "Gotcha."

Keeping to the shadows, she made her way toward the stairs. A row of windows ahead would expose her to the outside. She dropped to a crawl to stay out of sight. The hard floor bruised her kneecaps. Once inside the security of the stairwell she closed the fire door as quietly as possible.

She paused on the landing, listening to the heavy silence of the fireproof space. Blood rushing through her ears seemed to fill the silence with a roar. Then one real sound broke through. The sound of scratching. Faint, distant—a couple of floors down. Maybe the basement level. *Scratch. Scratch.*

The sound was innocuous but it filled her with dread. She remembered. An Edgar Allen Poe story. A woman buried alive, sealed in her family's underground vault, reanimated, scratching at the stone in a futile attempt to escape her premature tomb. Was Cristo scratching at the door? Not the Cristo she knew, the colleague she trained and worked with, but a walking dead man driven mad by a virus in his brain?

Sameer said the other victims had to be tied down...

The sense of horror couldn't be rationalized away. She swallowed it and started down the stairs.

As she neared the basement, the scratching stopped. She held her breath and listened. *Keep going.*

One more step triggered a flurry of scratching and scuttling sounds. She exhaled. She recognized the sound, and it wasn't a zombie.

White rats were in the stairwell, traveling through the tunnel to the Palacio. They cleared away at her approach and she entered the animal facility unmolested.

Nothing seemed to have changed since last night. Other than the loose rats, the only sign of the lab's former residents was a lingering stench. The door to the dog room was still closed. Afraid of what she would find behind that door, she steeled herself and went in.

"Cristo?" she said softly. She didn't want to scare him.

The reply was immediate. "Tessa?"

Cristo teetered forward from the recesses of the kennel. As he came into the light she examined him. He looked haggard, but not insane. His skin was not flushed and he was neither sweating nor shivering. He sank to the floor. *Weak, but not too weak to stand.* With cautious optimism she sealed the respirator mask against her face and moved a few steps closer to the cage.

"How are you doing?" she asked.

He sat leaning against the wall. "I feel like crap."

"You look better than you did." To be sure, his appearance was frightful: unkempt, dirty. But she watched for muscle tremors or twitches and saw none. His pupils were an appropriate size for the dim light of the cage. Most of all, the wild aggression he exhibited yesterday was gone.

"Better. That's not saying much," he said. "Had a helluva night."

She noted he wasn't wrapped in a blanket. "Do you think you still have a fever?"

"No." He touched his own forehead as if this would tell him. "I got pretty crazy, didn't I?"

"It wasn't your fault."

"I don't remember much." Pause. "I didn't hurt anybody, did I?"

"Heavens, no. I was afraid Dixie might hurt you."

She kept her distance. They stared at each other.

"Are you gonna let me out of this cage?" he asked.

She'd been asking herself the same question. How badly she wanted to! It was killing her to treat him this way. Yet seeing him calm and kind of comfortable made it bearable. She wouldn't improve his situation much by letting him out of the kennel. They were all prisoners now.

"I'm sorry, not yet," she said. "Too many variables."

"You think I've got what Maria had."

"And Juan, too. Sameer thinks it's an encephalitis virus from the chimp colony." She was aware her next words would sound cold, but they were both scientists. Facts mattered. "You're lucid now but we don't know anything about the natural history of this disease. Maybe it's temporary. Maybe you're still infectious."

Cristo snickered. "I don't have a virus."

"You were very sick—"

"It wasn't a virus," he insisted, anger in his voice. She took a step back, wondering if madness simmered just below a calm facade. He quieted and said, "I'm pretty sure it was the plack."

"Plack?"

"The Palacio's special house narcotic." He put his hand over his eyes. "Vargas uses it on lots of patients for post-op pain. He claims it's not addictive." A hollow laugh. "I was fool enough to believe him."

"You're an…" She was about to say, *addict*, but the word sounded so disparaging. "You've been using it."

"For months. No problems. Until this week."

It made sense. "Until you got cut off from your supply."

"Yeah."

Her heart went out to him. She didn't know much about narcotic withdrawal, but his symptoms probably fit. Maybe he wasn't infected with anything. Still, she was afraid to release him yet.

"Got anything to eat?" he asked.

"No. We gave the last to Gunnar."

"How about some fresh water, then?"

She passed the end of a hose through the metal mesh of the cage but did not open the door.

"You don't trust me," he said.

She wasn't taking any chances. Not with Gunnar upstairs. Gunnar, who was either in miraculous recovery or on the verge of death, depending on what you chose to believe.

Was there a way to prove that Cristo wasn't a danger to others? She had data from the nasal swab.

And I bet there are other samples in the freezers.

A testable hypothesis crystallized in her thoughts.

"I can't let you out now," she said. "But I'll be back after I do a couple of experiments. Just tell me one thing."

———————

Whether he liked it or not, Vargas needed to check on his troublesome patient-guest, Luis Angel de la Rosa. The partial dialysis treatment last night had bought them some time to break the siege, but de la Rosa was going to need more dialysis—or a new kidney—soon.

Vargas preferred to give him a kidney. That's what he'd promised. Even though it wasn't his fault the first donor was compromised and the second donor died in a plane crash, he had a bad feeling about discharging de la Rosa without fulfilling his end of the deal. He wanted the de la Rosa problem solved permanently. No unfinished business. No more gang takeovers of his hospital.

The Palacio's cutting-edge technology might offer a solution. Using the personalized medicine techniques that gave his paying guests superior medical care, Vargas was working to tissue-type all of the Mara Salvatruchas and other Sinaloa gangsters on campus. If he was lucky, one of them would be a partial match to de la Rosa. Perfect was no longer the goal. Close enough would be good enough. Rogelio, the transplant surgeon, was still here. They'd match some guy for blood type and a few major tissue antigens, pay him five figures in US dollars (out of Vargas's pocket if necessary), pop out one of his kidneys and send de la Rosa home on anti-rejection drugs. Not ideal for the patient, but better than the ongoing torture of dialysis.

And definitely better for Vargas than having the drug lord die on his watch.

He marched past the men guarding the entrance to de la Rosa's suite. Maybe one of these will match, he thought.

Elaborate tattoos marked all the men. Another complication, he noted. Unsanitary tattooing spreads hepatitis. *I bet half of these losers are infected. That shrinks the pool of potential donors even more.*

Luis Angel de la Rosa sat on a couch several meters back from the windows, gazing out at the besieged campus. He didn't bother to look at Vargas. "My doctor honors me with a visit at last."

Vargas squelched his irritation. Smoothly he grasped de la Rosa's wrist to count the pulse. "Your well-being is my top priority," he said. "Since your people failed to deliver a donor, it falls to me to guarantee your health."

"It wasn't my people who made me shiver like a child in the dialysis room," de la Rosa said.

"If you brought me a kidney, you wouldn't need dialysis."

A chilly pause. Then de la Rosa looked him in the eye.

"I have a reputation. In my business, I reap where I did not sow. You may need to do the same."

Vargas knew exactly what he meant and was not surprised that they were in agreement. "I've already begun. I'm scanning everyone on the peninsula."

"Good. The Zetas have us for now. My forces are new to this area. It's taking time for them to organize an assault from the outside."

"I understand."

"Do you also understand our position? I can't afford to lose the men I have with me."

Vargas swallowed this information. Was the drug lord suggesting the Zetas might actually fight their way in, get past the defenses? God forbid. The Zetas would wreck the place completely. It would be the end of the Palacio. And quite possibly the end of his life, too.

"We only need one man for a kidney," Vargas said. "He'll be back on his feet in a few days."

De la Rosa sneered. "You know, Doctor, I was born in a small village a day's walk from here. That was a simpler time, no? In those days we did not have monkeys of the kind my men described. Giant monkeys strong enough to tear a man to pieces."

Where was de la Rosa going with this? Vargas kept silent. *They're chimpanzees, you ass. Apes. Not monkeys.*

"Or maybe times have not changed so much. Maybe these monkeys aren't from here. Maybe they are, as they say in America, undocumented?"

"Perhaps," Vargas said.

With surprising vitality, de la Rosa rose to his feet. His head reached only as high as Vargas's nose but fearlessly he poked the doctor in the chest with an accusing finger.

"Don't mess with me, Manuel. I know these animals belong to you. Unlike me, you don't know how to control what's yours." He turned his back. "Whatever those monkeys do, I hold you responsible. You owe me for the deaths."

Vargas swallowed hard. "Sir, two of your men—"

"You took them away. They didn't come back. Why?"

Damn, de la Rosa's organization had good communication, if nothing else. If the drug lord already knew about the chimpanzee attack and the two injured men he'd left with Sameer, did he also know something about the virus?

"As I'm sure you know, the men's injuries aren't severe," Vargas said. "Dr. Desai is caring for them. But animals sometimes carry diseases. As a precaution we'll keep your men isolated for a day or two."

"My men tell me the monkeys are mad," de la Rosa said. "Like rabid dogs. Is this why you lost control of your monkeys?"

Again Vargas was unsure how much to reveal. He calculated it was best not to be caught in a lie. "One of my employees released the animals. I guarantee she is no longer in my employ."

"Perhaps this woman was mad, too?"

It dawned on Vargas that he'd underestimated what it took to become leader of a major drug cartel. Sinaloa was more or less a multinational corporation that operated with the extra handicap of being illegal. Even though this street-smart tough guy lacked Vargas's formal education, he had brains.

De la Rosa walked to his wheelchair and sat down. He signaled his bodyguards and said to Vargas, "I want to see my men. Show me."

"Your men are all over the campus," Vargas said. "The last group I saw was in the lobby."

"Not those men. The two you hid away."

Why did de la Rosa want to see those two? Did he dare to let the drug lord in the room with them? What if de la Rosa caught the virus? Would Vargas be blamed?

"Sir, I recommend—"

"I recommend you shut up and do what I tell you."

Vargas shut up. He led the entourage to the elevator. As they descended to the main floor he fantasized about getting his hospital back. *At the rate things are going, I'll be ready to give up a kidney just to get these people out of here.*

Once again he found the door to Sameer's treatment room locked from the inside. The appearance of weakness infuriated him—enduring de la Rosa's cold stare while he banged on the door and waited far too long for Sameer to grant them entrance.

Sameer was gowned from head to toe for protection: face shield, shoe covers, surgical cap. One hand was gloved in latex and held the glove he'd just removed from the other hand to open the door. "I'm in the middle—"

"It can wait," Vargas said, pushing his way in and holding the door for de la Rosa.

He assessed the room at a glance. The patient in the bed appeared to be sleeping; his chest rose and fell softly. The two injured Mara Salvatruchas sat, one on a couch, the other in a recliner. Next to the recliner was a tray of suture materials laid out on a sterile sheet: needles, thread, anesthetic, disinfectant. They'd interrupted Sameer sewing stitches in one man's torn scalp.

De la Rosa's guards wheeled him into the doorway. The MS on the couch sprang to his feet. De la Rosa's wheelchair propped the door open.

"What's going on?" Sameer said in a peevish tone that highlighted his accent.

"Our guest wanted to check on his—"

De la Rosa lifted a semiautomatic pistol. Vargas lost his voice.

Gunshots reverberated off the walls. *How many? Four? Five?*

The standing Mara Salvatrucha slumped to the couch. Sprays of his blood decorated the wall like a monochromatic Jackson Pollock painting.

Without a pause, de la Rosa turned his gun on the other victim of the chimp attack. *Bang.* A head wound that no suture could repair erupted in the man's skull. *Bang. Bang.*

Frozen with shock, Vargas lacked the sensibility to even move himself out of the splash zone.

"No!" Sameer lunged to put himself between the shooter and Juan, his patient in the bed.

Sameer moved too late. More shots. Juan's body shuddered. Sameer staggered back, shielding his face with his arms. The white bedsheet fluttered, fell, and blossomed red.

Then de la Rosa pointed his weapon at Sameer.

Vargas snapped out of it. He didn't posture himself as a human shield but he did put his hands up and shout.

"Wait! Don't shoot! We need him. *You* need him!"

De la Rosa paused, pistol raised. "I can't afford to let my men get sick. Not with enemies at the gate. This one's unclean."

Sameer raised a gloved hand. "I'm not infected. I've protected myself." Sweat dotted his forehead. "Look at me. I follow strict safety protocols. Medical practice. If you doubt it, you can isolate me until you're satisfied."

Vargas became aware of his own lack of proper protective gear. He covered his nose and mouth with his shirt and moved toward the door, away from the aerosolized blood. He leaned toward de la Rosa. "Your next dialysis treatment. I need him there. To give you the best care."

"The best care? Like last time?" de la Rosa snarled. "Doctor, from what I've seen you're good at only two things. Filling me with bad blood. And monkey farming. Can you do anything useful?" He lowered his gun. "But I'll give you and your boy another chance."

"Thank you," Vargas said, bowing.

De la Rosa's guards turned his chair and wheeled him out the door. "I'll be waiting for your surgeon," de la Rosa said. "In the meantime Sinaloa will solve your monkey problem for you."

You do that, Vargas thought. Just tell your morons not to touch the bodies.

The door closed, leaving Vargas and Sameer alone with the three dead men. Vargas pressed the fabric of his shirt tighter against his nose. He forced himself to wait for de la Rosa to go away, then opened the door and positioned himself as far out of the room as possible.

"You're welcome," he said.

Sameer looked at him, astounded. "I'm to thank you for this massacre?"

"I saved your life," Vargas said.

Sameer snorted. "Oh, yes, doctor, I'm so *grateful* you asked him not to kill me. Such *generosity* from you."

"You don't get it, do you? Until we replace his kidney, that psychopath has the power of life and death over both of us."

Sameer glared at him. "I understand," he said. "Why didn't you? *Before* you brought him here?"

"This wouldn't have happened if you hadn't lost control of the chimps."

"So it's my fault these men are dead?" Sameer gestured at the bodies around them. "And the boy in the MRI suite? And my friends on the airstrip?"

Vargas noticed Sameer was inching toward him with clenched fists and rising voice. Did he want to fight? Vargas couldn't remember being in a brawl in his whole life. But he was ready to take on the skinny Indian, if he had to. A geek slugfest.

Except that Sameer's gown was splattered with blood. No roundhouse punch could protect him from the invisible enemy in the room.

"Clean yourself up before it's too late. I'll check the latest typing data. There's a kidney here somewhere. We'll dialyze de la Rosa tonight and do the transplant tomorrow morning. All right?"

Sameer didn't look like he was "all right" with this plan. Vargas raised his hands in surrender.

"My friend, I need you to work with me on this," he said. "What's done is done. We've got to focus on the future. Work on getting Sinaloa out of our hospital."

"I'll give that monster the medical care he needs. Whether he deserves it or not. But you need to help me with Juan."

"Juan?"

"My patient. Your employee. The victim." Sameer's words dripped icicles. "We can't leave him like this. Or the other two."

Victim, my ass, Vargas thought. De la Rosa's bullets shaved maybe a couple of hours off that guy's natural life span. "Good point. You have my permission to do whatever seems appropriate," he said.

As he spun and strode away, he sensed that a half-second later Sameer was going to hit him.

CHAPTER 16

Lyle, Isabella, and Dixie were absent from their hallway camp when Tessa crept back to the laboratory from her visit to the basement. She figured they were probably trying to get Dixie to poop somewhere in the building.

No time to wonder about them. I've got work to do. She opened the laboratory door to the sound of wailing.

In a rush she closed the door and ran to Gunnar's little section of floor between the lab benches. He was sitting on his rump, half whining, half sobbing at the top of his lungs. His surgical mask lay crumpled a couple of feet away, as far as he could throw.

"I want Dixie!" he howled, tears rolling down his flushed cheeks.

A robust tantrum complete with kicking and screaming—it was such a normal, healthy kid thing to do, it actually brought a smile to her face. Six months ago he couldn't have pulled it off.

The smile faded when she saw Sigrun.

The boy's mother was on the floor next to him in their nest, cocooned in a blanket. Her face was even more pale than usual. Her right arm protruded from the layers of insulation as she tried to console her son by stroking his head.

Sigrun's outstretched arm was shaking.

Tessa went cold inside. *Maria had a tremor like that. Before she went mad.*

She rummaged through a cabinet, searching for something safe for Gunnar to play with. She found a roll of Parafilm, a long thin sheet of paraffin food wax that could be stretched and molded a bit like modeling clay.

"Here, Gunnar. Check this out." She tore off a piece of the film and showed him how to pull it to many times its original size.

It worked. The novelty of the wax was enough to occupy him. At least for a moment, he stopped crying. She turned her attention to Sigrun.

"Hey, are you okay?"

"I'm fine," Sigrun said. "Just a headache from sleeping on the floor."

Tessa touched the woman's forehead. Hot. "I'll get you some aspirin."

Until she did her experiments today, she wouldn't know for certain the meaning of Sigrun's fever, headache, and tremor. But the evidence she had so far suggested it was bad. Possibly very bad.

Even if Cristo isn't infected, Sameer believes there's a killer virus around.

As she fetched the pills, a tiny part of her brain stopped designing experimental controls and wondered what to do with Gunnar if—a big, inconceivable, never-let-it-happen if—his mother died. She had a vainglorious image of herself consoling the boy, taking Sigrun's place, loving and caring for the orphan with the terrible prognosis.

The image terrified her. She was unfit and unworthy to be a mother. If it was her destiny to save Gunnar, she would have to save Sigrun first.

After doing what little she could to comfort Sigrun and to settle Gunnar, she retreated to her lab bench. She'd come up with a possible explanation for the mysterious infection that had struck Maria and Juan. It was a "good" explanation in the scientific sense that she could test it. Beyond that, she did not allow herself to form an opinion about whether this explanation was desirable or not. Her experiments must first determine whether or not it was true.

Before leaving Cristo, she'd questioned him about the neuropathology work he'd done recently. She dug through the lab freezer in search of his samples. She found the small plastic tubes. They contained tiny droplets that thawed in seconds. She stacked the tubes in a bucket of crushed ice.

This morning I lost faith in science. I accused my microscope of lying.

But the science hadn't failed. The scientist had. She'd made a correct observation (Negri bodies) and drawn an incorrect conclusion (the boy is dying). She'd repeated the mistake with Cristo, seeing illness and assuming infection.

Not again. I'll trust my experiments but question my interpretation.

Something strange was happening in the microbial world around her. She'd better keep her mind prepared for the unexpected.

The kidney was a crappy match but it would do in a pinch.

Vargas sensed a pinch was coming.

He stared at the computer monitor in his office. One of the gangsters he'd screened was sort of, kind of a match for de la Rosa's tissue type. With enough anti-rejection drugs, the kidney would work. Maybe.

If they couldn't get de la Rosa out of the Palacio or get fresh dialysis fluid within twenty-four hours, good enough would have to be good enough. Not only for the patient, but to save Vargas's ass. If this kidney was the closest match available, so be it.

I'd better follow up with the potential donor now. Interview the guy about his health. And get a fresh blood sample to do a more thorough type and cross.

The name on the file was El Matador Rojo. Whatever. As long as the other gangsters could point out the guy.

He left his office to track down El Matador. To his relief he didn't have to go anywhere near de la Rosa's part of the building. It was best to avoid contact with the drug lord unless absolutely necessary. Just being in the same room with the man was unnerving.

The Mara Salvatruchas in the lobby told him El Matador was out on the grounds, probably on patrol.

He thanked them curtly and hustled out of there. As he crossed the lobby, he noticed a large, discolored rectangle marking the spot on the tile floor where a fine woven rug used to lie. He wondered where they'd taken the rug—and the body wrapped in it. He would have to find out later. He exited the hospital by way of the Serenity Garden.

The Palacio campus was quiet now but everywhere he could see evidence of the cartels' war. The road was littered with torn leaves and palms. The hospital's perimeter wall was pock-marked. In one section of the wall, a shell had blasted a hole large enough for a man to walk through.

So many repair jobs. Trivial, of course, in comparison to the damage to his Research Annex. He'd be lucky if he didn't have to tear it down. Money money money.

Yet suddenly it struck him that the financial cost of this regrettable deal with Sinaloa was no longer his number one concern.

He just wanted to survive.

Something rustled in the forest to his right. He thought of the Mara Salvatrucha lying on his beautiful rug in the lobby, bones crushed and guts spilled. Gangsters' guns weren't the only thing to fear on the grounds of the Palacio today.

His pulse quickened and he searched the road for a patrol. Some gun-toting toughs would be welcome company about now.

The crackling of foliage grew louder. He was alone on the road. The guardhouse at the main gate lay ahead. He picked up his pace to a jog, aiming for that shelter, where he hoped to find armed protection.

In his peripheral vision he glimpsed branches swaying. Something was moving through the trees toward him.

He ran.

CRACK.

"Freeze!"

The warning shot had cut close. He was pretty sure he'd felt the bullet's breeze. Obediently he froze and raised his hands.

"I'm Dr. Vargas," he said slowly, clearly, to the unseen patrolman in the woods. "I'm working under de la Rosa's orders. I'm looking for El Matador Rojo."

He took a chance, lowered his arms and turned around. Three scruffy guards wearing muddy boots were aiming weapons at him.

"El Matador?" The apparent leader shouldered his rifle. "He's on patrol. In the woods."

Great. "Can you find him for me?"

The man spat on the ground. "You got any cigarettes?"

"No, I haven't. Where is El Matador? I—your boss needs to bring him in."

"Hell if I know. His group's been gone for two hours."

"Can you lead me to where he might be?"

The leader looked him over from head to toe. "You sure you don't got any cigarettes?"

"No. Smoking isn't allowed at the Palacio." He looked down his nose at the man. *Good thing de la Rosa doesn't need a brain transplant because nobody out here has one.*

"Is that so," the man said. He slipped a cigarette out of the pack in his front pocket and lit it.

I will not be played. Wait for him to answer the question.

After a drag and a thick blow of smoke the man replied. "We're going back in the trees. You come."

Me? Vargas felt the perfect fit of his feet in his designer Italian shoes. He looked at mud on the men's boots and sighed. *Another expense.* "Take me to El Matador."

The ground was dry for his first few steps into the forest. As they moved deeper into shade, the earth grew damp and his feet sank into the loam. The smooth leather soles of his shoes were designed to tread the corridors of power, not guerrilla paths in the jungle. They slipped a little with each step. Mud slopped onto the sides of his shoes. The three Mara Salvatruchas led him without apparent purpose, strolling, sometimes laughing.

Maybe the noise will scare off the chimps, he thought. Then again, if they're mad, maybe it will attract them.

A shadow passed overhead. Too small to be an arboreal primate. Just a bird. "Did you hear about the chimpanzee attacks?" he said.

"Yeah. If we see one we'll kill it." The man confidently slapped the stock of his rifle.

You'll have to move fast, he thought. The chimps do.

Leafy branches brushed his pinstriped trousers, wetting them with dew. Butterflies vanished and reappeared as they flitted from sun to shade and back. Funny that he'd never walked in the Palacio's forest before. Not missing much, he decided. Bugs and snakes.

The hum of the outer electric fence told him they were getting close to the ridge, the edge of the no man's land between them and the Zetas down below on the mainland.

Something struck the ground in front of him. He recoiled, expecting it to blow up. It didn't, but a second object fell from the sky. It struck the leader of his little group. The man shouted a curse.

The missile was a fruit, some kind of guava. Overripe and rotten. It exploded on the man's shoulder, spraying him with smelly, sticky sap.

The other men laughed. Vargas didn't.

"*Idiotas!* Look for a chimp!"

Inhuman shrieks jerked his head skyward. Outlined against the bright sun he saw the shape of a chimpanzee in the canopy. Boughs rattled and swayed as it leaped in their direction.

"Shoot it!" he cried.

The three armed men swung their weapons around, firing wildly. The stream of bullets shredded foliage. He tried to run. Fragments of tree bark hit his face. The chimp shrieked again.

He managed one stride before his fancy footwear betrayed him. One leg slid forward, the other lagged behind. He fell. The back of his head hit the ground hard. Pain flared in his groin thanks to the twisted leg underneath him. Eyes looking up, he saw the chimp hurl toward the ground.

She landed—he could see now that it was one of the females—a few meters from him.

She was dead.

He scrambled through the decaying matter on the forest floor, trying to put distance between himself and the potentially infected corpse.

"We got it!" the Mara Salvatruchas celebrated. Vargas wasn't impressed. Given the number of rounds they fired, even he could've hit the thing.

"Good job," he said as he caught his breath. "Now let's find—"

Gunfire resumed. Confused, he glanced once more at his escorts. They weren't doing the shooting. The shots were coming *toward* them, from his left.

Zetas?

The Mara Salvatruchas ducked and hollered. Vargas did the same.

"Hold your fire! The monkey's down!"

Then he heard a blood-curdling scream. Another ape, just as deranged as the one they'd killed, came crashing toward them.

Except this one came on foot. Armed with an automatic rifle.

Because this ape was a man.

Based on the tattoos, the shooter was one of de la Rosa's soldiers. He advanced with jerky movements, uttering wordless cries of pain. He waved his rifle and every second or two randomly pulled the trigger. Terrified, Vargas flattened his body against the earth. Too-close hits kicked up mud droplets that splattered his hair.

The Mara Salvatruchas returned fire. A spray of bullets perforated the attacker's body. He keeled over.

Stunned silence washed over the survivors.

Vargas stood up. His escorts approached the fallen body with weapons ready, but there was no longer need for caution.

"We found your guy," the leader said, poking the dead man with his boot.

Vargas felt like he'd been punched in the gut. "El Matador?"

"The one you were looking for."

Pink foam trickled from the man's mouth. Bloodstains marked numerous bullet wounds in his torso.

"No, goddammit." Not that it did any good to say it. Even when he was in full control of the Palacio he couldn't resurrect the dead. El Matador Rojo's kidneys were of no use to anyone now.

He didn't know what upset him more. That he'd just lost his best chance to transplant de la Rosa and get him out of the Palacio alive.

Or that El Matador proved the encephalitis virus was spreading.

CHAPTER 17

Hunger was making Tessa light-headed. As she reached for the mouse at the lab's computer, her hand trembled.

I need sugar.

Data were coming in from her gene amplification and sequencing experiments. Data she hoped would explain things.

While the computer compared the gene sequences against a library of banked sequence data, she jotted notes. If her hypothesis was true, it was going to have to explain a lot.

She wrote.

Mysteries:

- Cristo: sick after exposure to bats in cave
- Cristo: recovery
- Cristo: sick again (??? plack withdrawal)
- Lab animals (esp. chimps): aggression and death
- Animal lab technicians: sick/dead
- Sigrun: sick

She hesitated, then wrote:

- Gunnar: Negri bodies in tissue
- Gunnar: clinical recovery

She had a hunch these last two were pieces of the same puzzle.

Light flashed from the screen. The computer had finished aligning the sequences.

For thirty minutes she swam through the data, manipulating, cross-checking, challenging. She'd analyzed samples from ten sources—some from multiple tissues—taken from humans and animals, now and in the recent past. She reviewed the list of samples and her notes about each.

Specimen #1:   **Bat (crushed tissue)**
Date: July 30 Tissue remnants extracted from Cristo's clothing after attack in cave. Sample previously tested by Cristo.

Specimen #2:   **Cristo (nasal swab; blood)**
Date: August 3   Early symptoms after bat bites

Specimen #3:   **Cristo (nasal swab)**
Date: August 22 Yesterday; symptomatic

Specimen #4:   **Dog (brain tissue; blood; liver)**
Date: August 21 Lab animal; aggressive (bit Juan); animal killed

Specimen #5:   **Gunnar (nasal swab)**
Date: July 15 Standard protocol biweekly sampling

Specimen #6:   **Gunnar (nasal swab)**
Date: August 1   Standard protocol biweekly sampling

Specimen #7:   **Gunnar (nasal swab)**
Date: August 15 Standard protocol biweekly sampling

Specimen #8:   **Gunnar (nasal swab)**
Date: August 23 Today

Specimen #9:   **Tessa Price (nasal swab)**
Date: August 23   Today

Specimen #10:   **Sigrun Baldursdottir**
Date: August 23   Today

She'd tested all of these for viral nucleic acids. The tests generated a huge amount of data. From this haystack of gene sequences, the computer program found not one needle, but three.

The specimens contained genomes from three viruses. The three viruses were related to one another.

She pursed her lips. She had expected two.

According to the sequence alignment, the first virus came from a bat that attacked Cristo in the cave. He'd tested the bats himself weeks ago. Her data confirmed his results. The bat was infected with an untyped *Lyssavirus*.

Which explained why the bats were in Mexico out of season. The whole colony was suffering from an infectious disease of the brain.

She moved on to previously untested material: the specimens taken from Cristo when he got sick after being bitten by the bats.

Here she found proof that the bats had infected Cristo with their virus. Four days after his ordeal in the cave, the *Lyssavirus* was inside his body. Almost certainly that's what had made him sick, kept him home from work, and prompted Tessa's trip to Mexico.

Lucky for him, the bat virus turned out to be nasty but not deadly in humans. Cristo recovered.

Her big question now: was he having a relapse?

She examined the information on the screen and papers in front of her. With a burst of pleasure, she clapped her hands. The nasal swab she took from him yesterday was virus-free.

No relapse. It really was drug withdrawal that brought him down. She could let him out of the makeshift isolation ward.

In addition to the bat virus, she had expected to find one other virus in her tests. This second virus dutifully turned up, in Gunnar. It was the modified rabies virus they were using to deliver his gene therapy. She'd created it herself and practically knew every nucleotide of its genome. This modified rabies was *supposed* to be in the boy's nose. And it was.

The computer showed that these two viruses were genetic cousins. No surprise. She knew rabies was related to the *Lyssavirus* family. Both kinds of virus were often found in bats.

But the surprise was, the computer had teased out a third viral genome. A new genome that didn't match any virus in the database.

A feeling of dread. *When it comes to viruses,* new *is not a good thing.*

Of course the gene sequence wasn't *entirely* original. The new virus looked an awful lot like rabies but also had pieces of the *Lyssavirus* in it. Like a poker hand with cards drawn from two decks, the new virus combined gene sequences from the other two.

Then she understood.

The third virus was a revertant.

No!

She'd suspected. Now here was proof. The bat virus and therapeutic rabies virus had traded genes. Like a couple hooking up in a bar, they met inside a cell. They had a lot in common. They swapped bodily fluids. Their genes mixed and shuffled into a new combination.

The result? A royal flush. Best cards from both viruses. The deadly infectious power of rabies plus the power to breed.

Gunnar's treatment virus which she'd carefully engineered to be infertile had found a way to replace the gene sequences she'd removed. It got the genes it needed to replicate from its wild cousin, *Lyssavirus*.

Her gene therapy rabies virus had reverted to wild type—or something worse. It was multiplying.

A rapid, patterned knock on the door interrupted her work. Lyle, Isabella, and Dixie let themselves into the lab.

Their faces were uncovered. *Fools.* "Stay in the hall," she shouted, "and get some masks on. I'll be right out."

Gunnar stirred. "Dog? Dixie stay?"

No one answered the child. As Dixie and her masters turned toward the hall, he started to cry.

She grabbed her notes and headed for the door. "Gunnar, I'll be right back." His plaintive protest increased in volume. The sound made her heart bleed. "I'll bring the dog."

Out in the hall, Lyle helped Isabella fit a respirator over her elegant cheekbones. Then he put his on. They looked at Tessa with a guarded expression in their eyes.

"You fixin' to tell us something?" Lyle said.

"I did some experiments," she said. "To find out if there's a germ going around, and if so, what it is."

"And?" Isabella said.

"You want the good news or the bad news first?"

"Good," Lyle said.

"Cristo's going to be fine. We can go downstairs and let him out."

"He's not infected?"

"No," Isabella said. "He's kicking the habit." She looked at Tessa for confirmation.

"That's what he says," Tessa replied, "and my data don't dispute that. How did you—"

"I talked to him about it. Because I could see it in his eyes," Isabella said. "Are his pupils back to normal?"

"Yes," Tessa said, amazed that Isabella had picked up on this side effect of narcotic use.

"So what's the bad news?" Lyle said. "No room service tonight?"

"I found a virus," Tessa said. "I think it killed Maria. And I think it drove the chimpanzees mad."

"Is it catchy?" Lyle asked.

She nodded. "I told you it was bad news."

"Well, if Cristo hasn't got it, what's the worry?"

Gunnar was howling on the other side of the door. She suppressed a surge of anxiety. *Think clearly. Lay it out logically.*

"The virus is here, among us. I can show you its history."

She opened a blank page in her notebook and wrote, in chronologic order, the result from each test and an explanation of what it meant.

Specimen #5:   **Gunnar**
> *Result:* + Rabies virus (gene therapy modified)

"I expected Gunnar to be carrying this rabies virus. It's what we use to treat him."

Specimen #1:   **Bat**

Specimen #2:   **Cristo**
> *Result:* + Lyssavirus

"Cristo caught this virus from a bat. It made him sick last month, but his immune system cleared it. I can't detect it in his body any more."

Specimen #6:   **Gunnar**
> *Result:* + Rabies virus (gene therapy modified) + Lyssavirus

She took a deep breath. "Gunnar was never anywhere near a bat or a cave. But he was around Cristo a lot. Cristo infected him with the bat *Lyssavirus*. Probably through the air, by breathing or sneezing on him."

Isabella's eyebrows rose.

Tessa continued. "Unlike Cristo, Gunnar didn't really get sick. Sigrun says he had some mild symptoms about that time. Two weeks later—"

Specimen #7:   **Gunnar**
> *Result:* + Rabies virus (gene therapy modified) + REVERTANT

"—Gunnar's body had cleared the bat *Lyssavirus*, but acquired something else."

"What's a revertant?" Lyle said.

It's a statistical impossibility, a freak, my worst nightmare...

"It's a combination of the virus I made crossed with the wild bat virus. A mutant, if you will."

"That doesn't sound good," Lyle said.

"Is this revertant dangerous?" Isabella asked.

Does that word begin to describe it?

"Genetically it's very similar to rabies. Rabies infects the brain, causes aggression, paralysis, and death." She paused. "Maria had those symptoms. Some of the chimpanzees, too. And—"

She wrote.

Specimen #4:   Dog
> *Result:* + REVERTANT

"—at least one dog."

"Dog? Which dog?" Lyle exclaimed, protectively reaching for Dixie.

"One of the lab animals. A beagle that was put down after it attacked Maria. According to my data, it was infected with the revertant."

"So it can spread!" Isabella said with alarm. "Cristo carried it to the animals?"

Tessa shook her head. "It's true the revertant was in the animal facility. But Cristo didn't bring it there."

Specimen #3:   Cristo
> *Result:* NO VIRUS

"He never tested positive for the revertant, not even yesterday," she said. "He was never a carrier."

Lyle tightened the seal of his mask around his nose. "Then where's it coming from?"

And that, my friend, is the heart of the matter. Her vision clouded. More tears, but not tears of joy this time.

Specimen #8:   Gunnar
> *Result:* + REVERTANT

As she wrote the words, this bit of molecular trivia spit out by a computer became real to her.

The source of this frightening new virus wasn't locked away in a basement cage, or hiding in the forests outside, or in a cave in distant mountains. It was here on the floor with them.

Gunnar.

The revertant was spreading *from him.*

A long silence followed. Lyle put a friendly hand on her shoulder. "Well if that don't beat all."

She swallowed hard and blinked a few times. "He's the source. The revertant was born inside him. The bat virus met the gene therapy virus inside one of his cells. While Cristo was home sick, Maria took Gunnar to visit the chimpanzees. I think that's how the revertant got into the animal facility."

"The kid bit a chimp?" Lyle said, trying to make light.

"This isn't an ordinary rabies virus. You don't need a bite to transmit it. It can spread through the air. Like flu."

"Good Lord."

The pity she felt for Gunnar became a physical pain in her shoulders and neck. *Poor child. Poor, cursed child.* As if he didn't have enough problems, this one-in-a-million biological disaster happens to *him.* And—

"There's more." She wrote.

Specimen #10:   Sigrun Baldursdottir
   Result: + REVERTANT

"Are you sure?" Lyle said.

"It's not just a test result," she said. "She's symptomatic."

"We've been with the boy!" Isabella cried. "And the mother." She clutched Lyle's arm.

Lyle put his hand on Isabella's. "What about you?" he said to Tessa. "You've spent the most time with them."

"So far I'm okay. I tested myself this morning. Negative for all three viruses. If you want, I can test you."

"And Dixie? Can you test her?"

"Yes, but I wouldn't worry about her. Are her vaccines up to date?"

"Are there tornadoes in Oklahoma? Hell yes."

"Good. I have a theory." *Or a selfish hope?* "I'm guessing that people and animals who are vaccinated against rabies will be immune to the revertant, too."

"What makes you think so?" Isabella said.

"The fact that Gunnar is infected but the virus isn't making him sick. Also, Cristo and I have been spared despite being around him so much. We both got rabies shots as part of the clinical trial."

Lyle bent down and gave his dog a hug. "If you're right, then Dixie's safe."

"But we are not," Isabella said.

"There's something we can do," Tessa said. "For Sigrun, and for you."

CHAPTER 18

Tessa's face was hot with emotion when she opened the lab refrigerator. For a moment the cool air and laden shelves made her think of a well-stocked kitchen—milk, eggs, a chilled bottle of chardonnay…

Forget it. Even if one of the bottles, tubes, boxes, or bags contained something edible, eating it would be unwise, to say the least. This refrigerator was plastered with garish orange biohazard stickers and a potpourri of diamond-shaped chemical hazard labels.

No matter. She wasn't scrounging for food.

Dozens of plastic boxes loaded with milliliter tubes were stacked in piles amid bottles of liquids, some red, some colorless. There were Petri dishes filled with sheets of gelatin-like agar, and a bottle of 190-proof ethanol. She made a mental note of the alcohol. It was intended for lab use but you never knew when such a thing might come in handy.

"Where are you?" she said to the clutter. Cristo must have this stuff organized in some fashion. Where would he keep the biologics?

The drawer. She yanked it open.

Where she kept cheese and deli meat at home, here she found drugs. She scanned the labels.

"Yes!" No one in the lab heard her rejoice. Gunnar was blubbering in his nest, calling out for Dixie. Sigrun dozed hot and shivering at his side.

She checked the expiration date on the box. The freeze-dried vaccine was still good.

On a less-happy note, so was the vial of plack she found in the drawer. *Cristo, you would thank me if you were here.* She dumped the drug down the drain.

"Gunnar baby, I'll be back soon." She didn't wait for a response.

Out in the hall, she triumphantly lifted her small prize in front of Lyle and Isabella. "Found it."

"Whatcha got there?" Lyle said.

"Rabies vaccine. If I'm right about the revertant virus, a shot of this should protect you and help Sigrun."

"A rabies shot for people?" Isabella asked.

"Yep. They don't make it just for dogs. Anybody working on my gene therapy project has had one. Even me. And believe me, I hate shots."

She dumped the contents of the box on the blankets. The wind went out of her sails.

Damn.

Two sealed pouches fell out. Lyle picked one up and read the label.

"One dose per package," he said. "Not enough."

"We need at least three. For both of you plus one for Sigrun."

"She's already sick," Isabella said.

"If she had ordinary rabies, it'd be too late for a vaccine to help. But this virus is something different. I'm hoping a shot will boost her immune system at least a little." *And give her a fighting chance at survival.*

"Give her my dose," Lyle said. "The boy needs his mother. I don't like shots, either."

"No," Isabella said, putting her arms around Lyle. "Take mine. I am young and strong. I will keep the mask close to my face."

Tessa fingered the two pouches. Each contained a vial with a trace of dried vaccine material, a bit of sterile liquid to dissolve it in, and the necessary syringes and needle. "It's possible to split a dose."

Lyle looked at Isabella. "One for Sigrun, one for us to share?" he said.

Isabella put her cheek against his chest. "Yes."

"She's the boss. Will half a dose work?" Lyle asked.

"I don't know," Tessa said. "I don't even know if a full dose will work. I don't know anything for sure. This is all guesswork."

The lovers clasped hands. Dixie licked their intertwined fingers.

"Let's do it," Lyle said. "In the arm?"

Oh my. I can't.

Such a simple thing, anyone could do it. Inject the liquid into the vaccine vial. Wipe the patient's shoulder with disinfectant. Withdraw the liquid with a needle. Stab the shoulder. Done.

Anyone except Tessa Price, med school dropout and extreme needle-phobe. Just the thought of doing one stab turned her stomach. Doing it on three different people was out of the question.

She could have them stick each other. Or—

"I'll be right back." Without explanation, she dashed down the hall toward the stairs.

Cristo can do it. I'm sure he's done plenty of injections into animals.

The white rats in the basement stairwell scrambled out of her way. A few doors later she burst into the dog room of the animal facility, startling its sole occupant.

Cristo rose to his feet inside the dog run. "You want to give me a heart attack?"

She approached the door and curled her fingers around the wire mesh. "How are you?"

"I'd like to join the human race again."

She grabbed the key and unlocked the door. "You're substituting one cage for another. You can't leave this building."

He stretched his arms over his head and stepped out. "I'll take it."

They shared a quick hug and headed for the stairs. As they climbed, she explained to him what she'd learned about the revertant and what she'd guessed about the protective power of the rabies vaccine.

"You might want to isolate yourself," she said. "Just in case."

"I've been sick with everything already. I'll stay with Gunnar."

They picked up a spare needle on their way. Lyle waved as they approached.

"You look much better," Isabella said to Cristo. Then she loosed a torrent in Spanish.

Tessa couldn't catch enough words to make sense of the speech but the tone was scolding. Cristo looked at his shoes and didn't respond. *Weird.*

"Glad to have you back with us, *amigo*," Lyle said.

"He's going to administer the vaccine," Tessa said. She didn't explain why. "You still want to share the dose?"

"You bet," Lyle said.

She helped Cristo organize what he needed but as soon as the first needle came out, she turned away. Lyle and Isabella didn't make a peep when he did the injections.

How do people do that? she wondered.

"Done," he said.

"Thank you," she said with real gratitude. *Now let's hope half a dose is enough.*

"I feel better already," Lyle said.

Isabella scoffed. He kissed her wrist. "Don't worry, hon, I don't do things halfway," he said. "When we get home, Dixie's vet can give you the rest of your share."

His girlfriend swatted him.

"We need to take this to Sigrun," Tessa said, collecting the last dose of the rabies vaccine. She considered asking if it was all right to take Dixie into the lab with her. She'd promised Gunnar she would bring the dog. But without solid proof that the dog was immune to the revertant, she couldn't risk putting Dixie in close contact with the boy.

The decision to return without Dixie pained her. In the past, she'd made too many promises she couldn't keep.

"Y'all have fun in there," Lyle said. "The lady and I are gonna find a barbecue joint."

Isabella rolled her eyes.

"Don't you dare leave this building," Tessa said.

———————

Sameer trembled with rage as he looked at the bodies of the two Mara Salvatruchas and Juan, the lab tech. So much needless death. Blood on Vargas's hands.

Vargas should never have allowed Sinaloa to control his hospital. These people are evil.

He predicted there would be more deaths. Though his life had been spared for the moment, he was pessimistic about his chances in the coming days. Between the virus swirling invisibly in the air of this contaminated room and the impulsive violence of Luis Angel de la Rosa, he did not foresee a happy ending.

He was a young man and had given little consideration to his own death. His Hindu family had cultivated in him a belief in life after death. He accepted that belief in an abstract way: other people's deaths, other people's souls. The thought that his own soul might soon make such a journey was strange to him. Might he be reincarnated here on earth? Or would his being transcend this world and move to the next?

There were no answers, and this was not the time for contemplation. It was a time for action. If he was going to die here at the Palacio, it was too late to attain self-knowledge through meditation, or to choose the blessed life of an ascetic. He could, however, accumulate the grace of good deeds in whatever hours or days he had left.

Vargas and de la Rosa twisted the people around them toward disgrace. Only by standing up to them could he keep his feet on a path of honor.

I will not submit. I will do what is right.

His first act of charity was to take care of Juan's body. A proper funeral for the man was impossible without relatives present. Nor could he arrange for Juan to be cremated until the siege ended. But he could prepare the body with a ritual cleansing. Nothing elaborate, nothing stupid. He'd wear double gloves and a tight mask. The hospital room was stocked with towels, gauze, and sponges that he could use. He gathered them and searched for a vessel to serve as a bucket.

His work was interrupted when the door opened. Two armed men hesitated to cross the threshold. They pointed their weapons at him. "Come with us."

Fear and anger tightened his gut. Time to choose.

He crossed his arms in defiance. "I'm tending to the dead." He pointed at the corpses of the MS. "Your friends? De la Rosa murdered them."

If his words made them feel anything, they did not show it. "Let's go," one said.

"I'm busy."

The larger of the pair put away his gun, strode into the room, and in one swift motion punched Sameer in the stomach.

Breath left him. He doubled over and dropped to his knees, stunned.

Unfamiliar pain type. Diffuse. Visceral. No one had ever hit him like that before.

The man retreated to the doorway. "You come or we shoot."

Hunched over and gasping, he tried to focus, to examine his conscience. *Do I go with these men or not?*

Do not submit. Choose what is right.

With his head down, the butt of the rifle came into view too late to brace himself. It struck his temple, twisting his neck. Flashes of nonexistent light danced in his eyes.

I know this kind of pain. Sharp. Somatic.

Both types of pain were astonishingly effective at changing his mind. A detached part of him realized he'd been coddled his whole life. He could give pain a name but until this moment he didn't really know what it was.

He managed to squeeze out two words before they could strike him again. "I'll come."

Gunnar shouted, "Cristo!"

Tessa closed the door of the laboratory behind her. The boy was so excited to see Cristo, he forgot about Dixie. For the moment she wasn't in trouble for failing to bring the dog.

Gunnar talked and talked, telling Cristo a tale in three- and four-word sentences. In ten seconds he spoke more words than she'd heard him use in the whole time she'd known him.

Then he grasped the handles of the cabinet drawers around him and pulled himself to his feet.

She watched in amazement. He let go. And stood. Without any help. Without hanging on to anything.

Wow.

"Look at you," Cristo said, "getting so strong!"

Clearly the kid was not about to die of rabies. She wanted to give him a hug. Cristo beat her to it.

"I'm hungry," Gunnar said. "Do you have crackers?"

"Sorry *mijo*," Cristo said. "No crackers until Christmas."

"Christmas?"

Cristo ruffled the boy's hair. "Just kidding. Not that long. But you have to wait a little longer."

"Mama's hungry. It makes her tired."

Two steps forward, one step back. Now it was Sigrun who lay weak and helpless in the blankets. Mother and son had switched roles.

"Give her the vaccine," Tessa said.

Cristo needed only a minute to do the job. Sigrun stirred and thanked them in a weak voice. Then Tessa and Cristo stepped to the other side of the room, out of Sigrun's hearing.

"You think she's infected with the revertant?" he said. "She's not acting crazy like Maria and Juan did."

"She tested positive so she must have it. Maybe it causes two different syndromes. Rabies does. Maria and Juan had the 'furious' form. Maybe she's reacting differently. With something milder."

"The paralytic form of rabies is not milder. You don't see the aggression but the animals end up just as dead," he said.

"I know." *I can hope. This virus is new. Anything's possible.*

He arranged a stack of papers on the desk. "You know the vaccine won't help her. It's too late."

"We can't be sure."

He didn't argue. There was no point. The evidence was on his side. Vaccines activated the immune system but it took days or weeks to mobilize a full response. At the rate Sigrun was declining, the virus would kill her first.

Ignore the facts. Find a way, somehow. Because Gunnar needs his mother.

"Look at him," she said. "Did you think he would ever stand again?"

Cristo smiled. "He got so much better while I was gone."

"No cause and effect," she joked.

But the correlation between Gunnar's remarkable improvement and Cristo's absence had been nagging her. Not that his absence had literally been good for Gunnar, but that Cristo fell ill and the revertant virus appeared at the same time the boy started to change.

Oh my God. What if...

"Cristo, why *did* he get better after you left?" she said.

"He tries harder when I'm not around?"

"Seriously. I saw changes under the microscope. His cells started to clear up right about the time you got sick."

He shrugged. "Coincidence. Maybe it takes six months for the gene therapy to work."

"I don't think so. Because the same time the Batten disease inclusions disappeared from his neurons, something else turned up. Negri bodies."

"The cellular marker for rabies?"

"Yes." Her ideas were coming together into a frightening, revolutionary explanation. "Our rabies virus didn't cause the Negri bodies. I think the revertant did. It started to grow inside his body at that time."

"That makes sense," Cristo agreed.

"He's the only person in history to have Negri bodies but not rabies disease."

"How does that explain that he can see and eat and stand up?" he said.

That was the question, and with each passing second she was more convinced she knew the answer. "It's the revertant."

He rested his chin in his hand, thinking.

She continued. "The revertant replicates. It multiplies in his body. He's probably got a thousand times more revertant virus in him than gene therapy virus."

"He's lucky to be alive," Cristo said. "That much should kill him."

"That's what I thought when I saw the pathology slides. But the fact is, he's better than ever. So we're back to the question: why?"

"Well, we made him immune to rabies. He must have enough antibodies in his blood to keep the revertant under control."

"Agreed. He's a carrier. He's carrying the revertant, spreading it to other people, and he's getting better." She quelled an urge to stamp her foot. *Come on, Cristo—am I on the right track?*

A flash of understanding in his face. "You sequenced the viruses?"

"Yes."

"The revertant shares DNA with your engineered rabies?"

"Yes."

"Does it have the therapy gene—the one that fixes Batten disease?"

"Yes!"

"*Ay, Dios.*" His assessment gave her a thrill of excitement and horror. "The revertant is a cure."

The words rushed from her mouth. "Yes, yes, that's what I think, too! When we made our treatment safe—by blocking its ability to replicate—we made it worthless. We traded effectiveness for safety. In order to work, the virus *must* be able to reproduce inside the patient. It's the only way to get enough of the good gene into his cells."

He put a hand on her shoulder. "Congratulations." His voice did not convey celebration. "You've lifted him from Hell to Purgatory."

That seemed about right. By accident she'd stumbled on a way to treat Gunnar's Batten disease. A treatment to save his life.

But at a terrible price.

It was a gift worthy of King Midas.

"A cure," she whispered. She glanced at Sigrun bundled on the floor. "A cure that kills everyone he touches."

———————

It's all Sameer's fault.

Vargas fumed while he walked back to the main hospital in his ruined shoes. If that damn Indian had done his job—properly managing the animal facility while Cristo was out—this would not have happened. No chimps running loose on the grounds. No deadly virus rampaging through the humans.

I can't do everything around here. I pay people to deal with this shit.

He resolved not to hire any more Indians. They were too full of themselves. Didn't take orders well.

Serves him right if he catches it. Whatever "it" is.

A long finger of vine stretched out from the forest into the roadway, groping for something to climb. His groundskeepers had only been away for a few days and the Palacio was already starting to look like an episode of "Life After People."

Get de la Rosa a kidney. Get him and his tough guys out of here. Cut a deal with whatever gang is running the show. Get back to business.

He tried to estimate how long it would be until he could admit patients again. He'd have to hire somebody to hunt down the chimpanzees, if any were still alive.

For a moment he wondered about the epidemiology of the mystery virus. In people, it acted fast—hours to days. It made them agitated, aggressive, and violent. It killed them in the end. How did it spread?

Juan, the animal tech, had close contact with the animals. He could've picked up the virus any number of ways. But that Mara Salvatrucha guy, El Matador, who was running around shooting up the forest? No way had he been playing with monkeys. Either the virus was in chimpanzee dung and El Matador had the misfortune to run into some. Or the virus was in the air.

Aerosolized from the chimps? Or could you catch it from another person? Airborne? Damn.

Movement about twenty meters ahead caught his eye. Something darted into the trees.

His breaths came quickly. It was too small to be a chimp, he reassured himself. A raccoon or something.

The shortest route back to the hospital entrance passed right by the spot where the creature had vanished. He paused and stared at the place. Nothing moved.

Squirrel, he thought, and resumed a trot to get indoors.

The gate to the Serenity Garden was just ahead.

Barking.

In a flash, his memory scanned the image of the animal. Yes, it might have been a small dog.

The forest erupted in barking. Not one dog. Many. In the forest right beside him.

Animals from the lab!

He ran. Something—several somethings—scrambled through the brush. Toward him.

The muddied, smooth soles of his fancy shoes gave him trouble again. He slipped in his first stride—didn't go down—found his balance on the second. The red LED of the gate's hand scanner was close.

Four—five—dogs flew out of the trees. Foam sprayed from their open jaws.

He slapped his palm on the scanner and shouted.

Green light. He yanked the gate and flung himself to the other side.

The lead dog literally crashed into the gate, slamming it shut.

The frustrated canine hunters bayed in dismay. Clutching his chest, Vargas backed away from the gate into the Serenity Garden.

———

Tessa and Cristo took turns looking into the microscope as they discussed Gunnar's "cure" and what to do about it.

"If he comes in contact with anyone who hasn't been vaccinated against rabies," she said, "they might catch the revertant and die."

"But if we find a way to clear the virus from his body," he said, "he will die of Batten disease."

It's so unfair!

Her feelings were a jumble of hope and fear, joy and disappointment. Yet one thought rose to the top: *he's alive and he's getting better.* She clung to this.

On the other side of the room, the child in question stirred. First she heard the rustling of sheets, then sighs and a yawn.

"I'm hungry," he said to no one in particular. Then he poked his mother. "Mama I'm hungry."

Tessa hastened to them as Sigrun sat up, a dazed look on her face.

Gunnar started to whine. "I'm hungry."

"We're all hungry, sweetie," Tessa said. She reached to pat his head.

Gunnar slapped her hand. "I want pudding."

"We don't have any—"

Before the words were out of her mouth, the boy hollered. He yelled and fussed and screamed and turned on a faucet of tears. He paralyzed Tessa as surely as rabies could. She knew a lot about a lot of things. But no school ever taught her how to shut down a seven-year-old's temper tantrum.

In response to the noise, Sigrun rose zombie-like from the blankets. Gunnar stood up and clawed at his mother.

"My keys," Sigrun said. "Where are my keys?"

Her eyes were vacant. Even Gunnar noticed something was wrong. He hit her to get her attention.

Sigrun's confused. It wasn't a good sign.

"Mama!"

Sigrun started to crawl away. Something caused her pain and she cried out. Tessa guessed it was muscle spasms. Sigrun sat down, dazed.

Gunnar got angry. He spoke fiercely with garbled words. His face turned red. Tessa had seen him like this once before, back in the United States. Batten patients were prone to extreme fits of rage. It looked like this was turning into one of those fits. One big difference this time: the boy was able to stand up. He screamed at his mother. She gave him no satisfaction. Frustration drove him—

To walk.

One unsteady step.

My God.

A second step. Shrieking. Trembling. Furious.

He fell into his mother. Driven by an instinct stronger than her confusion, Sigrun encircled him in her arms.

He walked! Tessa had witnessed a miracle of Biblical proportions.

But how to quiet him?

The lab door opened. "Sounds like y'all could use a little help," Lyle said. The door closed and help padded into the room.

Gunnar flailed and hollered, battering his poor sick mother, until the beautiful German shepherd silently came to his side.

"Dog!" He flung himself around Dixie's patient shoulders. The tears stopped.

"Thank you," Tessa whispered.

The cursed boy, the noble dog, the doomed mother. The scene broke her heart.

Once more she prayed she was right about rabies vaccine protecting against the revertant. If she was wrong, Dixie was another caregiver who would pay the price.

Sigrun lay back on the floor, keeping one hand in contact with her son.

Tessa couldn't deny the fact of what she saw. The revertant was killing Sigrun. Her death would leave Gunnar an orphan.

What devil's ransom is this, to trade the life of the boy for the life of the mother?

Cristo came and looked at Gunnar and Sigrun. He shook his head. "Too bad the boy can't give her some of his magic."

"Yeah," Tessa replied. Gunnar should be dead. The revertant should have killed him. It didn't, which meant he must have a really vigorous immune response. His little body had to be teeming with antibodies against the virus.

Antibodies.

In his blood serum.

Antiserum.

She grabbed Cristo's arm, startling him with her intensity. "You're a genius."

"What?"

"He *can*," she said. "With our help, he can save her."

"How?"

She dragged him back to the desk. "He's hyperimmune from chronic exposure to the rabies vector."

"So?"

"We can use his blood to make an antiserum. And give it to his mother." Her finger traced a row of medical books as she searched for the right title. "Vargas offers all kinds of experimental therapies here in this building. I remember one of them is an unproven treatment for autoimmune diseases. Plasmapheresis."

"Plasma—"

"It's kind of like dialysis. You take the blood out of a person, remove the antibodies, and put the blood back in. When they use it as a treatment, they're trying to clean out bad antibodies. We can adapt the process to collect good antibodies from Gunnar."

"And inject them into Sigrun."

"Exactly. She needs time for the vaccine to work. Even one dose of antiserum might beat back the virus long enough for her own immune system to kick in."

"Tessa, that's crazy. We're not doctors. You know how to do that?"

"No." She pulled a text off the shelf. "But I'm gonna figure it out."

If Vargas had a choice, he would never set eyes on Luis Angel de la Rosa again.

He didn't have a choice. Unhappy to the core, he entered the dialysis suite. De la Rosa was already there.

"Your BUN level is too high," Vargas said. "This dialysis treatment will bring it back down. You'll feel much better."

"What makes you think you know how I feel?" de la Rosa said. "I will always be stronger than you."

To prove his point, the drug lord rose from his wheelchair and transferred himself to the dialysis lounger. But not without stumbling.

Vargas resisted the urge to point out de la Rosa's weakness. "We did an extra purification of your solution. It won't cause us any problems this time."

De la Rosa grunted.

Vargas sensed the man was, in fact, weak and in extreme discomfort. Which was consistent with the blood test results. De la Rosa's blood urea nitrogen level was screaming for treatment. If the numbers weren't so bad, he would've delayed the dialysis. He was loathe to consume the last batch of de la Rosa's prescribed dialysate solution. Once it was gone, he could do nothing to treat the drug lord's kidney failure until the siege was broken or a compatible kidney turned up.

He checked the patient's vital signs and did a quick physical exam. No question, they had to go through with it. De la Rosa's blood was poisoning him.

The transplant surgeon showed up. With Sameer Desai quarantined, Vargas had to bring Rogelio in to help with the dialysis. They'd had a talk. Rogelio was going to behave himself in de la Rosa's presence.

The talk made a bigger impression than Vargas expected. The surgeon practically bowed and scraped his way to de la Rosa's side.

Jesus, he thought, get a spine. We're all afraid of Sinaloa but you're still a goddamn doctor.

"Dr. Rogelio, would you please insert the line?" he said. It made sense for the specialist to hook up the patient to the dialysis machine. It also gave Vargas pleasure to put the pressure on Rogelio.

"Of course," Rogelio said. He prepped de la Rosa's arm over the site of the implanted arteriovenous graft where he would insert the lines to extract and return the blood.

Vargas noticed Rogelio's hand was shaking. *That's gonna make it hard to get a clean stick.* He half hoped the surgeon would screw up. Failure would make Vargas look good. But sticking an AV graft was so easy a first year med student could do it.

Rogelio plunged the needle into de la Rosa's flesh. Both physicians looked for a flash of red in the tubing.

Nothing.

Amused, Vargas watched Rogelio sweat bullets as he pulled the needle out and tried again.

Still no blood flow.

The surgeon lost his cool and swore softly. De la Rosa didn't blink, maintaining a cold stare at Rogelio.

Vargas was less amused the second time. They really did need to get access to the patient's blood.

After the third stick failed to strike red gold, Vargas pushed the specialist aside. "I'll do it."

"Something's wrong," Rogelio said. "Let me—"

"I'll let you get out of my way." To de la Rosa, he put on his best compassionate physician act. "Sir, I apologize for that. We'll get your treatment started now."

His hands were not shaking. The needle landed precisely where he intended.

Therefore the absence of blood was a surprise.

"What the—"

Rogelio returned with a hand-held ultrasound scanner. "Move it."

Vargas moved.

The surgeon passed the scanner over de la Rosa's arm. Vargas didn't know how to interpret the readings on the scanner's screen. Rogelio repeated the motions. He stepped away from the patient and beckoned Vargas to follow him into the adjacent room.

Vargas followed, feeling a chill of foreboding. "What? What is it?"

"You clotted the graft," Rogelio said in a hush. "We don't have access."

He tried to keep his voice low so de la Rosa wouldn't hear. "I clotted the graft?" He wasn't an expert on this but he was pretty sure grafts sometimes filled with blood clots and blocked off on their own. It wasn't anything he'd done. Just extraordinarily bad luck. "That's bullshit. I didn't do anything."

"You messed up. His veins are shut down. We can't dialyze him."

Panic triggered dark spots in Vargas's vision. "You're the surgeon. Fix it."

"Fine. Tell me the Palacio stocks Quinton catheters."

"What?"

Rogelio folded his arms and indicted Vargas with his eyes. "I didn't think so. Fucking country hospital."

"The Palacio is a world-class institution." He got in the surgeon's face. "We don't take care of train wrecks."

"So you don't have the equipment I need."

This isn't happening, he thought. He tried to think of any research projects that might have the equipment for putting in a central line. Nothing. The Palacio wasn't set up to handle critically ill patients. It wasn't his business model. "Can you clean out the graft?"

"Takes too long to heal. He'll be dead before we can use it." The meekness Rogelio displayed to the drug lord had vanished. The bastard was all aggression now.

If he thinks I'm going to take the blame for this, he's got another thing coming. "You should've stayed for the last dialysis treatment," Vargas said. "You're the expert."

"You told me to leave."

"Did I put a gun to your head? Where was that superior clinical judgement you surgeons are always bragging about?"

Rogelio grabbed him by the tie and shoved him against the wall. Vargas became acutely aware that the surgeon was a couple of inches taller than he was, and brawnier. He gasped as Rogelio pushed the air out of his chest.

"This is your fuck up, not mine," Rogelio said.

Vargas nodded. It didn't matter what Rogelio thought. De la Rosa assigned blame the way a suicide bomber chose his victims. Broadly, with maximum carnage.

"He'll kill us both," Vargas squealed.

Rogelio let go. Vargas felt his full weight return to his feet. He smoothed his shirt and straightened the tie. "You can blame me. I don't care. But if we can't lower his BUN, de la Rosa is dead." He pointed at himself. "And I'm dead." He jabbed his finger into the surgeon's chest with needless force. "And you're dead. So we need to work together."

Rogelio put his hands against the wall behind Vargas and leaned forward. Vargas felt heat radiating from the man's skin.

The surgeon whispered into Vargas's ear. "Then unless you get me a catheter or a kidney, I'll see you in hell."

CHAPTER 19

Natural light was fading on the page in Tessa's lap, forcing her to squint to read the small print.

It's been two hours already?

She'd learned only a fraction of what she felt she needed to know to pull off this plasmapheresis with Gunnar and Sigrun. The procedure was complicated. Dangerous. She should forget about it. Surely the authorities were coming to rescue the Palacio. Outside help might arrive in time.

She closed the book. No, time was running out. Not just for reading. For Sigrun.

Nervous symptoms of doubt and fear crossed signals with hunger in her stomach. How long since she'd eaten? She needed her brain to function in top condition but her mental capacity was far from its best at this point.

With regret she left the comfy chair in the exterior room where she'd escaped to study. Cristo had stayed in the claustrophobic lab with Gunnar, Sigrun, and Dixie. He had his hands full. Gunnar's new-found strength was a miracle but under the circumstances it was not a blessing. Dixie could only do so much to distract the boy from boredom and hunger. He was restless and fussy. Tessa couldn't concentrate in the room with him.

Now she'd have to. Turning the lights on wasn't an option—it would give away her presence—and she couldn't read in the dark.

Back in the windowless lab, she found Cristo helping Gunnar build a tower with plastic storage boxes. Cristo's face was drawn. Good thing she'd disposed of the plack in the lab. The poor guy was coping with an awful lot right now.

He looked up, unsmiling. "Ready?"

"To do the plasmapheresis? Hardly," she said. "I've got the basic idea—"

"Unnngh." Sigrun groaned. One of her legs twitched and the other kicked, jerking the blankets.

Gunnar's tower of boxes collapsed. He wailed and beat Cristo with his little fists.

"She's going down fast," Cristo said. "You have to decide."

She knew what decision he meant. *Do I know enough to go ahead now, or am I going to watch Sigrun die?*

She leaned on a laboratory stool, fighting panic. The idea of making an antiserum from Gunnar's blood was a good one. As long as it remained an abstraction, an idea, she'd pursued it eagerly. But the thought of actually doing it...

She couldn't jab a flu shot in someone's shoulder. How could she possibly insert two large volume IV lines into Gunnar's tiny veins? Even health care workers without her hangups had a hard time sticking kids. She had neither the psychological fortitude nor the physical skill to set up the pheresis. And operating the machine, regulating the process—it was complicated. She needed time to study the guidelines, figure the variables. Account for Gunnar's small size. Don't clot him but don't let him bleed either. Take too much blood out at once and he'd go into shock.

Screw up completely and she could kill him.

"I—I'm not ready." She turned her back and went to her desk.

Cristo picked up Gunnar's building blocks. Gunnar viciously tugged at Dixie's short fur.

I can't do it. She hid her face in her arms. *Too risky.*

I can't hurt Gunnar.

Sigrun groaned again. For a moment Gunnar broke out of his childish egocentrism and noticed her pain. "Mama?"

The word cut her. She didn't want to hurt him. But what could be more cruel than letting his mother die when there was still a chance?

A couple of needle sticks versus life as an orphan with extraordinary special needs. Which was the true suffering?

Which inflicted more pain: to do nothing, or to act?

Benjamin, my angel, show me the way.

Head down on the desk, she listened to Gunnar and Cristo talking.

> *"What's wrong with Mama?"*
> *"She's sick."*

"Like me?"

"A little different."

"Will she get better? Like me?"

"Let's build another tower, okay?"

She lifted her head. She knew what she had to do. She didn't know how, but it had to be done.

Don't think about the needles. Just get the equipment set up. Cristo can do—that part. I'll run the machine.

Her colleague came over. He leaned against the wall and folded his arms. "What can I do?"

She clenched her fists. "Watch Gunnar while I prep the equipment."

The plasmapheresis treatment room was on the third floor and fortunately had no windows. As in other patient rooms in the Annex, tropical-themed art hung on one wall, in this case, an elaborate textured oil painting of a jungle that looked like a seek-and-find game. The pheresis machine resembled a control console from a 1960s science fiction movie, with dials, readouts, and a web of tubing over a nondescript tan housing that concealed the pump and blood spinner. A flat-screen TV faced the patient treatment chair, which was a padded, adjustable, vinyl-covered lounger.

The oversized chair swallowed Gunnar when Cristo laid him on it.

Tessa noted the mismatch between the size of the chair and the size of the patient. This treatment was not for kids. She reviewed her calculations, confirming she'd made adjustments for Gunnar's weight in all the right places. She checked the tubing and the needles. She had to gather them from other parts of the building because the materials kept with the machine were all adult-sized. She prayed these smaller replacements would work.

Dear, faithful Dixie sat on her haunches next to the chair on the side opposite the machine.

"TV?" Gunnar said hopefully.

"Sure," Cristo said. He powered up the TV but couldn't get a signal. "Sorry buddy, the satellite is down."

Gunnar whined and wiggled his legs over the side of the chair. "Go back," he said.

Time for the second-hardest part of this business.

"Gunnar, your mama is sick," Tessa said.

He blinked.

How could she possibly explain what was about to happen? It dawned on her that there were some major ethical issues here. Was it right to put the child in discomfort and danger to do something that had no medical benefit to him? Who gave her permission to make the decision? Should the boy have a say? Should she have discussed it with Sigrun, even in the mother's confused state?

Screw it. Posterity could judge, but in the here and now she had few options. Her mind was made up.

She sat on the chair next to Gunnar and stroked his hair. He looked at her with wide blue eyes.

"Sweetie, your mama needs a special medicine to get better."

His delicate nose wrinkled.

This was hard. "You want her to get better, don't you?"

"Yeah." He voiced the word like a question.

"Would you help me make her better?"

Suspicion in those blue eyes.

"There's a special medicine, a kind of magic, inside you." She touched a finger to his chest in emphasis. "If we can put it in a bottle and give it to your mama, she'll feel better."

"Oh."

She took this one syllable as approval and plowed ahead. "Cristo and I—I mean, Cristo is going to—" *how to say it?* "—to put a little tube in your arm. We'll take the medicine out through the tube." She didn't add, *along with all your blood.*

"Okay."

That's it? He said, okay?

"Okay," she replied and turned to Cristo. He was frowning.

He gave her a "come here" gesture. "I can't do it. I've never put in an IV."

"Neither have I," she said, which was a lie. During her short, disastrous stint in medical school, she *had* placed some IVs. First in people who were paid by the university to suffer through students' practice jabs. Then she'd poked a couple of real patients in the hospital. But it hadn't been many, maybe ten altogether. Plus, that was years ago. And none of the patients were children.

More important, all of that was before the accident in the operating room morphed her dislike of needles into a paralyzing phobia.

Cristo would have to do the sticks.

"You've drawn blood from animals, haven't you? It's pretty much the same. Just get a needle in the vein and I'll take care of everything else."

He looked unsure. Fair enough. This whole business was flirting with disaster.

Damn you, Vargas.

"Please. It's the only way."

Cristo knew about her phobia. What could she say to persuade him? Should she beg? Grovel? Make wild promises? Her anxiety rose on the crest of her desperation.

Then, he simply nodded.

With the urgency of a released spring, she opened the sterile packages and laid the items on a tray. She spoke gently to Gunnar and got him to lie back in the huge chair.

The trouble began when she tied a tourniquet around his upper arm.

"Ow! Stop it!" With his free hand the boy reached over and pulled off the strip of rubber. A wild look came into his eyes as he got the idea that she wasn't going to use magic to put his "special medicine" into a bottle.

"Sweetie, to help your mama get better you're gonna have to lie still for me." To Cristo she said, "See if there's any local reception on that TV. Anything."

Static filled the TV screen. She reached for Gunnar's arm. This time he jerked it out of reach.

"No!" He squirmed and moved away from her, trying to get off the chair.

Her stomach churned. *As if this wasn't hard enough already.* The noise of static from the TV sandpapered her nerves. "Forget it, Cristo. Turn it off."

Cristo playfully lifted Gunnar and set him back in the middle of the chair. Tessa whispered, "I'll have to hold him down while you do the stick."

For a dark-skinned guy, Cristo went positively pale in the face. "Can we sedate him?"

"Too dangerous. A sedative could affect his circulation. I can't make allowances for it. We're hanging by a thread here as it is."

She placed Gunnar's free hand on Dixie's head. Then she wrapped her hands around his wrists and pressed them against the padding of the chair. "I'll help you hold still, okay?"

Obviously this was not okay. Gunnar resisted. Cristo tied the tourniquet around the boy's arm. Gunnar wiggled his hips. Cristo wiped the arm with disinfectant.

Gunnar went nuts.

He kicked with both legs in every direction and put his entire strength against Tessa's grip. His shoulders lifted off the chair. He raised his head and screamed.

"Gunnar, it's okay! See, Dixie's right here!"

She might as well have told a hurricane to stop blowing. Gunnar couldn't overpower her but he generated enough force that she couldn't keep his arm still.

And for Cristo to hit a vein, the arm had to be motionless.

His screams were claws shredding at her sanity. Inflicting pain on another person wounded something deep in her psyche. Doing it to this child was torture.

Cristo leaned back from the treatment chair. "Forget it. We can't."

She let go of Gunnar.

Forget it?

Let Sigrun die?

Look beyond, she told herself. Focus on the big picture. Don't listen to the screams. You are helping him. Kids will scream over anything. You're not even touching him and he's screaming.

I've got to do this.

She snapped on a pair of gloves. "You hold him. If you get on the chair and straddle him it'll keep his legs down. You're big enough, you should be able to hold his arm still."

Cristo didn't speak. He climbed onto the chair and swung a leg over the squirming child, immobilizing Gunnar's hips. Without apology, he grasped Gunnar's wrists and leaned his body weight into the padding.

It worked. The poor boy was pinned.

His screams were so loud even Dixie looked agitated.

She filled her mind's eye with an image of Sigrun and Gunnar snuggled together. A happy scene.

Needles sparkled on the sterile tray. She felt light-headed.

"You can do it," Cristo said.

She forced herself into a regular breathing pattern. The world shrank. Gunnar's screams were the background static of the universe. Blackness filled her peripheral vision. A fat blue line rolled under the boy's skin.

She stabbed it.

The next minutes were a blur. She missed the first time but hit the vein on the second try. The scream-static rose in pitch. Halfway there. Three more stabs and she had placed a second intravenous line. Tubing and connectors confused her. One line out, one line in. Open the valve. Blood in the tube, rising like a flood toward the pheresis machine. Mechanical clunking from inside. Was it supposed to sound like that? Check the readouts. Check your notes.

Like waking from a nightmare, her sensibility gradually returned. She saw Cristo perched on top of Gunnar in that sadistic pose. Gunnar's screams subsided into whimpers.

The part involving needles was over.

"Good job," Cristo said.

No victory yet. Gloves off. She taped tubes and valves in place against Gunnar's arm. Her breathing returned to normal. She wiped her face clean of the tears she hadn't realized were flowing.

Check the patient.

"Are you okay, sweetie?" She touched his red, wet cheek.

He wagged his head no and sniffled.

They couldn't let Gunnar touch the IV site or equipment but as he quieted down Cristo was able to climb off the bed. He kept a grip on the boy's free arm, just to be safe. Tessa held the arm hooked up to the machine.

"Is it working?" Cristo said.

"As far as I can tell." The tubing was full of blood. The machine's internal centrifuge was spinning. She made adjustments to the flow. Gunnar was such a small person, taking out too much blood at one time or circulating it back too quickly risked sending him into shock, or worse.

Time passed. She and Cristo spoke softly. The loud clacking and whining of the pheresis equipment became less noticeable, white noise. Gunnar dozed off and lay still. Tessa relaxed her hold on his arm.

Something about his sleep disturbed her. He was too still.

Alarmed, she looked at his angelic face. His fair complexion had progressed to ghostly white. She lifted his hand. The fingertips were blue-tinged and cool.

"He's getting shocky." Consciously trying to stay calm, she reached for the machine's controls and cut the blood flow to a trickle. *Don't clot on me!* "Gunnar, baby, wake up."

Cristo jostled the shoulder of Gunnar's free arm. "Hey amigo, you in there?"

Feeling dizzy herself, Tessa stuffed a pillow under the boy's knees and tucked the blanket more tightly around him. "Help me rub his legs."

With pressured strokes they pushed from his feet toward his body, channeling blood into his core. Her hands grew warm from the friction against the blanket.

Gunnar's eyes flickered open. She moved back to his arm to protect the IV lines.

"Mama?" His voice was weak. Shivers ran down his body.

"You got enough antiserum for Sigrun?" Cristo asked.

"I don't know." There was no way to tell. She didn't have the time or technology to analyze the extracted serum for antibody content. Nor did she have any clue how much antibody was needed to save Sigrun's life—if, indeed, any amount would be enough. "Let's run it as long as possible."

How long was that? She tried to think like a doctor. What sign would tell her it was time to quit?

While Cristo did puppet tricks with his hands to entertain Gunnar, she checked the boy's pulse in several different places. It was faint in his lower legs.

What now? On the plus side, Gunnar was too weak to struggle and they didn't have to hold him down. On the minus side, she didn't know if he could stay like this for a while yet, or if he was on the verge of a crisis.

They only had one chance at this. She went back to rubbing his legs.

"You better pull the plug," Cristo said.

"Another minute." She re-checked everything she could think of.

"He's falling asleep again." He touched the boy's forehead.

Gunnar's skin started to look blotchy. Cristo shook him but his eyelids drooped.

Oh God, did I wait too long?

She stopped the extraction. The machine clanked along, spinning the blood already outside Gunnar's body and pumping it back into his slender arm. Cristo massaged the boy's forehead.

Come on, Gunnar. Show me how tough you are.

During the minutes it took to complete the cycle, she reviewed how to safely disconnect him and collect the antiserum.

Valves and switches. Get the sequence right.

Cristo set Gunnar's hand on Dixie's head. "There's a dog here needs petting."

Pulling out the IV lines, she untethered the boy from the machine. She pressed on his arm to prevent bleeding. His skin felt less cold. "Gunnar, Dixie's here."

Gunnar's skinny chest rose and fell in tiny, kid-sized arcs. Tessa and Cristo held their breath as they watched the boy's hand on the dog's head.

More miracles, please.

Little fingers twitched and discovered fur. He didn't open his eyes, but Gunnar started petting Dixie.

Tessa stretched a compression bandage around his arm. She'd done it.

CHAPTER 20

Tessa and Cristo both carried precious burdens.

At ten minutes past midnight, they returned to the safety of the laboratory. She carried a vial of Gunnar's serum, laden, they hoped, with antibodies that would save his mother's life. Cristo carried the listless boy, who looked like he'd survived a vampire attack. Barely. Dixie stuck close to his side.

While the plasmapheresis procedure didn't permanently remove any red blood cells from Gunnar's body, Tessa knew it might have damaged some of them and made him anemic. Maybe she'd made a mistake with the settings. Maybe the boy had too much or too little fluid in his system. She didn't know. But he did look utterly drained.

Kids bounce back, she told herself. Give him some water and rest and he'll be fine. Chocolate would help. Too bad they didn't have any.

Cristo lay Gunnar in his nest, next to his mother. Sigrun slept fitfully, twitching and groaning like a dreaming dog.

Tessa held up the vial. "Mission accomplished."

The adrenaline burst that fueled her courage to place Gunnar's IVs was over. She was emotionally spent, but there could be no rest until the serum was inside Sigrun. No doubt Cristo was even more exhausted than she, still reeling from the effects of plack withdrawal. But she couldn't—absolutely could not—put a needle in Sigrun. The phobia was back in control and no amount of will power she could summon would overcome it.

"Cristo, I—"

He finished tucking blankets around Gunnar and rose to look her in the face. Stubble covered his chin; his eyes were ringed in black. He touched her cheek.

"I know," he said. "This one should be easy. I'll do it."

The gratitude and fatigue and hunger she felt drove tears into her eyes. She hugged him and turned away.

Sigrun didn't resist.

"It's in," Cristo said.

Tessa refused to even glimpse the needle. She waited until she heard a tinkling sound in the sharps waste box. Then she rejoined the group.

Sigrun lay on her back. Her eyes were open. Tessa took her wrist. The skin was hot and dry.

"How you doing?" Tessa said as she massaged Sigrun's palm.

Sigrun stared at her with a blank gaze and parted lips. A tremor passed through her body.

"Take care of him," she croaked.

Tessa felt Sigrun try to squeeze her hand. "I will. Until you get better."

Cristo delivered a cup of water. She took it and lifted Sigrun's head. Sigrun turned, avoiding the cup.

Was it hydrophobia? Patients with full-blown rabies refused water and couldn't swallow.

"Come on, take a little."

To her relief, Sigrun relented and drank. They hadn't lost her yet. There was still time for the antiserum to work.

"How about you, buddy?" she said to Gunnar. He had to be dehydrated from the procedure. The guidelines she'd read all recommended rest, drink, and food during recovery.

Gunnar made a small whimper but didn't sit up or even open his eyes.

"Have a drink," she said.

He's really knocked out, she thought. Was she witnessing ordinary exhaustion from the circumstances and the time of day, or something more?

She managed to coax some water into Gunnar's mouth. Much of it spilled but he did swallow.

"Food," she said.

"Would be nice," Cristo replied.

"I'm not sure it's a luxury any more. Gunnar may be hypoglycemic."

"Low blood sugar?"

"It's a possible side effect of the pheresis." She listed the worrisome evidence. "He was half-starved when we took him in there. He burned up a ton of energy fighting us. He's tiny and skinny—no reserves. Even if I did everything right with the procedure, which isn't likely, the stress could've tipped him over the edge."

Cristo rubbed his chin. "Yeah."

"Can you think of anything we can feed him?"

No response.

She wanted to scream. Why, why did it have to be so hard? This should have been a time of triumph. The gene therapy was working! The Batten patient was recovering! But narco criminals and mutant viruses and crazed chimpanzees had driven her and Gunnar to this. He looked as fragile as he'd ever looked. For the absurd reason that they had nothing to eat.

She stood up and said, "Dixie. Come."

The risk calculation had changed. It was time to go outside.

————————

Tessa and Dixie went into the hallway. They found Lyle and Isabella spooning but awake in the darkness. Dixie broke up the couple, wagging her whole back end in happiness when Lyle rubbed her back.

"Tell me again what you saw on the security video," she said.

"Isabella watched it. I didn't have the patience."

Isabella loosened and retied her ponytail. "The chimps found food somewhere off camera. I don't know if it's a truck or a shed or a dump. If we go out the hole by the helicopter crash, we should be able to reach it without being seen."

"You say the boy needs food right now?" Lyle asked.

"I'm not a physician," Tessa said. "I don't know. I'm scared for him. If you two think there's a chance I'll find something for him to eat, I'll go."

"I will go too," Isabella said. "I've never been indoors so long in my life."

"There's no point in putting two of us at risk," Tessa said.

"Make that four," Lyle said. "Dixie and I are in. If you need some door kickin', Bella's your girl. If you need some ass-chomping, Dixie's the one you want."

"But if I'm seen—"

"If they see you," Isabella said, "we all lose, whether you are alone or not. They will come and search the building."

Lyle agreed. "So we might as well make a team for defense while we're out there."

Tessa remembered the images of the chimps attacking the two Mara Salvatruchas. The MS were armed and they still lost the fight. "Isabella, can you check the videos? Make sure there hasn't been any chimp activity around the building for a while?"

"Yes, I will check." She moved like a ghost toward the stairs to the security room.

Tessa found Lyle eyeing her.

"You doin' all right there, Doc?" he said.

"Fine. I'm worried about *you*."

"You just worry about Gunnar. And yourself. I'm a tough old bird," he said. "I came down here to get my mojo back and I am not gonna get myself killed before I have a go with that beautiful woman of mine."

In spite of everything, she laughed a little.

Lyle stood up. "Dixie. *Bleibsitzen.*" Dixie stayed where she was. Lyle leaned against the wall. "I suppose you've figured out I've got some spare change socked away."

"Most Palacio clients do."

"Did you wonder where I got it from?"

"Not really. Well, a little."

"Defense contracts, Doc. I was a soldier. Then I grew up and one day I realized I was mortal. I left the service and went into business." He chuckled and slapped his thigh. "A real Tony Stark, I am. Without the suit of course."

"Or the artificial heart thingy."

"No, but I got some other parts could use replacing." He put his hands on her shoulders. "You listen to me when we're out there—and to Bella too, she knows a few things—and we'll get that boy some food. Then we'll high-tail it back here and have a party."

His words lifted her spirits. "I'm partial to burgers at this time of day," she said.

"And I'm partial to sleep. We don't always get what we want."

Ten minutes later Isabella returned. She'd scanned the last hour of video surveillance on high speed. No chimpanzees or MS were in the area. "Let's go."

The smell of scorched plastic permeated the first floor of the Annex building. Isabella led the way toward the crash site. Dust and soot covered everything. Bringing up the rear, Tessa passed through a haze stirred up by the human and animal feet ahead of her. She coughed loudly. Lyle cringed. Isabella turned and frowned, a finger pressed to her lips.

Tessa nodded and tried to take shallow breaths. Crumbled chunks of wall crunched under her feet. Damp night air blew lightly through the gap, clearing the airborne dust as they approached the downed helicopter. She wondered who'd been on board, what stories ended when they died in the crash.

Isabella held up a hand. Wait. A hole in the building large enough to get through was at the top of the rubble pile. She climbed, picking a path through the jagged metal, concrete, and plaster. Tessa saw her flatten herself against the debris and peek out.

After a moment Isabella waved for them to follow. Lyle placed his feet with care, testing each point to confirm it could support his weight. Isabella disappeared through the crack into the moonlit night. Dixie followed eagerly and slipped only once. Tessa envied the dog's dexterity. With less grace, she made it up without slicing or skewering herself.

At the top she ducked under a crumpled rotor blade and emerged out-doors. She put a hand on the 'copter for support and hopped to the ground.

No one spoke. Isabella slinked cat-like along the building, darting from shadow to shadow. Lyle tried to imitate but couldn't match her supple movements. Tessa concentrated on moving silently. Stars filled the sky and moonlight illuminated the grounds. She shivered under the glare. If anything was watching, it would see them.

She scanned their surroundings for movement, or a pair of glowing eyes. Nothing.

Then there it was.

A vinyl shed about twenty feet long. Double doors at one end. One door was ajar. The other was wrenched out of position and dangled from a single hinge. Just enough room for a person—or a chimpanzee—to enter.

Isabella was already sprinting across the short gap to the shed. Lyle pushed Tessa in the same direction, ordering Dixie to stick close. In one breath Tessa dashed to the shed and ducked inside. The interior was dark. She bumped into Isabella, who had stopped just inside the door.

The shed stank of chimpanzee.

She froze, waiting for her eyes to adjust. Was there a chimp in the shed now? Subconsciously she calculated how long it would take to get out if something in the darkness attacked them. Too long. She backed up.

Dixie's claws clicked to a stop on the concrete floor beside her. The door creaked as Lyle squeezed through. They were all in. As far as she knew, they'd made it without being spotted by the drug gang. Had they just offered themselves as soft targets for a mad chimp? Would they find the food they were looking for?

The noise of her own breathing hampered her senses. She held her breath and listened.

Dixie growled.

Isabella whispered something to Lyle. Everyone stood stock-still. Tessa's heart fluttered. She thought of Gunnar, of his hunger, his weakness. *Do it for Gunnar.*

A sound. Ahead. To the left.

Her skin prickled. Whatever it was, it wasn't moving. But it was alive. The sound of breathing. Labored. Human?

A moan and the scrape of metal on concrete. More sounds—light scratching and shredding.

Her vision adapted to the dim light. Isabella had moved away from the entrance, deeper into the darkness. She squinted in the direction of the sound.

Light flared and she slammed her eyes shut, jumping as she did. The source of the sound cried out.

She looked.

An intense beam of light bombarded a ragged Mexican man huddled on the hard floor in a puddle of his own urine. Wild jungle rats, not the rotund white laboratory specimens, scattered from his legs and scuttled into hiding. The man was bald with a scalp so extensively tattooed for a fraction of a second she thought it was hair. A rifle lay across his torso. His arms twitched with a futile effort to seize the weapon.

Isabella kicked the rifle out of his reach and lowered the flashlight closer to the man's face. He turned his head and tried to pull away but seemed incapable of moving the rest of his body.

"Dixie! *Zur Wache!*"

Dixie leaped to Isabella and snarled at the man. She snapped her fierce jaws over his neck, daring him to try something. Then she went still and leaned over the man in a posture of unfailing readiness.

Isabella picked up the rifle and looped the strap around her neck. "Mara Salvatrucha," she said.

"Not having a good day," Lyle said. He approached their crippled enemy and looked him over. Dixie made a low noise in her throat. "He doesn't appear to be wounded."

The Mara Salvatrucha continued to moan and flop his head from side to side but uttered no clear speech. Tessa noticed he did not move his legs at all, and the motion of his arms did not appear purposeful.

"He's infected," she guessed. "Paralytic rabies."

Lyle said something to Dixie. The dog backed off a couple of feet but kept her attention fixed on the target.

Isabella spoke harshly to the man in Spanish. His eyes rolled in her direction but he didn't answer. His jaw was clenched and saliva dripped from his mouth. She pointed the rifle at him and shoved him with her foot. His only reaction was a grunt.

"He needs medical care." As soon as Tessa said it, she felt stupid. *Duh.* But what could they do for him? And what *should* they do? He was part of the drug gang, and now he knew about them. They couldn't let him tell their secret. They could put him in a dog kennel like they'd done to Cristo. But how to move him? Lyle couldn't carry anything heavy; he'd bleed again. And to drag him through the hole in the building—

"We leave him alive. Yes?" Isabella said.

As in, killing him was an option? Tessa was shocked. But Isabella was talking to Lyle, not her.

Lyle sighed. "Yes. I don't think he'll be tattling on us except to St. Peter."

Isabella directed the flashlight at the rest of the space. "Let's get what we came for."

The shed was about half full. Toward the rear was an assortment of groundskeeping equipment, bags of fertilizer, ladders, and ropes. Nearer the entrance were several pallets of cardboard boxes. A couple had been torn open. Some spilled basic supplies like paper towels and soap.

Others spilled snacks.

"Hallelujah," Tessa said. Chips and nuts and dried fruit and crackers, all in individual snack packages, bundled in larger bags, packed in boxes. The rats had certainly found them. Telltale gnaws marked the corners of boxes and bags. The smell proved the chimps had been here too, like Isabella said.

Her own hunger stirred and she immediately ripped open a package and dumped the contents into her mouth. Isabella did the same. Lyle first made a pile of chow for Dixie, who abandoned her guard on the Mara Salvatrucha only when her master commanded it.

"Junk food, eh girl?" he said. "Special treat."

"We should go," Isabella said, stuffing snacks into her clothes.

Tessa marveled at the way Isabella deftly shifted the rifle to her back. Like she had practice doing it before. Then Tessa, too, filled her pockets and pants. She gave a moment's thought to what might be Gunnar's favorite and grabbed an entire box.

She headed for the door and paused to let Isabella lead the way. But Isabella wasn't ready. She was bent over the moribund Mara Salvatrucha. Her hands explored his pockets and she lifted him, first one shoulder, then the other, to expose his back. Her effort netted a buck knife and what Tessa assumed was ammunition for the rifle.

"After you, ladies," Lyle said.

They found it easiest to pass the boxes through the narrow opening first. Then Isabella, Tessa, Lyle, and Dixie exited.

As they picked up the boxes, Dixie growled.

The growl was answered. Tessa straightened, cardboard box in her arms.

A circle of seven pairs of eyes, glowing with moonlight, stared at her and her companions. If she had fur on her back, it would've risen as tall and hostile as Dixie's.

The same as the fur on the pack of dogs that surrounded them.

Instinctively the humans clustered together. Dixie moved to the fore with bared teeth and tense muscles.

"No sudden moves," Lyle whispered. "Stay in a group. Tiny steps toward the building."

The dogs were small to medium-sized. Any one by itself would've been no match for Dixie. But over half a dozen?

Tessa recognized them as escapees from the lab. They should be tame, she thought. Hungry, sure, but...

She saw the foam at the mouths. *Not tame.* And worst of all, apparently not immune to the revertant virus.

In one horrified instant, her theory that rabies vaccine was protective crumbled to dust. A pack of rabid dogs. If a single bite broke the skin, it would kill.

Snarls mixed with the chorus of growls. One dog inched forward, lifting each paw in slow motion, the rattle of its growl unbroken as it came closer. Dixie matched the careful steps, putting herself between that dog and her people.

"Let's do it, folks," Lyle said. In micro-movements, they traveled less than a yard. The first dog in the pack raised the stakes with a bark. Dixie kept her cool.

Then the attack came.

Canine battle sounds filled the night. Vicious snarls from every direction. The snapping of jaws. The spraying of foam. The primal sounds of animal aggression ignited an ancient terror in Tessa's heart: the hunted's fear of the hunter.

Dixie dove into the pack and the human group broke up. Tessa spun to run toward the Annex. One of the dogs, some kind of terrier, gave chase. She heard it *rowr* and looked back just as it leaped into the air.

The dog wasn't big. She could beat it off. But its fangs were poisoned.

She lowered the box she carried to shield her legs. The mad dog collided with the box and she shoved the animal aside. She ran a few more steps—almost to the wall—but the rabid animal came at her again.

"Down! Back!" she screamed, as if this were a household pet playing rough. But rabies was in control. The dog lunged.

The only weapon she had was the box of food for Gunnar. She threw it as hard as she could. Her adversary was momentarily pushed back. She reached the crash site at the same instant as Isabella.

The same dog—*it won't give up!*—threatened them once more. Instead of charging, it lowered its head and stalked forward with fierce snarling barks and exposed teeth.

"Aaaiyah!" Isabella raised her heel and connected a powerful kick on the dog's head. It flew two feet and sprawled on the ground. This time it did not get up.

Where's Lyle?

"Get inside!" Lyle shouted.

To her surprise, he was still near the main fight, where the pack had coalesced around Dixie. He brandished the knife Isabella had taken off the dying man.

"Lyle, run!" Isabella screamed.

He won't leave Dixie, Tessa realized.

"Go," Isabella told her.

She scrambled up the helicopter wreck to get into the building. Halfway up, she looked back.

The German shepherd was a blur of motion. Dixie stood taller than the laboratory dogs but the leaping and twisting of canine bodies blended them all into one boiling pot of fighting dog. The minds of these dogs were enslaved to the will of a virus. The mission: to spread the virus. In saliva. To bite until they couldn't bite any more.

The dogs wouldn't stop until they were dead.

She reached the top of the debris pile. The shelter of the building's interior beckoned. Looking back she saw Lyle throw the knife into the whirling battle. A dog went down. She yelled at him, "Get out! Rabies!"

Isabella had stopped mid-way up the climb. She swung the stolen rifle forward, planted her feet on the unstable wreckage, and aimed at the dog fight.

No—the noise! "Don't!" Tessa shouted. "They'll hear!"

As far as she knew they'd evaded the security cameras, but gunshots would surely get the drug gang's attention. They would come. They'd find Gunnar and the rest of them.

Finally, Lyle was moving. He reached the wall. The dog fight rolled and writhed, exposing a bloodied dog body on the ground as it shifted to one side. Another dog staggered and fell, too lame to keep up with the action. Dixie fought on.

Lyle grabbed a piece of broken concrete and threw it at the pack. She couldn't tell if it hit anything but it drew the attention of one of the animals. The dog broke from the cluster and launched itself at Lyle.

A pit bull. Even without rabies it could kill a man. If it latched on to Lyle and injected him with the virus, the Texan would lose far more than a chunk of flesh.

Lyle started to climb the wreckage, his back to the attacker.

The pit bull was fast, eating up the ground between them with powerful strides.

It was going to catch Lyle.

"Watch out!" Tessa screamed.

BAM!

The flight of the pit bull ended with a thud as the dog's body fell to earth. It rolled forward until its momentum was spent, bumping into Lyle's ankle.

Isabella took fresh aim at the main dog fight.

"No." Lyle grabbed the barrel of the rifle. "You might hit her." His voice cracked with emotion.

Isabella shouldered the gun. Tessa ducked into the Annex. Seconds later Isabella and Lyle joined her.

She coughed and panted and mentally processed what had happened. They were a team of four, returning as a defeated group of three.

Lyle choked. Was he injured?

No. What she heard was body-shaking sobs. The big man was crying.

Isabella guided him through the rubble. "This is what she was born to do."

Tears welled in Tessa's eyes. *Dixie, Dixie. Good girl.*

She tried to count how many of the rabid laboratory dogs she'd seen killed or injured. Calculate how many Dixie was up against when they left her behind. She wasn't sure, but what difference did it make? If rabies vaccine didn't protect her against the revertant virus, the noble *Schutzhund* was as good as dead no matter how many of her foes she defeated in combat.

Lyle sat on the floor and buried his face in his hands.

"The dogs will try to follow us," Isabella said, gesturing at the fire-blackened opening in the building's wall. "Come, we must go."

He didn't respond. Isabella grasped his arm and gently lifted. "Come. She would want you to be safe."

Tessa could still hear dog-sounds outside. *We can't stay here.* "Please, Lyle. Gunnar needs us."

Lyle shook his head and sighed. Without speaking he rose and stumbled in the direction of the lab.

Tessa's senses were on maximum alert. The turmoil in her body and spirit made it hard to think. She needed to get behind a locked door and focus on the next problem.

Her first priority was obvious: Gunnar. They risked this whole misadventure for him, and they had little to show for it. None of the food boxes they collected had made it back to the Annex. In the flight and fight, they'd left too many precious calories strewn outside. She had some snack packs stuffed in her clothes. Good. Even a little bit might be enough to revive the boy.

But crackers were no salve for her other fear.

"That commotion was enough to wake the dead," she said. "The Mara Salvatrucha might investigate."

"You shouldn't have fired that shot," Lyle said to Isabella. He lagged behind as they hurried down the dark hall.

Isabella ignored him and responded to Tessa. "I fear this, too. You go to the boy. I'll watch the security cameras. If Sinaloa moves, I will tell you."

And what then?

They split up. Lyle and Isabella went to the video monitoring room. Tessa returned to the lab with all the food they had.

Cristo was pacing the room. He greeted her with an ashen face. "I heard a gunshot."

She told him what happened and shared her dread. "Those dogs were infected with the revertant, Cristo. That means I was wrong about the rabies vaccine. It doesn't protect, after all."

A bit of a smile came to Cristo's face. "No, Tessa. The opposite. I think those dogs prove vaccination matters."

"How can you say that?"

"Because I know Vargas stopped paying for rabies vaccines a long time ago. Said our animals never left the facility, so how could they ever get exposed?"

She put the heel of her hand to her forehead. Yet another item for her list of grievances against the Palacio's director. But this meant hope was not lost for Dixie—or for herself and the others who'd been exposed to the revertant by Gunnar.

Cristo eyed the cookies and crackers she carried. She gave him three packs and took the rest to Gunnar. He was lethargic and difficult to rouse. But when he spotted the miniature chocolate chip cookies she offered, he squealed.

"Don't eat too fast. I've got more." She gave him some water and tried to wake his mother.

Sigrun sat up weakly. "Dr. Price?"

Tessa took her hand. "Are you hungry, Sigrun?"

Sigrun nodded and gratefully accepted one of the crumpled little packets and a drink of water. Her eyes were bloodshot but she didn't seem confused. Was the antiserum taking effect? Was she over the worst?

"Cristo, we need to—" Tessa began.

A frenzied knocking on the door. Cristo opened it.

Isabella's face was taut. "They're coming."

———————

Vargas had to hand it to Luis Angel de la Rosa. The man had willpower. Not many people at his stage of organ failure would still be calling the shots.

Literally.

After they had to cancel the dialysis, Rogelio, the transplant surgeon, had pretty much gone into hiding somewhere in the hospital. Vargas left him alone. Which meant he had to answer de la Rosa's summons.

The old boss man was half dead, but he kept up appearances. He sat in his wheelchair with his gaze as energetic as ever.

"Do you remember our deal?" de la Rosa said.

"Yes," Vargas replied. That seemed the safest answer. A transplant operation in exchange for Sinaloa's protection and a steady supply of plack.

"You agreed to empty the hospital before my arrival."

Well, he hadn't exactly agreed, but he did do it. Under duress. "Yes, sir. Everyone except essential personnel was evacuated." He couldn't help adding a complaint. "On quite short notice."

"Then why do my men tell me there is someone in the other building?"

Because your men are idiots. "They're mistaken. The Research Annex is empty."

"No, Manuel, it is not. I'm sending the MS in now to find them."

Vargas kept silent. Who could be in the Annex? Had the Zetas infiltrated the peninsula? It couldn't be anyone from the Palacio. All the patients had been flown out. All the extra staff, too. He'd personally supervised the flight manifests. The planes carried—

Wait. One plane never left. The last flight out. The Zetas bombed it on the runway. Sameer said everyone on board was killed.

But what if not everyone was on board?

De la Rosa watched for his reaction. He tried to conceal his nervousness as he calculated the angles. If Palacio people had escaped the attack on the plane and holed up in the Research Annex, would de la Rosa blame him?

Would the Mara Salvatruchas kill them?

Cooking up a cover story about contaminated water had created some serious PR problems for the Palacio. He had ideas for how to deal with those problems later, after all this was over. But if Sinaloa murdered some of his rich foreign patients, the institution would never recover. He'd never see another medical tourist.

"Whoever they are," Vargas said, "keep them alive."

"Why should I do that?"

The answer was easy because it was also true. "One of them might be a match."

Tessa ran to Isabella at the door to the lab. "The drug people?"

"Less than ten minutes," Isabella said.

It was what she'd feared, what they'd been trying so hard to avoid. Their presence was no longer a secret. And she knew they were not welcome at the Palacio. They were supposed to be either gone, or dead. These Mexican gangsters had an international reputation for brutality. They tortured and murdered and disfigured—

"Hide," Isabella said as she sprinted away.

"Wait! Where? Shouldn't we stay together?"

Isabella merely waved. "I'm sorry," she said and disappeared around a corner.

Tessa looked at Cristo and panic took over. She hadn't realized how much Isabella, Lyle, and Dixie had given her a sense of security. They seemed so worldly, so powerful. What resources did she possess to face a situation like this? She felt her throat constrict.

"What should we do?"

"Split up and hide," he said. "Maybe they won't find all of us."

"No! I can't leave Gunnar and Sigrun." Gunnar could walk a step or two but no more than that. And Sigrun was weak. She couldn't run for cover.

"Then take the boy. I'll stay with the mother."

"But—"

"Tessa, take him. Go to the basement. Hide in the animal facility." He lifted Gunnar and forced him into her arms.

Her thoughts were in disarray. Gunnar willingly wrapped his arms and legs around her and buried his face in her neck. He was so light and frail.

"Hurry!" Cristo said. He swept through the lab, trying to clear away the evidence of human habitation.

Noises filled her head, memories of the explosions on the airstrip. Her smarts and logic failed her. The only solid thing in the universe was the small warm body pressed against hers. Cristo and Isabella had told her to hide. She would hide.

And if anyone tried to hurt Gunnar, she'd kill them.

Vargas got de la Rosa to excuse him and he retreated to his office. He was sick of surprises, sick of the loss of control, sick of being the whipping boy. Maybe the people in the Annex were game-changers—gangsters or soldiers or someone who would break the siege, in favor of one side or the other. He didn't care which. He just wanted it over, wanted de la Rosa either dead or fixed and gone from his hospital.

If the stowaways were merely some of his own people, he might still be able to turn this twist in his favor.

He opened a file to check the names of passengers assigned to the flight that never took off. The Texan with erectile dysfunction and his hot girlfriend. The Batten disease kid and his mother. Dr. Tessa Price. *That's unfortunate*, he thought. *I always liked Dr. Price.* Others. Because they were Palacio clients or employees, everyone on the list had been scanned and tested when they arrived. No need to do blood sampling like he did with the gangsters. He merely had to run the personal biochemical and genetic profiles of the people on the passenger list against de la Rosa's profile to see if any of them was a decent match for organ donation.

Once he had it set up, the computation was completed in an instant. He sorted the match scores from greatest to least and took a sip of coffee.

Involuntarily he spat coffee back into the cup. There was a name at the top of the list with a high score. An outrageously high score. A tissue match so close you'd swear de la Rosa was a brother. This kidney was *perfect*.

If those *were* the people in the Research Annex… He rose from his desk and hurried to give de la Rosa the news. He needed to emphasize that the Mara Salvatrucha better keep their fingers off their triggers on this operation. That perfect donor must be delivered to the Palacio unharmed.

After seeing de la Rosa, he'd track down the surgeon and prep the OR.

CHAPTER 21

Tessa raced for the stairs. Gunnar clung to her like a tick. The gangsters were coming. Where could they hide?

Down to the animal facility in the basement. The central room had cabinets. None were big enough to hold them both. She considered leaving Gunnar in one and finding another place for herself.

No. I won't leave him.

The dog kennels? Not really hidden, and an obvious place for the MS to look. The rat room was just an open room with metal racks—no good. Frantically she ran into the chimpanzee room.

That horrible chimp smell again. She quailed at the thought of staying here for long. But if she found the right nook or cranny…

Gunnar was cooperating, holding tight and still, but the burden of his weight was growing. She braced him with her knee to free a hand and open a latch. The old pig stalls were filthy and gave little cover.

Time was running out. Where?

Then she remembered the loading dock. It offered access to the outside. This posed a risk—the gangsters might come in that way—and also an opportunity. If for some reason it made sense to flee the building, she would have a choice.

She didn't want to be trapped with only one way out. They would hide in the loading dock area. Jogging away from the primate stink, she carried the boy out through the changing room.

The cavernous garage area offered no secret hideaways. Was she really lousy at hide-and-seek games, unable to spot a hiding place, or was she really good at it, unable to imagine a place the searchers wouldn't look?

They'd have to make their own hiding place.

The loading dock was designed to accommodate trucks backing up to the animal facility. A platform at the level of the doors was elevated to match the level of a truck's interior. She carried Gunnar into the dark empty space underneath. It was damp and dirty and smelled of mold. White rats scampered out of their way. Oily water trickled through a drain in the floor. She scrambled back as far to one edge as possible.

But they could still be seen. She set Gunnar down in the driest spot she could find. "Hold on for a second."

On the platform above was a stack of huge cut-down shipping boxes, strapped in bundles for recycling. Putting her weight into it, she shoved one, two, then three of these heavy bundles over the edge of the platform. The boom of their landing echoed in the room. Gunnar whimpered.

Hurry!

She pressed Gunnar back against the dank wall. He grabbed at her, frightened. She had to shake him off until the job was finished. She lugged the stacks of cardboard and struggled to stand them on end. Once all three stacks were ready, she squished herself next to Gunnar and arranged the cardboard over them. Her idea was to make it look like an out-of-the-way storage spot for waste. She prayed no one would guess there was a space behind the stacks, a space large enough to hide a person.

She sat on the cold, mildewy concrete and tried to get comfortable. Gunnar wiggled into her lap. She kissed his head. Jammed in this space so close to the boy, she was literally betting her life that rabies vaccination would protect her from the revertant virus leaking from his body.

The waiting began.

Minutes ticked by. Tessa's legs cramped. Gunnar got bored. He seemed to understand the need for quiet. He would start to speak in a whisper, but couldn't keep his voice low. She shushed him and his restlessness grew.

The silence was oppressive, the only sound a drip-drip of water. It made their breathing seem loud. If the gangsters had entered the Annex, they obviously didn't come in through the loading dock. She strained to hear anything that would give her a clue to what was happening. Nothing.

Questions filled her mind. Where would the gangsters begin their search? If they found Cristo and Sigrun first, would they believe no one else was in the building and give up the search? Where were Lyle and Isabella? How long should she and Gunnar stay in this dreadful place before it was safe to come out? If they came out of hiding, where would they go next? And the biggest question of all: what if they were discovered? What would the gangsters do to them?

She wondered if Sameer was okay, wondered if Dixie had survived, wondered if the antiserum was helping Sigrun... So many questions.

The only answer was the drip-drip of water.

————————

What was that?

Her ears could be playing tricks. Was it rats scratching around on the other side of their cardboard shield? Or was it something further away—movement in the stairwell?

"Can we go?" Gunnar said. The loudness of his voice startled her.

"Shhh," she said. The sound again. Muffled by the fire door. It was definitely on the other side of the door. In the stairwell.

She squeezed Gunnar close. "You must be very quiet now."

The vague noise resolved into the clomping of feet. They were descending to the basement.

"I want to go," Gunnar said. Louder than before.

"Hush," she repeated. How to keep him quiet? Should she try to make it a game, or should she frighten him into silence?

With her own heart pounding she was telegraphing fear. No way could she fake playfulness. "Sweetie, some bad men are coming. If they hear us they might—"

The heavy door to the stairwell opened. She stopped breathing. Men spoke in Spanish, in low voices. The door slammed.

They were walking right over her head.

Gunnar burrowed his face into her shoulder. She stroked his neck.

Drip. Drip. Drip.

The men broke up. Footsteps peeled off toward the animal facility. Others—belonging to one person? two?—creaked the metal stairs as someone slowly explored the loading dock.

This was it.

Unwittingly, she'd tightened her grip on the boy. He fidgeted. She adjusted her hold on him but squeezed tighter to keep him still. Did she make a sound?

The footsteps moved toward the garage door to the outside. Away from their hiding place.

She felt like she was going to explode.

Clop. Clop. Clop. Steps returning. Closer. Closer. Silence.

Blood throbbed in her ears.

Bam!

The slap against the cardboard startled her so much she hit her head against the wall.

Had Gunnar cried out? Had she?

The man's fingers scratched against the cardboard. He was trying to pry it back. She closed her eyes, choking back tears.

Voices from the animal facility. The other searchers were calling. The scratching stopped. She heard the man climb the stairs.

The loading bay fell silent.

Would the gangsters be back? Or would they leave the basement by way of the elevator in the animal facility? Was that man satisfied by the cardboard stack, or would he double-check?

Should she and Gunnar stay, or make a run for it?

An agony of indecision. Her gut told her the man would return. He would find them. They should—

"Are they gone?" Gunnar said.

He had the sweet, falsetto voice of an angel. A voice that could lift a prayer straight to heaven.

Or lift an innocent question to the ears of the gangster silently waiting on the platform.

"*Están aquí! Están aquí!*" he shouted.

No!

Running steps. More voices. Her mind screamed, run for it! Before they get here!

But she couldn't run with Gunnar in her arms.

The child started to cry.

Many feet stomped the stairs. The cardboard pallets were yanked away.

Sameer used a mirror to examine the spot on the side of his head where the MS had struck him last night. An ugly bruise marked the area. He touched it with his fingers and winced.

De la Rosa had taken him up on his "offer" of isolation. Vargas said de la Rosa needed Sameer. De la Rosa wanted assurance that Sameer wasn't infected. Thus he was now locked down, alone, in one of the Palacio's patient rooms. An armed guard outside the door passed him food and confirmed that he was not going berserk from encephalitis.

He'd had time to contemplate his pledge of honor. What was it Christians said? The spirit is willing but the flesh is weak. He understood. One swat to the belly and a club to the head was all it took for him to cave in yesterday. Fortunately, the only thing the devils had asked of him was to enter this room and stay there. That he could do gladly, given that every encounter he'd had with Sinaloa's people so far had resulted in violence. Let them lock him up and leave him alone.

He did wonder how Tessa and the others were getting on. He regretted not being able to check on them in the past days but he'd never had an opportunity to go to the Annex when it wouldn't raise suspicion. The last thing he wanted to do was draw attention to their presence.

Maybe he could turn this solitude and boredom into an opportunity. Yes. The circumstances were right to try meditation. He didn't know how to meditate. Most of the people he knew who meditated had a guru, a spiritual guide. Could a person teach himself? He sat on the floor and crossed his legs to try.

A knock on the door. "Dr. Desai." The voice belonged to Vargas.

His first reaction was irritation, followed closely by fear.

The door opened.

Vargas stared in surprise at him on the floor. "What are you doing?"

Sameer turned his palms up, touched his thumb to his first finger on each hand, and rested the backs of his hands on his knees. He hoped this yoga hand gesture, a *mudra*, would calm him, and annoy Vargas.

It seemed to work. "We've got a kidney," Vargas said. "Rogelio and I are going to do the transplant."

"Congratulations."

"I want you to assist with the operation."

"What if I refuse?"

Vargas squatted to eye level with him. "We cannot screw this up. Look. Sinaloa's bringing men into the region. In a couple of days, they'll blow the Zetas out of here. We get de la Rosa his kidney. He goes home happy. His organization is happy. I'm happy. We all win. Okay?"

Sameer closed his eyes.

This enraged Vargas. "Listen, you bastard. We don't need you. Rogelio can do a kidney transplant with one hand tied behind his back."

"Then let him."

Vargas grabbed him by the shirt. Sameer deigned to open his eyes.

"Rogelio's cracking from the stress," Vargas said. "I'm not taking any chances." He let go of Sameer's shirt. "You have good hands and good judgment. I want you in the OR in case something goes wrong."

"You haven't answered my question. What if I refuse?"

Vargas stood up. "Then I tell de la Rosa we don't need you any more."

The two physicians stared daggers at each other. Sameer looked into Vargas's eyes and decided the director wasn't bluffing.

So the moral dilemma was this. Should he do what he was trained and sworn to do—to use his medical skills to the best of his ability to help a sick person in need? Or should he refuse on the grounds that the patient and everyone associated with the operation was odious and morally corrupt—and then be martyred for his convictions?

He closed his eyes once more and imagined an executioner's bullet blowing his brains out.

Vargas had made it clear de la Rosa's transplant surgery would happen whether Sameer was in the room or not. If he was there, he could protect the health of the patients, both donor and recipient. Was that such a terrible thing?

He stood up. "I'll do what I can."

———

The Palacio patient room was equipped with a king-size bed. Plenty of room for an exhausted, terrified woman and child but Tessa was too frightened, too alert to sleep. Gunnar was worn down by the plasmapheresis procedure and the high-stakes hide-and-seek. He slept. She paced the room.

The armed, tattooed men had let her carry Gunnar through the tunnel to the main hospital. The men had asked questions, but she didn't speak Spanish and it seemed none of them spoke English. Unexpectedly, no one laid a hand on her or the boy. They simply forced her into this room and braced the door closed from the outside.

She had seen no one on the walk, not other gangsters, not Vargas or Sameer or Palacio staff. No sign of Cristo and Sigrun or Lyle and Isabella. She wondered if they were all still in hiding, or if they'd been locked in separate rooms.

Or killed.

No sense thinking that way. These people have done me no harm.

She was surprised to be alive but did not take that as a portent of what was to come. Probably the men had gone to report what they'd found to their superiors. What orders would they be given?

She marveled at Gunnar's ability to sleep. Truly the innocence of children. She watched his chest rise and fall. The snacks had done him a world of good. His color and muscle tone were better. Maybe these drug people would bring their prisoners a meal? Right now she would accept food from any hand.

A scraping and jiggling sound outside the door. Green LEDs lit up on the interior wall, indicating the hand scanner on the other side had been activated. She tensed and took a protective position in front of Gunnar. Someone from the Palacio was coming in.

The door opened and a man entered.

Vargas.

Had she really said she would accept food from *any* hand?

"Dr. Price!" he said, his arms extended as he stepped forward to embrace her. "Thank God you're alive. Sameer told me you'd perished in the attack on the runway."

She drew away from him. "Don't touch me."

He stopped. "Tessa, you should have come here. The main hospital is the safest place to be during an attack. Especially after the helicopter crashed into the Annex, why didn't you come over?"

Who did he think he was kidding? "I know what's—" She was about to say, *what's happening here, who's in control of the hospital.* But if it hadn't been for Sameer, Lyle, and Isabella, she would know nothing. Revealing all she knew might give away the fact that there were others still free on the campus and that Sameer had lied to Vargas. "I—I was afraid. I thought the Palacio had been taken over. Everywhere I looked out the windows I saw armed men." She tried to sound sincere. "I thought the people who bombed the airplane were everywhere. Was I wrong?"

Vargas sat down on the sofa. "Partly," he said. "The Zeta drug cartel has the peninsula under siege. But the men you saw here on campus are fighting against them."

He left the obvious question unanswered, and she did not ask who their "protectors" were.

"It won't be long now until this is over," he said. "I'm just so grateful you're okay. And the boy, too, of course. Where is his mother?"

She didn't miss a beat. "Dead. Hit on the tarmac."

He made a sorrowful face. "How terrible for the child."

"We're very hungry," she said. "Can you get something for him to eat?"

"Of course. Are you both well otherwise?"

How to answer that question? Did Vargas know about the revertant? He certainly didn't know about the miraculous improvement in Gunnar's Batten symptoms.

"I guess we are."

"Here, let me examine you." He rose from the couch, lifting a stethoscope draped around his neck.

Her revulsion surely must have shown in her expression. "No, I'm fine."

He paused. "Tessa, you've been through a difficult time. Let me check your vital signs."

"Check Gunnar, not me. All I need is a proper meal."

"Very well." He went to the bed and without even waking the boy, he did a perfunctory examination of his pulses, breathing, and heart sounds. "Now it's your turn."

"Is he okay?"

"He's dehydrated. Might need an IV. You're probably the same. Let me—"

"No way." She saw from his manner that he didn't really care about Gunnar's health. She questioned why he cared about hers. A drug gang was in control of his hospital, and no matter what he said, she didn't think they were friendly. Some plot was afoot and she wanted no part of it.

Particularly if it involved starting an IV.

She put her hands out, warning him to keep away.

"Dr. Price, don't be silly. You're distraught. Can I give you something to help you rest?"

"Don't touch me," she repeated. This time she really meant it. Her senses were so programmed to detect danger to Gunnar, it had taken her a while to notice that she—not the boy—was the focus of Vargas's noxious attention.

"All right." Vargas looped the stethoscope back around his neck. "I'll have someone bring you breakfast."

"Am I free to move about or am I a prisoner?"

He assumed his trademark expression of empathy and warmth. "Neither, Tessa. You're not a prisoner. But it's not safe outside. You and the boy must stay here for your own protection."

"Protection from what?"

He left the room.

She exhaled. A chill crept over her. She went to the window to see if there was a way out. She could probably get through the window, but they were on the third floor and she saw nothing to climb or grab hold of.

Her back to the door, she didn't see the LEDs at the door turn green. She spun around when she heard the door open.

Vargas again, only this time he wasn't alone. Four burly men accompanied him. They looked cleaner, less scruffy, than the ones who'd captured her in the Annex. They definitely had fewer tattoos.

She pressed her back against the window. It felt like the oxygen had just been sucked from the room. "What do you want?"

To her dismay, Vargas averted his gaze. Two of the men crossed the room. She'd run out of places to hide.

As they seized her by the arms, she screamed.

Gunnar sat up. She saw his wide eyes as the men dragged her to the floor. The men were strong. She kicked and struggled. Once she was down, the other two came and pinned her legs. The floor was hard and cold. Pain shot through her back and shoulders as they pressed her down with their weight. "Vargas! You son of a bitch! What are you doing?"

Vargas came into view. She was about to spit at him when she saw the hypodermic needle and syringe in his hand. Dizziness. Sickening terror. Her mind spiraled into chaos. Every muscle in her body flailed in total resistance.

"Hold her," Vargas said. "Give me some skin on the shoulder."

Pressure on the side of her neck. The sound of ripping fabric. Her teeth snapping, trying to grab, trying to bite someone. Snarling like an animal. Thrashing without movement. Burning muscles. Gasping. Shrieking.

Vargas coming close. There was no Gunnar. No gangsters. No Palacio. Only a needle.

A stab in her naked shoulder. Heavy, heavy weight crushing her entire body.

Blurred vision. Blurred thoughts. Screaming and screaming and screaming…

CHAPTER 22

Hot water tinkled in the giant stainless steel sink of the surgery prep room. Sameer looked past the armed guard to see the wall clock as he timed his five-minute surgical scrub. Vapors from the antimicrobial soap irritated his nose. He wanted to scratch, but that would contaminate his fingers and then he'd have to scrub for another five minutes. Not an option. Vargas was already in the operating room. Dr. Rogelio, the transplant surgeon, was almost done scrubbing at the faucet next to him. The kidney donor was prepped and under anesthesia.

Mentally he corrected his word choice. The unconscious patient on the table on the other side of the door almost certainly was not a "donor." He had no illusions about that. Vargas was desperate. He'd screened every gang member on the peninsula. When he found a match, he took it. Period. Maybe Sinaloa used carrots to reward the "donor" for "giving" a kidney. Maybe they used sticks. Either way, a kidney was coming out.

One more minute of scrubbing. He stroked a foamy sponge from his fingertips to above his elbow. Doubts resurfaced in his thoughts. Was he doing the right thing by assisting with this operation?

Right. Wrong. Ambiguity.

Life. Death.

He wasn't ready to die.

The man asleep on the table had made choices in his life that brought him to this unfortunate point.

It's not my fault he's here. And I can't stop the surgery.

Besides, the guy would do fine with one less kidney. Thousands of generous living kidney donors did. Especially if Sameer made sure the patient was properly sewed up and cared for post-op. That was how he could turn this evil into good. Do his absolute professional best to guarantee the "donor" had a smooth recovery back to normal health. He couldn't count on Vargas to do it. It was up to him to be the advocate for this patient.

He passed his arms through the warm flowing water. Iodine-stained brown suds drained from his elbows and gurgled down the drain. Keeping his hands high in the air, he backed into the door and pushed it open. Inside the cool stillness of the OR, he dried his hands on a sterile towel, donned a gown and sterile gloves. Then he turned to face Vargas and the patient.

As usual, the patient was entirely covered with sterile surgical drapes except for the body part where the surgeons were going to work. The shoulders and head were hidden on the other side of a vertical screen, creating a private space where the anesthesiologist worked.

The draped figure on the table was clearly female.

That's odd, he thought. He tried to remember seeing any women among the Sinaloa crowd. Certainly none of the Mara Salvatruchas he'd run into. He would remember if he'd encountered a woman with MS tattoo work. Maybe de la Rosa had brought a girlfriend with him to the hospital?

"Are you with us, Dr. Desai?" Vargas was fully gowned and wore goggles to shield against splatter. "If you're not, I don't want you in the room."

Anger against the director smoldered like coals in his belly. "I'm here to serve the patient. Not you."

A flicker of concern crossed Vargas's eyes, peering at him from above the surgical face mask. "Have it your way. Serving the patient is also my goal."

Of course it is.

Rogelio strode in, practically driving a wind before him. Sameer had a feeling the first word out of the surgeon's mouth was going to be an expletive.

"Turn on the damn monitor," Rogelio said as he gowned up and snapped on his gloves. He inspected the tiny cameras and tools arranged for him on a tray. He would remove the kidney laparoscopically, using those instruments inserted through small incisions in the donor's belly. He would see on a screen what the cameras saw inside the patient's body.

Sameer watched Rogelio mark the incision sites on the skin: three tiny ones and one about six centimeters long, just above the woman's pubic area.

"Vargas! You got the tank ready?" Rogelio barked. "I'll have this kidney out in no time."

Sameer felt an intense dislike for Rogelio. Arrogance was disrespectful. And it led to mistakes in the OR. By the time they were done with the two surgeries—on the donor and immediately after, on de la Rosa—he might grow to hate Rogelio as much as he hated Vargas.

The doctors gathered around the seemingly headless torso on the operating table. All that Sameer could see of the woman's body was a rectangular window of tender white skin in her midsection. With swift, skilled strokes Rogelio drew a scalpel across the flesh. The skin split. Blood pooled in the smooth cut. Sameer sponged it away until Rogelio came in with the tip of a Bovie. The electrosurgical device cauterized the tissue with a blast of energy. A sizzling sound, then a puff of smoke, and the smell of a tiny bit of burned flesh.

"Can't believe you found this match, Vargas," Rogelio said. His manner was manic, bordering on reckless. "Extraordinary, really. Virtually identical histocompatibility profile between donor and recipient. Normally I don't see matches like this unless I'm working with identical twins. Why the hell didn't you pull this out of your ass yesterday? Could've saved me a lot of stress."

Vargas blinked rapidly. "I—I didn't have access to—we tested some candidates late."

"That was stupid." The surgeon inserted one of his laparoscopes into the slit in the woman's skin. Several inches of the instrument burrowed into her flesh. "Why'd you wait around?"

Vargas shifted on his feet. Sameer looked up from the field of surgery and stared at him. Why did the director look so nervous?

An image of the woman's insides appeared on the monitor. The 'scope wriggled through her like a worm in mud. Sameer grew queasy. He'd participated in many surgeries; the gore didn't bother him. It was the perversity of this particular surgery. All surgery was a kind of violation, a penetration of the most private spaces. But this one was worse. This woman, whoever she was, received no benefit from what was being done to her. She had not freely given her consent to be used like this.

Rogelio cut open the six-centimeter site and put his hand inside her pelvis.

Vapors from the Bovie reached Sameer's nose. His stomach threatened to heave. He backed away from the table. Vargas looked at him.

"Vargas! Get your shit together!" Rogelio said. Vargas's eyes snapped back to the operation.

Keeping his hands sterile, Sameer took a few steps back in search of fresher air. He pitied the woman, depersonalized, objectified, being harvested like a ripe crop. Her advocate should treat her like a person, not a thing. He needed to know something about her.

He walked toward the other side of the screen that separated the anesthesia zone from the operating zone. Toward the woman's head.

"Hey! Don't go back there!" Vargas jumped away from the table, knocking a pile of bloody gauze and sponges on the floor. He placed himself between Sameer and the woman's head.

For a moment Sameer was shocked into immobility. Then a gut-wrenching fear seized him. What was Vargas doing?

Who was the woman?

"Get out of my way," he said.

Vargas held out his hands and shook his head no. They stood there, idiotically confronting each other without contact, not daring to break the sterility of their hands and gowns.

"Who is she?"

"She's a perfect match for de la Rosa."

"Who IS she?" Sameer thundered. He had to know. Now. Screw sterile protocol.

"What the fuck, Vargas?" Rogelio said, oblivious as he rummaged around in the woman's guts. "I need some help here."

Vargas's eyes narrowed and he stepped out of Sameer's way. "It doesn't change anything," he said as he returned to assist the surgeon.

With nothing standing between him and the truth, Sameer saw the patient.

A cry slipped from his lips. His focus left him and his hands touched things, unsterile things. He wanted to touch *her*, to comfort her, to tell her he was there. The anesthesiologist protectively rose from his chair. The patient was intubated, breathing through a tube down her throat, totally knocked out under general anesthesia. There was nothing Sameer could do that wouldn't make the situation worse, put her in greater jeopardy. He slammed the wall in frustration, leaving a bloody handprint on the paint, and howled at Vargas with every foul invective in the Hindi language.

Dr. Tessa Price slept through it all.

———

Warm water ran over Sameer's arms. He watched the clock. Five minutes. Five minutes to re-scrub. Five minutes to steady himself. Five minutes to prepare to act like this was an ordinary operation, to work with Vargas and Rogelio as if they were colleagues, to perform to the best of his ability and to care for the patient.

Because that's what the patient needed from him.

The patient. The victim. His friend. Why did he lie to himself? She wasn't just his friend. He was in love with Tessa, even if she didn't reciprocate his feelings. He couldn't help it.

He deeply, deeply regretted agreeing to assist with the operation. And yet, if he had refused, Tessa would still be lying there while one of her kidneys was taken from her. Was there anything he could have done differently? He scrubbed the skin on his palm until it stung. No. Nothing. He was awake, but in some ways as helpless as she was.

When had Vargas found her? Had Sinaloa captured the others hiding in the Annex, too? Where was Gunnar?

Calm, he reminded himself. You can't help Tessa unless you are in control of yourself.

Vargas was partly right when he said, *it doesn't change anything.* Sameer had already vowed to be the patient's healer and protector.

He let the water drip off his upraised arms and drew breath slowly through his nose. *Pranayama.* Yogic breathing. He exhaled the same way and repeated two more times. The fire of his anger turned to ice. A single-minded purpose conquered his will.

Tessa Price had more than an advocate. She had an avenger.

———

The warm, slippery kidney splashed into the wash and storage solution seconds after Sameer re-entered the surgical suite. The organ would bathe in that liquid until they moved Tessa out of the OR and brought de la Rosa in. Normally, two surgical teams would operate simultaneously in different rooms. The team working on the donor would deliver the fresh organ to the team working on the transplant recipient and the kidney would immediately be placed in its new body. That wasn't possible here, but it wasn't a problem.

Kidneys were hardy and could easily survive a day or longer with proper storage.

He didn't allow his emotions to be swayed by seeing Tessa's pound of flesh. *Focus on the sutures. Get her closed properly.*

First he took time to double-check the count. In every operation, they kept count of the number of sponges, needles, and other items that they started with and compared it with the number they had in the end. A mismatch would suggest something was accidentally left behind inside the patient, which was surprisingly easy to do during some procedures. Satisfied that Rogelio hadn't messed up, he turned on Vargas.

"I'll take it from here," he said coldly.

Vargas seemed to understand that interfering with Sameer now would be dangerous. He set down his tools and stepped away from the table. Sameer took up a pair of sharp-tipped scissors. He wanted to stab Vargas with them. Instead he used them to clip suture material as layer by layer Rogelio sewed up the tissue in the incisions. He scrutinized each movement of the surgeon's needle. If Rogelio's work wasn't perfect, he would make him do it over.

Rogelio *was* good with his hands. Even though he probably didn't care one whit about the person he was operating on, his experienced fingers automatically moved with efficiency and grace. Soon they had closed all the deep tissue layers and were stitching Tessa's skin.

The surgery was over. Vargas ripped off the soiled drapes and threw them away. Sameer's cheeks felt warm with embarrassment at Tessa's nakedness. He gently covered her with a clean sheet.

"Wake her up and put the next one to sleep," Rogelio declared. "I've got a kidney here that needs a home!"

Sameer was not going to let Tessa out of his sight. As he followed her toward the door, Vargas called out.

"We're not done yet. Help me prep the room for de la Rosa."

Words could not express what he wanted to say. He was done with words. Only actions mattered.

Without answering, he walked out of the OR with his patient.

————

"Tessa." Sameer trembled as he stroked her hand.

They were alone in one of the Palacio's surgical recovery rooms. He had removed the endotracheal tube and Tessa had been breathing on her own for a while as the anesthesia wore off. She'd opened her eyes and spoken garbled nonsense several times. He expected soon she'd wake up enough to be aware of her surroundings. He dreaded her questions. How much did she know?

He adjusted the blanket and confirmed that she was getting the right amount of pain medicine in her IV. Gently he placed a stethoscope on her chest and took her vital signs for the tenth time that hour. Praise God, she was doing well.

In a few hours, the same would not be true of Luis Angel de la Rosa. And that might be the end for all of them.

Since his initial shock at finding Tessa in the OR, he'd had time to ponder what happened. Sinaloa must have found her sometime during the night, shortly before the surgery. Which made him wonder, how did Vargas know she was a perfect match? When did he do the testing?

The answer came to him about an hour ago. Vargas didn't do the testing.

She was desperately afraid of needles. He remembered, when she arrived at the Palacio, she refused the standard blood screening.

At the time, he didn't want to fight about it. Who cared? She wasn't a patient. Nobody needed her medical information, except the computer demanded it.

He'd scanned her hand and then filled in fake data for the rest of her medical record.

Some of that data was easy to make up: blood levels of sodium and creatinine, for example. Just simple numbers in the normal range. But some of the tests yielded complicated results that were hard to generate at random and had to be consistent with each other.

Tissue typing, for example.

To fill in the blanks in Tessa's record, he'd cut and pasted test results at random from other patients in the database. An assortment, so her record would be unique.

Unique to her, but not *hers*.

It was the only possible explanation for the "perfect" match between her and the drug lord. He must have copied some of de la Rosa's information into her account.

Vargas didn't have to test her. When he found out she was alive, he simply went to the computer and checked her record for compatibility. Her record gave the illusion that she was a perfect match.

Tessa stirred and made odd noises. He massaged her forehead.

My fault.

The guilt was crushing. He had done this to her. She would never forgive him. How could he ever forgive himself?

He might not have to cope with these feelings for long. De la Rosa was going to die. If Sinaloa blamed Vargas and the Palacio for their leader's death, then all the doctors were as good as dead.

On paper the organ looked like a perfect match, but in reality it was not. It was possible that Tessa and de la Rosa didn't even share the same blood type. Once Rogelio hooked that kidney into de la Rosa's iliac artery and his blood flowed into her organ, rejection would begin. If the blood types were mismatched, the trouble would be hyperacute—symptoms within minutes. Acute rejection by the immune system would take a little longer—hours to days. Either way, without immune-suppressing anti-rejection drugs, the transplanted kidney would die.

De la Rosa would die along with it.

The only good thing was, the men of Sinaloa would probably vent their wrath on Vargas first. Sameer hoped he was there to see it.

"Where—what—" Tessa tottered toward wakefulness. He leaned over so his face filled her vision. "Sameer?"

"I'm here, Tessa. You're okay."

He gave her time and attention, shielding her from the shocking truth as long as possible. Eventually, though, the lights came on in all the rooms of her brain.

She looked at the intravenous line in her arm. "Vargas."

"Yes."

Her voice was dry and crackly. "What did he do to me?"

Sameer stroked her arm. A lie would not change the truth. "He took one of your kidneys."

Her eyes wrinkled in horror. "For a transplant."

He nodded. "But it's over. The surgeon did a good job. Used a minimally-invasive procedure. You'll be on your feet in a day or two."

She stared at him. "You were there?"

"Tessa, I couldn't stop them. Please, understand." The words spilled fast from his mouth. "I had to be there, to make sure they took care of you. That's the only thing I'm going to do from now on. Is take care of you until we get out of here."

She closed her eyes and sighed.

"Are you in pain?" he asked. "I can give you more plack."

"No more plack," she said. "Can you take that thing out of my arm?"

"I'm so sorry. It's too soon. A few more hours, okay?"

Her head seemed to sink deeper into the pillow. "What about the others?"

"The others?"

"They captured me and Gunnar together. I don't know what happened to the others."

"Nor do I. You're the only one I've seen. They had me locked in isolation until your operation."

"Why?"

"The encephalitis virus is spreading."

She clasped his hand. "I know what the agent is."

You are a remarkable woman, he thought.

"It's a revertant of Gunnar's gene therapy vector. Rabies. Airborne." Then her voice broke and she whispered. "Gunnar is the carrier. They must not know. They'll kill him."

Indeed they would. He remembered how close they came to killing him on the mere suspicion of infection.

"Rabies vaccine protects," she continued in a weak voice. "If you ever had the vaccine, you're safe."

He *had* been immunized against rabies. In the village where he was born, rabies was all too common in stray dogs. Once he'd foolishly played with a strange dog in the street and it bit him. His parents were educated enough to insist he get the vaccine immediately. They never found out whether the dog was rabid or not.

A distant rumble reached his ears. Tessa didn't react. He cocked his head to listen.

Another rumble. Louder.

"What is it?" she said.

The room was in the interior of the building, far from any windows. "I'll be right back," he said.

"Don't—" she pleaded.

"I won't leave you." He opened the door and peeked his head into the hallway. The noise became clearer. There were no people, no one to ask, and he would not venture out. So he paused and listened.

The subsequent blast needed no special effort to hear. A trace of dust tumbled from the ceiling. He closed the door and returned to Tessa.

"Another attack," she said.

"Yes."

"It's been quiet for a long time. Do you think it's the other gang?"

"Probably."

Her fingers quivered. He cupped them in his palms. So the battle of the drug cartels was hot once again. It could mean anything: Sinaloa had rein-forcements, or the Zetas had fresh support, or a new strategy, or anything. There was no winning side for him and Tessa. The only victory was to escape the peninsula and make it to Acapulco alive.

The explosions came more frequently. The lights in the room flickered.

He leaned over and kissed her forehead.

CHAPTER 23

In the OR, Vargas and Rogelio closed the incision low on de la Rosa's abdomen. Two of the drug lord's personal bodyguards hovered at the edge of the room. They looked less queasy now that the surgery was over. They'd been put in the room to protect de la Rosa and to keep the surgeons on their toes. Vargas felt no pressure from their attention. They knew nothing. Rogelio could've stuck a cow brain into de la Rosa's belly and those morons would've maintained the same stern, ignorant expressions.

Babysitters or no, the operation had been a success. For the first time in days, Vargas felt a radiant optimism. After all the recent surprises and setbacks, he was once again master of the situation. He had found a donor when Sinaloa could not. He had a skilled specialist to transplant the perfect organ in a flawless procedure. De la Rosa would wake up a new man, a man no longer tethered to dialysis.

The cartel leader will be grateful, Vargas thought. He'll want to reward me. Because of his line of work de la Rosa can't endow a chair at a university or name a public building in my honor, but maybe he'll pay for repairs to the Palacio. And give me a good deal on plack. And refer more rich patients—

He cut his fantasy short there. He would gladly accept money from de la Rosa. But he did not want contracts to work with any more gangsters. Too much risk. All he really wanted was to get these people out of his hospital and out of his life.

Completing the transplant brought him one giant step closer to that goal.

"I'll monitor the patient," Rogelio said. "You clean the room."

Vargas was feeling so good he didn't take offense at Rogelio's condescension. "Right."

Everyone else left the OR. He put a half-hearted effort into tidying up. This work was beneath him. Once things got back to normal, he would have his staff scour the place. To prevent a foul stench from sticking to the room before the staff returned, he made it a priority to clear out everything soiled with bodily fluids. He filled and sealed a large bag and marked it for sterilization.

Then the shelling began.

His mind raced as he tried to calculate the meaning of this fresh assault. But without information, he was in the dark. Under the circumstances, self-preservation was the only reasonable goal. The operating room was among the most secure locations in the building. If a bomb penetrated this sanctuary, the whole hospital was probably coming down. He decided to wait it out here.

The sounds of attack continued. Most hits were muffled and distant but a few flickered the lights and rattled equipment. His desire to know what was happening grew, nearly driving him to leave his isolation in search of news.

Don't be a fool. Stay put.

The door banged open. From behind a row of steel sinks, he couldn't see who had entered. He waited.

"Vargas?"

He recognized the voice. It was the chief of de la Rosa's bodyguards. Vargas came out. "What?"

"De la Rosa needs you. Come with me. Now."

They boarded the elevator and Vargas peppered the man with questions. Was there a complication from the surgery? Couldn't Rogelio handle it? Was it the bombing? The bodyguard said nothing and pushed the button for de la Rosa's floor. Nervous and annoyed, Vargas wondered why Rogelio hadn't taken the patient to one of the designated recovery rooms where they kept the proper supplies and equipment.

When the doors opened, air sucked into the elevator and sprinkled him with dust and smoke. Holy shit, he thought.

The floor had been hit.

They swept down the hall to de la Rosa's suite. The bodyguard opened the door. Vargas grimaced at the shattered wall where floor-to-ceiling windows used to be. Wind gusted into the room, creating visible eddies in the smoke and dust. Table lamps were overturned. Shards of something metallic stuck from an oil painting on the wall. Glass crunched under his feet.

The bodyguard hustled to the sofas. Vargas followed.

Luis Angel de la Rosa lay back on a fully-reclined lounge chair. He'd been extubated and was breathing on his own, but had not woken up yet. His body was covered with a sheet and thin blanket, except below the knee. Someone had peeled back the coverings there. Vargas saw why. De la Rosa's feet and lower legs were bleeding. Shards of glass were embedded in his soles. He stepped closer to examine the wounds.

Then he saw Rogelio.

Unlike de la Rosa, the surgeon had the misfortune to be standing upright in front of the window when it blew. Unwittingly he'd been a true "body" guard, and now he was sprawled belly down, bleeding profusely from multiple gashes in his back, head, and legs. The designer rug underneath him was soaked to capacity in red and the liquid stain was spilling over to the hard floor.

Rogelio's hand moved. Vargas knelt down in front of his colleague's face but was careful not to get blood on himself. The surgeon's eyes were open and his breaths came shallow and fast. "Help me."

Disgust and pity wrestled in Vargas. The whole scene was a mess and everyone expected him to fix it. What, did they think he was a miracle worker? He wasn't even an emergency room or trauma physician. And this suite was no emergency room. It had a cart and a cabinet with basic medical supplies. Plus his own bare hands. That was it.

Still, he had to do something. Getting the patient away from the hole in the wall seemed like a good start. "Move your boss into the hall," he said to the bodyguard, then turned back to Rogelio. "I'll see what I can do for this guy."

"No."

What? He looked up. The bodyguard had drawn a pistol and was pointing it at him.

"Leave him. Take care of de la Rosa," the guard said.

Rogelio was bleeding out before his eyes. He knew in a situation like this, every minute counts. Prompt action made the difference between life and death.

But what action, exactly? What the hell was he supposed to do?

He knew the bodyguard wasn't telling him what to do based on a rational assessment of the competing patients' injuries and likelihood of survival. This wasn't a medical triage decision. It was business.

If Vargas was anything, he was a good businessman.

He turned his back on Rogelio and scanned the room for a stretcher. They must have used one to bring de la Rosa to the room. "Let's get him in the elevator before another one hits."

With the help of de la Rosa's three personal bodyguards, Vargas lifted the drug lord from the lounge chair and transferred him to the stretcher. De la Rosa gurgled and his eyes lolled open and closed.

The chief bodyguard held the boss's head. "Is he okay?"

"Fine," Vargas replied. "It's the anesthesia. He'll be like that for a while."

They wheeled him away from the window. Vargas made them pause while he took a closer look at the injuries to de la Rosa's feet. He didn't think it was anything too serious. Possibly the glass had sliced a muscle or tendon. Nothing he could do about that; an orthopedist would have to repair it later. The bleeding wasn't as bad as he'd thought. The main thing was to extract all the shards from the flesh and protect against infection. Shouldn't be a problem. Most of the glass fragments were big enough to grasp. He grabbed some forceps and sterile gauze and pulled out all the pieces he could.

"I'll take him to a treatment room to wash the wounds," he said. "Second floor."

They lined up the stretcher to tug it through the doorway. He heard the *ding* of the elevator doors opening beyond.

Rat-a-tat-tat-tat.

The bodyguard at de la Rosa's head pitched forward on to the patient, blood spurting from fresh bullet holes in his back. The chief bodyguard at de la Rosa's feet screamed and yanked the gurney out of the doorway, back into the suite. Vargas found it prudent to help, keeping the stretcher as a shield while he backed further into the room. The wounded guard tumbled to the floor.

The clamor of gunfire filled his ears. Someone had exited the elevator with guns blazing. Was it the Zetas? If they found him with de la Rosa, would they kill him? Or could he hand de la Rosa over to buy their friendship?

The surviving bodyguards took up positions on either side of the doorway and returned fire. Vargas remembered there were a couple of Mara Salvatruchas hanging around the sitting area by the elevator. It sounded like they were in the gun battle, too. He opened a cabinet door in the entertainment console and huddled on the floor behind it. The door was made of thin pressed wood. Not enough to stop a bullet but better than nothing.

As suddenly as it began, the firefight ended. He peeked out. De la Rosa's bodyguards were still alive. And they were not in a posture of surrender. From this he concluded that their side had "won." He stood up.

"What the hell was that?" he said.

The men stepped out into the hall. Cautiously Vargas followed. Two Mara Salvatruchas were down. One had half his head blown away. The other still lived but Vargas could see that wouldn't be the case for long. Bullets had ripped up the furniture and walls. Blood and tissue were sprayed on the carpet.

The chief bodyguard approached the MS fallen near the elevator—the one missing part of his head. "*Loco*," he said.

Crazy.

"Is he one of yours?" Vargas asked.

"Yes."

"You're saying he went insane?"

"He's not the first."

The virus!

His chest tightened. Whatever those chimps had started wasn't finished. One by one, the Mara Salvatruchas were succumbing to the encephalitis. Some of them were going mad. Before the infection disabled and destroyed them, they were turning violent.

More violent than usual, that is. Like rabid dogs on the prowl. Armed with automatic weapons.

They were killing each other.

The glorious feeling of control that he'd experienced when they finished the transplant surgery was a dim memory. Nothing was in his control any more. His colleagues were either enemies or dead. His number one client was ready to kill him. There was an army outside the gates and crazed lunatics within. Even the hospital's air was laden with invisible agents of death.

What could he do? Keep calm and carry on?

It was as good a strategy as any to stay alive. "To the second floor."

Vargas wrapped sterile dressings around de la Rosa's feet. Just in time, too—the old man was coming around. He didn't want to be picking at de la Rosa's lacerations with him awake. Nor did he want to explain what had happened. In fact, he didn't want to be in the same room with de la Rosa or the chief bodyguard. The bodyguard was driving him nuts, hovering like an old woman in her daughter-in-law's kitchen, sticking his nose into everything Vargas did for the patient. Some actual help with the medical procedures would've been nice, but this was just interference. He wanted to have a man-to-man talk with the guy. Tell him they were on the same side. Remind him they both lost if de la Rosa didn't do well.

Instead he decided to go away for a while. He held up a sealed pack of gauze. "I'm going to get more of these."

The bodyguard flew to his feet, as if Vargas was making a run for it. "No. You stay with de la Rosa."

"Would you relax? The man's fine. He doesn't need me or you fussing over him." The kidney was perfect. Rogelio, God rest his soul, was a skilled surgeon. Nothing would go wrong.

"You're his doctor. You stay with him."

Vargas sighed. He could lie and say he desperately needed that extra gauze right now, but it wasn't worth it. Instead he sat down on the sofa and made a show of literally twiddling his thumbs. The gesture had some of its intended effect: the guard quit looking at him.

Explosions from the shelling had migrated into the distance, far from the hospital. Down near the airstrip, he guessed. If the bodyguard knew what was going on—and Vargas was pretty sure he did—he refused to talk about it.

"Do I have my kidney?"

The words jolted Vargas out of his pout. Leave it to de la Rosa to come out of anesthesia stone-cold sober. Other patients slurred and blabbered and hallucinated for a while until they got their wits back. Not this guy. He was steel.

The bodyguard immediately began speaking to his boss in hushed tones. De la Rosa raised a hand to silence him. "Save it. I want to speak to my doctor," he said in a croaky voice.

Vargas approached. "You have a new kidney, sir. The operation was a complete success."

De la Rosa's eyes searched from side to side. "Then why am I hearing about it from you, not Rogelio?"

Vargas looked at the bodyguard. The guard resumed his urgent whisperings. Fed up with both of them, Vargas crossed his arms and walked away.

Hours passed. Sinaloa members came and went from de la Rosa's room. Vargas sent blood samples out for analysis by the remaining Palacio staff, and tended to de la Rosa's hydration and analgesia. He wasn't surprised that de la Rosa scorned narcotic pain control and demanded it be kept to a minimum. The irony of a drug kingpin eschewing drugs was not lost on him.

A hesitant rap came on the door. Not the knock of a Mara Salvatrucha. A guard opened it and one of the Palacio's technicians stood there, his face a study in terror. He handed Vargas a printout of de la Rosa's first post-op test results.

He suspected trouble the instant he saw the tech. Why was he delivering the data in person?

Then he looked at the numbers.

Impossible. The lab screwed up.

Before he could open his mouth to chew out the technician, the tech spoke in his own defense. "Triple checked with controls. I swear these numbers are right."

Vargas stared at the page, trying to make his own face unreadable. He flipped to the next page of data. And the next. The numbers told a story. Or perhaps a sick joke, because there was a punch line to the tale.

The transplanted kidney wasn't working.

Again, the first word that came to mind was *impossible*. The tissue match was perfect. Rogelio was an experienced surgeon. There had been no complications.

And yet the kidney wasn't working.

Casually he upped de la Rosa's pain meds without asking for permission. *Let the old man sleep for a while. Give me time to make a plan.*

The chief bodyguard was not as easily sedated. He looked over Vargas's shoulder at the lab results, as if the numbers meant something to him. "How's he doing?"

Lying had become second nature to Vargas. "Stable. I see signs that the surgical pain is stressing his body so I increased his plack." He put on a closed-lip smile, turned and gently patted the guard's shoulder—reassuring gestures he'd perfected over thousands of patients. "Your boss needs rest. We can give that to him as long as things stay quiet." Pause. This was his chance to glean some news about the shooting war. "Can you tell me what's going on outside?"

"Don't put him under too far," the bodyguard said. "I may need to speak to him at any moment."

Have it your way, Vargas thought, seething with frustration. Who's shooting at whom isn't my affair. Focus on the medical problem. De la Rosa. Renal failure.

Maybe the transplanted organ needed more time to adjust to the shock. Plan: wait a few hours and recheck the labs. Watch for urine production. If de la Rosa started peeing, it would be a good sign.

Yes, that had to be it. More time. Lots could happen in the next few hours.

The visceral pain in Tessa's abdomen and pelvis wasn't strong enough to distract her attention from the IV line in her arm. She knew she ought to be most concerned about Vargas's theft of her kidney but she was fixated on the innocuous intravenous line sticking from her arm.

As he had been for the past several hours, Sameer was within reach. She touched his wrist. "Take it out."

"Not yet. I need to give you pain meds and fluids."

"No you don't. Take it out."

"Tessa, you've just had surgery. You might need drugs. Drugs I can only give by injection."

"Do I need any right now?"

"Normal saline, plack—"

"I don't want that shit in my body," she said. "What about antibiotics? Anything like that?"

"Not at the moment," he admitted.

"Then pull the line." Did he understand? The sight of it—not only seeing it, just *knowing it was there*, making a hole in her skin, connecting the inside of her body to the outside—overpowered any rational thought. The IV was driving her mad.

Is this how Gunnar felt when she and Cristo pinned him down and forced the plasmapheresis on him?

Don't think about that.

Apparently torn between good medical judgment and the desire to please, Sameer made no move.

"If you don't do it, I will." She grasped the IV tubing with her free hand.

"Okay, okay." He gently pressed her hand back to the bedding. "Let me do it."

She turned her head and looked as far away as possible. He ripped the tape from her skin and she felt the alien object slide out of her flesh. Nausea rose in her stomach. Pressure on her arm—Sameer was stopping the bleeding. The pressure felt good. She discerned two—maybe three?—different pain sources in her abdomen. Was it possible to feel the absence of a kidney? A gap or cavity or sensation of emptiness? Nothing she could notice now. The skin over her abdomen felt tight. Movement triggered sharp pains on the surface. Inside her, the pain was diffuse, nonfocal. Like a menstrual cramp or early labor contractions.

A few hours ago there were machines inside her. And human hands. She dared not think of it. She turned her attention to listening.

"It's been quiet," she said.

Sameer walked the remnants of the IV equipment to a trash can. "Whoever it is stopped shooting."

Having regained the integrity of her body, her thinking grew clearer. With conscious effort she prioritized her competing concerns. Anger, vengeance, any normal emotional reaction to what Vargas had done to her would have to wait. The kidney was gone. She couldn't get it back and she couldn't un-do the surgery. The important thing was she'd come through all right and Sameer was there to take care of her. If Sinaloa didn't murder her during the operation, she saw no reason to fear they would kill her now.

Gunnar's well-being flew to the top of her worry list. Had they left him in the hospital room where she'd last seen him? Was he alone? Had they found Sigrun and Cristo? Was Sigrun okay?

"We have to get out of here," she said.

Sameer gave her a tender look. "You're in no condition to go anywhere. Even if we had somewhere to go. There is no way off the peninsula."

"I want to find Gunnar." Her fingers searched for the controls to the bed and she raised the head end. "When they came for me, I think they left him alone."

"Where?"

"Room 118." She sat up higher and winced from the pull on her incisions. "He must be scared."

"Maybe they found his mother and brought her to him."

"If so, we still need to be there. Sigrun isn't well." She explained to him about Sigrun catching the revertant and her gamble to save the mother using the son's antiserum.

His eyes grew wide. Shock? Admiration? She figured he was feeling both.

"This room is set up for surgical recovery," he said. "I'd be more comfortable—"

"With all respect, my friend," she said, touching his arm, "I don't care about your comfort. Or mine. Gunnar is the only thing that matters."

"Very well," he said. "Let me see if we have the option of leaving."

He pressed his ear against the door. After half a minute, he cracked the door and peeked out.

"No one's there," he reported. "If they had someone watching us before, he's gone now."

"Bring me that wheelchair."

She tried to sit up. Black spots formed in her vision. He hastened back to her. "The bed has wheels," he said. "I can push it."

She would do anything for Gunnar but it was a relief to stay lying down. The plack was definitely wearing off.

He unlocked the bed's wheels and got the whole thing moving. She closed her eyes and for the first time wondered about Sameer's involvement in the surgery. She felt a flare of doubt and resentment. How could he? Why didn't he refuse? He said he did it to take care of her. Really? Was that the best he could do—let them, even help them, to cut her open, then patch her up and call it a favor?

Stop it.

He did what he believed was best. Surely he must have.

And who knows what they threatened him with?

"Coast is clear," he said as he jostled the bed into the hallway.

The emptiness was eerie. No patients, no staff, no Mara Salvatrucha. She fantasized that the hospital was indeed empty, that Sinaloa and its leader had left, that they were marooned here and safer for it. Sameer maneuvered the bed into a service elevator. As the doors closed, she heard a not-so-distant blast. The elevator rattled.

They were not alone. The combatants had taken up arms again.

Sameer squeezed her hand. She counted the seconds as the elevator traveled to the first floor. If they found Gunnar, maybe they should take him to the basement. Better protection from a direct hit.

The super-sized elevator, designed for transporting patients in private, opened in an out-of-the-way hallway far from the lobby. Sameer dragged her bed out head first so she was facing the back of the elevator, not the hallway. She couldn't see what caused him to gasp and stop moving.

But her nose guessed it. Her heart skipped a beat.

The reek of chimpanzee.

Sameer made no other sound after his initial start. She heard the animal vocalize, a kind of squawk, and pictured its long, hairy arms sweeping the floor.

The building had been compromised. Somewhere the bombs had cleared an opening to the outside.

Pain shot through her belly as she unconsciously tensed her muscles. If the chimp was aggressive—infected by the revertant—they were both as good as dead.

But the chimp was also surprised by the encounter. She heard it shuffle away.

"There's a broken window down the hall," Sameer whispered. "It went back outside."

"Get us to room 118."

He sped them past the hole where windows once had been. She saw no sign of animal life as they went by, but now they knew they had more to fear than Sinaloa inside the hospital's walls.

Sameer halted and whispered into her ear. "118 is around the corner. I will check for a guard. I think it's better if you are not seen."

Only seconds passed before she felt the bed move again. "They have the door handle braced so it cannot be opened from the inside. But no guard," he said.

So Gunnar was probably still there. She ached to see him, to know he was all right.

Sameer removed the jam from the door handle. The scanner accepted his handprint and the door opened.

"Ay, *Dios*," a voice said. "What happened to you?"

CHAPTER 24

The chief bodyguard leaned over de la Rosa's unconscious body on the stretcher in the treatment room. "Wake him up," he said.

Somebody wake *me* up, Vargas thought. I've had enough of this nightmare.

"He needs rest," Vargas replied.

"I told you not to put him under." The guard jabbed Vargas with his pistol.

Vargas didn't need this crap. He slapped the pistol and shoved the guard's arm away. So what if the meathead was twice his weight? What was the guard going to do, kill him? As long as Luis Angel de la Rosa was alive, Sinaloa needed him. In the few hours left, he damned well wasn't going to be pushed around.

"De la Rosa is my patient. I'll give him the care he needs. Not the care you think he should have."

The bodyguard's cheeks flushed and he raised a fist. Vargas half-wished the guy would cold-cock him, knock him into insensible bliss. Then when de la Rosa died, who would take the blame?

"Watch it, Doctor. I'm running out of patience."

Vargas didn't respond. They were all running out, out of patience, out of time. De la Rosa was indeed unconscious. What the guard didn't know was Vargas had no way to wake him up. This wasn't a drug-induced coma. De la Rosa was on his way to the great coca plantation in the sky. Kidneys failed, without dialysis, he was poisoning himself on his own metabolic waste. His blood was turning into urine.

"Wake him up," the guard repeated. "He can handle the pain." He lifted the gun again but didn't touch Vargas with it. "We can be friends, yes? You do your job. I do mine. The boss does his. He's got a decision to make. Wake him."

Laughter was not an appropriate response, but it disgorged from Vargas like vomit, unbidden, unwelcome, unstoppable. The act of laughing broke something inside him. Or perhaps the breakage came first, releasing the laugh. Either way, he laughed and laughed.

Smack.

He flinched and touched his head where the bodyguard had struck him. The laughs became whimpers, intermixed with giggles.

"Pull yourself together," the guard said.

He wanted to. He really did. But it was all so absurd, so out of control. What could he do? De la Rosa was going to die. Then Sinaloa would kill him. The end.

"Maybe this will get your attention." The guard touched the screen of his smart phone. A photo appeared. He pressed it into Vargas's face.

As if he'd been doused with ice-cold water, Vargas sobered up. No giggles, no whimpers. Stunned silence.

"The girl is pretty," the bodyguard said. "Is the mother a wildcat in bed?"

How did Sinaloa know? He hadn't seen them in over a year. They lived their own lives in Mexico City. There were other women in his life—*many* other women. But once upon a time, she was the only one. And the girl—well, what kind of man could deny his own flesh and blood?

"If de la Rosa dies, they die." The bodyguard holstered his phone.

The faces of mother and daughter disappeared from view but not from Vargas's mind. The giddy madness drained from him, leaving a hollow emptiness in his soul.

Before this moment, he would have denied that he loved them. Whatever he felt toward them was not what he would call love. And yet, they were bound to him. Sinaloa—*damn you!*—was taking that bond one step further. The two women's fates were now linked to his. Life or death would come to all of them the same.

He didn't want to die. And he didn't want *them* to die because of him.

The guard must have seen the effectiveness of his threat. With nothing else to prove, he put on a bored, disinterested air. "Wake him up."

"I can't."

He felt the man weighing his truthfulness. "Believe me. It's not the drugs. He's in a coma."

The guard grilled him with his stare a moment longer. "The girl's death will not be painless."

"You goddamn fool. Your boss is dying." Vargas clenched his fists. "The transplant failed. There's nothing I can do!"

"You lied to me."

"I thought after a few hours the kidney would take."

"Do something."

Once again Vargas laughed. "Right. You think I'm fucking Jesus Christ? I don't know why it's not working. Rogelio might know, but he's dead. We took our best shot." *Why wasn't it working? A perfect match. It's so unfair.* He thought he might explode from frustration. "Look at me. I'm a doctor. I don't want any of my patients to die. I want de la Rosa to walk out of my hospital feeling twenty years younger. I know what happens to me if he dies. Don't you get it? I can't help him. Not even to save myself."

A surprisingly pensive look came over the bodyguard's face. *Thinking? The guy was thinking?*

He practically held his breath, wondering what would come out of the man's mouth next.

"The new kidney isn't working," the guard said.

Didn't I just say that? "No, it isn't."

"So he still needs a transplant."

"Right."

"Give him another one."

"What?"

"Put another kidney in." The bodyguard paced the room with growing excitement.

Having an idea must be a novel experience for him. Too bad it's a stupid idea. "And how are we supposed to do that?"

The bodyguard stopped moving and faced him, his eyes alight. "You still have the donor?"

"Yes."

"She has two kidneys."

"Yes, but we don't have a surgeon."

"Aren't you a doctor?"

God, does he really think…

"And you have another doctor here, that Indian guy?" the guard continued.

"It's not a question of how many doctors. Neither of us is a transplant surgeon."

Animated by the power of his idea, the bodyguard couldn't resist pulling out his firearm and twirling it in Vargas's vicinity. "You did the surgery before."

"I was assisting Rogelio. I didn't do the surgery."

The guard waved the gun dismissively. "You will operate on de la Rosa."

"You might as well put a bullet in his head," Vargas said.

Click. The cocked pistol pressed cold and hard against his temple.

"I might put a bullet in yours. But by that time, you'll be begging for it." The bodyguard's rancid breath choked him. "Unless you have a better idea, you and the Indian will do another transplant."

A better idea? How about I wrap my fingers around your throat and force you to kill me now?

He heard an echo of his daughter singing. She had a beautiful voice.

"Whatever you want," he said.

It didn't matter. All roads led to the same destination.

Death.

———

Tessa recognized Cristo's voice coming from the room where she'd originally been taken with Gunnar.

So the MS found Cristo in the Annex. At least he's alive.

Softly, Sameer opened the door. He narrowly missed a blow from Cristo, who hesitated just long enough before striking with a table lamp, the closest thing to a weapon in the room. Cristo cringed when he saw Tessa in the hospital bed and helped Sameer push it into the room.

"Don't close the door," Cristo said. "They locked us in and the hand scanner doesn't work."

"They put a crude mechanical device on the handle," Sameer said. "I'll make it look like the door is still locked."

Tessa painfully raised herself on her elbows, looking for Gunnar.

"Hi!"

A blond head popped up from the bed in the room. A weight lifted from her chest. The boy seemed none the worse since she was taken. And he was not alone.

"Mama's here!" he said as Sigrun rose from lying at Gunnar's side.

"Dr. Price!" Sigrun cried, aghast.

I must look terrible. Certainly worse than Sigrun, who seemed to be in better shape than when they'd last been together. *Was it the antiserum?*

"I'm okay," Tessa said. She most definitely did not want to talk about the… about what happened. *Compartmentalize. Ignore. Focus on what we have to do now.* Cristo and Sigrun had been captured but were unharmed. She knew first-hand how quickly that could change.

Sameer re-entered the room and gently closed the door with the fake lock in place on the outside. Quietly he explained to the others what had happened to Tessa.

"What are we going to do?" Sigrun said.

"We've lost the advantage of secrecy," Tessa said. "Sinaloa knows we're here."

"The group is more dangerous than ever," Sameer said. "I have reason to believe their leader will soon be dead. That will make their behavior even more unpredictable. And violent."

"What if the other side, their enemy, gets through?" Sigrun said. "Haven't they been firing at the hospital?"

"We don't know what's happening outside," Sameer said.

"If the Zeta gang takes over, we won't be any better off," Cristo said. "I've had dealings with them. They'll kill anything that moves."

Sigrun wrapped her arms around Gunnar. "Hide. We must hide again."

What we need to do is get off this rock, Tessa thought. But how? Even Sinaloa was trapped on the peninsula. What could this pathetic bunch do to save themselves? She and Gunnar could barely stand, much less walk. Sigrun was at death's door only yesterday. Cristo was emerging from opioid withdrawal. Sameer was fit and whole but—

He said he would not leave her. She believed him. He was their best chance. He should know the hospital like the back of his hand.

"Any out-of-the-way holes in this building where they might have trouble finding us?" she asked.

"If we split up—"

Swiftly pounding footsteps in the hall went silent at the door.

Too late already?

She locked eyes with Sigrun and saw her own panic reflected there. *Is there somewhere to hide in here? The bathroom?*

The intruders found the lock disengaged on the other side of the door. Someone cursed. Sameer slinked to one side of the entryway. Cristo picked up the lamp.

The door flew open, striking the bed on which Tessa lay. The jolt made her gasp in pain.

Cristo swung the lamp at the first man through the door. The lampshade crumpled; the burly man did not. He grabbed the lamp and wrenched it from Cristo's hands, then body-slammed him against the wall.

More men spilled in. Two wrestled Sameer to the center of the room and held his arms tight behind his back.

Manuel Vargas marched in.

"There you are," he said. "When you weren't in the recovery room, I figured we'd find you here." He gestured to the Sinaloa guards holding Sameer. "Bring him. Push the bed."

Ignoring the pain, she tried to get up. Two men shoved her down into the mattress. She saw stars.

"Vargas!" she screamed. "Leave us alone!"

What? What did he want now?

Cold suspicion stoked the terror in her gut.

Why did Sameer say the leader would soon be dead?

"Leave me alone!" As they pushed her bed into the hallway, she grabbed at the doorjamb, tearing her fingernails. "Sameer!"

They dragged him through the door next. His stricken expression gave no comfort.

Cristo managed to land a single kick on one of the men holding Sameer. The man pinning him to the wall whacked an elbow into his cheek. Cristo's head slumped.

"Stop it!" she sobbed.

Sigrun cried out, "Where are you taking them?"

No one paid any attention to her. Apparently they didn't want Sigrun and Gunnar.

Maybe the boy and his mother would be okay.

Tessa's last glimpse of Room 118: Cristo on the floor. Tears on Sigrun's face. The door closed and locked.

The gangsters wheeled her into the service elevator. "Sameer!" she screamed.

Where was he? *He said he would stay with me!*

"Tessa!" he called.

The men held him back, waiting for the next elevator.

The doors closed. Sameer had abandoned her. She was alone.

They tied her arms and legs to the bed. A profound mental anguish seized her. It wasn't the raw terror of an exposed needle. It was the deep, knowing fear of the needle yet to come.

A digitized female voice announced their floor as the elevator doors opened.

On the surgical ward.

———————

The Indian was making a scene.

Vargas looked with disdain on Sameer's squirming and shouting of Tessa's name. The behavior was unbecoming of a man as educated as Dr. Desai.

Doesn't he understand that we are no longer masters of our fate?

"You'll see her soon," Vargas said. He waited for the elevator doors to close on Dr. Price, then pushed the button to call the car back.

Sameer's eyes followed the elevator's floor indicator light. The elevator stopped in the basement: the surgical floor.

"I know what you want," Sameer said.

"It doesn't matter what I want," Vargas replied.

"De la Rosa is rejecting the kidney."

A tinge of inquisitiveness piqued amid Vargas's bland acceptance of his end. "The patient is still in renal failure, yes. But not rejection. The donor kidney is a perfect match."

"It is rejection." Sameer stopped struggling against the men who held him. "I *know*. The second organ will also fail."

No doubt it will, Vargas thought, because neither of us is trained to do the surgery. "Perhaps."

Sameer persisted. "The tissue typing is a lie. She was never tested."

"What do you know about it?"

"Her data in the computer are fake. There is no perfect match. Her data are de la Rosa's own. I randomly created her medical record using other patients' information."

He looked at his former colleague in surprise. Yesterday, or even a few hours ago, he would have been enraged by this news. Sameer's deception had set him up to fail.

But now, all was lost. This world would soon pass away. The information was a mere curiosity.

Sameer pressed toward him as if to strike. The Sinaloa guards held him fast. "Did you hear me? If you take her other kidney, they *both* will die."

"You say that like it matters."

Red rose in Sameer's cheeks. "I'm telling you the truth. You must find a different donor. Test her yourself if you don't believe me!"

A grotesque mirth rose in him and he laughed. "Believe you? What difference does it make what I believe?" He flicked a speck of lint from his sleeve. "You think the truth matters. You're wrong. The truth is irrelevant."

Poor fool, he doesn't understand, Vargas thought. Reason had abandoned the Palacio. The men of science had lost control. Years and years of building a reputation, of providing the highest quality, cutting-edge medical care and recreation. Of education and research. Of interior designers and trained chefs. Of bribery and protection rackets. Everything he had built was lost.

Do what Sinaloa asks. Get them away from my daughter. Surrender to the inevitable.

"Sinaloa wants de la Rosa to have another transplant," he said. "From a perfectly matched donor."

"Impossible. Tell them!"

The elevator opened. He walked in and held the doors while Sameer was hauled inside.

"Medically speaking, it's the best option we have to offer."

Sameer strained against his captors. "Have you gone mad? If Rogelio moves another kidney all you'll do is go from one patient in renal failure to two."

"Rogelio won't move the kidney."

That shut Sameer up for a moment.

"So Rogelio isn't going to do a transplant?" Sameer asked, confused.

The doors closed. "No. You and I are."

Sameer felt faint as the elevator seemed to shrink around him. What the hell was Vargas saying?

The director explained. "Rogelio's dead. We're the only doctors left. And we've been told to take a kidney from Tessa Price and put it in Luis Angel de la Rosa."

"You are insane," Sameer said. The Sinaloa guards tightened their already fearsome grips on his arms. "Even if the kidney matched, we aren't trained to do a transplant."

"I'm aware of that."

"So why are you doing it?"

"Because they told me to."

"Who told you? A bunch of plack-brained thugs like these?"

"The acting boss of the Sinaloa cartel. I was persuaded."

Sameer bounced on his toes. "You can't force me to do this."

Vargas held up his palms. "It's out of my hands."

"I won't," Sameer said. Truly. No matter what. Even if Tessa survived the hack job Vargas's surgery would be, she would immediately go into total renal failure. Without dialysis she'd die. And they couldn't dialyze her at the Palacio. Not while under siege.

And yet, fear filled him as they exited the elevator. He wasn't afraid of making the wrong decision. His mind was made up; his moral purpose was clear.

He was afraid of what Vargas meant by *I was persuaded.*

They took him to the patient prep room outside the OR. Tessa wasn't there. A thousand practical questions flooded his thoughts. Details about how two men could perform an operation alone. He could easily compile a list of a hundred problems with no solutions. He and Vargas couldn't do this even if both of them were mentally and emotionally committed one hundred percent. They lacked the skill. They lacked the support staff.

"Your plan is murder," he said.

Vargas shrugged. "Someone's going to die today. I'd prefer it not be me."

Anger seized him. "You black-hearted dog—"

The guards threw him back, smashing him into a metal storage cabinet. The handle dug into his side. One of the doors jolted open. Surgical kits clattered off the shelves.

Someone yanked him upright as a well-dressed hulk of a man entered the room. He recognized the man from the last operation. It was de la Rosa's personal bodyguard.

"You found him," the bodyguard said to Vargas. "How soon can you begin?"

"Never," Sameer grunted.

The bodyguard marched toward him. With effort, Sameer stood straight and tensed his belly against the blow he expected to come. He sensed that unlike de la Rosa, this man was not cold steel. He was dry tinder, primed for any spark.

The guard leaned into his face. "Did you say something?"

He felt like he was melting.

Find your center. Find the goodness. The strength of a martyr.

He swallowed and when he spoke his voice sounded unnaturally high-pitched. "I will not operate on these people."

He wanted to explain about the tissue mismatch but the words died on his tongue. He blinked hard and could say nothing else.

The guard glanced at Vargas. Sameer saw Vargas yawn and look away.

"Vargas says he can't do it without you," the guard said.

"Is that what he said? Then I will tell you a secret. He cannot do it at all. With me or without. He is no surgeon."

Spark. Swing. He braced for the fist.

In a nick of time, the guard restrained himself. "My boss needs you because your boss says you are necessary."

"Then you have a problem," Sameer said. "If you kill me, I cannot help him. But while I live, I will not."

"You think those are the only choices?" The bodyguard stepped away. "You need imagination. Bring them in!"

The door opened.

———

Tessa prayed for something to focus on. A goal. A task. A face. Anything to anchor her from drifting into delirium and terror, frenzied terror. Her mind was spinning out of control. The world was becoming a dreamscape, a nightmare. Nothing had substance except palpable fear and the crush of the restraints against her limbs. They were moving the bed. She smelled the disinfectant odor of an operating room.

The knives and needles were coming.

A wordless scream as she thrashed against her bonds. Pain exploded in her belly. A mental image of the stitches she'd just torn. She retched. Her mind was a prisoner to terrible suspense.

Somewhere a voice called, "Bring them in."

Them?

A gust of cold air swept over her from the open door.

Kill me. Just take a gun and shoot me now.

"Mama! Mama!"

Another voice. In the hall. A small, soprano pleading. One word. Many wails.

She needed a counterweight to wrest her attention from her own intolerable anguish. A cruel-eyed Mara Salvatrucha delivered what she'd asked for. She profoundly regretted her wish for a distraction.

He brought Gunnar.

The boy screamed and kicked but his size and weakness made him helpless in the man's arms.

Her splintered consciousness crystallized. There was no "me." Only him. Why had they brought him here?

Her prison-bed moved again. The other people in the room came into view. Vargas. Sameer, still held by two men. More gangsters. Gunnar.

She felt like she was breathing motor oil.

"Here we are." One of the men, apparently the leader, spoke. His eyes were on Sameer. "Of course you're right, Doctor. I can't force you to work. I can only encourage you to make the right choice."

He gestured and Gunnar was slapped onto a plastic chair. The Mara Salvatrucha pinched his thin wrists together behind the chair's back.

Gunnar cried out. She felt *his* pain in *her* shoulders.

"De la Rosa has no time," the chief bodyguard said. "You have to start on the woman now."

"I refuse," Sameer said.

"Then I will torture the boy until you do."

The spinning sensation returned.

No! Stay awake! Protect Gunnar!

The man drew a slender black-and-chrome object from his pocket. She heard the click when he opened the blade.

"Stop! Please!" she said.

He was swift. She didn't see the cut, only the blood dripping on the floor. Behind the chair. From Gunnar's arm or hand.

The child howled like a cat in the night. Stomach acid burned her throat. Between gasping sobs she repeated, *no!*

Sameer's head pitched forward. He was fighting them. They hit back.

Stop it stop it stop it!

"Normally, Doctor, I'd give you time to think things over. To watch slowly. But not today." The leader held high the silver blade stained with Gunnar's blood. "My next cut will cause permanent damage."

Only one way out.

"Sameer! Take it! Take my kidney!"

She poured her heart and soul into the plea. He had to do it. He wouldn't want to. But he must. The knife—it must cut her, not Gunnar.

And in that instant, she yearned for a needle. Finally, she could do what she'd wanted to do for Benjamin. To transfer the suffering of another into her own body. To relieve a child's pain by welcoming it as her own. Not metaphorically, but physically, literally, to experience agony in order to spare the life of a young innocent.

She was empowered at last. A choice. Herself, or Gunnar. The needles and knives for her, not him.

Sameer was still slumped, not acknowledging. The torturer laid his blade against Gunnar's ear.

Benjamin, my angel, pray for us.

Every drop of maternal rage and despair channeled into her desperate scream. "Sameer! Do what they ask."

He looked up, his tear-streaked face a window to his empty soul.

"Please. Please," she said. "Do it. Sameer. Don't let them hurt Gunnar." Sobs broke her speech. "If you love me—"

―――――――

Sameer loved her.

This love was the one ray of light in the darkness of the room.

He would do anything for her.

Even kill.

No more struggling. On his knees, he sagged limp in his captors' grip.

"Don't harm the boy," he said.

The bodyguard lifted the knife, leaving a bloody print on Gunnar's pale skin. "You'll do the operation?"

He nodded. The men dragged him to his feet. Tessa wept.

From a detached position on the other side of the room, the zombie who once was Vargas floated over and said, "We'll have to do an open procedure. Get a general abdominal surgical set."

Yes, that would work.

"I'm keeping the boy here," the bodyguard said. "I'll be watching you."

Watch. Watch and learn.

He felt Tessa's eyes on him. He avoided them. She understood too much.

Sealed, sterile surgical kits had spilled from the cabinet into a pile on the floor. The men released him. He sorted through the pile, searching for what he needed.

"I'll prep the organ storage device," Vargas said.

Is he talking to me? Everything seemed unreal.

Small sobs now from both Gunnar and Tessa. One of them understood that someone was about to die.

Steel forceps, clamps, and scissors stiffened the pouch of surgical tools like bones inside a carcass.

"Did you find it?" Vargas said, carrying a pile of linens and sterile drapes.

I found it. The only solution.

"Let me see." He peeled apart the plastic packaging that kept the equipment sterile.

"What are you doing?" Vargas said. "Don't open that out here."

Sensing trouble, the bodyguard shifted his weight.

The handle of the scalpel balanced lightly in Sameer's right hand. His left hand touched his neck. A healthy systolic pulse throbbed in his carotid artery.

He counted three beats. Turned his head to the right. Plunged the scalpel into his flesh just below the jaw. Drew the blade down until it hit his collarbone. A sharp, clean cut yielding a sharp, clean pain that exploded, far-reaching and multifaceted like fireworks.

"Goodbye, Tessa."

———

Vargas was pleased to be out of range of the fountain of blood spurting from Sameer's neck. In the first few seconds, both the volume of blood and the distance it sprayed were impressive. But as his blood pressure fell, Sameer Desai collapsed to the floor and the blood geyser diminished to a burbling spring.

He cut exactly the right spot, Vargas thought. Good anatomist. Would've made a decent surgeon.

De la Rosa's bodyguard roared and flew at Sameer.

A little late. With his carotid flayed open, Sameer would lose consciousness in about a minute. Cardiac arrest from exsanguination would follow a few minutes later.

Not much you can do to threaten a dead man.

The bodyguard put his hands on Sameer's torn throat. Vargas noted the motion could be either strangulation, or an attempt to stop the bleeding.

Good luck. A vascular surgeon and a dozen units of blood for transfusion might be enough to save the doctor in the next five minutes. Direct pressure to the neck would do nothing.

Tessa let loose a hysterical cry, carrying on like she was the one who'd been cut.

Women.

Well, if nothing else, Sameer's bold stroke had upset everybody's plans. *Time to recalculate.* What was the next move?

He had reason to worry. He truly, truly could not even pretend to do the kidney transplant without Sameer. He could essentially rip the kidney out of Tessa Price, but even these idiot Sinaloa guys would see that such techniques would not help their boss when his turn under the knife came. The transplant operation was off.

Whom would they blame?

The list of candidates was short and matched a roster of the people in this room.

In a few seconds, the bodyguard will give up on Sameer. He'll turn his attention to me.

If I let him kill me in anger, will he spare my daughter?

Unsure, he decided to keep his options open and inched toward the door that led to the OR. A quick exit and his familiarity with the hospital could win him an escape, if he chose.

As expected, Sameer's life force drained onto the hospital floor and the bodyguard lost interest. The guard stood up, whipped out his knife, and went on the move. Vargas shrank back against the door, still undecided about whether to stay or to run for it.

Then he realized the Sinaloa brute intended to vent his anger on the child.

Splattered and dripping with Sameer's blood, his face purple with rage, and the open blade in his hand, the bodyguard was a vision of Satan himself.

Vargas closed his eyes. In recent days he'd witnessed horrors, but this was too much. He heard Tessa scream his name. She wanted him to do something. Funny. Hadn't he done too much already? Everything he did ended in death. The first donor—Juan—Rogelio—Sameer...

Weeping, he sank to his knees. He pressed his hands against his ears but could not shut out the world.

Tears obscured Tessa's vision. *Sameer!*

No time to mourn. The man with the knife was going for Gunnar.

She had only one ally left, one person who had the power to save the boy. "Vargas! Do something! For God's sake, stop him!"

The restraints on her legs loosened slightly. The extra inch of movement did nothing for her. Still she pulled and twisted against the straps.

The door to the hallway whooshed open and hit the wall with a bang. Commotion. Movement.

The noise jolted Vargas from his stupor. He opened his eyes to bedlam.

Crashing and blasts and chaos. The gangster who'd shackled Gunnar to the chair went down in a puddle of blood and gore with a gunshot wound to the head.

Voices yelled in a babble of languages. A low, dark, fast-moving shape flew into the room, aiming straight for the knife-wielding bodyguard. It leaped into the air and attached itself to the Sinaloa demon's arm. The knife tumbled from the man's grip. He cried out and was dragged to the floor by the shape which now resolved in Vargas's eyes. A dog. German shepherd.

Gunshots from his right. The other Sinaloa men were firing back.

The Zetas! They're here!

No question now. It was time to get out. He lifted the door latch behind him and slipped away.

Tessa heard a familiar voice.

"*Fass!*"

Dixie's paws barely touched the floor. She covered the distance from door to target in a heartbeat, a blur of teeth and black-brown fur. Tessa looked in awe as the *Schutzhund* brought down the monster with the knife.

"Get down get down get down!"

Isabella!

Deafening gunfire erupted from every direction. She flattened against the mattress and fervently prayed Gunnar was making himself as small as possible. A bullet ricocheted off the bed rail. She squeezed her eyes shut and painfully flexed every muscle in her body.

In seconds, it was over. Her ears rang with the echoes such that she could barely hear Gunnar crying.

Cautiously she lifted her head.

Isabella sprang through the door, her long dark hair pulled back from her face. The stock of a rifle was planted against her shoulder. Tessa followed its aim and saw the gangsters who'd been guarding Sameer sprawled on the floor on either side of his body. A sickening quantity of blood covered them all.

Was there still time?

"Isabella! Cut me loose—Sameer—"

Lyle dashed in and gave a word to Dixie. Then he grabbed the fallen knife and ran to Tessa's bed. The sharp blade sliced through the four restraints that held her down.

Tessa threw a quick glance at Gunnar—sitting upright on his own, crying but okay—and swung her feet over the side of the bed to go to Sameer. Isabella was already on her knees by his body.

She'd moved too fast for her condition. Instead of standing and running, she tumbled to the floor.

"His neck—stop the bleeding—"

Ignoring the pain and dizziness, she crawled toward him.

Isabella held Sameer's wrist in her hand. Gently she laid it down, then reached for the undamaged side of his neck.

Tessa saw Isabella's head bow. "No."

"He's gone, Tessa." Isabella stood and wiped the blood off her hands.

"No." *He can't be dead. Not because of me. Why didn't he—*

"We have to go." Isabella put her hands on Tessa's shoulders. "Can you stand?"

Sameer. So humble. So brave. She clutched his ankle and cried.

"Bella, I need a hand here," Lyle said.

Isabella patted Tessa's back and went to Lyle. "We don't have much time."

Dixie growled through teeth clenched on the Sinaloa man's arm. The man berated them in Spanish but had the good sense not to move a muscle.

Lyle crossed his arms and glared at the bodyguard from a safe distance. "We can't leave this *hombre* on the loose."

Tessa remembered the gleam of the knife when this fiend threatened Gunnar. The tortured expression on Sameer's face before he died.

Sameer didn't deserve to die. This man did.

"Kill him," she said.

"Not a bad idea," Lyle responded smoothly, "but we've got another trick up our sleeve. Darlin', would you do the honors?"

While Dixie held the man still, Isabella used rubber tubing and tape to tie his wrists to the bed.

Tessa wobbled to her feet, keeping her head down so she wouldn't faint. Small arms wrapped around her thighs.

"Gunnar." She dropped to hug him, caress him, examine him. "Dear boy."

The knife had slashed a straight, clean cut about two inches long across his little forearm. The cut wasn't shallow, but it didn't look too deep, either. Stitches were needed but the best she could do was reach into the nearby cabinet for a surgical dressing to cover the wound.

Isabella and Lyle stepped away from the prisoner.

"*Lass!*"

Dixie let go. With snapping barks, she backed away from her prey until she was at her master's side.

Isabella grabbed a wheelchair and swung it behind Tessa. "You two, sit."

They were leaving? With Sameer's body prostrate and broken on the floor?
"We can't just leave him like that."

Isabella gently pressed her into the seat. She kneeled before Tessa and held her hands. "If we don't go now, he died in vain. More danger is coming."

Tessa tried to resist. She felt woozy, disoriented, nauseated, weak. Sameer's body didn't look like Sameer. She heard his lilting voice call her name.

"Let me go to him," she said.

Then Isabella set Gunnar on her lap, and the urgency of getting him to safety wrenched her focus away from Sameer. She wrapped her arms around the boy, positioning him to protect her belly as much as possible. Blood oozing from her incisions glued the flimsy hospital gown to her skin.

"The tunnel." Isabella led the way, rifle ready. Dixie trotted alongside.

Lyle pushed the wheelchair. "Hang on, folks. The Mexican Federal Police are bringing a little gift for de la Rosa and we do *not* want to be here when it arrives."

Tessa remembered. "Wait—Sigrun and Cristo are in the building, too."

"Not any more," Lyle said. "Dixie found them first and we let 'em out. They'll meet us in the tunnel. An aerial bombardment's coming. Safest place to be is underground between the buildings."

How does he know that?

"Where's Mama?" Gunnar said.

She held the boy tight. "Just ahead."

They passed the service elevator and followed the basement hallway to where it ended at a fire door. The door was programmed for hand print access, but it was already ajar. She could see into the tunnel beyond, where bare concrete floor and walls replaced the warm, faux-jungle decor of the main hospital.

Isabella tugged at the door to widen the gap. The door didn't budge. "Tessa, see if it recognizes your hand."

She placed her palm in the reader. The indicator lights were already green, so nothing happened. "It must be jammed."

Lyle and Isabella both put their full weight into pulling the door—only a little more space would make all the difference—but to no avail.

"I can go back and find a lever," Isabella said. "Something to open it wider—"

"The bombs could start falling any second," Lyle said. His rugged face was set. "I bet you can get your pretty little fanny through there. 'Course Dixie and the boy, too." He looked at Tessa. "Doc, you up to a little squeeze?"

She looked at the crack. She looked at Isabella. Lyle was a good guy. Just being polite. Isabella was slender and fine-boned. If she could get her head through, the rest of her could follow.

But not me, Tessa thought. I don't compress that much.

"Go on without me," she said. "This looks like a safe place."

"Now, nobody's gonna leave you here," Lyle said. "I don't have a snowball's chance in hell of gettin' through that slot." To confirm, he put his skull against the opening and peered to the other side. "Bella, take Dixie and the kid and keep going."

"What about you?"

"See those stairs entering the tunnel right over there? We'll find 'em and get in that way, from the first floor." He lifted Gunnar from Tessa's lap and handed him to Isabella. "Dixie. *Geh voraus.*"

Dixie slipped through the door. Her wet, black nose peeked back at them as she awaited her next command.

Lyle kissed Isabella on the head. "The boy'll stick to that dog. You stay with 'em." He grasped the handles of Tessa's wheelchair and turned it around.

"Wait," Isabella said. "Take this."

She handed him the rifle.

He nodded. "See you later."

CHAPTER 25

Vargas skulked into the OR, eager to escape the gunfight between Sinaloa and the Zetas.

Despite all your bluster, Luis Angel de la Rosa, your gang is weak. You lost. Your enemies are here.

If the Zetas moved quickly, they'd get the pleasure of killing de la Rosa before he died on his own.

But now what about me?

He had a good relationship with the Zetas before Sinaloa took control of the region. Could he win their trust again? Or at least convince them not to kill him?

When they found him, it was going to be hard to get a word in before somebody pulled a trigger. Explaining why he'd dedicated his entire hospital to the service of a rival drug lord would be even harder.

He trotted through a series of connected surgical suites and prep rooms. At first, he had no goal except to put distance between himself and the shooters. Then he concluded that the smartest place to be was his personal office. Being found there would help establish his identity, at least.

He didn't want to get trapped in an elevator so he chose the stairs. Before he reached the first floor, bombs began to fall.

The Zetas definitely had gotten reinforcements—and bigger guns. This bombardment made the earlier one seem like a simulation. Noise and vibration rattled the Palacio, even in the stairwell.

Now, hanging out in his office on an upper level didn't sound like such a good idea. He exited the stairs on the main floor. On the bright side, if the Zetas were bombing the building, maybe they didn't have many of their men actually inside yet.

He crept into the main lobby and hid behind a huge pot of bamboo while he scanned for Zetas. The room was empty.

Top priority: shelter from the bombs.

Where? Somewhere without windows, with good structural support. Idea: the walk-in refrigerator in the hospital's main kitchen.

He sprinted across the lobby.

A blast. He dropped to the ground, hands over head. Plaster dust showered him. Sunlight streamed through what used to be a solid wall. He got up and kept going.

————————

Luis Angel de la Rosa was awakened by the panting.

Awakened from deep unawareness to a dream-state part real, part poisoned-brain fantasy. He remembered there was supposed to be an operation.

Was that the reason his belly hurt so?

The belly pain peaked in rhythm, in rhythm with his bouncing head. Head upside down, he realized. He was flopped stomach-down over a man's shoulder. The man was carrying him. The man was breathing hard. They were going up stairs.

This didn't seem right. He had a question but couldn't organize a thought. And the loud noises were distracting. Scary.

Light. Warm sunlight. A new loud noise, getting louder. Wind. Voices shouting over the noise.

"I've got the boss! Help me get him in!"

He was no longer flopped over that shoulder. His belly hurt like hell. One word formed amid the chaos of his brainwaves.

Helicopter.

Now he was lying on his back. Being lifted, pressed against a hard surface beneath him. Intolerable confusion.

Then all at once, noise and heat and pain pain pain nothing.

————————

Vargas kept his arms up, protecting his head as he ran. The exquisite tile work he'd commissioned had become a thousand ceramic and glass missiles. The Palacio, a monument to his own glory, was coming to pieces around him.

He felt an incredible lightness of being, stripped of personal artifice, levitated by a primal instinct to survive. He floated through the smoke and dust, not heeding the sounds of destruction, aiming for the sanctuary of the kitchen.

I really liked that painting, he thought as he saw an ornate frame drop heavily from its mount on the wall.

The artist—she smelled of lilac. I remember. Her lips tasted of sea salt.

His life had become past tense.

The expansive lobby receded behind him. His route took him through less-public areas of the hospital, past the service elevator. He met no one. Where had the Mara Salvatruchas gone? Dead? Diseased? Battling on the front line, wherever that was?

Weird odors blew through the hallways, fanned by gusts from the blown-out holes in the walls and rolling pressure waves from the ongoing blasts. Burning, smoky smells mixed with floral fragrances and rotten garbage and ruptured sewer lines. Not what he was used to in this part of the building. Most days the kitchen area smelled of fresh bread and roast chicken.

The kitchen. He'd made it. Giddy, he didn't care that the place looked nothing like a safe haven. Copper pots and saucepans had been knocked from their hangers, dented and strewn across the stone countertops. Something had tipped over the compost bin, spilling decomposed banana peels and coffee grounds and tomato skins that attracted a cloud of flies.

Maybe I'll start over and become a chef.

The door to the walk-in refrigerator was ajar, allowing him to see how reassuringly thick the walls were. Yes, this was the place to hide. Air conditioning, food, and shelter. He could live the rest of his life in such a place. Maybe he *would* spend the rest of his life in this place.

He opened the door wide and was disappointed to see his chilly apartment already had a tenant.

The chimp was squatting on its haunches, cradling a grapefruit in its hands. It bared rows of enormous teeth that glared white against its black lips. The mouth opened alarmingly wide and revealed acres of pink gums.

Some of the teeth were very pointy.

The sight shocked some sanity back into Vargas. Slowly, silently, he took a step backward.

The chimp rose up, exposing a pale penis lying atop enormous black testicles. Vargas took another step away. The chimp howled.

The ferocious noise snapped his fragile psyche. No more cautious retreat. He panicked. And ran.

The chimpanzee gave chase, using all four limbs to cover ground in half the time it took Vargas on two legs.

Sameer Desai, this is all your fault.

He made it as far as the compost heap. His left foot landed on something mushy, slippery. Lost his balance. Went down in the decaying mess.

He had half a second to notice the comedy of slipping on a banana peel while fleeing an ape.

Then the chimp sank its teeth into his face and massive synaptic activity in his lower brain overwhelmed all higher cortical functions.

––––––––––

Tessa heard a fresh wave of blasts. The hospital itself was getting hit. Time was running out.

They were in front of the service elevator in the basement hallway. Lyle pressed the button.

"You take the stairs," she said. "The power might go out while we're inside."

"We stick together," he said. They both knew she couldn't sprint up a flight, nor could he carry her up stairs.

The wide doors opened. Lyle pushed her wheelchair into the cavernous car. Anguished memory struck. The last time she was in this elevator, Sameer was alive. She'd left him at the door, calling her name.

She was leaving him again.

Every second of the ride one floor up ticked in her mental clock. *Don't get stuck. Not between floors.* The floor indicator blinked "1" and an eternity passed before the doors actually opened. Lyle burned wheelchair rubber getting them out.

"The stairs to the tunnel should be this way." He rotated the chair. "According to that sign, over by the kitchen. Too bad we don't have time to rustle up some grub."

Indeed they did not. Bombs were hitting the Palacio. She thanked God Gunnar was in the tunnel, underground, out of reach of the explosions.

They barreled down a hallway, searching for a stairwell.

"It's got to be here somewhere," Lyle said.

They checked every door but none led to a staircase. All were dead ends except a pair of swinging double doors that led to the kitchen.

"Those stairs must be for the kitchen staff," he said. "Maybe we'll get a snack after all."

His frantic movements belied the levity of his words. Tessa suspected he knew much worse than the current strafing was on the way. If they wanted to live, they had to get into the tunnel.

Lyle backed into the swinging doors, dragging the wheelchair in reverse. As the doors swung shut, air from the kitchen was drawn past Tessa's nose. The atmosphere was foul and she vowed that if they found any food, she wasn't going to touch it. But the stench was more than just spoiled food—something else nasty was in the air, too.

Not again!

"Watch out," she said, "It smells like—"

Clattering of metal pans. An animal screech and a man's shout. The wheelchair jerked and spun.

"Lyle!"

A short, massive, hairy form knocked Lyle to the floor.

It was the male chimp.

Horrified, she remembered what that chimp had done to the female of his troop back in the animal facility. What he'd done to the Mara Salvatrucha outside the Annex.

Lyle was a big man. He didn't go down without a fight. Hollering with all his might, he thrashed and pushed against the ape's chest. A punch landed with no effect. She saw him stick his fingers out, aiming to poke the chimp's eyes.

The chimp howled and bit down on Lyle's arm. Blood dripped from its mouth. Lyle screamed and tried to bring a knee up into the monster's groin.

It's going to kill him!

But what could she do, frail and crippled as she was?

The rifle! Where is it?

Under Lyle. The weapon was hanging from his side when the chimp ambushed him. He landed on top of it. With the weight of the animal and the mortal struggle, there was no way for him or her to get it free.

In a few more seconds he'd be incapacitated. A minute later he'd be dead. She had to act. Now.

Don't faint don't faint don't faint!

She staggered out of the wheelchair to a counter two steps away. A wooden block, full of kitchen knives. She snatched the largest handle and swung around, screaming.

The chimp released Lyle's arm and rose up, its gaze fixed on Lyle's face, ready to—

There was only one way to get the animal's attention. She put both hands on the knife handle, lifted the blade over her head, and collapsed her whole weight to bring it down on the chimp's back.

She felt the disgusting sensation of the blade plunging into flesh and hitting bone. She lost her grip and tumbled back.

It worked. Shrieking other-worldly cries, the enraged chimpanzee abandoned Lyle and turned on her.

"Get up! Lyle!"

The tables were turned. If he didn't get up and use that rifle right now, she was a goner.

Lyle barely moved. The chimp came at her with the speed of a hurricane. Hopelessly she raised her arms over her head. In an instant, primate incisors would impale her tender skin. She braced for the bite.

Rowrrr!

That was no chimp sound.

She saw another set of open jaws and sharp teeth. Spittle splashed her arm.

Like a cannonball, Dixie slammed into the chimp. Her powerful jaws clamped onto its thigh. She snarled and the chimp howled in a bestial cacophony.

Tessa skittered across the floor, trying to get away. Her hands touched something soft and slippery. Flies flitted in her face. Her eyes were glued to the battle.

The chimp struck Dixie with its oversized hand. Its strength was such that the big dog lost her grip and tumbled away, tearing the chimp's leg as she went. Every hair on Dixie's back stood on end as she faced the ape, angling for her next attack.

But the chimp was wily. It had twisted and lunged, tricking Dixie into exposing her flank. If the chimp connected with her rear leg, it had the strength to rip it completely from her body.

Tessa gasped. Dixie seemed to realize her mistake, tried to turn, not enough time—

Blam. The chimpanzee was thrown off balance. It missed the dog and crashed into a cabinet. *Blam. Blam.*

"Don't mess with my girl."

Lyle stood, blood dripping from his arm to the barrel of the rifle he was aiming point-blank at the chimp. He fired again and again, until it was clear that creature was never, ever going to hurt man or beast again. Then he fell to his knees and wrapped his arms around Dixie.

"*So ist brav,*" he said over and over as he wiped his tears on her fur. She responded with eager licks.

A fly brushed against Tessa's nose. There were dozens buzzing around, attracted by the foul stink. What slimy mess had she backed into?

She turned to look.

Atop a pile of days-old kitchen rubbish lay a freshly-mangled human body. A victim of the chimpanzee. She scrambled away on a wave of nausea.

The chimp had paid special attention to the body's face and groin. Both were a bloody mess, obliterated by the attack. The abdomen, too, had been ripped open, exposing the viscera. Loops of sausage-like bowel lay next to a maroon-colored organ swathed in fat. A kidney.

It was more than she could take. She vomited, ripping open another one of her surgical incisions.

"Move! This way!" Isabella called from a door on the other side of the kitchen.

The stairs to the tunnel!

Dixie ran for the door. While Tessa was still heaving, Lyle picked her up and carried her away from the carnage, toward the safety of underground. As they left the kitchen, she got one last glimpse of the faceless corpse. The feet were still clad in designer shoes.

She recognized Vargas's footwear and felt a little less sick.

Dixie led Lyle and Isabella as they half-carried Tessa down the stairs to the tunnel. Blood dribbled from Lyle's torn arm. Once underground, they staggered halfway down the tunnel toward the Research Annex and collapsed in a heap with Cristo, Sigrun, and Gunnar, who were waiting for them. They were a ragtag bunch, every one of them bloodied or bruised and weak and hungry.

For a minute they sat panting without speaking. Tessa sank down next to Sigrun, both of them on their backs against the concrete. Gunnar sat cross-legged next to her. He put one hand on Dixie, stroking the one part of her fur that weren't torn, bitten, or scabbed. His other hand stretched toward Cristo, who was dressing the knife wound on his arm.

"Got any more of that gauze?" Lyle said to Cristo.

Cristo's eyes widened when he saw the bite on Lyle's arm. He taped the gauze to Gunnar and hastened to put what he had left on Lyle.

Tessa knew she was bleeding, too, but she didn't care. So what if she had a few cuts? They weren't going to kill her. Not like Sameer. Sameer—

She curled into a ball and cried.

While the muted sounds of warfare rumbled above, the others shared their stories. Cristo described his capture by the MS. He'd hidden Sigrun in the small cell culture room off the main lab, and squeezed himself into a cabinet. It was no surprise that they were quickly discovered and herded to the hospital.

As he finished his brief tale, the lights went out in the tunnel. The bombing stopped.

Rather than being afraid, Tessa felt comforted by the blackness. She needed her senses shut down. This was the end game. The time for doing was over; it was time only to be. As adrenaline cleared from her system, the nausea passed and the post-surgical pain worsened.

She smelled her friends' sweat and the odor of dog, and wondered about Lyle and Isabella.

"How did you find us?" she asked.

She heard Lyle shift position on the hard surface. "When Sinaloa went on the move, Bella and I lit out for the woods. Sorry about that. Hated to leave y'all but, well, it had to be done. That's where we found Dixie, out in the woods. She was banged up but good to go. Once the coast was clear, I set her on Gunnar's scent. She's a pretty decent tracker. Led us first to that room where Cristo and Sigrun were locked up. Then she took us to—to the place where we found you."

Thank you, Dixie. She owed the dog an enormous debt. If only they'd gotten there a few minutes sooner.

Cristo spoke. "You're with the *Federales*," he said. "That's why you kept asking me for plack. That's how you knew this attack was coming."

A pause before Isabella answered. "I'm Brazilian Federal Police, not Mexican. On an exchange program to American Drug Enforcement. Believe me, if this had been a Brazilian operation, our forces would've been here days ago." Her tone was bitter. "I told the Mexicans when de la Rosa arrived at the Palacio. But there is so much politics and corruption, they did not act at once."

They quietly pondered the cost of that delay.

Tessa felt Sigrun put an arm around her. "You saved my life," she whispered. "You saved my son's life. God bless you."

She let the love mix with her grief. Sigrun had turned the corner in her battle with the revertant. She was going to survive.

Then, she heard voices in the tunnel. The tramping of booted feet. A flash of approaching light. Isabella stood up with the rifle in hand, and called out in Spanish. A man replied.

She shouldered the rifle and smoothed her hair. "It's over."

Tessa squeezed Sigrun's hand.

They were *all* going to survive.

CHAPTER 26

E ven hospital food tasted good.

Tessa savored a spoonful of *flan*. The rich caramel custard finally sated the hunger that had built up over the preceding days. An ocean breeze blew through the window of her private room at the hospital in Acapulco. Yesterday, when the Mexican Federal Police transported her here, the bed felt like heaven and she thought she could sleep forever. Now, it was a sign of her rapid recovery that she was thinking about taking a walk.

"Want some?" she asked.

Isabella shook her head. "Lyle told me to wait. He has something special planned on the flight."

"You're flying back to the States together?"

"Yes." Isabella gave her a confused look. "He chartered a plane for us."

"Wow, that'll be nice. But you're not really—I mean, the two of you, it was an act, right? You came to the Palacio on an undercover mission or something. You're not a couple."

Isabella laughed. "You are a very good scientist, Doctor Price, but you are no expert in matters of love."

No, she thought, but thanks to Sameer I understand it better.

"Lyle spends much time in Washington, D.C. That's where I met him. He is a foolish romantic. I fell in love. He planned a trip to the Palacio for the experimental treatment—you know. When I told my boss at the DEA where I was going, he asked me to investigate a little. They suspected Vargas was using the Palacio to launder money for the drug cartels. I was to ask a few questions, learn what I could, and make a report. None of us knew Sinaloa was coming."

Tessa heard a scuffle in the hall and looked to the door. Lyle and Dixie marched in, sporting matching white bandages on their various wounds.

Poor Dixie. The cone was back.

"Dixie. *Gib laut!*"

Her piercing bark rang through the room. Tessa laughed nervously. "I never, ever, want to be on the business end of that."

"Don't you worry, Doc, she's always on the side of the good guys."

She stroked the German shepherd. "Did your master get his rabies shots?"

Lyle held out his arm. "They saw these monkey holes and thought that made me a pincushion. Shot me up with more things than I can count. Somewhere in there was rabies stuff." He grabbed Isabella's buttocks. "Good thing, 'cause I might bite."

Isabella hugged him. "I got my vaccine as well."

"What did you tell the police?" Lyle asked Tessa.

"I told them there was a rabies-like virus in the air. They know that anyone who was on the peninsula that day needs to be treated to prevent infection," Tessa said. "That should break the chain of transmission. After they hunt down any dogs and chimps that are still alive on the grounds, the revertant will disappear."

Lyle walked to the window and looked out. "So they don't know about the boy."

And they never will. "I told them the virus came from Vargas's illegal chimpanzee colony."

"But the child is dangerous," Isabella said.

"That's why I also told them he has a rare immune disorder. Everyone thinks he has to be isolated for his own protection. The fact that he's actually a danger to people, not the other way around, doesn't matter. Cristo and Sigrun are making sure no one gets near him."

"For now," Isabella said. "But what will they do?"

That was the million-dollar question. Gunnar was a walking—yes, walking—medical miracle and a medical disaster. She had defeated the enemy in his DNA. He was no longer fated to decline and die a young, horrible death. But his cure was a curse. As long as the revertant rabies virus replicated inside his brain, he would stay healthy. And as long as that virus was alive inside him, he could not be in the presence of any person or animal not vaccinated against rabies. He could never go out in public. His mother would be his only companion. Cure him of the virus, and he would die.

"I don't know," Tessa said. "They can't travel. For now Cristo is going to take them to his house. He's developed quite a bond with Gunnar."

"If I can help, call me." Lyle shook her hand. "Well, darlin'," he said to Isabella, "me and my girl got a plane to catch. You coming with us?"

"Against my better judgment," Isabella said.

"Hey, a private jet can make up for a lot of sins," Lyle said. "And we've got some serious sinning to do."

The most remarkable trio Tessa had ever met kissed—or in one case, licked—her and departed. She knew she'd talk to Lyle Simmons again. Gunnar would need his resources. But first she had to make sure Sameer's remains were returned to his parents, and the story of his heroism was told. Then she would get back to her laboratory and start working on the next most important project of her life: an unequivocal cure for Gunnar.

In the meantime, she rejoiced in the astonishing victory she'd won for him so far. Her research had saved his life.

Benjamin, my angel, I did it for you.

The doctors at this hospital wanted to keep her for another day or two. She agreed on one condition: no needles. Period.

Though if she thought about it, the prospect of a little jab didn't seem like such a big deal anymore.

The End

SCIENCE OF REVERSION

Reversion is a real biological phenomenon.

To *revert* is to return to an earlier state. "Revert" is even a command option under the File menu of the computer program I'm using to type this.

In biology, reversion is the reappearance of an earlier characteristic in an organism or species. The term is most often used to describe a microbe that loses some function due to mutation, but regains that function after a second mutation corrects or compensates for the first.

Reversion occurs in nature. The DNA sequence of viruses and bacteria can change (mutate) a lot in a short period of time because microbes reproduce in enormous numbers. Each time a new virus or bacterium is produced, there is a chance for errors in the copied DNA.

However, the reversion people care about is related to a particular category of vaccines.

In the mid-20th century, America was engaged in a very real war against paralytic poliomyelitis, or polio. This terrifying virus attacked healthy children in the summertime, and could leave them dead or paralyzed. The March of Dimes was founded in 1938 as a way to raise money to fight polio. In 1952, there were 58,000 polio cases in the US.; 3,145 of those children died, and nearly half were left with mild to disabling paralysis. Money poured into vaccine research. In 1955, Jonas Salk presented to the world his polio vaccine. Thanks to vaccination, by 1962 there were only 910 polio cases in the US. Today, polio has been eradicated from the Western Hemisphere.

The Salk polio vaccine is given by injection and is made from a preparation of killed poliovirus. Salk is a good vaccine, but vaccines that contain live virus are better. In 1960, the oral polio vaccine (OPV), or Sabin vaccine, was licensed.

OPV is made from live, attenuated poliovirus. Attenuated polioviruses have been purposely mutated in the lab. They have precise changes in their DNA that allow the virus to live and reproduce harmlessly in a person's gut, but not to infect the nervous system and cause disease.

Oral polio vaccine is given by mouth (as the name implies), and the attenuated virus in it takes up residence in the intestines for as long as several weeks. During that time, the person develops excellent immunity against the natural (or wild-type) virus. The person also is shedding attenuated virus in their feces, and can infect other people with the vaccine virus. (This is how polio spreads naturally.)

This propensity for the Sabin vaccine to spread just like wild-type polio is wonderful for public health, because one vaccinated person can naturally vaccinate another.

But, there's a problem.

At a small but measurable frequency, the attenuated virus mutates. Sometimes, a mutation restores the ability of the virus to infect the nervous system. In other words, the attenuated virus can revert. Therefore, very rarely, the oral polio vaccine (*not* the injected one) can actually *cause* polio.

OPV (the Sabin-type live vaccine) reverts to wild-type at a rate of about 1 in 750,000 doses.

In countries where the risk of catching wild polio is higher than that, the OPV is the best vaccine to use because it is more effective than the injectable vaccine at stopping outbreaks in the community, and it provides better immunity in the gut.

In countries where wild polio has been defeated, the tiny risk of vaccine-associated paralytic polio is unacceptable. In such countries, the OPV is abandoned and children are only vaccinated with the killed virus.

A dead virus can't revert.

The United States discontinued use of the oral polio vaccine in the year 2000.

ACKNOWLEDGMENTS

With much gratitude I thank my critique group, The Warp Spacers, for their specific comments on this manuscript, and for all I've learned from them over the years: Judy Prey (who offered the name "Dixie"), Steve Prey, Lee Garrett, Dennis Grayson, Jane O'Riva, James Czajkowski, Caroline Williams, Chris Crowe, Christian Riley, Leonard Little, Sally Ann Barnes, and Scott Smith.

Thanks also to my friends and cheerleaders who served as beta readers for *Reversion* when it was still called *Revertant*: Tina Bonilla, Elisa Arostegui, Sharon Malecki, William Rogers, Jason Rogers, William Pevec, Christi Graham, J. Christopher Brown (who came up with the marvelous name "Luis Angel de la Rosa"), and fellow science thriller writers Brian Andrews and Mark Alpert.

If you enjoyed *Reversion*, you might like other titles
published by ScienceThrillers Media.

ScienceThrillers Media specializes in page-turning
stories, both fiction and popular nonfiction, that have
real science, technology, engineering, mathematics, or
medicine in the plot.

Visit our website and join the STM mailing list to learn
about new releases.

ScienceThrillersMedia.com
publisher@ScienceThrillersMedia.com

Share your thoughts about *Reversion* by leaving a review on
your favorite social media, or the book sites:

GoodReads
Barnes & Noble
amazon
iBooks

Visit author's website AmyRogers.com

Made in the USA
San Bernardino, CA
06 August 2015